The Regiment That Lost Its Soul

Tulloch at War
Book 2

Malcolm Archibald

For Cathy

Therefore, put on the full armour of God, so that when the day of evil comes, you may be able to stand your ground, and after you have done everything, to stand.
Ephesians 6:13

Yes – it's Jock – Scotch Jock.
He's the fellow that can give or take a knock.
For he's hairy and he's hard,
And his feet are by the yard,
And his face is like the face what's on a clock.
But when the bullets fly you will mostly hear the cry –
"Send for Jock!"
A.B. Paterson

Prelude

KEREN, ERITREA, MARCH 1941

"That's Cameron Ridge," the battered Rajputana lieutenant indicated the rocky ridge. "We used to call it Feature 1616 until the Cameron Highlanders captured it from the Italians. We named it in their honour."

Lieutenant Douglas Tulloch of the Lothian Rifles lifted his binoculars and surveyed the ridge. "That's an impressive place," he said. "I don't envy the Camerons' task in capturing that."

"Capturing it was one thing," the Rajputana lieutenant said quietly. "Holding it was quite another. The Italians badly wanted it back and threw in counterattack after counterattack. My lot, the Rajputana Rifles and the Camerons, held on by our fingernails."

"But you held on," Tulloch said.

"We held on," the lieutenant confirmed.

They both looked up as the *Forze Armate*, the Italian Army, reminded them of its presence by firing a salvo of artillery shells.

"105 millimetres," the Rajput lieutenant said immediately. "They'll be firing at the supply trucks. They do that a lot." He

1

nodded to the heights above. "The Italian artillery is good. They are accurate and brave and give us no end of problems."

"We found that in the Western Desert, too," Tulloch said.

They watched the shells land astride the road, two miles from where they stood.

"You had a rough time in the desert, I heard," the lieutenant said.

"Mixed," Tulloch replied. They looked up again at the sharper bark of an Italian 75 mm gun.

"That one is closer," the lieutenant observed.

Tulloch threw himself onto the hard ground as three shells exploded nearby, with a mixture of shrapnel and shards of rock hissing through the air.

"I reckon they've seen us," the Rajputana lieutenant spoke from the ground nearby.

"I reckon they have," Tulloch agreed.

They moved away from the mound on which they had stood as more 75 mm artillery shells hammered down.

"They certainly don't like us," Tulloch remarked.

"Welcome to Keren," the lieutenant grinned, sliding down the scree slope. "There's your objective tomorrow." He stopped behind an outcrop of rock and nodded to a prominent spur. "We call that the Spike because of its shape."

The Spike overlooked Cameron Ridge, rising in a series of naturally terraced ridges to a point that seemed to thrust into the abyss of the Eritrean sky. Tulloch studied it through his binoculars, seeing the snouts of artillery pieces covering the approaches and the sun glint on the muzzles of 20 mm Breda machine guns. He lifted his gaze higher and saw the huge Italian flag on a white pole, defying everything the British and Empire forces could throw at them.

"Has anybody tried it before?" Tulloch inquired.

"We all have," the lieutenant said dryly. "Many of my men are still up there."

Tulloch grunted, traversing his binoculars. He could see, faint against the dark rocks, the khaki bodies of British and Indian dead. "I understand," he said.

The lieutenant nodded. "I don't understand," he said quietly. "If we couldn't take the Spike, I can't see any point in sending your boys up. After all, you didn't exactly cover yourselves in glory in Libya, did you?" His basilisk gaze pierced Tulloch with a level stare. "We know you as a broken battalion, the regiment that lost its soul."

Chapter One

Despite the wartime blackout and the plethora of military uniforms on the street, Edinburgh had never looked so good. Tulloch stood on the Waverley Bridge outside Waverley Train Station, with the ridge of the Old Town silhouetted against the starry sky and the great bulk of the Castle looming over Princes Street Gardens. He took a deep breath, coughed in the smoke of the steam-powered trains, and strode northward towards the New Town.

"On leave, sir?" A tall policeman eyed Tulloch up and down.

"A few days," Tulloch confirmed.

"Just back from France, are you?" The policeman seemed inclined to talk. "A bad business, yon."

"Bad enough," Tulloch agreed.

Nodding, the policeman stepped on, watching everybody and ignoring returning soldiers' slight breaches of the law. Tulloch crossed Princes Street and headed up the steep hill to George Street, then downwards. It was only a ten-minute walk to Nelson Street through the blackout-darkened streets, where policemen and air-raid wardens eyed him suspiciously until they noticed his uniform and treated him to a grudging nod.

Tulloch noted sandbagged defences at strategic corners and windows boarded up in preparation for German bombs or invasion; he was unsure which. Tulloch frowned as he passed a couple of shattered shops with smashed windows and smoke-blackened doors.

The Germans must have dropped bombs on Edinburgh. I hope my parents are unharmed. The sight made Tulloch hurry in sudden anxiety until he forced himself to calm down. Surely, somebody would have notified him of death or injury in the family.

He passed the gates to Queen Street Gardens, strangely upset to see the once private sanctity had been disturbed and a sandbagged air-raid shelter sunk into the once pristine turf. A small body of elderly men passed, with one holding a shotgun and the remainder armed with a variety of implements that the charitable could call weapons. All had armbands with the letters LDV displayed: Local Defence Volunteer. Hitler's war had extended even to the sheltered life of middle-class Edinburgh.

Tulloch remembered the ruthless, highly trained German soldiers he had encountered and wondered how these old men would fare if Hitler invaded. He knew they would fight as best they could, pitting their raw courage, patriotism, and anger against the most professional army in the world.

Thank God for the Navy, Tulloch thought. *And the RAF.*

Despite the early hour, the lights were on in the Nelson Street house, seeping through a gap in the blackout curtains. Tulloch smiled as he tapped on the door and waited for his mother to answer. His father never answered the door.

"Douglas!" Mrs Tulloch stepped back, with a hand to her mouth. "Douglas!" She stared at him for a moment as if he were a stranger in the family home. "We didn't expect you."

"Leave was unexpected," Tulloch entered the house. "I didn't have time to phone."

Mrs Tulloch touched his arm as if checking he was real. "You look older," she said. "And you've lost weight."

"I'll soon put it back on," Tulloch reassured his mother.

Everything in the house was as he remembered, except slightly smaller and shabbier. The longcase clock ticked softly in the background, with flowers enclosing the maker's name: Robert Green. The telephone sat on a marble table in the inner hall, with a gilt-framed mirror above, a sign of status to prove the Tullochs had made it in status-conscious Edinburgh.

Tulloch smiled; such things as class didn't matter a twopenny damn when Britain was fighting to save the world from the forces of Nazi evil. He took a deep breath of the smell of beeswax polish. The carved wooden settle still sat in the outer hall, with the scratch marks left by their long-deceased cat, and the picture of the Thin Red Line dominated the wall, as it had all through Tulloch's formative years. That picture had encouraged Tulloch to become an army officer, and he viewed it now through different eyes.

Sutherland Highlanders, eh? I know how you lads felt facing the Russians.

"Your father is on duty tonight," Mrs Tulloch said. She did not hug her son, for the Tullochs were not a demonstrative family. "He's an air raid warden, you know."

"That's an important job," Tulloch placed his kit bag neatly in a corner. His mother liked to keep the house tidy, war or no war. She would not allow some Austrian upstart with a silly moustache to disturb her life.

"Your father checks houses for blackouts," Mrs Tulloch said, watching her son. "He lets people know if he can see light through the windows."

Tulloch nodded. "Father will be good at that." Tulloch knew his father would enjoy the petty power of telling people what to do.

"How was the war?" That was the nearest Mrs Tulloch could get to expressing her continual worry.

Tulloch considered his reply. "I'm with some very good men," he said.

"Was it as bad as the news made out?" Mrs Tulloch ushered her son to the kitchen, the beating heart of the house. "You'll want a cup of tea."

"I do," Tulloch agreed with a smile. "It was bad at times, but I got through without a scratch."

Mrs Tulloch bustled around the kitchen, glancing continually at her son; within a few minutes, she produced a tray holding a teapot, two bone china Willow Pattern tea cups, and a plate of McVities Digestive biscuits. "We're rationed for biscuits, I'm afraid. And for milk and sugar."

Tulloch nodded. "I know," he said. "The war's affecting everybody now."

"I don't suppose you've had time to meet a girl," Mrs Tulloch said, questing over the rim of her cup.

"I might have," Tulloch said guardedly.

"You might have?" Mrs Tulloch smiled encouragingly.

"There's a girl I have bumped into here and there," Tulloch said.

"What's her name?" Mrs Tulloch affected only slight interest as her eyes brightened.

"Amanda," Tulloch said. "Amanda Clark."

"Amanda? That's a nice name. Where does she live?" Mrs Tulloch began her gentle interrogation, which Tulloch knew would draw every scrap of information from him before she finished.

"I believe she's working in London," Tulloch said.

"Oh," Mrs Tulloch looked disappointed. "That's a long way from here. How often will you see her?"

"As often as I can," Tulloch said. "It depends on the war."

"Everything depends on the war," Mrs Tulloch agreed.

They both looked up when the front door banged open.

"That will be your father," Mrs. Tulloch said with a touch of fatalism in her voice.

"What's that kitbag doing in the hall?" Mr. Tulloch looked as prosperous as ever as he closed the door with a bang and strode into the kitchen. "Oh, you're back, are you, Douglas?" He stood in the doorway with his ARP armband on his suit. "You lot made a Dickens of a mess of things in France, didn't you?"

"We'll do better next time," Tulloch promised, remembering the blood and confusion of the retreat to Dunkirk and the good men who had died.

"I hope so," Mr. Tulloch said. "You should be defending the country, not sitting in your mother's kitchen drinking tea. When are you going back to the front?"

"There isn't a front to go back to," Tulloch replied.

"No; the Germans pushed you out of Norway as well as France," Mr. Tulloch reminded.

"So I believe," Tulloch agreed.

"Where are you trying next?" Mr. Tulloch asked. "Or will you wait for Hitler to come here?"

"Let Douglas settle in first before you send him back," Mrs. Tulloch said. "He's only just arrived."

Mr. Tulloch sat down. "He shouldn't be here. He wanted to join the army and be a soldier, so why isn't he fighting rather than leaving everything to civilians like me?"

"I'll be fighting soon enough," Tulloch said quietly. He remembered the carnage of the final few days in France, with his company of the Lothian Rifles fighting desperate rearguard actions against overwhelming German forces.

"Allowing the Germans to push you out of France," Mr. Tulloch said. "Thank God we have a navy."

"It's not Douglas's fault," Mrs. Tulloch defended her son.

"I noticed some damage on Rose Street," Tulloch remembered the wrecked shops. "Have the Germans bombed Edinburgh?"

"They tried to bomb the Forth Bridge last year," Mrs. Tulloch said.[1]

"Damaged shops?" Mr. Tulloch shook his head. "That would

9

be the Italian shops. Fifth columnists, the lot of them. We don't want that sort in the country, spying on us all the time, so the patriotic people of Edinburgh smashed their businesses."

"Some of the Italian men have been here for years. Old Joe from the chippie fought in the Royal Scots through the Great War!" Tulloch remembered Old Joe Spiteri, who always had a smile on his face when he served his fish and chips.

"We can't trust them," Mr. Tulloch said.

Tulloch caught his mother's headshake and closed his mouth. He held his father's hostile glare. "How is the legal practice getting along, Father?"

"Business is steady," Mr. Tulloch said and launched into details of his solicitor's practice. "Once this foolish war is over, you can leave the army and join me in the business. I have left a chair vacant for you."

Tulloch caught his mother's eye and knew she was warning him not to antagonise her husband.

"Thank you," Tulloch said. "Let's win this war first, and then we can discuss the future." He saw the relief in his mother's face.

Mr. Tulloch nodded, partially mollified. "At least we have a decent Prime Minister. Winston Churchill is an inspiring man," he said. "His speeches certainly woke us all up. We shall fight on the beaches indeed."

Tulloch said nothing.

"Churchill was partly to blame for our unpreparedness for war," Mrs. Tulloch reminded. "His ten-year rule, remember?" She looked up with the light of battle in her eyes. "He constantly claimed there would be no war in Europe for ten years, so we did not need to modernise the army."

Douglas hid his surprised smile as his father looked nonplussed. In the nation's current mood, any criticism of Churchill was viewed nearly as treason.

"Let's not argue about a politician," Tulloch realised he was acting as the peacemaker, not his mother. "I've only got a few days' leave, and then I'm back on duty."

"Yes," Mrs. Tulloch nodded. "Let's not argue."

Mr. Tulloch grunted. "Mr. Churchill is a great man," he said.

"Yes, dear," Mrs. Tulloch said. "But not as perfect as the newspapers would have us believe."

Tulloch looked away. He did not care about the Prime Minister's imperfections as long as he helped them win the war.

TULLOCH RECOGNISED THE OFFICIAL KNOCK ON THE DOOR AND stumbled from his bed, momentarily unsure where he was. He fumbled in the dark, thinking he was back in France and waiting for the scream of a diving Stuka.

"Will somebody answer that door!" Mr. Tulloch complained. "I'm up in three hours and need my sleep!"

"I'll get it," Tulloch fumbled down the stone stairs, gripping the polished wooden bannister for support. The ticking of the long-case clock was a familiar friend, and for a moment, he glimpsed himself in the mirror, with tousled hair above an unshaven face and his dressing gown flapping loosely around his lean body.

Mother was right. The war has changed me, and I've lost weight.

"I'm looking for Lieutenant Douglas Tulloch of the Lothian Rifles," the constable said. He was middle-aged with a world-weary look in his eyes.

"That's me," Tulloch admitted. "What's the trouble, officer?"

"Do you know a man by the name of Hogg?"

"I know a Rifleman named James Hogg," Tulloch confirmed. "He's in my platoon."

"That's the fellow," the policeman said. "He's causing trouble and asking for you."

Rifleman Hogg was one of Tulloch's best soldiers when the battalion was in action but could be troublesome in the barracks. He was middle-sized, truculent, and often violent when he didn't get his way.

Tulloch sighed. "Wait until I get dressed," he opened the door wider. "Come in."

"What's happening? Are we being bombed?" Mrs. Tulloch had run down the stairs, fastening the cord around her nightgown.

"No, we're not being bombed," Tulloch said. "It's one of my men getting into trouble. Go back to bed, Mother."

"Oh," Mrs Tulloch eyed the policeman, automatically straightening her hair. "What will the neighbours think with the police coming here at all hours of the night?"

"The neighbours can think what they like," Tulloch said. "They shouldn't be looking out the window anyway." He dressed hastily. "Right, officer, I'm all yours."

At four in the morning, Edinburgh was quiet, with the dawn not far off and blackbirds calling from the trees. Some men were slouching to their work with early trams on the roads and a slight wind cooling the streets.

The police had a car waiting for Tulloch and drove him west-ward to the tenements and industries of Gorgie.

"Here we are, sir," the constable said as they pulled up on a dark street. An elderly police sergeant waited with four tall constables and two military policemen.

"Hogg's inside the house and refusing to leave," the sergeant said as he stood at the entrance to a tenement with the flint-eyed military police in support. "We were about to break into the stair when Hogg demanded we bring you."

"What's he done?" Tulloch asked, looking up at the building's cliff-like face, where windows glared out like dark entrances into another world.

"He got into a fight with a couple of lads and damaged them," the sergeant said. "When we tried to arrest him, he knocked down Constable Stanton and ran in here."

Tulloch nodded wearily. "That sounds about right. Let me talk to him."

"He's refusing to come out until you come, sir," the sergeant said.

"Do you have a key for the tenement door?" The outside door to every common stair had a simple latch which a key opened. The residents of the tenement would possess a key, and the beat policeman would also have one.

The sergeant produced a key.

"Open it," Tulloch ordered. "Follow me up, but don't do anything unless I say so."

"Very good, sir," the sergeant agreed.

The stairwell was unlit and smelled of dampness and decay, with flights of worn stone steps leading upwards into stygian gloom. Borrowing a policeman's torch, Tulloch climbed upstairs, checking each step before he trusted his weight. Each landing held three houses, and Hogg was in the middle house on the top floor. Tulloch stopped outside the door.

"Hogg!" he roared, "what's all the fuss about?"

"Is that you, sir?" Hogg replied from behind the door.

"Yes, it's me. What are you up to?"

"Just a wee disagreement, sir, and the polis tried to make out it was something more."

Tulloch glanced at the sergeant, who raised his eyebrows. "He broke one man's jaw, sir, and the other's nose," the sergeant explained.

"What was the argument about, Hogg?" Tulloch asked.

"They said the Germans chased us out of France, and we were all cowards, sir," Hogg replied.

Tulloch stiffened, remembering the British dead on the road to Dunkirk. The words of *We're no awa' tae bide awa'* drifted into his head. Rifleman Brown had sung that song as he died behind a crumbling wall. "Is that what they said?"

"Aye, sir," Hogg replied.

The sergeant glanced at Tulloch, reading his change of mood. "Were you there, sir?"

"We were," Tulloch confirmed. "We lost too many good men in that debacle, and not a coward among them."

"I see, sir," the sergeant nodded. "I was at Ypres, sir, and through the March retreat in the last war."

"You'll know how Hogg feels, then."

The sergeant raised his voice. "Hogg! Who raised his fist first, them or you?"

Hogg did not reply.

"Answer the man, Hogg!" Tulloch snapped.

"I'm trying to think, sir," Hogg said. "Them, sir. One said we were all cowards, and I said, would he want to prove that outside the pub? The other tried to put the heid on me, and I hit him."

"Self-defence," Tulloch said quietly. He eyed the constables who were preparing to storm the door and tackle Hogg. "Private Hogg was with me in France," he murmured. "He saw some of his friends killed and fought hand-to-hand with German soldiers. He's one of the toughest soldiers in the battalion."

Two constables had followed Tulloch up the stairs and now glanced at each other as he had intended. "Do you wish to try and arrest him? Or shall I take him off your hands?"

The sergeant only considered for a moment. "Can you keep him quiet and return him to the barracks?"

"I can," Tulloch said with more confidence than he felt. He raised his voice. "Did you hear that, Hogg?"

"Aye," Hogg replied. "I dinnae trust the polis."

"They won't touch you," Tulloch promised, looking at the sergeant for confirmation.

The sergeant nodded. "Just get him away from here."

"Out you come, Hogg," Tulloch ordered. He heard the rattling of a chain and the rasp of a bolt being drawn, and the door opened. Hogg stood a few paces back with a brass poker in his hand.

"I'll break the heid of the first polisman to touch me," Hogg promised.

"You won't need that," Tulloch told him.

Suspicious-eyed, Hogg glared at the police. "If any of youse try anything," he lifted the poker threateningly.

"You won't need that," Tulloch repeated. "The police are just leaving as long as you promise to behave yourself and return to barracks. Isn't that correct, Sergeant?"

"That's correct, sir," the sergeant agreed. "Come on, lads, we're not needed here."

"That goes for the Redcaps as well," Tulloch nodded to the military police.

Hogg waited until the police stomped down the stairs before he lowered his poker. "I cannae stand the polis," he said. "What happens now, sir?"

"Now, we get you home before you cause any more trouble," Tulloch told him.

"Yes, sir," Hogg glowered at Tulloch. "Are you going to charge me, sir?"

"What for?" Tulloch asked. "Self-defence?" He felt Hogg relax. "Is this your home?"

Hogg looked back at the flat. "This was my home, sir, but my Ma died when we were in India. I only found out from the neighbours the day."

"I'm sorry to hear that, Hogg," Tulloch said. "How about your father?"

"He died years ago, sir. He got gassed in Ypres, and it killed him back in thirty-one. He died coughing up blood."

"I see," Tulloch did not press further. He tried to imagine Hogg's feelings when he returned home to find his mother dead. "Where will you stay now?"

"I'll go back to the barracks, sir. The regiment's my only home now."

"I'll take you back," Tulloch said. "Gather anything you need."

Hogg tossed the poker inside the flat and pulled the door shut. "I've nothing here, sir. The flat's empty without my ma, and everything inside is rented anyway. Let's go."

Chapter Two

"Did you hear the news, Douglas?" Mr Tulloch carefully folded the newspaper before placing it beside his plate.

"Not yet, Father."

"Our Navy has bombarded the French Fleet in Oran," Mr Tulloch said.

"Have they?" Tulloch replied. "That's rather a drastic move."

"The Admiralty thought they might throw in their lot with the Vichy French," Mr Tulloch continued. "Admiral Somerville sent in aircraft and sunk the battleship *Bretagne*, running *Dunkerque* and *Provence* aground and chasing *Strasbourg* out to sea." He nodded in plump satisfaction. "Those ships won't help Herr Hitler!" He looked at his son. "And while the Navy and RAF do all the work, young and fit army officers wake up God-fearing people at all hours of the night to help a drunken brawler."

Tulloch saw his mother's face colour with embarrassment. "I'm heading back to the battalion tomorrow," he said quietly.

16

"About time," Mr Tulloch replied, biting into half a slice of toast.

Tulloch's mother slid her hand across under the table and patted Tulloch's thigh in wordless sympathy. "We'll miss you," she said. "Ignore what your father says. He'll miss you just as much as me."

Tulloch smiled. "I know you will," he kept his reply deliberately ambiguous. He looked around the room, wondering when he would be back home. The last day was always the worst, with the knowledge that every minute diminished his time. It felt like the last Sunday of the school holidays, with the system stretching out constricting arms.

LOTHIAN BARRACKS, DALKEITH, JUNE 1940

The Lothian Rifles reassembled in their barracks outside Dalkeith with the sun casting short shadows and sparrows flitting from the trees. Tulloch toured the familiar buildings filled with memories and watched the men arrive, one by one and in small groups. He heard the familiar voices from Edinburgh and the Lothians, with a few Borderers with broad accents, and pushed away the sadness when he remembered the gaps in the ranks.

The Lothians had suffered during the retreat, with a third of the men killed, wounded, or captured, and those that remained were quieter than Tulloch remembered. He glanced into Four Platoon's room and saw Connington sitting on his bed, head down and with a cigarette cupped in his hand.

"Attention! Officer in the room!" Sergeant Drysdale shouted, and the men jumped to attention.

"Easy, men," Tulloch said quietly. "I'm not here on an inspection. I checked on Aitken, and he's still in hospital after he was wounded in France. How are you all?" He noted the grim faces.

"We're all right, sir," Drysdale replied.

"Very good, carry on." Tulloch walked away, hearing his footsteps echo in the long corridor. Colonel Pringle had called a meeting in the Officers' Mess for noon that day, and Tulloch did not want to be late.

The Officers' Mess reeked of history, with the huge picture of the Lothians at the Battle of Alexandria dominating one wall and a glass case holding silver trophies of various sporting events.

"We're receiving new drafts as replacements." Captain Muirhead had been wounded in France and recently returned to the battalion with a promotion to captain and new responsibilities as the adjutant.

Muirhead continued, "Some of the replacements are from our territorials, so they might know the basics, and others are fresh recruits who won't know which end of a rifle the bullet comes out of. A few may be trained soldiers, but I doubt it. The War Office relies on us to teach them and make them into Lothians."

The officers nodded. Tulloch saw Colonel Pringle filling his pipe. He looked older, with new lines on his face.

"With Hitler poised on the other side of the Channel, we can expect an invasion any day," the adjutant continued. "As long as we're based in Dalkeith, our job is to guard the Lothian coast from Musselburgh to Dunbar."

"That's a fair stretch of coast for one battalion," Lieutenant Kinnear observed. Tulloch did not know Kinnear well but remembered him from the fighting in France.

"After Dunkirk, we have four hundred and forty-two men," the adjutant said, "and remember, the replacements are on their way."

"How many?" Kinnear asked.

"I'll tell you when they arrive," the adjutant replied. "We're luckier than some units as most of our men retained their personal weapons."

The Lothians had fought hard to escape from France, and Tulloch thought the survivors looked worse for wear. Nobody was singing when Tulloch walked around the barracks, and even the NAAFI was quiet, with only a couple of off-duty men slumped over their beer.

This is not the regiment I remember, Tulloch thought.

Dr Mercer, the battalion's new surgeon, inspected each man, recommending some for hospital treatment and marking others fit for service.

"Are you sure Orr is battle-worthy?" Tulloch said doubtfully. "He's a bit shaky under pressure."

"He's got two arms, two legs, and a head," Mercer was tall, slender, and punctilious. "In this time of national emergency, we must make the best with what we have."

"An unfit man will jeopardise the rest of his section," Tulloch said doubtfully.

"All he has to do is pull a trigger," Mercer replied. "Even a man with one leg and one arm can do that. A private soldier doesn't require brains; he only obeys orders." He looked up. "You do the thinking for him."

"I don't agree with you, Doctor," Tulloch said. "One unfit man can be a burden; he might fall asleep on guard duty or fail to watch his front and allow the Germans to advance unseen."

"Fit for duty," Mercer decided.

"I'll refer Orr's case to the company commander," Tulloch told him.

Tulloch's new company commander, Captain Kilner, had been transferred from the Territorial Army. He was a middle-aged man who had seen much service during the 1914-18 War and listened to both men before making his decision. "I see your point of view, Tulloch," he said, "and in other circumstances, I would agree with you. However, the battalion is short of men, and Orr is an old soldier like me. During the last war, we didn't mollycoddle men to the same extent. Good God, man, he's not a child!"

"No, sir, but he fought under my command in France, and we had to dig him out of a trench after a German shell buried him alive."

"Is that all?" Kilner smiled. "That was a daily event at Ypres. I agree with the doctor's decision. Return Orr to duty. Dismissed."

"As you wish, sir." Tulloch saluted and left. Army discipline left him no choice, but he resolved to watch over Rifleman Orr as best he could.

The Lothians organised defences along the south coast of the Firth of Forth, working with the Local Defence Force, a mixture of the elderly, the medically unfit, and the very young. Many older men had served in the First World War and proudly sported their medal ribbons. A few of the even older had fought in the Boer War or had served in the Edwardian army in India or other imperial outposts. Others were civilians, angry at having their routines disturbed and determined to take out their frustration on the first Germans to land.

"God help the Germans if this lot get at them," Rifleman Hardie said, looking at a man in his seventies with a splendid moustache and a fierce glare.

"God help us if the Germans get this far," Rifleman Cummings replied. "We have pikes, shotguns, and rifles to defend ourselves against Panzers and Stukas."

The Lothians organised themselves into standing and mobile patrols and helped the Royal Engineers position concrete pill-boxes at strategic points. They placed roadblocks along the coast roads and X-shaped girders as tank obstacles behind the beaches, along with six-foot-high coils of barbed wire. They liaised with the Local Defence Volunteers, the Navy, and the RAF at Drem. They helped train the Local Defence in patrol work, ambushes, and the use of cover and dead ground while watching for Germans by land and sea.

After touring their operational area, Colonel Pringle decided the Lothians would only position half the battalion on the beaches.

"I don't want a static defence line on the beaches, whatever Winston Churchill thinks," Pringle said. "I want a thin defensive line on the coast and the bulk of the regiment as a mobile reserve, ready to rush to wherever the Germans land."

Tulloch agreed with Pringle's strategy. He organised his platoon, choosing landmarks for strongpoints and creating defences from whatever was handy. The men filled sandbags and created killing zones for their personal weapons, rolled out barbed wire across the beaches, and helped the Royal Engineers place concrete obstacles to prevent German tanks from landing. Every day, Tulloch thought the country was slightly better defended and that the Germans had less chance of a successful invasion.

It was not all plain sailing. There were no heavy guns, for the army had abandoned most on the Dunkirk retreat, and the War Office prioritised the south and east of England where the Germans were expected to land.

"They might not mount a full invasion here," Pringle said, "but they might stage a raid, and if they do, I want to be ready for them." He grinned without humour, puffing foul-smelling smoke from his pipe. "Of course, Hitler may surprise us all and attack Scotland; I heard he wants Edinburgh Castle as his summer palace."

"God save us all," Major Hume growled. "Half the kings and queens of Scots have lived there, and now some jumped-up pipsqueak of an Austrian corporal wants our castle." He shook his head. "Over my dead body."

Muirhead smiled. "Maybe over all our dead bodies," he said quietly. "I heard that Churchill has no intention of defending Scotland if Hitler lands here. When he and General Ironside discussed a possible invasion, they said they didn't have sufficient troops to defend Scotland. England should receive total priority for defence." He lit a cigarette and looked up. "If the balloon goes up, we're on our own, chaps, so let's make sure we make a good job of it."

Tulloch nodded. "We'll do our best."

"Let's hope it's good enough," Kinnear said.

"That's enough of that kind of talk," Colonel Pringle rebuked wearily. "We're British soldiers, and we do our duty."

The replacements arrived in two drafts, mostly bewildered young men who looked around at the barracks with a mixture of belligerence and apprehension, with some resigned old soldiers who had seen it all before and had no intention of returning to the fold. Tulloch watched as they were fed and watered, shown to their rooms, and NCOs explained what the battalion expected of them.

Remembering his early days at Sandhurst, Tulloch felt a pang of sympathy. Yet he knew it was necessary to toughen up men softened by civilian life before sending them into war. With a German invasion expected daily, there was no time to break recruits in gently.

The men from the Lothians' Territorial battalion knew a little about soldiering with the recruits just out of basic training, the loudest and most useless. They wore ill-fitting uniforms and were unfamiliar with their weapons or anything except for simple drill.

"We've got a lot of work to do," Tulloch addressed his platoon, with the new men frantically trying to behave like veterans. "We'll only succeed if we pull together and remember we are all Lothian Riflemen."

The men stared at him, some with hope in their eyes and others guarded or suspicious.

"When the RSM, the Regimental Sergeant Major, is finished with you, we'll all go for a little stroll in the countryside," Tulloch promised, smiling at his veteran's expressions. "A twenty-mile route march over the Pentland Hills should bind us together."

The RSM herded the entire battalion onto the barrack

square and welcomed them with an intense drill session before sending them to the range for shooting practice.

"That's the way, RSM," Hume approved. "We need the men fit in case the Germans land. Bayonet practice next!"

"As you say, sir," the RSM agreed.

Most of the new officers were as raw as the men, pink-faced second lieutenants straight from Sandhurst, keen to demonstrate their ability and all certain that they could alter the course of the war single-handed. Two young men differed from the others. One was so nervous that Tulloch wondered how he had survived the rigours of Sandhurst, and the other kept himself apart from the others and did not visit the Officers' Mess.

"What's that fellow's name?" Tulloch asked.

"Which one?"

"The loner," Tulloch knew that a loner would never be popular in the Officers' Mess.

"Erskine," Muirhead said. "He was in the First Royals in the Holy Land, and I heard he did a lot of cloak-and-dagger work."

"Why come to us?" Tulloch asked. "Why not return to the Royals?"

"Ask him," Muirhead said as Erskine found a corner seat and ordered a whisky. "I was just glad to accept an experienced officer into the battalion."

Tulloch eyed the new officer for a few moments before walking across. "Erskine, isn't it?"

"That's correct," Erskine looked up. He was a suntanned, handsome man with an elegant moustache and disturbingly steady eyes. "Tulloch, isn't it?"

"That's also correct," Tulloch said, settling into a seat beside Erskine. "Welcome to the Lothians, Erskine."

"Thanks," Erskine said without dropping his eyes.

"You'll soon fit in," Tulloch said. "We're quite a friendly bunch here."

Erskine grunted, finished his whisky, rose, and strode away.

Muirhead strolled over, smiling. "Did you ask him?"

"No," Tulloch replied. "He didn't seem inclined to talk."

"That's how I found him," Muirhead said. He shrugged. "We'll see what he's like with the men. If he steps out of line, I'll slap him down. If he causes the men problems, I'll transfer him to the Camel Corps in the Falkland Islands."

Tulloch took out his pipe and began stuffing tobacco into the bowl. "I'll give him the benefit of the doubt first," he said.

Muirhead shook his head. "I won't," he said quietly.

The nervous officer sat alone in a corner of the Officers' Mess, slowly sipping at a glass of beer.

"I didn't catch your name," Tulloch said cheerfully.

"Atkins, sir. I'm Peter Atkins."

"Douglas Tulloch, and you don't call anybody sir in the Mess. It's your home." Tulloch wondered how many subalterns had made that identical mistake.

"Sorry, sir," Atkins said.

"Welcome to the Lothian Rifles," Tulloch sat beside Atkins. "What brought you to us?"

"I wanted to join the infantry, sir, Tulloch, and the War Office sent me here."

"Our good fortune," Tulloch said as Major Hume loomed over them.

"Was it good fortune? Or did somebody dump you on us?" Hume glowered at Atkins. "What skills do you bring, Atkins, apart from drinking our beer?"

"None, sir," Atkins admitted. "I did some mountaineering and rock climbing before Sandhurst, sir."

"Rock climbing?" Hume stepped back. "That will come in handy when we fight Hitler on the beaches." He walked away, shaking his head.

"Don't mind him," Tulloch tried to soothe Atkins' fragile nerves. "I'm sure you'll soon settle in here."

TULLOCH HATED KIT INSPECTION WHEN HE HAD TO WALK through the barrack room looking for flaws. He knew it was essential for discipline to keep his men on their toes, but when his duty was to reprimand an old soldier with half a chest full of medals for some minor oversight, he often turned a Nelsonian eye.

Does it matter if a man's toothbrush is turned the wrong way or his bed sheet is out of alignment? We need soldiers, not blasted housekeepers.

The barrack room was quiet when Tulloch entered. Men stood at attention beside their beds and all their kit was laid out in immaculate order. Tulloch walked through the room with nods of encouragement to the replacements, trying not to show favouritism to the men he had fought beside on the Frontier and in France.

Orr is shaking; he looks like he might fall at any minute.

Rifleman Hardie's kitbag was slightly, and uncharacteristically, out of place, and when Tulloch corrected its placement, it tipped over, and the contents spilled onto the floor. Rather than snarl at Hardie, Tulloch automatically stooped to tidy the mess. Two pamphlets had escaped: *The Art of Guerrilla Warfare* and *The Partisan Leader's Handbook*, both written by Brigadier Colin Gubbins.

"Are you interested in such things, Hardie?" Tulloch asked mildly.

"Yes, sir," Hardie replied, standing at attention and staring at a fixed point an inch above Tulloch's head.

"Do you think guerrilla warfare would work in this country?"

"We might have to if Hitler invades, sir," Hardie replied.

Tulloch nodded. "Let's hope we stop him before he reaches our coast."

"Yes, sir," Hardie said.

You're an interesting man for a private soldier, Tulloch thought. He handed the pamphlets back to Hardie. "Carry on."

"Yes, sir."

Tulloch had already noted Hardie as being different from the average Lothian Rifleman. He was quiet, self-contained, and a crack shot.

"What unit did you say Hardie was in before he joined us?" Muirhead asked as they sat in the Officers' Mess that evening. When he lifted his finger, the mess waiter poured him a Glenkinchie whisky.

"He once mentioned the King's African Rifles," Tulloch said, "and then he clammed up. I think he regretted telling me."

Muirhead raised his eyebrows. "When was that?"

"I don't know," Tulloch admitted. "He never mentioned it again, and Hitler has made things a little too interesting for me to pry into his life."

"The KAR is from East Africa," Muirhead said. "The men are all natives, led by British officers, good lads, from what I've heard of them. Either Hardie is lying, and he wasn't in the KAR, or he was an officer."

"He had no reason to lie," Tulloch said. "But why would an officer become a private soldier in the Lothians?"

Muirhead smiled. "You have a mystery on your hands. Agatha Christie would love it: the Mystery of the Commissioned Private." He sipped at his whisky. "Unless he was asked to resign his commission and knew no other trade than soldiering. What did Kipling call them? A gentleman ranker, wasn't it?" He lifted his crystal tumbler and quoted Kipling's poem *Gentlemen-Rankers*.

"We're little black sheep who've gone astray,
Baa—aa—aa!
Gentlemen-rankers out on the spree,
Damned from here to Eternity,
God ha' mercy on such as we,
Baa! Yah! Bah!"

"That sounds familiar," Tulloch said, recognising the poem

from his school days. "I never thought I'd meet a gentleman ranker, though."

"Does he not want promotion?" Muirhead asked.

"I've suggested it to him more than once," Tulloch said. "He's not interested."

Muirhead smiled. "We can't force anybody to accept the King's Commission. Just be thankful you have a good Rifleman."

"I have a few good Riflemen," Tulloch said. He stood up as Colonel Pringle entered the Mess.

"Sit down, Tulloch," Pringle waved him back to his seat, walked to a table at the head of the room, and perched on it. He thrust tobacco into the bowl of his pipe with a calloused thumb and looked over his gathered officers through tired eyes.

"Good evening, gentlemen," he said quietly. "Some of you have been in the regiment for years, and others have recently been posted here and might find our way of doing things a little bit strange." He scratched a match and applied it to the tobacco, sucking and puffing until his pipe was alight. "Well, you are all Lothian Rifles now, and I'm sure we'll all get along just fine."

The officers glanced at each other, the veterans of Dunkirk and the Northwest Frontier and the new members in pristine uniforms, wondering how they would fit in. Tulloch thought Erskine looked slightly bored and decided he did not like the man.

"You all know the current situation," Pringle puffed out aromatic blue smoke. "The Germans are poised on the other side of the Channel, waiting to invade, and we are building up our forces to repulse them."

The officers nodded, with the newcomers muttering about their willingness to fight and the veterans looking grim as they remembered the scenes from France.

"However," Pringle continued. "There are other threats we have to face. While the RAF will take the first strain against Hitler's Nazis and the Royal Navy will fight to keep the sea lanes safe, Britain also has to maintain the oceans and highways of the world. You know that since Italy declared war on us, Mussolini's armies threaten the Suez Canal and the oil fields of the Middle East. General Wavell has a vastly outnumbered force guarding everything from British Somaliland to the Holy Land."

Tulloch listened intently. Wavell was in overall command in the Middle East, with a vast area under his control, from Iraq to Somaliland and the Sudan, including Egypt and the Suez Canal.

Colonel Pringle puffed out more smoke. "General O'Connor commands our forces in Egypt, facing the Italians, and we are sailing out to reinforce him. We're leaving in a few days, so ensure your men are ready, but in the meantime, we'll continue with coastal defences. Are there any questions?"

"Yes, sir," Kilner asked. "Who is taking over here?"

"A Polish unit and the local Home Guard and Territorials," the colonel replied. "We have five days to acquaint them with the area before we leave."

The officers glanced at one another, unhappy at the thought of elderly men and strangers guarding their wives and families. Atkins was white-faced, while only Erskine looked untroubled as he fitted a cigarette into the end of a long holder and lit up. Aromatic smoke trickled to Tulloch's nostrils.

Pringle gave them a few moments before he continued. "With every day that passes, we are more ready to face and defeat Hitler's invading forces. Every pillbox we erect, every gun emplacement, every strand of barbed wire strengthens our defences. Think of that when we're in the Middle East. Our people are in good hands, gentlemen."

Tulloch felt the tension rise within him as the memories of Dunkirk returned. *I don't know if I am ready to return to war yet.* When he closed his eyes, he could hear the terrifying whine of a descending Stuka and see the shocked faces of the columns of Belgian and French refugees as the Luftwaffe bombed and strafed them.

"Are you all right, Tulloch?" Muirhead asked sharply.

"Perfectly," Tulloch replied with an automatic grin. "Just raring to get at the Italians."

"That's the spirit, old man," Muirhead said, with his eyes scrutinising Tulloch. "You looked a bit concerned there."

Tulloch shook his head. "Not at all," he lied.

Erskine leaned back in his chair. "No reason to be concerned, Tulloch. After all, we're the Lothian Rifles, aren't we?" He drew on his cigarette holder and smiled.

Colonel Pringle allowed the officers a few more minutes.

"That's all, gentlemen. Dismissed."

Chapter Three

LOTHIAN COAST, JULY 1940

"This is our last day on home defence, sir," Atkins said. He pushed back his helmet and touched the revolver in its holster. They stood on the shore at Seton Sands, with the Forth lapping at the beach and clouds flitting across the scimitar moon.

"That's correct," Tulloch lifted the Italian army-issue binoculars he had picked up on the Northwest Frontier and scanned the firth. He passed over the dark islands with their minimal anti-aircraft and anti-ship defences and over to the southern shores of Fife. An unseasonal wind flicked the tops from the waves, creating a slight haze on the water's surface and distorting sounds. "This time tomorrow, we'll be on our way to pastures new."

"Yes, sir," Atkins said. "Sometimes I wish the Germans would come so we can fight them on the beaches, as Winston said."

Tulloch glanced at the young second lieutenant. "Wars are better fought in somebody else's country," he replied. "We don't want the destruction and civilian casualties in Scotland."

As Atkins closed his mouth in embarrassment, Hogg

stamped his boots on the ground and hitched his Lee-Enfield further over his shoulder. "Do you think the Germans will come, sir?"

Tulloch had heard the same question posed a hundred different ways over the past few weeks. "I don't know, Hogg. If they do, we'll be ready for them."

"Aye," Hogg said. "Cummings in the NAAFI said Hitler was over in Denmark, just beyond the horizon, planning to invade Scotland. Cummings said he was using the build-up at Calais as a feint to draw our defences down south while he lands here. He knows Churchill hates Scotland since the folk in Dundee voted him out. That's why he sacrificed the 51st Division in France."

"Ignore these rumours, Hogg," Tulloch advised. "We're all in this together."

"Aye, maybe," Hogg said. He stamped his boots on the ground. "I hate the Germans after what we saw in France, sir."

"I don't think anybody likes them much, Hogg," Tulloch said. "Atkins, you patrol to the east, ensure the men are alert and look for anything unusual."

"Yes, sir," Atkins responded eagerly.

Tulloch walked on, inspecting the men in the solitary pillbox guarding this section of the coast. Innes stood inside with his Bren gun and three spare magazines, while Elliot, his loader, and the enigmatic Hardie waited in patient boredom.

"I wish the buggers would land so we can have it out with them," Innes said.

Tulloch smiled. "If they do, we'll be here," he said.

The Local Defence Volunteers patrolled the next section of the coast. They were a group of flint-eyed veterans of the Boer and Great Wars, armed with pikes and sharpened miner's spades, while the moustached corporal held a twin-barrelled shotgun.

"You should have handed that to the authorities," Tulloch said.

"Let them try and take it," the corporal growled, "and I'll give them both barrels."

Tulloch grinned. "I'm sure you would, corporal," he said. He looked up when he saw a flashing light out on the Forth. "What the devil's that?"

"A returning fisherman, perhaps," the corporal replied. "Or a Royal Navy patrol. Dinnae worry, Lieutenant; we'll keep an eye on it."

"Maybe," Tulloch said. He glanced behind him, hoping to see one of his platoon, but their patrol had taken them in the opposite direction. "Come with me, corporal."

Six of the LDV followed as Tulloch strode towards the shore, removing his revolver from its holster.

The light came closer, accompanied by the murmur of voices drifting on the wind.

"Spread your men out," Tulloch ordered in a tense whisper. "Where's the corporal with the shotgun?"

"Here, sir!"

"Stand behind that tree," Tulloch indicated a twisted birch. "Don't fire until I give the order. You!" he pointed to the unit's youngest member, a boy who looked about fifteen and probably was even younger. "Run that way and find one of the Lothians. Ask for Lieutenant Atkins and tell him what's happening. Move!"

As the boy ran away, Tulloch stepped forward with his pistol ready. The beach defences consisted of a few concrete blocks to impede landing tanks and a double string of barbed wire, which was all the government could find for this section of the coast.

When the voices grew louder, Tulloch levelled his revolver and ducked as a huge explosion broke the silence of the night. The intense flash starred Tulloch's vision, and the concussion staggered him.

"What the hell!" Tulloch swore and cursed again as a deluge of sand, stones, and water cascaded down on the beach.

With his ears ringing from the explosion, Tulloch barely heard the shouts from his right, where Atkins's platoon guarded the coast.

"Somebody's screaming," the LDV corporal said quietly. "He sounds badly injured."

Tulloch swore and increased his speed. The first man ran past him, helmetless and without his rifle.

"Mitchell!" Tulloch recognised the recruit. "Stand fast!" Another panicking Lothian passed him, and then a third, all youthful Lothian replacements. The screaming continued an inhuman, high-pitched wail that rose the tiny hairs on the back of Tulloch's neck.

"Corporal!" Tulloch roared. "Round these men up!" He strode forward, snarling as another soldier fled in his direction.

"Halt! Where the hell do you think you're going?"

The man was another recruit, a wide-eyed youth with a face badly scarred by acne and a shock of dark hair. Tulloch grabbed him roughly. "Hold still! What's happened!"

"The Germans have landed! They're firing at us!" The boy tried to push Tulloch away.

"Stand fast!" Tulloch held the boy. "You're a soldier now! Act like it!"

The man was still screaming, the sound dominating the coast. Tulloch sensed movement behind him and knew the LDV were close by.

"Corporal!"

"Sir!" The Home Guard corporal slammed to attention.

"Did you get these running men?"

"We did, sir. We're holding them secure."

"Good. Send a man to bring three men of my platoon here. I want Sergeant Drysdale and two men!" Tulloch wanted men he knew around him. "You!" He addressed the frightened youth. "Where's your rifle?"

"I dropped it, sir!"

"Well, pick it up again and come with me!"

Another recruit rose when Tulloch approached. "Who goes there?"

"Friend," Tulloch responded. "Lieutenant Tulloch. Identify yourself!"

"Private, sorry sir, Rifleman Scott."

"What's happening here?" Tulloch was pleased to see Scott was prepared to fight, with the safety catch off his rifle and his voice and eyes steady.

"I don't know, sir. There was an explosion, and some of the men ran away."

"But you didn't run," Tulloch approved. "Where's Lieutenant Atkins?"

"I don't know, sir," Scott replied.

There had been no more explosions and no sound of gunfire or German voices. Holding his revolver, Tulloch headed for the screaming. "Who's injured? Where's Lieutenant Atkins?"

"I'm here, sir!" Atkins' voice came from behind a gorse bush. "Be careful! The Germans are firing at us!"

"Where?" Tulloch looked around. "And who's injured?"

"Over there, sir," Atkins indicated the beach. "It's Orr."

Tulloch looked around. In his experience, night operations were always confusing, but if the Germans had landed, he would have expected more than a single explosion.

"Orr! Hold on, man; I'm coming!"

Orr lay on his face, holding his steel helmet in place with trembling hands. Tulloch could not see any blood or sign of a wound. I knew he was not fit to fight. Tulloch knelt at Orr's side and touched his shoulder. "Orr! It's all right, man. Lie quiet now."

Orr looked round with his eyes wide. "Lieutenant Forsyth, sir!"

Forsyth had died during the retreat to Dunkirk. *Orr doesn't recognise me; he's not with us.*

Tulloch stood up. "Corporal! Look after this man!"

"Yes, sir," the LDV corporal had seen shell-shocked men during the 1914-18 war and knew how to respond. "Come along, lad. Let's be having you."

"Atkins! Come out from behind that bush."

Tulloch waited for Atkins to emerge and moved on, ordering the rest of Atkins' platoon to remain where they were. The replacements looked scared, with one man shaking, holding his rifle in white-knuckled hands. "Don't fire without orders!"

Orr's screaming faded to an occasional whisper, mingling with the wind that blew clouds across the moon, leaving the land in darkness. Tulloch headed towards the explosion, holding his revolver in his right hand.

"Sir!" Sergeant Drysdale hurried up with Hogg and Cummings.

"Take over the section here, Sergeant. You two, come with me!" Tulloch loped forward, relieved he had two veterans at his back. He stopped at the site of the explosion, a five-foot-wide crater at the edge of the water, and saw phosphorescence gleaming offshore.

"There's a boat out there, sir," Hogg knelt, aiming his rifle. "Bastarding Nazis!"

"Don't fire yet," Tulloch cautioned and raised his voice. "Out there! Identify yourself!"

"Who's that?" The voice came from the darkness.

"Lieutenant Douglas Tulloch, Lothian Rifles," Tulloch replied.

"It's about time you Pongos showed up!" The voice said in a rich English West Country accent. "Midshipman Redcap, HMS *Shearwater!*"

"What are you playing at, firing guns at the shore?" Tulloch wished he had a torch to shine on the boat.

"We've not fired at anything. We've blown up a mine," Redcap replied cheerfully. "It looks like one of ours that broke free of its mooring. Better safe than sorry, eh?"

The wind shifted again, uncovering the moon and revealing a small rowing boat a hundred yards offshore. A teenaged midshipman balanced in the stern, with four oarsmen staring at Tulloch and the still-threatening Hogg.

"Where's HMS *Shearwater*?" Tulloch peered out into the Forth. He could only see a trawler quarter of a mile offshore.

"That's her," Redcap indicated the trawler. "An armed trawler." He laughed. "Not quite HMS *Hood*, but she does the job!"

Tulloch watched as the tiny boat rowed away. The German army might have pushed Britain out of France, but with men like Redcap in the Navy, she was a long way from defeat. He remembered how HMS *Glowworm*, a 1,350-ton destroyer, had fought two German destroyers and a heavy cruiser in an unequal battle.

Thank God for the Royal Navy.

Orr was quiet now, and the LDV escorted the shamefaced young soldiers to Tulloch.

"What a bloody shower," the LDV corporal said to the youngsters. "In the last war, you'd have been lined up against a wall and shot."

"Get back to your section of the coast," Tulloch snarled at the corporal. "Leave this lot to me."

The corporal opened his mouth to reply, but years of army discipline forced him to snap to attention. "Yes, sir," he said and marched away.

"You men return to your duty," Tulloch ordered the replacements. "Captain Kilner and Sergeant Naesmyth will speak to you tomorrow." Naesmyth would make life hell for the young soldiers for the next few days, but imposing some discipline now might save their lives later.

The news of the Lothians' behaviour had already spread when Tulloch returned to barracks, and the next day, the *Edinburgh Evening News* carried the story.

"Local Regiment runs from British mine. Last night, a platoon of the Lothian Rifles fled in near panic when the Royal Navy detonated a rogue mine. Only the actions of Corporal Michael Spalding of the Local Defence Volunteers saved the situation."

"Did you see this?" Erskine tossed the newspaper across to Tulloch. "Pringle's precious regiment is a laughingstock. The journalists are asking how we can defeat Germany when our regular soldiers run from a British mine."

"They were children," Tulloch said. "Seventeen-year-old boys just a few days out of basic training."

"Their officer was at fault," Erskine said loudly. "He didn't take command."

"He was too inexperienced," Tulloch tried to defend Atkins.

"That was Colonel Pringle's fault," Erskine said. "He should never have given him a platoon." Erskine stretched on the chair. "This regiment is not fit to fight at present, Tully."

"Tulloch."

"Didn't I say that? Do you know why General What's-his-name is sending us to Egypt? It's because we're a liability here. Half the men are only eighteen, and the other half haven't recovered from Dunkirk yet."

Tulloch grunted. He could not blame Atkins for succumbing to his fear or the young half-trained recruits for panicking. "The replacements just need more time to bed themselves in before they face the enemy."

"They won't get it if Hitler invades," Erskine said with brutal honesty. "I spoke to Pringle yesterday about teaching officers and men more realistic self-defence and sniping, and he turned me down."

"Why?" Tulloch asked. "Colonel Pringle is an experienced officer and loves the Lothians. Why did he turn down your offer?"

Erskine lit another cigarette and fitted it onto his long holder. "He said my techniques were ungentlemanly and unworthy of a British officer." He drew on his cigarette, giving Tulloch a questioning look.

"Are they?"

"Undoubtedly," Erskine said. "As long as the British officer is more concerned with hunting, balls, and gentlemanly behaviour than actually winning wars, then my techniques are not worthy."

Tulloch began to understand Erskine a little better. "What are they?"

Erskine blew a perfect smoke ring into the air. "Eye-gouging, testicle squeezing, joint dislocating, and the like." He began to discuss details.

Tulloch winced, then remembered the SS murdering prisoners-of-war and the Luftwaffe deliberately machine-gunning columns of civilian refugees. "If the colonel ever changes his mind, teach my platoon first, will you?"

Erskine blew another smoke ring. "I am not sure about you, Tulloch, but you might have promise." He stood up. "We'd better get our men ready for the fray, Tully. Or as ready as we're allowed."

Tulloch nodded. "Let's hope we can restore the Lothians' reputation."

"You can hope that," Erskine replied. "I'll hope we can defeat the enemy before they destroy everything we stand for." He grinned and smoothed a finger across his moustache. "Whatever that is."

Chapter Four

PORT SUDAN, SUDAN, AUGUST 1940

The Lothians filled the tenders, old soldiers and wide-eyed replacements side by side as the flat-bottomed vessels churned to the quayside. Flights of seagulls floated above, wingtips quivering as they looked down on the seeming confusion of khaki-clad men, weapons, and sundry kit. Already, the sun forced sweat from hot bodies, adding to the perpetual stench from the dockside.

"Here we are again," an old soldier chanted a refrain that had been old when he learned it in the Flanders' trenches twenty-odd years previously. "Here we are again. You made us jump at old Dunkirk, but here we are again."

"Aye, here we are, but where's here?"

"Port Said," Sergeant Drysdale said.

"What did the port say?" came the inevitable response.

"It said you're on first stag tonight, Cummings, and I'll be watching you!"

Most men stood or sat in silence, glad to be free from the confines of the troopship with its always-present fear of being torpedoed but apprehensive of the future in this new continent.

"Ready, lads?" Tulloch ran his gaze over his men, concentrating on the replacements. Rifleman Scott replied with a steady nod while most of the others dropped their eyes.

We have a long way to go yet.

"Are you all ready?" Tulloch repeated louder.

"Yes, sir," Four Platoon, a mixture of familiar soldiers and raw faces, agreed without enthusiasm.

"Think of the women, boys," Rifleman Elliot advised. "The bints here are willing, ready, and cheap. They'll fall over themselves for a fresh British soldier."

"Ignore Elliot's nonsense and remember the MO's lectures," Tulloch called. Dr Mercer had given a series of talks warning the younger soldiers of the dangers of sexually transmitted diseases in the East. Many of the men had looked ill and shocked at the end, which was Mercer's intention. The Army needed every soldier it could get, and sick men were a waste of resources.

The increasing smell of North Africa crossed the dark water to the Lothians, vaguely familiar to the old hands but chokingly unpleasant to the replacements.

"Welcome to the exotic East. You'll get used to the stink," Sergeant Drysdale said. "After a few weeks, you won't even notice."

Tulloch looked forward, where Egyptian anti-aircraft gunners manned the harbour's defences. The Lothian Rifles were returning to the war.

How will we cope when we meet the enemy? The battalion has changed since France. We've lost too many good men and some confidence. The experience of Dunkirk shook us to the core.

The Lothian Rifles disembarked in the dark, with only a handful of porters to witness their arrival, no cheering crowds, and no brass bands. The anti-aircraft gunners stared skyward, not interested in the arrival of another British infantry regiment.

"Here we are then, back in the East," Kinnear said.

"Ship me somewhere East of Suez, where the best is like the worst,

Where there ain't no Ten Commandments and a man can raise a thirst," Captain Kilner had not been with the Lothians on their pre-war tour of India and looked around with as much interest as the youngest rifleman.

"We're not East of Suez," Muirhead said. "We're here to stop the Italians from getting to the Suez Canal."

"What would they do if they got it?" Atkins asked, greatly daring.

"God knows. Ask Mussolini; he's the man who wants it," Kinnear said. "He'd probably ship it back to Rome as a trophy of war."

"Mussolini?" Atkins repeated. "At least he got the Italian trains to run on time."

"Did he?" Kinnear asked. "We could do with him here, then. I heard the Egyptian trains are always late."

Tulloch hid his smile, glad that Atkins was gaining some confidence. The young second lieutenant had hardly said a word on the outward voyage.

After the confusion of disembarking came the anticlimax of waiting for a train. As the sun rose to its apex, it brought increasing heat that swept across the waiting Lothians. The arrival of a fresh British battalion attracted a swarm of beggars and vendors who tried to squeeze every penny from the impoverished soldiers.

"Don't buy anything," Tulloch advised Four Platoon, knowing his words would be unheeded. British soldiers loved souvenirs from places they considered exotic. Given luck, the knickknacks the riflemen purchased from the quayside vendors would end up on mantelpieces from Leith to Loanhead and Broxburn to Belhaven.

"I have lovely clean ladies," one grossly fat man promised until Sergeant Drysdale sent him staggering with a mighty kick to his backside.

"Get away, you dirty bugger, and take your poxed-up hoors with you."

Erskine chuckled. "Aye, who needs Dr Mercer's lectures when you have Sergeant Drysdale's more direct methods?"

When the train finally arrived two hours later, the Lothians scrambled on board, cramming onto bare boards in ramshackle compartments, jostling for space and snarling happily at one another. The train moved in fits and starts, stopping every few moments and emitting clouds of steam to add to the smut-ridden smoke from its smokestack. While the old Indian hands played cards or tried to sleep, the new men stared excitedly out of the windows, exclaiming in wonder at every novel sight. Young men who had never been out of Edinburgh or the mining villages of Midlothian pointed to camels, canals, and water buffaloes even as they swatted at the insects that buzzed around their heads.

"Quassassin Station!" An iron-voiced station master announced.

"This is our stop," Colonel Pringle said, looking for any sign of the trucks. "There should be lorries waiting to take us to the transit camp."

Major Hume grunted. "It looks like we're marching."

"In this heat?" Pringle asked. "The men will be dropping out."

"I don't think we have much choice, sir," Hume said.

The battalion emerged, hot and sweaty, and looked around at the depressing starkness of the desert.

"Form a column of fours and march," Colonel Pringle ordered.

The heat was punishing, hammering on the heads of the Lothians as they obeyed. They moved on, kicking up dust, coughing, and swearing until the welcome sound of engines heralded the arrival of the trucks.

"Sorry we're late, lads!" a cheerful Geordie shouted. "Bloody sand in the carb!"

"In you go, boys!" Tulloch ushered in his platoon, ensured nobody was left behind, and climbed in beside the driver.

The convoy grumbled over the road, with each vehicle sucking up its quota of dust to irritate the tired and disgruntled men under the canvas covers in the back.

The trucks carried the Lothians to El Tahag, a British transit camp that was the sole feature beside a sand-smeared black tarmac ribbon that seemed to stretch from nowhere to nothingness.

"Right, boys," Tulloch said as the truck ground to a dusty halt. "We've arrived."

Four Platoon stumbled from their trucks with a great deal of swearing and looked around them as the dust gradually settled.

"Where are we?" Connington, a stocky ex-miner, asked.

"El Tahag," Sergeant Drysdale replied. Middle-aged and vastly experienced, Drysdale had been with the regiment since the Somme in 1916.

"It looks like the arse end of bugger all," Drummond, the one-time fisherman, said. "There's nothing here."

"That's what I said," Drysdale told him. "El Tahag is the Egyptian for 'bugger all.'"

"Is it, Sergeant?" Bryson, one of the new men, asked.

"Ask Hardie, he's been in Africa before."

Hardie, quiet, serious, and self-effacing, smiled and said nothing.

"I'm going to learn some Egyptian," Bryson announced.

Tulloch could only agree with Drummond. A barbed-wire fence surrounded groups of tents, each collection clustering close to an ugly water tower. There was nothing else in the transit camp of El Tahag, a bleak, hot place surrounded by a featureless stretch of dust and grit ruled by flies and ants.

"Right, lads," Tulloch said. "Let's get settled in."

"Well, bugger this for a game of soldiers," Hogg said. "I thought Dalkeith was grim until we came here."

Each tent was dug into the ground as protection against enemy bombing, and scores of flies settled on each spread of white canvas.

"We should be in Blighty," fair-haired Cummings said, "defending the country against Hitler, not sweating out here hundreds of miles from the war."

"We're defending civilisation from fascism," Innes informed him. "Without us, Mussolini's millions would walk across the frontier, grab the Canal, and control half the world's trade. But no," he said. "The Lothians are in El Tahag. I must stay in Libya, Abyssinia, and Eritrea and do nothing except eat spaghetti and drink vino."

"He can keep the spaghetti," Hogg said, "but send the vino to us."

While the old soldiers soon acclimatised to the heat, the replacements suffered from sunburn, cracked lips, and peeling noses. As they wore unfamiliar shorts, their bare white legs itched from a combination of sand and sun, and every man resented the humiliation of wearing huge topees that immediately marked them as newcomers to Egypt.

"How long do we have to wear these things for?" Connington indicated his topee.

"Only a week," Tulloch told him. "Then we can discard them."

"Thank God for that," Connington said.

Sand got everywhere: into the tents, into every article of clothing, into eyes, noses, ears, mouths, and other less obvious places. Men scratched, swore, and flapped frustrated hands at the millions of flies.

"Did Moses not bring a plague of flies to Egypt?" Smith asked.

"He did," Elliot, a Selkirk Souter, replied.

"I wish he had taken the buggers away with him when he crossed the Red Sea," Smith said, swatting furiously.

Added to the flies and the sun glare that hurt men's eyes was the dreaded Gyppy Tummy, dysentery spread by the flies. The old hands remembered Delhi Belly from India but still succumbed, and the medical officer ordered more latrines dug to ensure there were no queues.

"Whatever happens out here," Dr Mercer said, "we'll all succumb to Gyppy Tummy at some time. It's one of the pleasures of the East."

The Lothians learned how to conserve water, reuse shaving water to wash socks or underwear, and how to use the four-gallon petrol cans issued by the War Office.

"These are marvellous things," an enthusiastic, bespectacled artillery officer told Tulloch. "The powers-that-be decided to make them single-use and very thin. They leak like sieves, of course, and lose half the contents before they reach their destination, but apart from that, they have a hundred uses."

Tulloch grinned. "I notice you're sitting on one."

The artillery officer patted his makeshift seat. "Oh, yes, my seat is made from three petrol cans. Fill them with sand and they can revet the trench walls, build latrines or anything else; they make excellent wash basins and are useful for everything except holding petrol. Wait, and I'll show you something else you'll need to know."

Tulloch watched as the gunner lifted a tin from behind him and handed it over.

"Note the punctures?" the artilleryman asked.

"I do," Tulloch said solemnly.

"I made them with that very adaptable tool, the eighteen-inch bayonet," the gunner said. "Find a suitable tin, stab the thing with a bayonet, half fill it with sand – there's plenty going around – and pour in a pint of petrol. Stir it into a paste; the bayonet is excellent as a stirrer, light a match and drop it in." He looked up with a smile. "It's better to throw the match in because the petrol ignites with a bit of a whoomph, and you might lose your eyebrows."

"I'll pass your advice on to the men," Tulloch said. "What is it?"

"It's a cooker, easy to use, and simple to make. It burns for about twenty minutes, half an hour if you stir it with a bayonet," the gunner said, "and that's your cooking worries over out in the Blue."

"The Blue?" Tulloch queried the word.

"The desert," the gunner explained. "We call it the Blue because all you see is blue sky." He stood up. "And sand," he added. "Lots of sand."

While the Lothians suffered and gradually became accustomed to life in Egypt, Colonel Pringle put them on a war footing. He organised desert marches, set up Bren guns in case of air attack, and ordered firing drills to ensure the men were used to the different clarity in the desert.

"We have an advantage over most of the units already in Egypt," the colonel told them. "Many of us have already seen action on the Frontier and in France. We know the reality of war." He paused for a moment. "But we are not yet desert worthy."

"Or battle-worthy," Erskine murmured.

Pringle did his best to rectify the Lothians' lack of desert experience. He sent his men on route marches, increasing the distance every time. The colonel organised tactical exercises, company against company, and platoon against platoon. He ordered night marches using the compass and the stars, borrowed desert veterans from other units, and had them lecture and train the officers and men.

After a week, the men thankfully discarded the topees. After two weeks, checking their boots for invasive scorpions in the morning became second nature. After three weeks, their transport arrived to take them closer to the border with Libya, where the Italian Army, Mussolini's vaunted *Forze Armate*, waited.

The Lothians waited patiently beside the road, wondering what the future held.

"What are the Italians like as soldiers?" Atkins asked.

"Nobody knows for sure yet," Hume replied. "They can be ruthless when they wish. They conquered Abyssinia without much difficulty, and some of their men have experience fighting for Franco's fascists in Spain, so they'll know what they are doing."

Tulloch watched Atkins' face. The youngster had still not recovered from the incident on the East Lothian beach and was more hesitant than Tulloch expected in an officer.

"However good they think they are," Tulloch said quietly, "they're not as good as us." He looked up as a convoy of trucks pulled into the camp. "Here comes our transport. Look to your platoon, Atkins."

Tulloch sat beside the driver, a nasal-voiced New Zealander with a long chin, an impressively large slouch hat, and a Lee-Enfield rifle propped up in the cab at his side.

"Going up the Blue, mate?"

About to remind the driver that he was an officer, Tulloch saw the New Zealander's steady eyes and realised he was being deliberately provocative.

Tulloch nodded. "Yes, we're headed there."

The driver grinned. "Best of luck, Scottie. Mussie wants our Egyptian sand."

"Does he not have enough of his own?"

The driver nodded. "Too true, mate, but he wants ours too."

"We'll ensure he doesn't get it," Tulloch said.

"That's the way, Scottie," the driver replied. "As long as he doesn't blow up any mines then."

That story's spread out here, has it?

Tulloch forced a laugh. "We're fully trained in mine avoidance," he said. "That and being impudent to officers."

The New Zealander laughed. "That's the way," he replied. "We'll make Kiwis of you yet, Scottie."

Chapter Five

Nobody regretted saying goodbye to El Tahag as the Lothians travelled past Cairo without stopping and a dozen miles closer to the frontier with Libya. The road was bumpy, with the trucks crashing into rock ledges hidden by sand, throwing the men against one another and testing their temper with each passing mile.

"I thought the Edinburgh Corporation buses were bad," Cummings grumbled.

"Bugger this for a game of soldiers," Hogg said, holding onto a strut that supported the canvas cover. "I'd prefer marching."

"We'd prefer you marching, too," Smith told him.

The convoy moved slowly, each truck throwing up a curtain of fine orange dust that settled on the vehicles behind, covering every surface, sticking to the men's sweat so individuals were lost in a general view of orange, dusty, ill-tempered humanity.

They camped beside the road, with fewer flies but a new hardship with water rationed to two gallons daily for all purposes.

"Where are the sand dunes?" Hogg asked, gazing in disgust at the desert. "I thought we'd have sand dunes and Arabs on camels."

Tulloch grunted. He was also disappointed with the Egyptian geography. This section of the desert was a plain of rock topped by a thin layer of sand. Unlike the romantic visions of P.C. Wren's *Beau Geste*, it was featureless, dry, and uninspiring. An occasional dwarf scrub did little to alleviate the monotony, and Tulloch unfolded his map and tried to pinpoint their position.

"It seems a strange place to want to fight when Hitler is paddling his toes in the English Channel," Kinnear said.

Tulloch nodded. "It seems a strange place to fight for any reason. Who wants a desert?"

"We do," Kinnear replied. "The Egyptians do, and now the Italians also want it."

"The Italians are still in Libya," Tulloch said.

"Marshal Graziani is building a formidable force there," Kinnear reminded him. "His army is at least three times bigger than ours, with huge armoured reserves and aircraft."

Tulloch nodded. "Quality is better than quantity," he tried to sound optimistic.

"Size might not be everything," Kinnear said soberly, "but it helps."

Tulloch noticed Atkins a few yards away, listening to everything they said. "Man to man, we were better than the Germans in France," he said. "We'll be better than the Italians, too, and this time, we haven't got unreliable allies."

Kinnear shrugged. "Maybe," he said, stood up, and sloped away.

The Lothians scraped holes in the sand that night, with bivouacs stretched over them and the chill of the desert night keeping many men awake. Tulloch thought of home and wondered if Amanda remembered who he was. He could hardly remember the last time he had seen her.

The bugle woke them half an hour before dawn, and the men stood to, grumbling as they pulled up the collars of their greatcoats and watched for an enemy who was many miles away. None had expected the desert nights to be so cold and stamped their feet to restore hampered circulation.

"The Italians might send a raiding force," Hogg said hopefully as he peered into the dark. Dawn carried spreading light that revealed scattered vehicles and sinister shapes that became innocent rocks. The sun rose swiftly, dispersing the dew and heating the men, so they discarded their greatcoats and began to sweat.

"Come on, Mussolini," Innes cuddled into the butt of his Bren gun, "I'm waiting for you."

Tulloch walked along the line occupied by Four Platoon, checking Sergeant Drysdale had put the experienced men between the replacements.

"All right, Sergeant?"

"Nae bother, sir," Drysdale replied.

Hardie heard the sound first, "Aircraft, sir!" he shouted. Within minutes, the Lothians stared into the sky as a lone aircraft passed. It disappeared, turned, and passed again, much lower.

"That's the *Regia Aeronautica*," Tulloch warned. "It's a Meridionali, an army co-operation aircraft."

"That's a hostile aircraft!" Tulloch shouted.

The veterans immediately dived into their trenches, with those with Bren guns aiming them skyward.

"Give him a burst, Innes," Tulloch said, remembering the terrifying Stuka dive bombers on their retreat to Dunkirk.

Elliot lay at Innes's side with spare magazines.

"He's going to bomb us," Cummings warned.

"He's not," Hardie reassured them. "The Meridionali doesn't carry any guns. He's probably only spotting."

"Aye?" Innes grunted. "Well, spot this!" He fired a short burst, with three other Lothian Bren guns following his lead. The aircraft abruptly rose, twisting as the Lothians' fire rose towards it.

"It's getting away!" Hogg said.

"He's going to fetch his friends," Hardie said soberly. "We'll have half a dozen fighters hammering us in a few moments."

Tulloch eyed Hardie curiously, wondering how he knew so much. *A gentleman ranker from the King's African Rifles who knows Italian aircraft at a glance? Who the hell are you, Private Hardie?*

Tulloch brought his mind back to the present and passed the information to the other officers. "Stay in the trenches," he ordered Four Platoon. "Bren gunners, get ready to fire. The rest of you, keep your heads down."

When he saw Atkins shouting desperate orders, Tulloch gave him a reassuring wave. The Lothians waited, watching the sky, with some silently praying and the Bren gunners wiping the sweat from their eyes and traversing their weapons from left to right and back. The drivers threw camouflage netting over their trucks and scuffed the tyre marks as much as possible, hoping to hide them from the aircraft. They worked rapidly, glancing upwards.

A distant hum grew more menacing, with the sound of aircraft engines increasing. Again, Hardie was first to see the distant black specks.

"Here they come!"

The Lothians prepared for the *Regia Aeronautica*, with the veterans hiding their fear and the replacements trying to appear nonchalant.

Tulloch could taste the apprehension as the Lothians wondered if the Italians were as formidable as Mussolini's propaganda claimed.

"Bugger this for a game of soldiers," Hogg fiddled with his bayonet as if he hoped to leap into the air and skewer the approaching aircraft. Erskine sat on the edge of a trench, calmly smoking a cigarette.

"Here they come!" Hardie repeated.

The four tiny dots grew larger, with a faint hum that increased as the aircraft approached.

"What are they, Hardie?" Tulloch asked.

"Fiat CR32 fighters," Hardie replied calmly. "They have eight machine guns and can carry one 220-pound bomb."

"Formidable," Tulloch said.

The aircraft seemed to approach slowly and suddenly were diving at the Lothians' positions. Their machine guns hammered, raising spurts of sand as men crouched in the bottom of trenches that seemed far too shallow. The Brens fired back, with the number two men providing fresh magazines as bullets thudded into the sand or ricocheted from the rocks.

"Come on, you bastards!" Innes snarled.

Tulloch saw Rifleman McAllister lying on his back in his trench, firing his Lee-Enfield at aircraft travelling over two hundred miles an hour.

Unsure whether to keep under cover or stay above ground as an example to his men, Tulloch felt a strong hand pull him down.

"Keep down, you bloody fool! You're doing no good above ground!"

Colonel Pringle glared into Tulloch's eyes. "A dead officer is no good to anybody."

The Italian fighters flew low across the Lothians' position, firing long bursts with their machine guns as the Brens fired back. Tulloch closed his eyes, trying to burrow deep into the suddenly friendly sand as bullets burrowed into the ground all around.

The noise seemed to engulf him, swallowing him so he could think of nothing except escaping. He felt his hands clawing into the ground, grabbing great handfuls of sand as if that would save him from the hundreds of bullets the aircraft pumped out.

As one CR32 passed, another took its place, and Innes and the other Bren gunners returned fire, with the loaders calmly holding spare magazines.

The raid seemed to last for hours, yet when he checked his watch as the aircraft flew away, Tulloch saw it had only been a few moments.

He stood up and took a deep breath to control himself. "Any casualties?" He counted the men of Four Platoon as they emerged from their holes in the sand. The aircraft had hit one of the trucks, which blazed furiously as Captain Martin, the Motor Transport Officer, organised a party to quench the flames.

"None, sir," Sergeant Drysdale reported calmly. "Not in our platoon. The Italians wounded Leishman, the Bren gunner of Three Platoon."

Tulloch knew Leishman as a steady man with a wife and two children. "Did we get any of them?"

"No, sir," Innes reported, clicking a fresh magazine into the Bren. "I don't think we even nicked them."

"As long as they didn't nick Four Platoon," Tulloch replied. He saw Dr Mercer with Leishman and hoped the man was not severely hurt.

With one truck less, the Lothians moved on thirty minutes later, heading inexorably west towards the frontier. Tulloch noted the men were more wary, watching the sky for further Italian air raids.

Nobody panicked; nobody ran away, and now the replacements have some experience of being under fire. Except for Leishman, the attack probably helped us as a battalion.

The convoy halted after a five-hour drive of dust and apprehension, with men stretching stiff limbs, holding their rifles ready to fire and looking for cover. The dust gradually cleared, leaving the sky clear and blue above, with neither a cloud nor the sinister black specks of enemy aircraft.

"A thirty-minute break," Colonel Pringle ordered, "and then we're on the move again. When we stop next time, I want the lorries to be more dispersed. The closer we are to the frontier, the more chance the *Regia Aeronautica* will pay us another visit."

When they moved on, one of the battalion's pipers played the regimental tune, *The Flowers of Edinburgh*, with the familiar notes helping to alleviate the alien environment.

"Trust the Pipie to make things worse," Smith grumbled. "I cannae stand the pipes."

"I cannae stand you, Smith," Connington said, "but I don't moan about it."

They halted thirty minutes before nightfall, with the men scattering and the drivers dispersing and hauling camouflage netting over the trucks.

"Set up the Brens for anti-aircraft," Pringle ordered, "and dig shelter trenches before we do anything else."

After the brief air raid, the Lothians worked willingly, with the replacements throwing sand around like men demented.

"Get these trenches deeper," Atkins ordered, "and make sure they face the right way."

Tulloch walked over. "It's all right, Atkins," he said quietly. "A trench against enemy aircraft can't face the wrong way."

"In Sandhurst, the instructors taught us that trenches must face the enemy," Atkins said, flushing.

"This enemy is in the sky," Tulloch reminded gently and walked away.

"HOW DO THE FIGURES STACK UP, SIR?" KINNEAR ASKED.

Colonel Pringle puffed at his pipe before replying, "On paper, the Italians have all the advantages," he admitted, looking around his officers. "Let's go over the three services: land, sea, and air. Before the French surrendered, our combined navies outnumbered the Italians in the Mediterranean. Now that the French have packed it in, that is no longer the case, and the Italian *Regia Marina* outnumbers the Royal Navy in every department, especially in submarines, where they have 115 against our twelve." The colonel paused for a moment. "They have six battleships, seven heavy and twelve light cruisers, and around 130 destroyers."

"How many do we have, sir?" Kinnear asked.

"Four old battleships, two aircraft carriers, plus cruisers and destroyers," Pringle gave his gentle smile. "If you want to know the exact number, you'll have to ask the Navy because they don't tell me."

Tulloch heard Atkins' high-pitched laugh.

Pringle continued, "The Italian ships are also faster than ours, and Italy is centrally placed in the Med. That means they have a decided tactical advantage in deciding when and where to fight."

Atkins looked pale. "Is there any good news, sir?"

Colonel Pringle nodded. "We have Admiral Cunningham," he said quietly. "You'll know his reputation as a destroyer commander in the Kaiser's War and again in the Baltic to ensure Latvian independence."

Atkins nodded.

Pringle smiled again. "And our ships are Royal Navy, the best in the world."

Some of the officers laughed, but all knew the army in the Middle East depended on men and supplies from Great Britain, which meant the Navy had to protect the merchant ships from a larger Italian Navy. Nobody mentioned the possibility of Vichy French bringing the powerful French Navy onto the Axis side. Tulloch remembered his father mentioning the Royal Navy bombarding the French fleet in Oran and understood why.

"Air next," Pringle said. "The Italians are numerically superior to the RAF in the air in fighters and bombers. Their aircraft are also more modern, generally faster, and can be reinforced from Italy faster than our fliers from the UK." He paused for a moment. "We met some Italian aircraft on our journey here. Some have recent experience of battle in Spain and Ethiopia, and with the RAF fully occupied in the Battle of Britain, they won't have many spare aircraft for this theatre."

The officers looked serious. Erskine lit one of his aromatic cigarettes and blew his usual perfect smoke ring.

"Lastly, to the land forces," Pringle said. "The Italians

comfortably outnumber us on land as well. We have 36,000 fighting men in Egypt, as well as the Egyptian army, who will only defend their own land. The Italians have some 200,000; with France out of the war, Mussolini can concentrate them all against us."

The officers listened quietly. Erskine blew another smoke ring.

"The army is stretched pretty thin," Pringle continued. "We will be attached to the Fourth Indian Division, but at present, we're on our own." He lifted a sheet of paper from his desk. "We have orders here from headquarters. Some are confidential to me, but I will read out the final paragraph."

The officers waited. Tulloch noticed that Atkins looked like he was about to be sick.

"Although the utmost aggressiveness will be displayed, it is important to avoid becoming engaged with superior enemy formations."

Tulloch spoke without thought. "Surely that can't refer to us, sir," he said. "No Axis formation will ever be superior to the Lothians."

"I presume they mean superior in numbers," Pringle replied with a wry smile. "Or maybe they read the newspaper account of our behaviour before we left Scotland."

Atkins stood up until Hume shoved him back down. "Sit, Atkins. We all make mistakes the first time we're in action."

"It wasn't a real action, sir," Atkins said.

"You didn't know that."

Tulloch met Atkins' gaze and winked.

"The army commander is General Richard O'Connor," Pringle said. "I think it's important for the officers to know about the general in charge, so I'll tell you O'Connor is of Irish stock but with strong Lowland Scottish connections as he served with the Cameronians in the last war."

The officers nodded in approval for the Cameronians were a fine fighting regiment.

"I knew nothing about General O'Connor," Major Hume said. "I had to ask one of the old Egypt hands for details. They call him the Little White-Haired Terrier, apparently."

"Why?" Tulloch asked the obvious question.

"Because once he decides on something, he never lets go," the major replied. "That bodes well for us and badly for Graziani. O'Connor's an Indian-born Irishman who won the Military Cross, the DSO, and the Italian Silver Star of Military Valour during the Kaiser's War."

"The Italians honoured him?" Tulloch asked.

"He captured an island from the Austrians for them," Major Hume replied.

"And now he's fighting his old allies."

Hume smiled. "We all will be." He was quiet for a significant moment. "We lost a bit of our reputation recently, and the influx of raw men into our ranks has created confusion. Fighting the Italians will allow us to find ourselves."

Tulloch saw Atkins stir in embarrassment. Erskine blew another smoke ring as he looked at the brilliant stars above.

Chapter Six

The following morning, the Lothians moved again, basing themselves a few miles from the border with Italian-owned Libya. They dug in with rifle pits and machine gun nests, strung barbed wire in front of their positions, and contacted the Royal Engineers to come and lay a minefield.

"Well, gentlemen," Colonel Pringle said. "We're at the sharp end here." He began to fill his pipe. "I suggest we learn all we can about the area."

They studied maps of the Egypt-Libya border, marking their position and that of the other Imperial units holding the line.

"We're spread very thin," Tulloch said. "If the Italians come over in force, we're not strong enough anywhere to hold them."

"We're sufficiently strong to hold them for a while," Hume said. "Let them come."

"The 11th Hussars have been on the frontier for months," Colonel Pringle said. "They've been patrolling on both sides of the frontier." He thrust his pipe into his mouth and grinned. "Well, anything the Cherry Pickers can do, we can do better.

58

Kinnear and Tulloch, take the carriers over the frontier and see what mischief you can do. Keep the Italians on their toes and show them that the Lothians are here."

Tulloch and Kinnear glanced at each other. "Yes, sir," Tulloch said. It was an ideal order for any junior officer, allowing him to act on his initiative.

"But remember the orders from above," Pringle added an immediate qualifier. "Don't take on a superior force and avoid casualties."

"We'll do our best, sir," Tulloch agreed. He saw Hume frown behind Pringle's back and wondered if the colonel and senior major had an acrimonious relationship when out of earshot of the junior officers.

"When do we leave, sir?" Kinnear asked.

"Tomorrow night," Pringle said. "Familiarise yourselves with the terrain first."

"Yes, sir," Kinnear agreed.

Tulloch watched a patrol of the 11th Hussars advance to the frontier in their Rolls-Royce armoured cars. The Hussars drove in a stately line with their old-fashioned-looking vehicles that had seen service with the army since 1924.

Imagine that lot meeting the Panzers. The Germans would mince them. We're fighting this war with weapons that are fifteen years out of date.

The armoured cars had a tall, ungainly turret and a Boys anti-tank rifle probing hopefully outward.

With Hardie driving, Tulloch took a carrier in the wake of the Hussars, observing them closely and learning all he could. The Hussars headed straight to the long wire fence known as the Wire that marked the boundary between Egypt and Libya and dismounted.

"Why the rubber-soled shoes?" Tulloch asked when the leading lieutenant changed his army boots for a pair of rubber overshoes.

"The Italians might have electrified the fence," the lieutenant said nonchalantly, took a pair of wire cutters from inside the car, and cut a dozen strands of wire. As Tulloch watched, the lieutenant returned to his post, pressed the nose of his vehicle against the nine-foot-high barrier, and pushed until the fence collapsed. Dragging the strands of wire away, he repeated the procedure until he created a wide gap for the remaining armoured cars to drive through.

"As easy as that, sir," Hardie said.

"As easy as that," Tulloch agreed as the Hussars roared across the frontier into Libya.

And as easy for the Italians, with their much larger army, to invade Egypt.

Tulloch had the battalion's fitters check the Bren gun carriers before he took them across the Wire. The battalion had six Scout Mark 1 carriers, a relatively new addition to the British Army, introduced in 1938. Weighing three and a third tons, the carriers were tracked vehicles with a crew of three or four, lightly armoured and with a top speed of thirty miles an hour. In theory, the carrier could carry a Bren Gun and a Boys anti-tank rifle, but with the perennial shortage of armament in the British Army, the Lothians' vehicles had one or the other. Two of Tulloch's carriers carried Brens; the third was armed with a Boys.

"Smith, you're best with the Boys; I want you in Carrier two. Innes and Elliot, you're with me, and Hardie, I want you as my driver." Hardie was experienced in driving in rough terrain. Tulloch knew having four men in a carrier would be a squeeze, but he could not simultaneously command and act as driver or loader.

Tulloch felt the usual tension as he checked his patrol for petrol and ammunition. He had decided to bring one replacement, the steady Scott, with him, while all the others were veterans of France and the Northwest Frontier.

"Ready, lads? Let's show the Hussars that we can drive in the desert as well as they can."

The men nodded or smiled, looking to the west.

"Let's go." Tulloch led his three carriers through the gap and into Libya. The Hussars and other units had been raiding Libya since June when Mussolini declared war, so Tulloch did not expect to find any Italians near the frontier.

"According to the Hussars, the Italians mostly keep inside their series of heavily defended forts," Tulloch said. "All the same, keep an eye open and watch for aircraft. Our dust will attract them like bluebottles to a pile of dung."

Innes grinned and adjusted his Bren. "We'll watch for them, sir." He glanced behind him. "As long as they don't hit the petrol."

Tulloch insisted that each vehicle carried spare fuel to enable him to penetrate further into Libya.

They moved cautiously, stopping every mile to inspect the surroundings and check their position with the stars. After three hours, they reached a track that hugged the escarpment that marked the end of the coastal plain.

"Halt here," Tulloch ordered. When the carriers cut their engines, Tulloch scanned the road that snaked into the distant haze. The sun rose behind him, its rays penetrating the gloom and reflecting from something ahead.

"That could be glass, sir," Hardie said. "Or metal. Either could be from a vehicle."

"Quite possibly," Tulloch agreed. "Are you ready with the Bren, Innes?"

"Ready, sir." Innes traversed the barrel, working out his angles, while Elliot readied spare magazines.

Tulloch dismounted and warned the other two carriers.

"Keep hull down and watch the road. Don't do anything until I lead."

The men nodded, with Smith smoothing a hand across the clumsy Boys. "My elephant gun is ready, sir," he said.

With the sun behind him, Tulloch knew the light would not reflect on the lenses of his binoculars. He focused on the road, watching the ribbon of dust that announced the approaching vehicles. The sound of engines soon reached him, a reassuring growl that rose as a small convoy approached.

"Six trucks," Tulloch said to Hardie. "Tell Smith to take the leading vehicle with the Boys and then the last truck; Innes and Connington will take the vehicles in between."

Hardie nodded and slipped away with the message, returning within a few moments. The heat increased, baking the men inside the steel carriers. They waited, feeling the tension rise.

The Italians approached steadily, with a space between each truck and dust nearly concealing the vehicle at the back. Tulloch waited until the convoy was almost level with his carriers and shouted, "Fire!"

Innes fired first, raking the second vehicle with his Bren. Tulloch saw the bullets hammer into the truck and raise spurts of dust from the road. Connington concentrated on the third vehicle, firing a long burst that smashed into the driver's cab, breaking the windscreen glass and puncturing the radiator. Smith fired the Boys a few seconds later, with the anti-tank bullet missing the leading vehicle by a handbreadth, but the shock caused the driver to slew sideways, effectively blocking the road. Both Brens altered their target, concentrating on the fourth vehicle, bursting a tyre and puncturing the door with holes.

"Get the last truck, Smith!" Tulloch shouted above the rattle of the Brens, the roaring of engines, and the screams and yells of the Italian soldiers. He saw the rearmost truck halt an inch from the vehicle in front and try to reverse. Through his binoculars, Tulloch saw the driver's frantic face as he sought to turn and flee from the ambush.

"Fire, Smith!" Tulloch bellowed.

A second later, Smith fired again, with the shell crashing into the body of the truck, which skidded to one side but continued a three-point turn, with flames licking from the rear.

"He's getting away!" Scott shouted. "Don't let him get away!"

Innes switched targets and fired a long burst at the fleeing vehicle. When he ceased firing, Elliot handed him a fresh magazine.

"I think I got him, sir!" Innes said.

"Let him go," Tulloch ordered. "He'll spread panic among the Italians. Concentrate on the leading three vehicles."

The convoy halted, with men spilling from the trucks to scatter on the ground. A few brave soldiers attempted to return fire, throwing themselves under the trucks or lying prone on the ground. The remainder fled into the desert, some dropping their weapons in their haste to escape.

"Keep firing," Tulloch watched Scott as Italian rifle bullets whistled around the three carriers. The youngster appeared as calm as any of the veterans.

With the leading truck jammed across the road and the rear-most truck ablaze, the rest of the convoy had nowhere to go. When Smith fired his Boys again, hitting the second vehicle, the last of the Italians dropped their rifles and threw up their hands in surrender.

"Cease fire!" Tulloch shouted, with a hand on Innes' shoulder.

The Bren guns stuttered into silence; dust drifted across the desert road, mingled with the smoke from burning trucks. One wounded man moaned piteously as the prisoners stood, hands raised, nervous, afraid, unsure what was going to happen.

What the hell am I going to do with prisoners? Tulloch asked himself. He stepped cautiously from the carrier. "Cover me, Innes. If any of the Italians try to attack me, shoot them."

"I will, sir," Innes aimed the Bren at the prisoners.

"I hope one of them speaks English," Tulloch said as he stepped forward, revolver in hand.

"I speak a little Italian, sir," Hardie volunteered.

"The devil you do!" Tulloch said. "You're a lad o' pairts, aren't you? Don't let them know you speak their language yet. Come with me."

Hardie leapt from his seat and joined Tulloch, marching with his shoulders back and a Lee-Enfield in his hands.

The seven Italians waited in a group as Tulloch approached. "Can anybody speak English?"

One man nodded eagerly. "I speak some." He was about thirty, with wide brown eyes, a smooth face, and a ready smile.

"Who is in charge here?" Tulloch asked. "Who's the officer?"

The smiling man nodded. "I am, sir," he introduced himself. "Capitano Peppino Galuzzo." He saluted.

"I am Lieutenant Douglas Tulloch of the Lothian Rifles." Tulloch returned the salute as Hardie kept his rifle pointed at the Italians. He considered for a moment. "You can come with us, Capitano Galuzzo." Tulloch decided. "The rest of your men can go free. We'll patch up the wounded man."

"Too late, sir," Hardie said.

Tulloch realised the wounded man had died. "At least he's out of pain." He saw Capitano Galuzzo look concerned.

You may not be the best soldier in the world, but at least you care for your men.

Tulloch lifted his voice. "Search the vehicles for maps and documents and destroy them," he ordered. "Take the officer as a prisoner, and let's get away before the smoke alerts the Regia Aeronautica."

Tulloch sent Elliot into the second carrier, put Galuzzo into his vehicle, and headed back across the desert, pleased with the success of his first patrol.

"What's your unit?" He asked the prisoner.

"I will not say," Capitano Galuzzo lifted his chin defiantly.

"You fought bravely," Tulloch did not press his questions, knowing the battalion's intelligence officer would interrogate Galuzzo.

"We are a transport unit, not a fighting unit," Galuzzo said. "The MVSN will give you a better fight."

"Who?" Tulloch already guessed the answer.

"The *Milizia Volontaria per la Sicurezza Nazionale*," Galuzzo explained.

"Is that the Blackshirts?" Tulloch asked. He saw Hardie stir uneasily when Galuzzo nodded. "Have you heard of the MVSN, Hardie?"

"Yes, sir," Hardie admitted without explaining more. "May I ask Captain Galuzzo a question, sir?"

"Go ahead," Tulloch allowed. "He understands English."

"Thank you, sir," Hardie replied. "Captain Galuzzo, have you heard of an MVSN battalion commanded by Tenente Colonnello Lorenzo Rotunno?"

Galuzzo crossed himself before replying. "Tenente Colonnello Rotunno is a fascist hero," he replied enigmatically.

"Perhaps," Hardie said. "Is he in Libya?"

Galuzzo spread his hands expressively. "He may be, or he may not be. I do not know where every Blackshirt unit is." He smiled. "Wherever Colonnello Rotunno may be, there will be fighting, and Italia will triumph."

Hardie nodded. "That may well be correct, Capitano."

Tulloch eyed Hardie curiously. "You seem to know a lot about the Italians, Hardie."

"I picked up a little bit here and there, sir," Hardie said.

"Where?" Tulloch asked bluntly. "How do you know about this fellow Rotunno?"

"It was a name I heard, sir," Hardie replied evasively.

"Not in the NAAFI, I suspect," Tulloch said. "Where?"

Before Hardie could reply, Innes pointed upwards. "Aircraft, sir!" he warned.

The tiny dots looked innocent against the clear blue sky, but Tulloch remembered how deadly an air attack could be. He guessed the carrier's dust would be visible from above and knew the aircraft would spot them in moments.

British or Italian? They're coming from the West, so they are probably Italian. Is it better to keep moving? Or find somewhere sheltered?

Tulloch looked around. He could not see anywhere to hide in the flat, featureless desert.

"Spread out and keep moving!" Tulloch ordered, waving his hand in a gesture he hoped the other carriers would understand.

"They're coming this way," Hardie warned as Galuzzo looked concerned.

"Stand by the Bren, Innes," Tulloch ordered.

"I am, sir," Innes lifted the Bren from its mounting and pointed it upward, balancing himself against the bouncing carrier.

"Capitano Galuzzo," Tulloch said evenly. "Some of your countrymen may be visiting us shortly. I recommend that you keep your head down."

"Fiat Freccias," Galuzzo said.

"Are they dangerous, Hardie?" Tulloch asked.

"Very, sir. Freccias have four machine guns and one 20-millimetre cannon," Hardie replied. "I am unsure if our armour is proof against a cannon."

"Thank you, Hardie," Tulloch said. He watched as the four aircraft came lower, flying over the three British carriers. "They're checking to see who we are," Tulloch said. "They don't want to fire on their own men." He raised his voice. "Wave to them, Innes!" Tulloch hoped the dust would help mask their identity.

The aircraft buzzed overhead, with the Italian markings distinct on their wings. Galuzzo stood up, balancing in the rear of the carrier as he waved at the Freccias.

"They're not sure what we are," Tulloch said. "Keep waving, Innes. Hardie, make more dust!"

"Yes, sir," Hardie moved the carrier from side to side, stirring up the desert sand. Following Tulloch's example, the other carriers followed, so all three vehicles moved within a dust screen.

Let's hope the pilots recognise Galuzzo's uniform and think we're all Italian.

The aircraft circled and returned, flying so low that Tulloch could make out the pilots' faces as they scrutinised the vehicles.

"They're going to attack!" Innes shouted.

"Keep waving!" Tulloch wished he had an Italian flag to display.

The aircraft passed again and then roared away, leaving the Lothians relieved. Tulloch closed his eyes, checked his compass, and headed back to Egypt with the other carriers close behind.

Well, that's our first foray into enemy territory, and we survived. Hopefully, we've restored a little regimental pride, although it will take more than one patrol to regain our confidence.

Chapter Seven

WESTERN DESERT, EGYPT, SEPTEMBER 1940

Colonel Pringle leaned back. "You destroyed a convoy and brought back a prisoner."

"Yes, sir," Tulloch said.

"Yet you allowed other Italian soldiers to escape."

"I had no room for them in the carrier, sir, and I thought they could spread dissent when they returned to their units."

Tulloch saw Hume frown. "You could have made them walk," he said.

"We were deep inside Italian territory, sir. They'd have slowed us down."

Pringle glanced at Hume before he spoke. "I appreciate your predicament, Tulloch, but the more prisoners we take, the fewer Italians there are to fight us."

"Yes, sir. I believed taking prisoners would have put my men at risk, contrary to orders." Tulloch felt Hume's gaze burning into him.

"I see. Apart from the prisoner situation, you did well for your first patrol in the desert, Tulloch. You had quite a reputation in France and Belgium; let's see if you can do even better here."

"I was lucky, sir."

"So were the Italians you allowed to go free," Hume murmured, lighting a cigarette.

"Dismissed, Tulloch," Pringle said.

The following night, Colonel Pringle sent out two more fighting patrols, with Erskine leading one and Atkins the other.

"Sir," Atkins sought out Tulloch. "I've never led a patrol. What do I watch out for?"

"You've been on training exercises," Tulloch reminded him. "Don't be too ambitious the first time. Don't attack anything you might not be able to handle, and watch for enemy aircraft."

Atkins listened, shifting his weight from foot to foot as Tulloch gave the benefit of his experience.

"Best of luck, Atkins," Tulloch said. "Keep calm, and you'll be fine."

"Thank you, sir," Atkins replied.

"No need to call me sir," Tulloch reminded him. "Now, remember, don't be scared to withdraw if the odds are too great. You have three decent vehicles there, but carriers have limitations. They are not tanks."

"I'll remember, sir," Atkins smiled with what Tulloch guessed was false confidence.

"Best of luck, Atkins," Tulloch said.

"Thank you, Tulloch," Atkins said. "I won't let the Lothians down."

"I know you won't," Tulloch agreed.

Tulloch saw the Riflemen frowning at Atkins as he took command of the leading carrier. *The men don't trust him anymore. Atkins will have to regain their respect somehow.*

"Come on, men," Atkins shouted.

Tulloch watched the two patrols set off, raised worried eyebrows to Kinnear, and checked the standing patrols. So far, no Italian aircraft or raiding parties had disturbed the Lothians' peace, but he wanted to ensure nobody caught Four Platoon off guard.

"What do you think, Tulloch?" Kinnear asked.

"About what?"

"Atkins," Kinnear replied bluntly.

Tulloch thought for a few moments before replying. "I think he's trying too hard after that debacle in East Lothian. He wants to prove himself, which might lead him into bigger trouble."

Kinnear began to tamp tobacco into his pipe. "You give him too much credit, Tulloch. I think he's a born bloody fool, and the sooner some friendly Italian puts a bullet in him, the better for the battalion."

Tulloch flinched. "He's one of us," he said. "Give him a chance to learn the job."

"Aye," Kinnear extracted a cigarette from a silver case, tapped it on the back of his hand, and lit it with a silver lighter. "As long as he doesn't get anybody else killed while he's learning."

Tulloch watched the three carriers, with the sound of their engines lingering long after the vehicles vanished in the dark.

"Now we wait," Tulloch said.

"And pray," Kinnear added.

"And pray," Tulloch agreed.

ERSKINE WAS BACK BEFORE DAWN, WITH TWO OF HIS CARRIERS bullet-scarred and two Italian prisoners, both of whom looked happy to be out of the war.

"We came across a couple of supply trucks," Erskine said. "They put up a bit of a fight."

"Was there an escort?" Colonel Pringle asked.

"A small tankette and a truckful of infantry," Erskine brushed off the question.

"Tankette?" Tulloch asked. "What's a tankette?"

"A baby tank," Erskine explained. "A tiny little thing I could have put in my pocket, but Black disposed of it with his Boys."

Tulloch nodded. "Well done, Black."

Hardie provided more details: "They call them tankettes; I have no idea what the Italian term is. Carro Veloce 3/33 vehicles, they might be useful against unsupported infantry or for scouting. They weigh about three tons, the same as our carriers, and carry a couple of 8-millimetre machine guns."

"Thanks, Hardie," Tulloch said. "We'll probably run into them sometime."

Atkins limped in two hours later, with one carrier missing and a dead man in another.

"What happened?" Tulloch glanced over the battered patrol.

"We were doing well," Atkins looked dazed, with wild eyes and his helmet missing. "I tried to emulate your ambush, sir. I saw a convoy coming along the road, but when I opened fire, more Italians appeared from behind us."

"They're learning," Tulloch said. "What did you do?"

"I tried to fight them," Atkins replied.

"How many were there?"

"I don't know," Atkins admitted.

Tulloch nodded. "If that happens again, don't linger. Either go for them or withdraw. We're not there to engage in a stand-up fight when the opposition can whistle for reinforcements, and we can't."

"Yes, Tulloch," Atkins said.

"You got out, engaged the enemy, and returned with most of your men. That's all positive. Now go and report to the colonel."

"Yes, Tulloch." Atkins obeyed as two stretcher bearers carried away the dead man. The smell of raw blood was strong in the morning air.

"THAT OFFICER IS NOT THE RIGHT STUFF."

Tulloch heard Pringle's comment as he approached the colonel's tent. He paused, not wishing to eavesdrop, yet wondering to whom they were referring.

"I don't agree, sir," Hume replied firmly.

"I'll give him another month and then decide," Pringle said. "Now, this Atkins fellow."

"The man's a liability. We should transfer him," Major Hume snarled.

"No," Pringle shook his head. "I won't do that." He nodded to Tulloch, who stood two feet from the colonel's desk. "I think Lieutenant Tulloch could be the answer."

"Me, sir?" Tulloch had only heard the tail-end of the conversation.

"You, sir." Pringle gave a half-smile. "Maybe," he said. "Now that you've proved yourself in the desert, I want you to take young Atkins under your wing."

"In what way, sir?" Tulloch did not hide his dismay.

Pringle nodded. "Atkins is not fitting in well. He's awkward with the officers and unpopular with the men, yet I think there's a decent soldier there."

"I'm not a nursemaid, sir," Tulloch said.

"I am aware of that, Tulloch," Pringle told him. "Atkins is young and keen, yet not quite ready to take independent command. When we gave him an opportunity yesterday, he lost a valuable carrier and men's lives."

Tulloch could not argue with the colonel.

Pringle continued, "I want you to show him the error of his ways, Tulloch. Teach him how the Lothians fight."

"Yes, sir," Tulloch said.

How the hell can I teach a fellow officer how to be a Lothian Rifleman? Don't I have enough to do looking after Four Platoon?

"Atkins!"

"Yes, Tulloch?" Atkins nearly ran up to Tulloch.

He's as eager as a puppy.

"You have Three Platoon, don't you?"

"That's right."

"I have an idea for a joint training exercise with both our platoons if you're agreeable."

"That's an excellent idea, Tulloch."

"We'll brush up their scouting and desert navigation," Tulloch decided. "If any of our men get separated from the main body out in the Blue, they'll have a fighting chance of returning safely to base."

Atkins nodded eagerly.

"Five o'clock tomorrow morning," Tulloch said. "Unless the colonel has other plans for us."

A VISITING HUSSAR OFFICER TOLD THE LOTHIANS OF EARLIER operations on the frontier when a small British force comprising units of the 7th and 11th Hussars moved deeper into Italian Libya. The British had already captured Maddalena, one of the Italian frontier forts, and now moved against the fort of Capuzzo.

That operation was less successful, for the British force hit a minefield that knocked out three tanks. The Italians attacked with units of tankettes, which the Boys anti-tank rifles destroyed without much trouble. When the Italians raised the white flag, the British tanks probed forward, to be met with concentrated artillery fire that failed to destroy a single British tank.

"I've heard people say the Italians are poor soldiers," the visiting Hussar lieutenant said. "Well, their artillerymen are as brave as anybody I've ever met, and men who attack Matilda tanks with tankettes are anything but cowards."

Tulloch nodded. He noticed Atkins sitting on the fringe of the conversation, saying nothing, and motioned him closer.

"Come into the body of the kirk, Peter!" He noticed Atkins' pleasure at the use of his Christian name.

"Fill us in, Lieutenant," Kinnear said. "Tell us what happened on the border before the Lothians arrived."

The Hussar lieutenant accepted a large Glenkinchie with a smile. "Thank you. I should have known a Scottish regiment would have the best whisky." He continued with his selected history of the desert war so far.

"The next encounter with the Italians came when a British unit known as Combe Force, led by Lt Colonel John Combe, came against an Italian force of armour, infantry, and artillery formed into a fighting square in the desert."

"A fighting square?" Erskine queried.

"Exactly so. Shades of Waterloo or Ulundi," the Hussar replied with a smile. "The Seventh Hussars had only five tanks still operable, three light and two of the heavier cruisers, but they advanced in a cloud of sand and dust. The Italians responded by sending seven tanks from the square to meet us in a duel."

Erskine shook his head. "Sir Lancelot would have approved."

"Indeed," the Hussar sipped at his whisky. "The Seventh Hussars destroyed the Italian tanks without difficulty and circled the square, firing into the infantry and artillery."

"Dear God, it's like a Western at the flicks!" Erskine said softly until Hume ordered him to keep quiet.

The Hussar coughed at the sting of whisky and continued. "The Italians placed their artillery at the corners of the square, and they engaged our tanks. When our fire set the ammunition trucks ablaze, the Italian officers and Eritrean gunners stood at their posts until we destroyed them. They were brave soldiers, gentlemen, and don't let anybody tell you anything different."

Tulloch nodded. He noticed that Atkins was listening intently.

"With their artillery out of action," the Hussar said, "the Italian infantry could not fight back against our tanks. They jumped into lorries to escape, only for the Hussars' armoured cars to intercept them. The Italian tanks attempted a brave attack on the heavier British armour. The odds were too great, and we smashed them." The Hussar finished his whisky with a flourish and looked up. "And that, my Scottish friends, is how we won the Battle of Ghirba. All liquid contributions to the Hussars' Officers' Mess will be greatly appreciated."

"Overall, how would you rate the Italians as soldiers?" Tulloch asked, adding a generous spoonful of sugar. "After all, you Eleventh Hussars are already renowned as experts up the Blue."

The Hussar pondered the question for a few moments before he replied. "I have heard people calling them cowards," he said quietly. "I don't agree at all. The men who say that are usually from the back areas, armchair heroes who have never heard a gun go off in anger. The Italian artillery fought to the end, and their light tanks came out to face our cruisers gun to gun. That took genuine bravery."

"We captured their frontier forts with little trouble," Tulloch reminded.

"We did," the Hussar agreed. "The Italians are as brave as anybody when they want to fight, but they are poorly trained, badly led, and have inferior equipment."

"We'll bear that in mind," Tulloch glanced at Atkins, who nodded eagerly.

While the British and Italians sparred across the frontier, General O'Connor was as busy as any of his men. Basing himself at Maaten Bagush, he travelled extensively, visiting the rear areas and the more forward units.

Small in stature and eager as the terrier of his nickname, he left his staff car, spoke to Colonel Pringle, and toured the Lothians' defences.

"Minefields and barbed wire," O'Connor said. "You have sent some patrols across the Wire into Libya, I hear."

"Yes, sir," Pringle replied.

"Good. Keep the Italians on the hop." O'Connor turned to

an elegantly dressed aide-de-camp at his side. "What do you say, Worthington?"

Brigadier Worthington wrinkled his nose. "The Lothians are too static, in my opinion, sir," he said. "Too defensive, which we may expect after their experiences in France. Maybe they are too accustomed to retreats and defeats." He smoothed his luxurious moustache. "I am sure they are a decent battalion at heart, but they lost confidence at Dunkirk, then there was that business with a British mine in Scotland and the recent loss of a couple of valuable Bren Carriers." He looked away. "I think the Lothians lack the offensive spirit we need."

O'Connor frowned. "I don't agree, Worthington."

"We can discuss it later, sir," Worthington said.

Colonel Pringle sent four more patrols into Libya, twice without result and the third time engaging in a skirmish with a mobile Italian unit. The *Regia Aeronautica* caught the fourth patrol in the open desert, with a flight of Fiat CR.32s machine-gunning the carriers and hitting two men. One died, and an ambulance transported the other to a hospital in Alexandria.

"We still have a lot to learn about fighting in the desert," Tulloch said.

"We still have a lot to learn about fighting a war," Erskine corrected.

They stood side by side with the desert stretching before them and a faint wind lifting the surface of the sand.

"Those self-defence classes Colonel Pringle does not approve of," Tulloch said. "How effective are they?"

"Very," Erskine swept his gaze across the horizon, focusing on anything that might prove hostile. "You'll know the government has issued booklets on techniques of British champion wrestlers."

"I do," Tulloch nodded.

"That's only the start," Erskine said.

"Could you teach Four Platoon?"

"Yes." Erskine lowered his binoculars. "Pringle won't approve."

"No, he won't," Tulloch said. "I'll risk the colonel's disapproval if it helps my men be better soldiers."

———

THE SEA SPLINTERED INTO SILVER SURF AS FOUR COMPANY stood in front of Erskine and Tulloch, wondering what new torture the officers planned for them.

"Who is the toughest man among you?" Erskine asked.

The men glanced at each other. "Hoggie," Innes said. "Rifleman Hogg."

Tulloch agreed. Hogg had been a street fighter from childhood, brawling in the dark streets of Gorgie in Edinburgh and taking his boots and fists to Orange Lodge marches in Glasgow and Belfast.

"Step forward, Hogg," Erskine ran a finger over his immaculate moustache. "Let's see how good you are."

Tulloch sensed a ripple of anticipation among his platoon. Everybody knew Hogg's reputation, and the men expected him to defeat the elegant, cocksure new officer easily.

"Hit me, Hogg," Erskine invited.

Hogg glanced at Tulloch, who nodded.

"It's all right, Hogg. You won't get charged with assaulting a superior officer."

"If you say so, sir," Hogg said doubtfully, throwing a half-hearted punch.

Erskine blocked the punch, caught Hogg's arm, and threw him over his shoulder to the ground.

"My granny could do better than that," Erskine mocked, "and she's been dead and buried for ten years. Try again."

Hogg stood up, eyed Erskine with more respect, stepped back, and came again. This time, he feinted with his right, then launched a left hook that glanced off Erskine's ribs. The officer gasped, jabbed an elbow into Hogg's face, and chopped the edge of his hand lightly at Hogg's throat. As Hogg fell, gasping, Erskine stepped back.

"If I had done that with any force, Hogg would be dead." Erskine waited for his words to sink in. "You have all had some sport boxing in the army, and some of you may have boxed at school or brawled in pubs or the streets. That's all fine and dandy, but what I will teach you now may save your life."

The men watched Hogg slowly rise to his feet, gasping for breath and holding his throat.

"Boxing and wrestling are all very well," Erskine motioned for Hogg to return to his place, "but they all have rules and are essentially sporting contests. Even street brawls have some rules, for few people die in a pub fight. I am going to teach you how to kill with your bare hands."

For the rest of that morning, Erskine taught Four Platoon the gentle art of murder with an array of techniques that would have shocked Tulloch had he not seen the dirty side of war on the Northwest Frontier and in France. Every time Erskine showed a new method of gouging, mutilating, or killing, Tulloch remembered the SS murdering British prisoners of war and the Luftwaffe machine-gunning columns of civilian refugees.

We need to be ruthless to win this war.

By the time Four Platoon returned to the camp, the men were tired, battered, and sore, but they had learned some skills that set them aside from the ordinary British soldier.

"WE'RE MOVING OUT!" THE WARNING SPREAD ALONG THE Lothians' ranks the following day. "All officers report to the Mess. The Colonel wants to address us!"

Tulloch hurried to obey the order, arriving just as Colonel Pringle began to talk.

"You all know that the Fourth Armoured Brigade has been

active on the Frontier for some time, months before we arrived," Pringle told his officers. "They have been successful but have suffered many mechanical breakdowns. They are being withdrawn to refit, and Brigadier Strafer Gott's Support Group is taking over the frontier watch."

The officers listened, waiting to hear where the Lothians were involved. Tulloch caught Atkins watching him and grinned.

That man gets more like a puppy every day. I am sure if I threw a ball, he'd fetch it back for me.

"We are the new boys here," Pringle said. "We are joining Brigadier Gott's Support Unit."

The officers grunted, nodded, or said nothing.

I wonder if Brigadier Worthington was involved in that decision.

"General O'Connor has ordered the Support Group to establish a line of observation between Sollum and Madalena. The Lothians will be part of that line," Pringle said. "We all know that the Italians outnumber us and have been building up their forces near the frontier. Our hit-and-run tactics may have delayed them a few days or weeks, but we have barely scratched their strength."

"Will the Italians attack, sir?" Captain Kilner asked.

Pringle nodded. "Undoubtedly. Our orders are to delay them without getting seriously involved."

Tulloch smiled. "Are we allowed to expend any ammunition, sir?"

Hume grunted. "As long as you don't tell the quartermaster, Tulloch. Quartermasters believe the army should store ammunition in secure boxes, not fired at the enemy."

Pringle consulted a sheet of paper in his hand. "Gott has three motor battalions, two 25-pounder field batteries of twelve guns apiece, two anti-tank batteries, one section of medium artillery, plus the usual quota of engineers and machine gunners. Add one very weak cruiser tank battalion and us."

The officers were silent, contemplating the relative strength of Gott's force and that of Marshal Graziani.

"We are occupying forward positions two miles from the frontier, with the Eleventh Hussars still probing into Libya." Pringle held Tulloch's gaze. "We have to stop our patrols crossing the border and concentrate on creating a defensive perimeter."

"How about the Jock Columns, sir?" Kilner asked. "Can't we join one of them?"

Named after Lt Colonel Jock Campbell, a Thurso-born artilleryman who commanded one such column with great skill, Jock Columns were mobile units of mixed arms that harassed the Italians. They had proved to be very effective in the desert.

"Apparently not, Kilner. General Wavell has ordered O'Connor to halt all forward movement. He wants us to sit tight for the present." "When do we move, sir?" Kilner asked.

"Dawn tomorrow," Colonel Pringle replied. "Have your men ready, gentlemen." He glanced at the calendar. "It's September the 11th, gentlemen, and we're part of Wavell's front line."

On the 13th of September 1940, the Italians moved forward in great strength. They crossed the frontier and invaded Egypt.

Chapter Eight

WESTERN DESERT, EGYPT, SEPTEMBER 1940

"**D**ust, sir."

Tulloch looked up from his map, knowing Hardie had more to add.

"It looks like something is approaching us at great speed," Hardie said.

"Thank you, Hardie." Tulloch folded the map. "We'd better warn the colonel."

"I sent Scott to him, sir."

"I thought you might have." Tulloch left the trench to check Four Platoon. He glanced upward where a squadron of Bristol Blenheim bombers roared majestically towards the west. "It looks like the RAF are busy today."

"I'd say so, sir," Hardie agreed.

Marshal General Graziani had gathered the Italian 10th Army near the Egyptian frontier, with only the Maletti Group slow to muster at Sidi Omar. RAF spotter aircraft and forward British patrols had watched Graziani's army advance and advised higher command. General Wavell sent the RAF to bomb and strafe the Italians as they gathered.

"Keep alert, boys," Tulloch swatted at the swarm of flies that circled his head. "We might have visitors."

Hogg patted his rifle. "Let them come, sir," he said.

Colonel Pringle walked calmly to the forward positions and peered forward through his binoculars. "Whoever they are, they're moving fast," he said.

"They're ours," Kilner said laconically. "That's the Cherrypickers. The 11th Hussars."

"Pass the word to the men to let them in," Pringle ordered.

The Lothians had left a space in the barbed wire, with a Bren and a Boys trained ready on the gap. They watched suspiciously as the vehicles approached, unwilling to alter their aim until they could see through the curtain of sand.

"They're ours," Smith said in disgust, lowering the Boys' barrel.

Two armoured cars of the 11th Hussars powered through the gap and halted in great clouds of dust.

"The Italians are coming!" A red-faced lieutenant shouted as his head and shoulders protruded from the hatch.

"How many?"

"Thousands and thousands; hundreds of acres of them," the lieutenant said. "Tanks, lorried infantry, and artillery." He lifted his head. "Can you hear artillery?"

Tulloch heard a distant rumble, recognising the sound of scores of guns firing simultaneously.

"We hear it," Pringle said quietly, packing tobacco into his pipe. "We've been waiting for this." He raised his voice. "You know the drill, gentlemen. Let's welcome our guests!"

Tulloch echoed the colonel's shout. "Come on, Four Platoon! We're moving forward!"

Leaving their prepared positions, the Lothians piled into their trucks, negotiated the dog-leg gaps in the wire, and moved the few miles to the frontier. They were not alone, for the third battalion of the Coldstream Guards, a battery of the Royal Horse Artillery, a section of medium guns, and a motorised company of the King's Royal Rifle Corps also waited on the border.

"Bugger this for a game of soldiers," Hogg grumbled. "That's the second time we've dug ourselves into the desert just to abandon the position."

"We did the same in Belgium," Innes reminded soberly, "when we left our fixed positions and advanced towards the Germans."

"I remember it well," Smith said. "We'd better prepare for the next retreat, then."

"Enough of that rubbish," Tulloch ordered. "Get ready to meet the invaders. Check your ammunition, boys."

They halted on the border, with the Wire stretching from the coast in the north to seeming infinity to the south.

"Now we wait once more," Kinnear said. "And hope the units on either side hold out."

Colonel Pringle loomed behind them. "Ignore what's happening elsewhere," he snapped. "Our concern is what's happening in front of us and nothing else."

"I could take a patrol in front, sir, and find the Italians," Tulloch offered.

"We stay still and follow orders," Pringle said.

The sound of artillery increased, with flashes visible beyond the horizon. "Somebody's getting a pasting," Kinnear remarked.

"It might be our turn next," Atkins said, laughing nervously. "But we can take it."

"Personally, I'd rather we didn't have to," Erskine smoothed a finger over his moustache. He lit a cigarette and placed it carefully in its holder.

"I'd prefer we were handing it out," Major Hume said, and Atkins laughed again, too loudly.

As Tulloch peered ahead, the RAF and *Regia Aeronautica* battled above. Tulloch could see the vapour trails and heard the occasional rattle of machine guns. Twice, he saw an aircraft fall from the sky, leaving a spiralling trail of smoke.

"Ours or theirs?" Kinnear wondered. "The guns have stopped."

Tulloch nodded. The silence was slightly unnerving. He slapped at the questing flies and sniffed at Erskine's tobacco smoke. "What the hell are you smoking, Erskine?"

"Egyptian tobacco, old chap." Erskine wafted his cigarette in Tulloch's direction. "Do you like it? You should try some, a mixture of incense and sandalwood, nothing like the rubbish you stuff into your pipe." He waved to one of his platoon. "Fairbairn! Bring up a fifteen hundredweight truck and a set of stepladders."

Fairbairn, a tousle-haired man with a freckled face, looked confused. "Where will I get ladders, sir?"

"Use your initiative, man! Try the quartermaster."

Fairbairn returned within ten minutes. "The quartermaster says he wants a receipt for the ladders, sir."

"He knows what he can do with his receipt," Erskine said. He opened the ladders in the back of the truck and swarmed up, binoculars in hand. "That's better! I can see further now." He scanned the horizon to the west. "Hello! The Italian guns are firing."

The Italian artillery barrage began again, with the guns hurling hundreds of shells at a small village.

"What the hell are they firing at?" Kinnear asked.

"The village of Sollum, I think," Tulloch had his map spread on the sand before him.

"It's empty," Kinnear said flatly. "All the inhabitants have gone. Why are the Italians wasting ammunition?"

"Maybe they think we're sheltering there," Tulloch said.

"They're making sure," Erskine balanced on his ladders, focusing on the distant explosions.

"Tulloch!" Colonel Pringle approached. "Take your carriers forward, see what's happening, and report to me. On no account engage the enemy."

"Yes, sir!" Tulloch had hoped for the order.

"Take Atkins with you. Two officers are better than one."

"Yes, sir. Come on, Atkins; you're with me. Take charge of Number Three carrier."

Atkins ran over with one hand holding his steel helmet in place.

"Come on, lads!" Tulloch had trained his men to move quickly, and all three carriers moved forward within five minutes.

"Keep your finger on the trigger, Innes," Tulloch ordered. "But don't fire unless the enemy fires first."

Occasionally glancing to ensure Atkins was following, Tulloch drove to within five miles of Sollum and halted, with Elliot and Innes hauling the camouflage net over the carrier. Simultaneously, Hardie tried to obscure the carrier's tracks.

The Italian shelling increased and abruptly ended, leaving a pall of dust and smoke above Sollum. A few moments later, three tankettes appeared, leading a long column of trucks into what remained of the village. Tulloch lifted his binoculars to the rear of the column.

"Dear God, would you look at that!"

"What's that, sir?" Innes asked.

"Mussolini's sent his family to visit," Tulloch said.

What seemed like half the Italian Army waited to the westward, neatly drawn up, waiting for the order to advance.

"Light tanks, tankettes, motorbikes, and huge trucks," Tulloch said as he scanned the Italian army through his binoculars. "How many are there?"

"Thousands upon thousands, sir," Innes said.

"They're moving, sir," Hardie said quietly.

With a cloud of motorcyclists in the van and medium tanks guarding the flanks, the Italian army began a slow advance. High above, Italian fighters continued to contest the skies with the outnumbered RAF.

"Come on, lads. It's time to report to the colonel," Tulloch decided. He signalled to the other carriers to follow as he withdrew.

Hardie pressed down the accelerator with what seemed like

half of Italy a few miles behind. Tulloch had the carrier manoeuvre within a few yards of Colonel Pringle's position before he reported what he had seen.

"Do you think it's the main advance, Tulloch?" Pringle asked calmly.

"I'd say so, sir."

The colonel considered for a moment. "Take your carriers forward again, Tulloch, and slow these motorbikes down," he said. "Don't engage their tanks unless you have to."

With vivid memories of facing the invading Germans in Belgium, Tulloch ordered his three carriers forward. Since his previous patrol into Italian territory, he had created a system of giving orders by using hand signals to the other carriers.

"Bren gunners, target the motorbikes. Smith! Use the Boys to hit the tankettes and light tanks, but only if they attack us first." Tulloch pushed forward in an arrowhead formation, standing in the back of the leading carrier. Despite the danger, he felt some of the old exhilaration. He was leading his men into action, following the life he had chosen ever since he had viewed the picture of the Thin Red Line as a boy.

"Come on, Four Platoon! Let's show these Italians that the Lothians are back!"

Atkins copied Tulloch, standing in Number Three carrier.

The Italians advanced slowly, with the long columns of trucks well back from the motorcycle screen.

"That's the Bersaglieri, sir," Hardie said. "See the plumes on their helmets? They're one of the elite regiments."

"We'll soon see how good they are," Tulloch growled. "Ready, Innes?"

"Ready, sir!" Innes held the Bren to his cheek.

When they were in range, Tulloch lifted his right hand, waited for a few seconds, and dropped it suddenly.

"Fire! Let them have it!"

Both Brens opened with short, aimed bursts into the mass of Italian motorcyclists. Not expecting an attack, the Italians scattered in all directions, leaving two men lying on the sand and three destroyed motorcycles.

"That's the way!" Atkins shouted.

"Give them another burst!" Tulloch ordered.

Both Brens hammered again, kicking up dust and knocking another motorcyclist from his machine.

"Regroup!" Tulloch ordered. "They'll recover."

The Italians circled and returned, firing at the three carriers without dismounting from their motorcycles.

"Tank!" Hardie warned. The dust acted as a screen, so only the turret was visible. "I think that's a Carro Armato L6/40."

"Armament?" Tulloch asked.

Hardie screwed up his face. "A twenty-millimetre gun and a couple of machine guns, sir. It's one of their light tanks, if I am correct."

Innes gave it a burst with the Bren.

"You're wasting ammunition," Tulloch said. "Leave the tanks to the Boys." He glanced to his right, where Smith was waiting with the anti-tank rifle.

When the motorbikes withdrew, the Carro Armato fired, with the shot passing over Tulloch's head to explode thirty yards away.

"Missed!" Innes jeered and added the inevitable. "You couldnae hit a bull's arse with a banjo."

"Don't encourage them, Innes," Tulloch said as a second tank emerged from the dust and then a third.

"Christ alive, man! How many of the buggers are there? Mussolini must have sent half his armour against us!" Elliot ducked as small stones and sand rattled around the carrier.

"Smith!" Tulloch roared. "Fire at the damned things!"

In reply, Smith fired the Boys, with the heavy projectile missing the first tank by a foot. The tank reversed, with its gun traversing towards Smith's carrier.

Tulloch saw Smith struggling to reload and Atkins shouting encouragement to his Bren gunner.

"Pull back!" Tulloch ordered as he saw a group of tankettes appear on the left flank. He saw Smith fire again, with the missile striking the first tank. Then the tankettes began to fire, with machine-gun bullets hammering off the carrier's thin armour.

"Get us out of here, Hardie," Tulloch ordered. "Innes, target the tankettes."

"I am, sir!" Innes replied, firing short bursts with the Bren.

The tankettes moved in a long line, firing at the carriers as two tanks followed at a more sedate pace. One fired, missing by twenty yards.

"Can't you go any faster, Hardie?"

"No, sir. That's our top speed!"

Tulloch swore, "Do your best, Hardie."

"Yes, sir."

All three carriers were swerving from side to side to avoid the Italian fire when a shell exploded beside the second Italian tank, ripping off the track. The crew bailed out as a second shell landed beside the third tank.

"Thank God for small mercies," Tulloch said. "Who's firing?"

"It's coming from over there, sir," Hardie nodded to his left.

Tulloch saw the muzzle flashes of artillery and heard the whoosh of shells passing overhead before he saw more bright orange flares of explosions.

"That's a twenty-five-pounder, one of ours. Head for the guns!" Tulloch ordered. "Make sure they know we are British!" *How do we do that? Sing "Rule Britannia"? Fly the Union Flag?* He ducked as a shower of dust and gravel cascaded onto the carrier from another Italian shell.

"Keep weaving, Hardie!"

"I am, sir!" Hardie replied, throwing the carrier from side to side as machine-gun bullets bounced and rattled all around.

As all three carriers raced for the British guns, twisting and turning to put any Italian gunners off their aim, Tulloch saw British armoured cars racing out on either side of the artillery.

"11th Hussars, I think!" Tulloch said.

"Let's hope they know we're on their side, sir," Hardie shouted as an Italian shell exploded fifteen yards away, sending shrapnel clattering against the carrier's armour.

"That was close!" Innes said.

"Nearly there! Hold on to your hats!" Hardie twisted the carrier from left to right and back, with the other two carriers following, retaining their V formation.

Three twenty-five-pounders stood behind camouflaged netting with the gun crews loading and firing with mechanical precision.

"Who the hell are you?" Tulloch halted his carriers and stepped onto the disturbed sand beside the guns.

A tall, broad-chested officer looked at Tulloch through twinkling eyes. "I am Lieutenant Colonel John Campbell. Who are you, Lieutenant?"

"Sorry, sir!" Tulloch straightened to attention. *This officer is the famous Jock Campbell, who has been giving the Italians such a difficult time.* "I am Lieutenant Douglas Tulloch of the Lothian Rifles, sir."

Campbell looked more amused than anything else. "Tulloch of the Lothians, eh? And what are you doing swanning around in a trio of Bren carriers among a hundred enemy tanks?"

"I'm trying to get away, sir," Tulloch said, starting as the twenty-five-pounders banged out again.

"Does Colonel Pringle know you're here?" Campbell had not flinched at the sound.

"I'm on a forward patrol, sir," Tulloch realised he was speaking to himself as Campbell darted away to supervise the returning Hussars' armoured cars. A moment later, Campbell was speaking to a leathery-skinned major in charge of four truckloads of infantry.

"Is he always like that?" Tulloch asked a watching subaltern.

"What? Jock Campbell? He's a livewire, that man." The subaltern returned to his duty.

"Are you still here, Tulloch?" Campbell strode towards him. "I am sure Colonel Pringle wants you back."

"I thought you might need our help here, sir," Tulloch said.

An Italian shell exploded nearby, sending up a fountain of sand. Campbell brushed loose sand from his shoulder.

"You have your duty to do," Campbell said as the dust cleared, and two of the twenty-five-pounders replied with a ferocious bark. "That's another Italian tank damaged. Report to Colonel Pringle, Tulloch; that's an order."

"Yes, sir," Tulloch said. "Come on, lads. Colonel Campbell has things well in hand here."

Pringle filled his pipe as he listened to Tulloch's report. "You met Colonel Campbell, then," he said.

"Yes, sir," Tulloch agreed.

"God help the Italians who cross that man," Pringle said. "He's got the energy of three men and the courage of six." He fiddled with his pipe, watching Tulloch through musing eyes. "How did Atkins act?"

Tulloch considered the question before replying. "He was fine, sir. He obeyed orders and acted like a British officer."

"Good." Pringle nodded slowly, took a small knife, and began scraping out the charred tobacco from the bowl of his pipe. "I want a weekly update on his progress, Tulloch."

"Yes, sir," Tulloch nodded.

Chapter Nine

EGYPTIAN LIBYAN BORDER, SEPTEMBER 1940

As the seemingly endless columns of Italian troops powered across the border, the vastly outnumbered British withdrew before them. On the first day of their invasion, the Italians bombarded and occupied Sollum, then pushed along the main highway, the coastal road that probed further into Egypt.

The Lothian Rifles defended their section of the thin khaki line, skirmishing with the oncoming Italians as they slowly fell back.

"Bugger this for a game of soldiers," Hogg said as Four Platoon clambered onto their trucks for another withdrawal. "This reminds me of bloody Belgium."

"We can't withdraw forever," Hardie told him. "We must hold the Suez Canal at least, or the Italians will control one of the most vital waterways in the world."

"Bugger the Suez Canal," Hogg said.

The Lothians motored another three miles deeper into Egypt and halted, with the men sullen and the officers short-tempered with frustration.

"Tulloch!" Colonel Pringle snapped. "You too, Kinnear. Take out the carriers and do what you can to delay the Italians."

"Yes, sir," Tulloch agreed.

"We'll do our best, sir," Kinnear said.

"Atkins!" Tulloch gestured to the young officer. "Look after Four Platoon when I'm away." He turned away before Atkins could reply, ordering his men to follow.

With three Bren carriers against light and cruiser tanks, Tulloch could do little. Twice, he waited in ambush, with his single Boys' anti-tank rifle able to destroy the little Italian tankettes but less useful against the cruiser tanks.

Undaunted by the relatively slight losses the British rear-guard inflicted, the vast Italian army pushed slowly, remorselessly eastward.

"There are too many of them," Kinnear said, mopping the sweat from his face. "If we destroy one, another half dozen appear on the flanks."

Tulloch nodded, again remembering the retreat through Belgium earlier that year. *Is our war to be one of continual withdrawal?*

"The RAF is doing all it can, and I'm sure the Navy is snapping at the Italians' heels along the coast," Tulloch said. "How is your ammunition?"

"Enough for one more encounter," Kinnear replied, "then we'll have to return to base to re-equip."

"We're the same," Tulloch said, glancing skyward, where an RAF flight headed westward. "Ready?"

"Ready," Kinnear said.

They moved on, heading for the dust cloud that blanketed the Italian advance.

Concentrating on the coastal plain, the Italians occupied Bug Bug, and Halfaya, and moved remorselessly east towards Sidi Barrani, while the 1st Libica Division occupied Maktila. The 64th Catanzaro Division reached Nibeiwa, while the 62nd

Marmarica Division and 63rd Cyrene Division occupied Bir Rabia and Sofafi, driving the British rearguard before them.

The RAF took a toll on the long columns of ten-ton trucks and supply vehicles, leaving burning wreckage along the coastal road, but Marshal Graziani ignored his losses and thrust eastward. On the 16th of September, the third day of their assault, Graziani's Italians powered into the village of Sidi Barrani, with Italian radio boasting of their major success.

"They're claiming that Sidi Barrani is a large city," Kinnear scoffed, "with streets of houses and shops, and a working tram service."

Tulloch smiled, remembering the sweltering village with its battered mosque, small police station, and a score of huts. "Let them enjoy their victory," he said. "We'll be back soon enough."

"I hope so," Kinnear said. "Although I don't know how. We don't have the manpower."

Tulloch saw the fitters working on his number one carrier, on which sand had clogged the filters. "We could certainly use some reinforcements and more vehicles," he grinned. "One thing, though, the more the Italians advance, the further they are from their base and the longer their supply lines." He glanced at his platoon. They looked weary and disconsolate after retreating through Egypt following their experiences in Belgium and France.

"We've got the beating of these bastards," Hogg said. "Why are we retreating? If we stood our ground, we could stop them cold."

"There are millions of them," Connington said. "Graziani has more men than we have bullets."

Hogg grinned, showing misshapen teeth. "They'll run long before we're out of ammunition."

"Leave it to O'Connor," Innes said. "The general knows what he's doing."

"Does he? A general that knows what he's doing? That would be a change," Hogg replied.

In the air, the RAF continued to strike at the long columns of heavy Italian trucks, leaving smoking ruins on the roads and dead and injured men. The *Regia Aeronautica* fought back, with dogfights above the desert and casualties on both sides. Tulloch grew used to watching two or three RAF fighters dive into twice their number of Italian aircraft, scatter them, shoot one down, and retire.

"Thank God for the RAF," Elliot said. "The Brylcreem Boys might get all the best women, but at least they're giving the wops a run for their money."

Tulloch remembered his men cursing the RAF in France and the bravery with which the air force had flown outdated and slow machines against German anti-aircraft defences. "Thank God for the RAF," he agreed quietly. "It takes a lot of guts to fly against these odds."

"Tulloch!" Colonel Pringle shouted. "Are your vehicles refuelled and ready?"

Tulloch saw the fitters step back, with one giving him a thumbs-up. "Yes, sir."

"Get forward. I want range markers up to a thousand yards. General O'Connor wants us to delay Graziani, and we need every bullet to count."

"Yes, sir," Tulloch replied. "Come on, Four Platoon!"

TULLOCH WIPED THE SAND-SMEARED SWEAT FROM HIS FACE. "Ready, lads?" They were five hundred yards in front of the Lothians' position, with the sun nearly directly above and the carrier's metal hot to the touch.

"Ready, sir," Innes and Hardie replied.

Elliot, the last man, hurried back to the carrier, having hammered in the white posts Tulloch used as range markers.

"What now, sir?"

Tulloch grinned. "That depends on what Graziani sends

forward. If it's infantry or motorbikes, we'll stand and fight. If he sends tanks, we'll return to the battalion and let the artillery sort them out."

"Let's hope he sends infantry," Innes said, running a hand across the butt of his Bren.

"You bloodthirsty bastard," Elliot said as he checked and rechecked his stock of Bren magazines.

They heard the Italians before they saw them, a constant roar of engines as the tankettes and motorcycles shielded the motorised infantry. Then Tulloch saw a flash through the yellow screen of dust, and then another, and the leading motorcycles burst through, heads down, as they manoeuvred their machines over the uneven ground.

"Here they come," Innes murmured.

"Fire when they reach the seven-hundred-yard marker," Tulloch ordered.

Innes bowed over the Bren, ignoring the ever-present flies that feasted on his sweat.

Hardie lifted his rifle, pressed forward the safety catch, and aimed at the approaching Italians.

"Come on, Bersaglieri," Hardie said.

The sound increased as the motor bicycles advanced at a steady fifteen miles an hour, with half a dozen tankettes emerging from the dust a hundred yards behind.

"The sand is obscuring the markers," Innes said.

Tulloch grunted when his third carrier opened fire.

"Fire, Innes."

Both Brens opened up, with Smith a few seconds later with the Boys. As before, the leading motorcycles scattered, with the tankettes pushing through to engage the Lothians.

"These wee toy tank things are pointless," Innes said as Elliot passed him a spare magazine. "Their armour is paper-thin." He aimed the Bren, hammering the nearest tankette until Smith fired his Boys and stopped it dead. "Whoever said Italians are cowards has never gone to war in a thing like that."

The Bersaglieri dismounted, lay on the sand and began disconcertingly accurate rifle fire, with the bullets rattling from the carriers' armour.

Tulloch grunted. His three carriers were no match for the numbers ranged against him, and the Italians seemed determined to press on.

At least our firing will alert the battalion that Graziani is here.

"The Bersaglieri are getting round the flanks, sir," Hardie warned.

"So they are. Pull back," Tulloch ordered.

Following Tulloch's example, the other carriers withdrew, followed closely by the tankettes and the Bersaglieri on their motorcycles. Tulloch ducked as a bullet whistled past his ear, and another smashed against the armour plating at his side.

"These Bersaglieri are good shots," he remarked.

"Yes, sir," Hardie replied. "The name means marksmen."

Tulloch was relieved when the Lothians supported his retiral with heavy machine gun fire and the blast of the Royal Artillery's twenty-five-pounders.

The Italian advance faltered as Tulloch led his carriers into the Lothian's positions.

"They've turned back," Major Hume announced. "Dig in, lads; we're not withdrawing another inch."

"Thank God for that," Hogg said. "I've had enough of running away from these bastards."

WHEN THEY REACHED THE VILLAGES OF MAKTILA AND SOFAFI, some sixty miles inside Egyptian territory, the Italians halted and began constructing strongly fortified positions.

The British had made them pay for their advance with some three and a half thousand casualties, including seven hundred prisoners.

Tulloch lay back in his trench, trying to ignore the flies that buzzed around his head and landed on his face and shoulder. He stared at the envelope, putting off the incredible pleasure of slitting the seal and pulling out the letter inside. He blew away an inquisitive fly and read the name on the front.

Lieutenant Douglas Tulloch, Lothian Rifles.

The sender had not known in which arena the Lothian Rifles were based. They could have been defending Great Britain from invasion or on garrison duty in Gibraltar, Malta, or Cyprus. They could have been in Palestine, Iraq, Aden, Hong Kong, India, or any other far-flung bases that Britain had assumed the responsibility to defend. Tulloch did not know when the sender had posted the letter or how long it had taken to find him.

Tulloch did not recognise the writing, but he guessed the writer's identity. Only two people would write to him, and he knew his mother's writing from the twice-weekly letters she sent. The other person was Amanda Clark.

Carefully, Tulloch took the fighting knife from inside his tunic and slit open the envelope. He replaced the knife, savouring the experience of extracting the single sheet of paper inside. Finally, he pulled out the letter, unfolded it, and began to read.

"Dear Douglas," it began.

"I have thought about you often during these dark days when Hitler threatens invasion, and we are all pulling together to fend off the terrible evil of Nazism. I do not know where you are or what you are doing, but only that you are doing your bit for freedom."

Tulloch reread the opening paragraph, looking for a clue as to Amanda's whereabouts in London. The first time he met her, she was working for her father in the Indian intelligence service, and he wondered if she had returned to that type of occupation.

"Wherever you are, Douglas, I hope you are well and keeping safe. I also hope you have put our earlier misunderstanding behind you and can remember only the good things we shared. I thought I would never see you again until I met you on the shore when you returned from Dunkirk."

Tulloch smiled at the memory of when he and the survivors of the Lothian's rearguard had landed in southern England. Amanda had been one of the ladies giving succour and hot tea to the bedraggled soldiers.

"Then your unit was sent abroad, and I lost touch again. If you receive this letter, please reply. I can no more give you my location than you can give me yours, so if you want to keep in touch – and I sincerely hope you do – then write to my parent's home address:

Kirklands

Meigle

Perthshire.

I do so hope to hear from you.

Your friend,

Amanda Clark."

Tulloch read the letter three times, waving away the flies that wanted to land on the paper, and closed his eyes.

Wartime is a strange thing. I'd never have met Amanda in peacetime, and now she is the only person apart from my mother who cares sufficiently to write. I don't know Meigle, but I can get there when this war ends.

The shelling began again, desultory yet irritating. The Italians had shelled the British positions ever since they halted their advance, with the British responding with patrols and Colonel Campbell's Jock Columns. Tulloch glanced along the line of trenches with the barbed wire strung in front and the engineers busily laying mines, unconcerned about the occasional Italian shell that came close.

I never realised how much we depended on the Royal Engineers or what a dangerous job they had. All credit to them.

A shell exploded twenty yards in front of the British wire, with a stiff breeze blowing the dust away. Tulloch focused his binoculars. Out there in the Blue, the Italians had fortified camps and a massive preponderance of men and equipment. Someday soon, they would surely decide to advance again, pressing at the overstretched British defences with their out-of-date armour and outnumbered aircraft.

"We haven't done well in this war so far," Kinnear might have shared Tulloch's thoughts.

"No, we haven't," Tulloch agreed. "The Navy's covered itself in glory by defeating *Graf Spee*, the Battle of Narvik, and HMS *Glowworm*, and the RAF won a remarkable victory in the Battle of Britain, but we've got no reason to be proud."

"The Germans defeated us in Norway and France, and now the Italians have shoved us back in Egypt and out of Somaliland," Kinnear said. "What happens next?"

Tulloch thought he saw movement and rose to study the ground ahead through his binoculars. "Next? Do you believe the Italians are better than us?"

"I don't know," Kinnear said.

"I don't believe so," Tulloch said. "Nor do I believe the Germans are better. Next, we'll counterattack the Italians and shove Graziani back into Libya. We'll retake Somaliland and maybe even invade Italian territory to ensure the oil wells and Suez are safe."

"Unless the Germans invade Britain," Kinnear said.

Tulloch forced a laugh. "The RAF and Royal Navy have ended that pipe dream."

He thought of the defences along the British coast and the makeshift Local Defence Volunteers, now known as the Home Guard, and hoped he was right. Tulloch shivered at the prospect of Nazis goose-stepping along Princes Street or the swastika floating above Edinburgh Castle.

"Why have the Italians stopped?" Kinnear asked.

"Maybe Mussolini thinks they've gone far enough," Tulloch replied, lowering his binoculars. "The further into Egypt they come, the longer their supply lines, and with the RAF bombing their trucks on land and the Navy bombarding them from the sea and mining their ports, they'll have serious problems soon."

Atkins hurried over. "Maybe that's as far as they're going to come. Maybe we've stopped them."

"Maybe we have," Tulloch said. "Our job is to strengthen our defences here and make them pay for every mile they penetrate."

While the British consolidated their positions, Colonel Campbell took his Jock column into the desert. Campbell's information, added to the mainly New Zealand-manned Long Range Desert Group's work and the RAF's aerial observations, enabled the British to create maps of the Italian defences.

"The Italians are superb engineers," Captain Kilner observed. "They've built solid defended camps as if they intend to remain in Egypt forever."

"Maybe they do," Tulloch said. "Think of Hadrian's Wall. The Romans marked the edge of their empire with solid defences and launched attacks into Caledonia from their secure position."

Kilner looked along the line of barbed wire and trenches. "We're hardly Hadrian's Wall," he said, "but I am sure we can stop the barbarian hordes here."

Graziani's Italians created a chain of eight defensive camps from Maktila to Sofafi, built up their forces, sat tight, and mounted limited patrols into the desert.

O'Connor's British withdrew a few miles, settled in, and sent out fighting patrols.

Luckier than some regiments, the Lothians found a fine collection of Roman ruins to use as a headquarters. Colonel Pringle and his staff moved to underground tombs, with the battalion's scanty collection of vehicles scattered among the ruins under camouflage netting. Within a few days, the Royal Signals had added a telephone network while the Engineers unrolled barbed wire and began to plant more minefields.

"We are more and more like Hadrian's Wall every day," Tulloch said, "except the Romans are on the other side."

"Weren't they always?" Kilner asked, smiling. He looked up. "Here comes young Atkins, and he looks agitated."

"Sir," Atkins said. "Tulloch. The colonel wants to see you."

"Keep an eye on my platoon, will you, Atkins?" Tulloch asked as he left.

"I'll make sure he's all right, sir," Sergeant Drysdale said softly, nodding towards the subaltern.

"I know you will, Sergeant," Tulloch replied.

The colonel pushed forward a map as Tulloch descended to the echoing tombs.

"Tulloch," Pringle said. "I want you to probe forward from our defences and see what's in front of us." He prodded at the map. "You'll have to skirt our minefield and watch for anything the Italians have planted."

"Yes, sir."

"Take your three carriers, see what you can find and avoid any serious trouble."

"Do you want me to take Atkins, sir?"

The colonel contemplated for a moment. "Not this time."

Tulloch moved off soon after dark, using the stars to guide him and a rough map that showed the main Italian positions. He drove slowly to conserve fuel, with a space between each carrier, stopping every few moments to check his route with the stars. The carriers carried dimmed lights that gave sufficient illumination to be seen by their companions but not enough to alert anybody from a distance. Only the sound of their engines might give them away as they motored over the desert.

The nearest Italian camp to the Lothians was Nibeiwa, and Tulloch halted a mile away and allowed the engine noise to fade and dust to settle before he gave further orders.

"Hardie, stay here with three men. The rest come with me. We'll go on foot the remainder of the way."

The men dismounted, cursing softly as they checked their weapons and looked around at the featureless desert.

With five men at his back, Tulloch headed for the Italian

base at Nibeiwa. He could see the dim glow of the fort's lights across the desert and hoped his men remembered their training. They lifted their feet high and placed them down carefully to avoid kicking loose stones and spoke only in whispers.

Tulloch knew that the British soldiers were inveterate talkers at night, and nothing he had done had cured them. Instead of imposing draconian punishments, he allowed them to converse in whispers. A whisper could be clearly heard within a five-yard radius but not beyond, while even the lowest murmur was audible at ten times that distance in the stillness of a desert night.

You're learning, boys. The veterans of the Northwest Frontier don't need me to teach them the basics, but there are fewer of them now.

Tulloch raised his hand to halt the patrol when he reached a small ridge half a mile from Nibeiwa. Motioning the men to form a defensive circle, he lifted his binoculars and studied the Italian camp.

Every scrap of information could be helpful.

The Italian engineers had excelled themselves in building their new frontier fort. By Tulloch's reckoning, Nibeiwa was rectangular, a mile wide and nearly a mile and a half long. Anti-tank obstacles covered the ground outside, preventing British armour from coming too close, while the camp perimeter was walled, with sangars for additional protection.

Nibeiwa will be a hard place to take if the Italians decide to be stubborn.

Tulloch could see machine gun emplacements at various points along the wall, with the heads of sentries silhouetted against the growing light.

The rising sun reflected from barbed wire entanglements placed seemingly at random, and Tulloch guessed there would be minefields as well, although he had no means of knowing where.

Tulloch took notes with a stub of a pencil in a small note-book. The main anti-tank obstacles were about a hundred and fifty yards outside the walls, concentrated on the southwest and southeast, with a stone and mud wall behind a trench.

Nibeiwa is weakest in the northwest, which must be where the supply trucks enter. That information could be useful if General O'Connor decides to attack.

The dawn rose while Tulloch examined the defences, and an Italian patrol left Nibeiwa from the southwest and picked its way cautiously through the minefields and barbed wire. Tulloch watched the three AB 41 armoured cars with their 20-millimetre guns following the command car, carefully spaced out with the head and shoulders of each vehicle's commander protruding from the turret. Ten yards behind the armoured cars, a small Fiat lorry followed, with the driver casually smoking a cigarette and his companion poking a rifle through the open window.

"Do we shoot, sir?" Innes whispered hopefully.

Tulloch shook his head, wordless. He doubted the Italians could hear him above the sound of their engines, but he did not want to take the risk.

The Italians looked professional, as if they knew what they were doing. Tulloch kept them under observation as they circled the camp, with an Italian flag hanging limply from the command car and the dust slowly rising to drift behind them in a long yellow ribbon. He sketched their route on his plan of the defences, hoping to find a safe route through the minefields.

"They're coming this way, sir," Innes warned as the command car turned towards them.

"So I see."

The command car moved three hundred yards and stopped, with a smartly dressed officer climbing onto the bonnet to scan the surrounding countryside through his binoculars. Tulloch remained still as the officer's gaze swept across his position, wavered momentarily, and continued. He sensed Connington lifting his rifle and motioned for him to keep still.

One of the Italians laughed, the sound clear across the sand, and half a dozen men dismounted from the Fiat truck. Led by an officer, they lifted a hatch in the ground and descended into a concealed observation post.

That's worth knowing. Tulloch added details to his plan while wondering how many more observation posts the Italians had placed around Nibeiwa and if anybody was watching him.

The patrol commander lingered for a few moments, then waved his hand and led the armoured cars back to the camp.

That was a short patrol: three armoured cars to take a small unit to an observation post.

Tulloch waited for three hours until his men were baking in the heat and plagued by flies, and then he led them back to the carriers.

Hardie looked relieved when Tulloch appeared. "I was going to look for you," he said.

"Here we are," Tulloch replied. "Back to the battalion, lads."

Another patrol, a little more information gained, and I've done my bit for King and Country. I hope I have helped win the war, although there seems to be an awful lot yet to do.

Chapter Ten

"**M**ussolini's happy with himself," Kinnear remarked. "He's boasting about the great Italian army defeating the British and winning glory for Italy."

Tulloch grunted. "He's trying to regain the days of the Roman Empire at our expense."

"We've retreated far enough," Atkins said. "It's time we began to retaliate."

"I agree," Tulloch said. "The navy and RAF are doing their best, but so far, all the army's done is patrol work and a few raids."

"If the Italians want to advance further, they'll have to build a new road," Kinnear said.

They stood beside the highway to Mersa Matruh with the Mediterranean Sea glittering blue to the north and a single Royal Navy gunboat cruising offshore.

Even in its heyday, the road had only been a track, with primitive bridges across the wadis so some enterprising mapmaker could colour it red as a highway. After the Royal Engineers had come and gone with their bulldozers, mines, and booby traps, the road was impassable for anybody except the foolhardy and the ignorant.

"Aye, Graziani will have fun rolling his tanks along that highway," Kinnear smiled. "He'll have to import some of his old Roman engineers to fix that mess."

"I heard a rumour that Wavell has planned an advance into Cyrenaica," Atkins said.

"I presume he has," Tulloch said, staring westward towards the distant Italian lines.

"I wish he'd get on with it," Kinnear said. "He ordered his staff planners to avoid the slow ponderosity that characterises British operations." He grinned, "those were his exact words."

"How do you know that?" Tulloch asked.

"I know people on the staff," Kinnear said casually. "I plan to go to the Staff College myself. That's the way forward, Tulloch. Sitting in a regiment never gets you a promotion, and I intend to end this war as a general. What is your ambition?"

Tulloch considered for a moment. "To survive the war," he said soberly, "and defeat the pure evil of Hitler's Germany."

"Of course, we all want that," Kinnear said. "But on a personal level, what rank do you hope to achieve?"

"I hadn't thought about it," Tulloch admitted. "Maybe a major." He shrugged. "Defeating Hitler and Mussolini seems more important at present. I will consider my career later."

Kinnear smiled. "How very noble of you. Don't you know the old naval toast, 'Here's to a bloody war or a sickly season?'"

"I've never come across it," Tulloch admitted.

Kinnear shook his head. "What a sheltered life you have led, Tulloch. One must use whatever opportunities come one's way. You see this war as a Crusade against evil, whereas I see it as a stepping stone in my military career."

"More important than what either of us want," Tulloch said, "is what General O'Connor wants."

Kinnear looked up as three Italian Breda 65 bombers growled past. "I don't know about O'Connor, but Archie Wavell wants two armoured divisions, a brigade of heavy tanks, and two mobile divisions with strong artillery and air support."

Tulloch thought of the depleted British Army after Dunkirk. "We've precious little to defend Britain, let alone send men and tanks out here."

"Oh, Hitler won't invade now. The RAF has seen to that," Kinnear said with breezy confidence while Atkins nodded, trying to join the conversation.

"I hope you're right." Tulloch thought of his parents in Edinburgh and Amanda Clark, wherever she was, facing a unit of Nazi Germans. He didn't know much about Hitler but guessed he had not given up on his plan to invade Great Britain. "I wish we were closer to home. If the Germans invade, I want to be there to face them, not stuck thousands of miles away in Africa."

"If the Germans invade," Kinnear said, suddenly sober, "it will all be over before we get there."

"God forbid," Tulloch replied. He felt Atkins' gaze on him.

"Amen to that," Atkins said quietly. Tulloch noted that his hands were twisting together, his fingernails ragged where he had bitten them.

LOTHIANS' HEADQUARTERS, EGYPT; NOVEMBER 1940

The three Gloster Gladiators flew low overhead, the biplanes that made up much of the British fighter force in Egypt. Tulloch watched them growl towards Libya when he saw Atkins hurrying towards him.

"Did you hear about the raid on Taranto?"

"I did," Tulloch replied. "The Royal Navy Fleet Air Arm hammered the Italian Fleet."

"That's right." Atkins nodded eagerly. "The Italians had five battleships, eight cruisers, twenty destroyers, and an array of smaller craft. Could you imagine if that lot attacked one of our convoys?"

"I can imagine," Tulloch said. "They would brush aside the escort and sink every ship."

The army could only function because of the constant stream of supplies from Britain, with the hard-working merchant ships carrying everything from food and clothing to tanks, fuel, and reinforcements. The Italians still far outnumbered and outgunned Admiral Cunningham's Royal Navy, which fought to keep Malta, the Middle East, and Egypt supplied while still having warships to bombard the Italian troops in Libya and Egypt.

"No merchant ships means no supplies, no ammunition, no reinforcements, no parts for the tanks or trucks," Atkins said.

Cunningham hoped to entice the Italian fleet out of their base in Taranto and engage them in a general action. His ruse failed, and the Italians stayed put, remaining a threat to every convoy without putting themselves in danger. Cunningham knew he could not allow the *Regia Marina* to hazard British convoys, so he took the war to them, using a first in naval warfare. Admiral Cunningham planned the novel idea of an aerial attack with his aircraft carriers *Illustrious* and *Eagle*, launching their Swordfish biplanes against the pride of the Italian Navy.

"Imagine piloting one of these rickety aircraft against some of the most powerful battleships in the world," Atkins marvelled.

"I only admire their courage," Tulloch agreed.

Cunningham's battle took careful arranging. He sailed from Alexandria with one aircraft carrier, four battleships, and a strong force of cruisers and destroyers to escort an inward-bound convoy. When the *Regia Aeronautica* followed the British fleet, HMS *Illustrious* sent up aircraft to shoot down the Italian aircraft. Meanwhile, British scouting ships did not find any enemy surface ships, and Cunningham sailed into Grand Harbour in Malta unscathed, if slightly frustrated.

With additional ships joining him from the UK,

Cunningham sailed from Malta towards the Italian coast to try and tempt the *Regia Marina* out of their harbour. Cunningham had a screen of Fulmar fighters ready to shoot down any Italian aircraft that ventured too close. On the 11th of November, he reached his position 170 miles from Taranto, where aerial reconnaissance revealed a sixth Italian battleship in the harbour.

At six that evening, Rear Admiral Lumley Lyster in *Illustrious*, with escorting cruisers and destroyers, detached from the remainder of the fleet, and two and a half hours later, the first wave of Swordfish aircraft was airborne.

The Fairey Swordfish was a torpedo bomber nicknamed the Stringbag by its crews. A biplane that already looked outdated when it first flew in 1936, twenty Swordfish flew against the pride of the Italian Navy. Flying through intense anti-aircraft fire, the Swordfish achieved spectacular success, sinking one Italian battleship, severely damaging two others, and damaging a cruiser and two destroyers for the loss of two aircraft and four men.

"Everybody's winning except the army," Atkins complained.

"Our time will come," Tulloch reassured him. "Wavell and O'Connor won't want to sit about forever." Yet even as he spoke, Tulloch wondered what the army could do against the huge numbers of men, tanks, and guns the Italians could muster.

Man to man, we're better than them if only we had the opportunity to prove it.

While the British and Italians sat in their fortified positions and skirmished in no man's land in between, Wavell prepared for Operation Compass, a five-day raid into Italian-held territory. Reinforcements arrived in Egypt, including some Matilda tanks, although they would be desperately needed in Britain if the Germans invaded. However, Matildas were just as essential if O'Connor was to break through the Italian defences and push them out of Egypt.

The Matilda was a twenty-five-ton Infantry support tank with heavy armour, a two-pound gun, and a 7.92-millimetre Besa machine gun. The Matilda was designed to be proof against most anti-tank guns of the period.

"Wavell is planning something big," Kinnear said.

"I hope we're involved," Atkins said.

"We will be," Tulloch said quietly. "General O'Connor has so few men compared to Graziani that he'll have to use us all." He tapped Atkins on the shoulder. "You'll get your chance, Peter, never fear." He felt Atkins shaking under his hand.

The poor lad is terrified underneath the bluster.

"Operation Compass is supposed to be a secret," Kinnear shook his head. "Are there any secrets in North Africa? How can the Italians fail to notice the movement of ships, equipment, and men into Port Said and Alexandria?"

"I am sure half the Arabs east of Tobruk are feeding information to Graziani," Tulloch agreed. "The Italian intelligence service will know before Wavell tells us."

Wavell ordered the newly arrived tanks to Heliopolis near Cairo, where busy men painted them in desert colours, and the crews attended classes in desert navigation and how the Italians fought. From there, the tanks shifted to Maaten Bagush, not far east of Mersa Matruh, making final preparations for the five-day raid.

Tulloch, along with half a dozen Lothian officers, spent a day with the 7th Royal Tanks to view the newly arrived Matildas.

"Are they as good as I've heard?" Tulloch asked. "I remember our tanks giving the Germans a fright at Arras during the retreat to Dunkirk."

A sunburned lieutenant grinned. "They're beauties," he said. "They'll knock spots off anything the Italians have and probably Hitler's Panzers as well."

The officer's enthusiasm impressed Tulloch, as did the actions of the regimental camouflage officer who covered each tank with EPIP tents [1] and sent motorcycle despatch riders to tow rough sacks over the area so any inquisitive Italian airman could not see the tank tracks.

"The tankies seem confident," Atkins commented as they returned to the Lothians' base.

"They seem itching to have a go at the Italians," Tulloch said.

When Tulloch returned to camp, Kinnear greeted him with a smile. "O'Connor's pulling us out of the line," he said. "We're going to be involved in Operation Compass."

The Lothians grumbled as they left their carefully prepared positions and moved southwest of Mersa Matruh, deeper into Egypt.

"Bugger this for a game of soldiers," Hogg said as he helped load a truck. "Move, dig in and move again. If I wanted to be a removal man, I'd never have joined the army."

"Are we retreating again?" Connington asked. "We beat the Germans and had to retreat, and now we've beaten the Italians and have to retreat. Are our generals scared to move forward in this bloody war?"

"Aye; they want to keep close to the hoors in Alex," Smith said. "Bints and French champagne is all they're good for."

"Sharrup, Smudger," Elliot shouted. "You're making me jealous."

"Keep the noise down!" Sergeant Drysdale ordered. "You lot gabble like a bunch of bairns on a school holiday!"

General O'Connor had a mixed force of British, Indian, New Zealanders, and Free French, the newly arrived armour, and a high degree of confidence and energy. Facing him, Marshal Graziani had the advantage of numbers in men and equipment and secure defensive positions.

"This is Training Exercise Number One," Pringle explained to the officers as the NCOs supervised their arrival at the new camp. "General O'Connor will lead us against the Italian positions soon, and he wants everybody to be familiar with the topography."

The Royal Engineers had created a replica of the Italian defensive positions at Nibeiwa, using the information Tulloch and others had provided. The British and Indian forces inspected the models and then practised attacking the mock forts. They learned where the machine gun nests and barbed wire entanglements were placed and worked out the best routes for tanks and infantry.

"We are not leading the attack," Pringle said. "We're leaving that to the tanks."

"Why?" Kinnear asked. "It's accepted military practice for the infantry to lead in any attack."

"That is General O'Connor's decision," Pringle said. "I suspect he is taking a leaf from the Germans' book. Their tanks smashed through the defenders in Poland and France."

Tulloch nodded. The art of warfare was evolving, and he had to move with the times. Lessons he learned on the Northwest Frontier of India did not apply to this new mode of mechanised warfare.

"O'Connor has decided to forgo a preliminary bombardment," Pringle again surprised the traditionalists who recalled the Somme and Ypres. "The armour will rely on surprise and shock to achieve their objectives. We will create a diversion to the east of Nibeiwa and follow up on the tanks' success."

"What about the mines, sir?" Major Hume asked.

"Our patrols, led by Tulloch, Kinnear, and Erskine, have plotted the position of the minefields, and the leading tanks will be supplied with a device to clear the minefields in front of them."

Tulloch listened with interest, for minefields were one of the most feared forms of defence, and anything that could neutralise them was good news.

The colonel did not mention Atkins. That omission will not do the lad's confidence any good.

"Tulloch!" Colonel Pringle said softly. "I'd appreciate a word with you in my tent after the exercise."

"Yes, sir," Tulloch said, wondering what sin of omission or commission the colonel had discovered.

The colonel was waiting for him, leaning back in a camp chair.

"I heard you allowed Lieutenant Erskine to teach Four Platoon some filthy tricks, Tulloch," Pringle's eyes were as hard as Tulloch had ever seen.

"Yes, sir," Tulloch admitted.

"You knew I had banned Erskine from teaching these things."

"Yes, sir, but we must be ruthless to win this war."

Pringle frowned. "We are British soldiers, Tulloch, not murderers. If we descend to such methods, we are no better than the enemy. We are here to fight evil, not embrace it."

"Yes, sir." Tulloch knew he could not argue with the colonel.

Pringle sighed. "You have been doing well until now, Tulloch. Your patrols have been successful, and you've taken young Atkins under your wing. I had considered promoting you to captain, but I cannot promote an officer who disobeys my orders."

Tulloch remained at attention. "Yes, sir."

Colonel Pringle stood up. "I am disappointed in you, Tulloch. You have let me down. However, I haven't given up hope. You may recover my good opinion and show yourself as a true gentleman and officer."

"Yes, sir."

"That's all, Tulloch. You are dismissed."

Promotion? Does that matter when there's a war to win? Yes, it does. Kinnear was right. The higher rank I achieve, the more significant the part I can play in defeating Hitler and Mussolini.

When Tulloch left the tent, the sun seemed stronger than ever, yet the bustle around him seemed surreal, as if he did not quite belong. Shaking away the momentary despondency, he marched back to his platoon.

Damn the man! Colonel Pringle's gentlemanly ideas do not belong in this modern war. Or has the war already changed me for the worse?

THE LOTHIANS JOINED THE 4TH INDIAN DIVISION, WHICH pleased the old soldiers who had served in Peshawar and along the Frontier. With its badge of a red eagle against a black background, the 4th Indian contained some famous regiments, Indian and British. The officers greeted the Lothians cordially, with a few remembering them from the pre-war days in India. Tulloch recognised the Punjab Regiment and the Rajputana Rifles, although some of his men growled at the Cameron Highlanders, for Lowland and Highland regiments had a long history of animosity.

"None of that!" Sergeant Drysdale snarled. "The Camerons are on our side!"

Hogg glared at a wiry Cameron, who seemed happy to trade insults or blows. "Yes, Sergeant. That Cameron is getting smart."

"He thinks the same about you," Drysdale shoved Hogg away from trouble. "Come on, there are a hundred sandbags needing to be filled."

The Lothians were brigaded with a regiment of Rajputs, and after an ugly sandstorm that made some men lose their bearings, they practised assaulting the mocked-up Italian fort. After two days of constant training, the Lothians and Rajputs knew the Italian defences intimately and could anticipate the Italians' response to every angle of attack.

"We're the diversion," Pringle told the Lothians. "The Rajputs and us will make a lot of noise at this flank while the tanks attack from the rear, the weak spot Tulloch noted." The colonel jabbed the stem of his pipe at the replica of Nibeiwa. "I hope your intelligence is accurate, Tulloch, because a lot depends on the outcome of this battle."

"I am sure it is, sir," Tulloch said.

"So am I," Pringle seemed to have forgiven Tulloch's self-defence training.

"When do we do the real thing, sir?" Atkins asked.

"We have Training Exercise Number Two first," the colonel replied. "And then probably the assault."

The Lothians' officers dispersed to their duties or to the tented Officers' Mess, where Tulloch listened to the conversation.

"There's no Training Exercise Number Two," Erskine said flatly. "We'll be heading for the real thing soon."

Tulloch nodded. He did not think the army could continue with so much secrecy without something leaking through to the enemy. Many Egyptians did not like the British presence in their country, and they would happily inform the enemy of what was happening, uncaring that the Italians would be less amenable colonists.

"I hope it's soon," Atkins said, looking around at his fellow officers for approval.

Nobody commented.

Tulloch looked west, where the Italians waited inside their heavily defended forts.

Chapter Eleven

WESTERN DESERT, DECEMBER 1940

Shortly before two in the morning on December 7, 1940, the Lothian Rifles clambered into a convoy of lorries and headed west. As the vehicles grumbled along the road, a big yellow moon floated in the sky above while the desert stretched forever on either side. Tulloch sat beside the driver, eyeing the long convoy, each truck packed with men or supplies.

Somewhere in the convoy, a piper struck up the regimental song, and the words of the final verse of *The Flowers of Edinburgh* eased into Tulloch's mind.

> *"All joy and mirth at our return*
> *Shall then abound from Tweed to Tay;*
> *The bells shall ring, and sweet birds sing,*
> *To grace and crown our nuptial day.*
> *Thus bless'd wi' charms in my love's arms,*
> *My heart once more I will regain;*
> *Then I'll range no more to a distant shore,*
> *But in love will enjoy my darling swain."*

Tulloch thought briefly of Amanda but knew the memory would weaken him, so he returned his attention to the war. He glanced out the window, where the dark was fading, and the lights of hundreds of trucks glistened as far as he could see.

There was something exciting about driving to war with such a force of men. He watched regiment after regiment of tanks advancing in line astern, like armoured ships of the desert. The dust and night obscured much of the scene, but Tulloch saw the pennants flying from the tanks, the faces of the tank commanders, and moonlight gleaming from the long barrels of the guns.

Here we go again. Once more into the breach, dear friends.

"We're all going to die!" Rifleman Bryson said with an attempt at humour.

"Maybe you are, you ugly bastard," Cummings retorted, "but I'm going to live. These Italian lads have plenty of bottles of vino, and the first is mine."

Tulloch smiled. Looting from the enemy was as much a part of warfare as fighting or going on sentry duty. He remembered Aitken, the battalion's best scrounger, who was wounded in France and wondered how he was progressing.

"You have the vino, Cummie," Elliot said. "I want their women. I've heard the Italian officers all have personal hoors with them."

"Away you go, man!" Innes scoffed. "They never do!"

"They do, I'm telling you, Innes! The higher-up ones have half a dozen each, like a twelve-point stag and his harem."

Tulloch leaned back, closed his eyes, and allowed the driver to follow the truck in front. One of the rules he had learned on the Frontier was to take every opportunity to sleep, eat, or relieve himself, for one never knew when the next chance might appear.

The convoy halted in a barren patch of nowhere, with the stars fading above and the officers and growling NCOs mustering their men into order. Tulloch realised they were on top of the escarpment, fifty miles west of the Matruh-Siwa highway. The Lothians shivered in the pre-dawn chill, with the engines grumbling in the background and men stamping their feet, lighting cigarettes, and talking in low monotones.

"This piece of nowhere is Piccadilly Circus," Colonel Pringle told them. "Our gathering point. The Italians are over there," he pointed west, "but we have thirty thousand quality men and squadrons of the best tanks Britain can produce."

"How many men do the Italians have here, sir?" Erskine asked.

"We are aware of about sixty thousand Italians and Libyans manning their forward positions," Pringle replied.

"Twice our number then, and dug into prepared positions," Erskine said.

"That's correct," Pringle told him with a faint smile. "Only twice our number, so it should be a walkover."

"That's what they said about the Somme," Erskine said dryly, ignoring the colonel's hard glare.

"We're going right through the centre of the Italian lines," Colonel Pringle said. "General O'Connor plans to capture the forts of Nibeiwa and East and West Tummar, then strike northward towards Sidi Barrani and Buq Buq," Pringle began to scrape out the bowl of his pipe.

"We hope to cut the Italians off in Sidi Barrani and Maktila and retake these villages." He tapped his pipe on his boot, inspected the bowl, and thumbed in fresh tobacco.

"The army will not be operating in isolation. The RAF will attack the enemy airfields to reduce their capability to attack us and will bomb the forts as we approach, masking the noise of our tank engines."

The officers nodded in approval.

"In the meantime, the Navy will bombard Maktila," Pringle said. "That's all, gentlemen."

The meeting broke up with officers murmuring to one another.

"We should be involved in the main attack, not footling about with a diversion," Atkins complained.

"We obey orders," Pringle said with a meaningful look at Tulloch. "We do our duty."

General O'Connor moved his headquarters to the front, basing himself in a truck to increase his mobility.

"We'll soon see if the general is a terrier or a poodle," Erskine said cynically.

"He's as busy as a terrier," Tulloch replied.

"Playing with raids and patrols is one thing; commanding an army in a major operation is another," Erskine said, placing a cigarette in his holder. He smiled without humour. "Our generals have not covered themselves in glory so far."

"Let's see if we can help them," Tulloch said. "Who's taking us toward the fort?"

"4th Reserve Mechanical Transport Company," Kinnear replied. "Kiwis. We're moving with the Rajputs."

"How the hell do you know everything before I do?" Tulloch asked.

"Friends in high places, Tulloch, remember," Kinnear replied.

"I remember," Tulloch said.

The New Zealanders were efficient, laconic, and helpful as they loaded the Lothians into their trucks. Each vehicle held nineteen privates and one NCO. On Pringle's orders, they lifted the canvas cover and tied it around the central support, leaving the back open to the sky.

"If any Italian aircraft comes, we'll greet it with hundreds of rifles and Brens," the colonel said. "They won't find the Lothians a soft touch."

"Hundreds of rifles, he says," Connington grumbled. "And here we are, breathing in sand instead of air for the next God knows how many hours."

The long convoy headed west, forty miles across the desert, with the dust choking the men and obscuring the drivers' view. The piper had long since stopped playing, so the only sound was the growling of the engines and the rumble-thump of wheels across the rough road.

"I spy aircraft," the driver said, and Tulloch stared upwards. He saw the tiny dots high above and sighed in relief when they passed overhead and disappeared toward Libya.

"Probably ours," the driver said. "Going to give hell to Mussolini."

"Probably," Tulloch agreed. "Softening up the opposition before we arrive with the bayonet."

After a nervous few hours camping in the desert, on the night of 8th December, O'Connor's force marched westward towards the Italian positions.

"Bugger this for a game of soldiers," Hogg grumbled. "Drive all bloody day and march all bloody night."

"Aye, that's right, Hogg. If you're not careful, we'll expect you to fight next," Drysdale said. "Now shut your mouth and get on with it."

Tulloch marched at the head of Four Platoon, glancing at his compass occasionally to ensure they were on the correct route. He heard the growl of engines in the distance and wondered if the tanks were moving to the attack.

"Where are we going, sir?" Hardie asked.

"Our final position. We'll soon be attacking Nibeiwa or making the Italians believe we are," Tulloch said.

"What if the Italian armour attacks us from the south, sir? Our flanks are horribly exposed, and the Italians have forts at Sofafi and Rabia." Hardie once more revealed too much tactical awareness for a Rifleman.

"The Seventh Armoured Division is covering our flank," Tulloch reassured him. "They'd welcome a crack at the Italians if they try anything."

Hardie nodded. "Yes, sir. We don't know much at the sharp end."

"I can imagine how frustrating that must be for an ex-officer," Tulloch said. "You were an officer, weren't you?"

Hardie was quiet for a few moments. "I was, sir. In a different time."

Tulloch nodded. "The army always needs good officers, Hardie."

"I don't want promotion, sir."

"Even if you'll know what's happening?"

"Yes, sir." Hardie walked on, seemingly effortlessly, over the desert.

What secret are you hiding, Hardie, most private of all private soldiers?

The moon faded, leaving the desert in total darkness. For a moment, Tulloch thought of the blackout in Edinburgh and the fear of German bombers, and then he heard, soft in the distance, a faint purring from the outflanking British tanks.

There's no mistake this time. The assault is going in soon - our first major attack since the armour at Arras.

"All right, Tulloch?" Captain Kilner padded soft-footed to Four Platoon. Major Hume was at his shoulder, grim-faced as he checked the Lothians' dispositions.

"These poor Italians don't know what's going to hit them," Tulloch said. "O'Connor has organised this well."

"We could have done with him in France," Kilner said.

"We could have done without allies in France," Hume said sourly. "Leave your men here; the colonel wants us. Come with me."

"Right, gentlemen," Colonel Pringle struck a match and lit his pipe. "Zero hour. Time for us to move. Nibeiwa is three miles away, and we're going in on foot. Remember, our job is to distract the defenders so the armour can break in on the opposite side. The more noise we make, the better." Pringle puffed smoke into the air. "If we all do our duty, the day will go well. Don't fire until I give the order. Good luck, gentlemen."

Here we go. Once more into the breach.

The officers returned to their men, gave brief orders, and headed forward by compass bearings and the stars. Every man in the Lothians had participated in Training Exercise Number One and knew the ground and their part in the operation.

The music of *The Flowers of Edinburgh* eased into Tulloch's head as he returned to Four Platoon, and he thought briefly of Amanda before pushing her memory to the back of his head.

Duty first, but I hope she's all right with all the bombing in London.

"Come on, lads. This is the real thing. Leave any casualties for the stretcher-bearers and remember your training."

Hogg hawked and spat on the ground. "This is more like it, sir."

Although Tulloch knew the 7th Rajput Regiment was on the flank, performing the same advance, he heard nothing. For a moment, he felt very lonely in the desert, although he knew hundreds of men surrounded him.

Somebody stumbled and swore, with Drysdale rebuking the offender with a hushed snarl.

"Keep the noise down, you clumsy bastard!"

Tulloch's men moved as he had trained them, high-stepping and making the minimum of noise. Tulloch checked his watch. It was nearly three in the morning, the deepest and darkest hour of the day when people were at their lowest ebb.

"*Allarme!*" the word was startlingly clear in the silence, and somebody, British, Indian or Italian, fired a single shot. "*Il nemico è qui!* – the enemy is here!"

"We've bumped a listening post!" Tulloch said as the Italians opened fire, startlingly loud in the dark. "Lie down, lads!"

The Lothians sunk into the sand as the entire east side of Nibeiwa crashed into flame. Rifles, machine guns, and artillery opened up as the Italians manned their defences and fired at the approaching British and Indian infantry.

"I don't think they like us very much," Connington said as bullets hissed and cracked above the Lothians' heads.

"I don't think I like them very much either," Innes replied, easing his Bren Gun forward.

"Open fire!" Colonel Pringle ordered, and the Lothians joined the Rajputs in firing at Nibeiwa. Brens stammered, rifles cracked, and Smith fired his Boys, with the Italians retaliating with every gun they possessed.

"Keep them busy, lads!" Captain Kilner shouted.

Tracer bullets flicked towards the Lothians, rising in slow motion from the fort, then speeding up as they zoomed over the infantry's heads. Artillery and machine guns crashed out, with flares lighting up the desert, casting harsh shadows on the featureless, nearly level plain.

"Cease fire!" Pringle ordered, and the Lothians stopped firing. The Rajputs did the same, and a few moments later, the Italian fire also slackened.

"They think they've seen us off," Hogg commented, reloading his rifle.

The infantry lay still, allowing the flares to die down and the defenders to believe they had beaten off an attack. Somebody laughed nervously, and a Rajput shouted his war cry, the sound ominous in the starlit night.

"*Bol Bajrang Bali Ki* Jai! Victory to Lord Hanuman!"

"Advance," Colonel Pringle said, and the Lothians and Rajputs moved forward, found a small ridge three hundred yards closer to Nibeiwa, and opened fire again.

"That'll fool Mussolini!" Elliot said as the British and Rajput musketry hammered at the Italian fort.

The Italians responded at once, firing furiously at the infantry. Artillery shells arced overhead to explode behind the British and Indians in glaring orange flashes. Smoke and dust rose, chokingly.

"Careful, lads, or they'll throw the kitchen sink at us next!"

"My ma could do with a new sink," Cummings said, loading his rifle. "Ours is cracked and leaks like a politician's promise." He raised his voice. "Come on, Musso! Give us a new sink!"

"Cease fire," Colonel Pringle bellowed, and the Lothians

again stopped firing. The Rajputs continued for a few moments, and then they also stopped. Italian bullets and shells hammered at them, mostly passing overhead.

"Keep your heads down!" Tulloch reminded. He saw one man rise, give a little grunt, and fall into the sand. He knew that one home in an Edinburgh tenement or a mining row in Newton-grange or Rosewell would be mourning for their son.

Was it worth it? Was it worth losing a man to demonstrate against an obscure Italian fort in a country most people have never heard of?

"Advance!" Pringle ordered, and the Lothians pushed forward another two hundred yards until Nibeiwa's walls were clear under the stars.

Tulloch heard an order from the Rajputs, and they opened fire again. The Lothians were fractionally slower, hammering at the defenders with rifles and Bren fire. After ten furious minutes, Pringle ordered another ceasefire, followed by a staged withdrawal.

"What's happening?" Connington asked. "Have they beaten us?"

"Not a chance," Sergeant Drysdale replied. "We're just keeping Mussolini on the hop."

The Lothians settled on the ridge they had recently vacated and fired again, listening to the Rajputs shouting their war cries and firing alongside.

"*Bol Bajrang Bali Ki Jai!*"

"Good lads, the Rajputs," Hogg said. "I'm glad they're on our side."

Innes laughed. "They won't cut and run like the French, that's for sure."

The infantry continued to distract the Italians until six in the morning, when both regiments withdrew to their starting point, having achieved their objectives.

"Withdraw? Bugger that for a game of soldiers!" Hogg said. "Are we not going to attack the buggers?"

"No," Drysdale explained patiently. "We're keeping them busy while our armour moves around their camp. If the Italians are firing at us, they won't hear our tanks."

"We could have taken them without the tanks," Hogg said. "The Rajputs are right handy lads in a dust-up."[1]

Tulloch noted the nods of agreement from most of Four Platoon.

"Take over, Sergeant," Tulloch said and strolled across to the neighbouring platoon. "Are you all right, Atkins?"

"Yes, sir," Atkins looked drained by the morning's excitement.

"That's another action to tell your girl about," Tulloch said. "You've fought the enemy, been under fire, and survived to tell the tale."

Atkins smiled. "So, we have, Tulloch."

"Keep your chin up," Tulloch said and returned to Four Platoon.

"Listen!" Sergeant Drysdale lifted a hand. "The tanks are engaging the Italians!"

Too far away to participate, the Lothians could only listen as the armour entered the Italian camp and attacked the defenders. They heard the rattle of machine guns and the deeper crump of the tank's guns, both British and Italian. The flashes of explosions lit the sky above the fort, with a red dawn rapidly spreading over the battlefield.

"It sounds like the tankies are having all the fun," Hogg said. He looked towards Nibeiwa, shifting his feet as if he wanted to run across the desert and join in.

The firing inside Nibeiwa continued until ten that morning, sometimes rising to a crescendo, then fading away to erupt again until it finally ended.

"Come on, gentlemen," Colonel Pringle said. "We're going into Nibeiwa."

The Lothians sighed, hitched up their trousers, restocked

their ammunition, filled their water bottles, and marched to the smoke-blackened ex-Italian strongpoint.

Tulloch learned that the Matildas of the 7th Royal Tank Regiment had powered into the gap he had noticed in the fort's defences, only to find twenty-three Italian M11 tanks already there.

Thankful they were dealing with tanks rather than hidden mines, Major Henry Rew, an English rugby international, led the 7th RTR straight at the Italian tanks. In the tank-to-tank action, the Matildas proved their worth, destroyed the M11s within ten minutes, and burst into Nibeiwa.

Many of the Italian defenders fought bravely, with General Maletti running from his tent firing a machine gun, only for a Matilda to kill him. The Italian artillerymen fired their guns and died at their posts, frustrated that their weapons were ineffective against the British armour. The colonial infantrymen were not so brave, with the Libyan soldiers surrendering en masse.

Among the few British casualties was Major Rew, who left his tank to accept the garrison's surrender when some of the defenders hoisted a white flag. An Italian shot Rew dead, killing a man who could have played a notable part in the war.

Tulloch looked around the interior of the camp the Italians had constructed with such pride and skill. Dead and wounded colonial troops filled the perimeter trench, with tents ripped and torn by British bullets. British soldiers were organising burial parties for the dead, with some Italian officers still wearing their pyjamas, either as casualties or prisoners. Tulloch saw at least two thousand prisoners sitting in bewildered groups with half a dozen British soldiers on guard.

"What next, sir?"

"We're going onto Tummar West," Colonel Pringle said cheerfully. "That's the next Italian fort in the centre of their line. The tanks need infantry support."

"I'll organise the men, sir," Major Hume said.

Tulloch could see that the Italian gunners had frequently hit the Matildas without any significant effect. The tanks were battle-scarred but unbowed, with the crews talking cheerfully as they repaired the most obvious damage.

"How are we moving?" Hume asked.

"By truck. The Italians left behind quite a few vehicles," Colonel Pringle said. "The Royal Tanks kindly left us a few."

"Come on, lads! No dawdling for souvenirs!" Tulloch gathered Four Platoon together. "Elliot! There are no women here for you; get on board the bus!"

Leaving Nibeiwa's chaos, the Lothians boarded the trucks and followed the tanks northward into the desert. The men were tired but in high spirits after their victory.

"We let the armour enter first," Pringle said when the trucks halted and the men disembarked. "We're here in support again."

Tulloch could plainly see the enemy fort, with the Italian flag held proudly above the walls and the sun reflecting from the barrels of the defenders' guns. The Matildas lined up west of Tummar West in an impressive display of armoured might. For a few moments, both sides stared at each other without firing a shot.

"What's happening here?" Erskine asked, sotto voce. "Is it a battle or a blasted military parade?"

"Here they come," Kilner murmured as an Italian gun fired. Tulloch heard the bang of the shot a full second before he saw the explosion well in front of the tanks.

"Ranging shot," he said.

The Italians fired again, with the explosion closer to the Lothians than to the tanks. "Over," Tulloch said. "The Italians have bracketed the armour. The next salvo should be directly on target."

"They're too late for that," Kilner said as the tanks headed forward, kicking up sand and with the sound of their engines loud in the desert.

"What do we do, sir?" Hogg asked impatiently.

"We wait for orders," Tulloch replied curtly.

He felt himself tense as the tanks moved in. Suddenly, the infantry seemed very vulnerable, stuck between a regiment of armour and a fortified base with machine guns and artillery. The desert provided few places to shelter.

Chapter Twelve

When the tanks moved towards Tummar West, the Italian defenders opened fire with everything they had. Machine guns, 37 mm solid shot, and 105 mm high explosive all hammered towards the thin line of British Matildas. Tracer whipped through the air, and even 20 mm anti-aircraft guns joined in the barrage until it seemed the tanks would disappear beneath the terrible fusillade. The shots kicked up dust and rattled like hail on the tanks' armour.

"They can't survive that!" Cummings breathed.

"Whoever said the Italians could not fight were talking nonsense," Innes said.

Tulloch agreed as the defenders' fire grew even heavier as the tanks drew closer. He lifted his binoculars and focused on the battle, expecting to see an array of destroyed and burning Matildas. He saw a tank judder as an Italian shot hit it dead on, but then it continued without any apparent damage.

"These Matildas are indestructible!" he said. "The Italians haven't destroyed a single one!"

"Go on, the Royal Tanks," Hogg roared. "Shabash the tankies!"

The British tanks roared on, bumped over a shallow anti-tank ditch, and entered the fort with their two-pounder guns firing and machine guns spraying its interior.

Colonel Pringle checked his watch. "Right, lads!" he stepped forward, shouting to be heard above the noise of battle. "Here we go! Fix bayonets and follow me!"

The Lothians obeyed, with their rifles extended and the sun glinting from their bayonets. Tulloch glanced to the right and left, seeing the long line of khaki-clad men, some with their steel helmets angled to shade their eyes, others with the helmets at the back of their heads, but all striding purposefully forward. For the first time in the campaign, the battalion's pipers played them into battle, with the distinctive sound of the Lowland pipes a homely reminder of Scotland as they trod over the shifting desert sand.

After a rendering of *The Flowers of Edinburgh*, the pipers changed to *The Black Bear* and *Hey Johnnie Cope*, stirring music to urge the men forward.

"Aye, that's the way, pipie," Hogg said. "Let the Italians know we're coming so they can shoot us to bits."

"It's broad daylight, you moaning-faced bastard," Sergeant Drysdale growled. "They can see us."

"Even so, why advertise our presence?" Hogg said.

"That's what the pipes are for," Drysdale replied. "They're to let the enemy know how long they have left to live."

"Double!" Pringle ordered as they neared the fort.

The Lothians increased their speed, closing the distance to Tummar West. Hogg shouted something inarticulate, adding, "The Gorgie Boys are coming!"

Other Lothians yelled, with Sergeant Drysdale roaring the regimental slogan, "Gin ye daur," and others taking it up as they rushed for the gate.

Tulloch heard the clamour as the Matildas fought it out with the Italian defenders, machine guns, and two-pounders busy. The Italians responded with artillery and machine guns. Tulloch heard the sharp crack of the Italian anti-tank guns and the rattle of British Besas. He listened to the confused gabble of men shouting in panic or anger and the long, drawn-out scream of a mortally wounded man.

"Inside!" Colonel Pringle was first to enter Tummar West with his revolver in his hand and his pipe clenched firmly between his teeth. Tulloch brought Four Platoon at his back, searching for the enemy and expecting a blast of Italian fire.

"Extended order," Tulloch shouted. "Watch for snipers. Sergeant, take the left flank." He saw Atkins striding forward on his right.

You're doing all right, Atkins.

The inside of the fort could have been a sight from the third panel of Hieronymus Bosch's *Garden of Earthly Delights.* Dead and wounded men lay among a shambles of destroyed trucks, tents, caravans, and artillery pieces. The tanks had powered in, shooting at everything with their two-pounders and Besa machine guns. Tulloch saw one Italian soldier screaming after a Matilda ran over his leg and the horrible remains of another, flattened by a tank. Others stood with their hands raised or sat in disconsolate groups, wondering what had happened.

A massive explosion made Tulloch start. He looked to the east of the camp, where an Italian ammunition lorry vanished in a terrible burst of fire. The Italians were firing well, but their guns failed to penetrate the Matildas' armour. The tanks ran the entire length of the camp, firing their two-pounders at anything that looked like resistance and finishing the job with their machine guns.

There's little for us to do here.

"Mop up, lads," Tulloch ordered as the Lothians spread out in the tanks' wake. "Take prisoners where you can and end any enemy that fights back."

Elliot and Innes worked together, moving purposefully with the Bren gun, searching for targets.

Three Italians emerged from behind a burning truck, firing their rifles at the Lothians. Hogg shot the first, with the bullet knocking the man off his feet. As he worked the bolt of his rifle, Sergeant Drysdale shot and wounded the second. The third glanced at his companions, shouted something, and charged forward. Hardie killed him with a single shot to the head.

"Keep moving," Tulloch said.

Many of the Italian gunners died at their posts, persisting in their hopeless tasks like the brave men they were. Seeing that resistance was pointless, the surviving infantry surrendered to the tanks or the Lothians.

After twenty hectic minutes, the firing ended as disconsolate Italian and Colonial troops threw down their weapons and surrendered.

"Where the devil are we going to put all these prisoners?" Kinnear asked.

"More to the point, how will we feed and water them?" Tulloch asked. "The Navy is already hard-pressed to supply us, let alone hundreds of Italians."

"Don't you worry about the prisoners," Kinnear advised. "Just enjoy the victory; God knows we've had few enough of them."

"Hopefully, it's the first of many," Tulloch said.

With the camp secure in British hands and a handful of British and Indian soldiers guarding the thousands of prisoners, the Lothians reformed in the desert. The tank crews were talking excitedly among themselves, pleased with their victory. Tulloch noted that the Italian gunners had hit every tank, but their artillery had lacked the power to penetrate the armour.

"With better weapons, this battle might have turned out differently," Tulloch said. "These Italian lads fought well with what they had."

"We'd have still won," Atkins replied.

Tulloch nodded. "I think so."

"We'll defeat the Germans next," Atkins claimed.

"One step at a time," Kinnear cautioned. "We've only won a single battle against the Italians. Let's not get ahead of ourselves." He looked up as Pringle arrived with his pipe firmly clasped between his teeth.

"What next, sir?" Kinnear asked.

"On to Sidi Barrani," Colonel Pringle said and grinned around his pipe. "Not Four Platoon, though, Tulloch."

"What are we doing, sir?"

"You are accompanying a section of tanks to persuade Tummar East and Point 90 to surrender," Pringle told him.

Tulloch fought his surprise. "It's taken a full-scale attack to capture Tummar West, sir. What makes the general believe the other forts will surrender to a few tanks and a handful of infantry?"

"General O'Connor knows his enemy," Pringle said. "Off you go, Tulloch. Your Matildas are waiting for you." Removing the pipe from his mouth, he jabbed the stem toward the fort's entrance.

"Yes, sir," Tulloch said and passed the news on to his men.

Sergeant Drysdale nodded. "Yes, sir," he accepted the news without emotion.

"Is the colonel sure you need all of us, sir?" Connington asked.

"Enough of your lip, Connington!" Drysdale admonished.

Hogg stamped his boots on the sand, withdrew his bayonet from its scabbard, and thrust it back in, wordless.

"Right, lads, let's be having you," Drysdale said.

Rather than a section of tanks, Tulloch found only one battered Matilda waiting for him.

"Are you Tulloch?" A sand-smeared lieutenant asked.

"I am," Tulloch said.

"Tom Craig," the lieutenant cheerfully introduced himself. "You and I have to persuade Tummar East to surrender." He seemed to find the idea highly amusing.

"Where are the rest of your tanks?" Tulloch asked.

"We are all the tanks," Craig said and leaned closer. "And our turret is stuck. An Italian fired his blasted 20 mm as we were in full recoil, and their round is stuck in the mantlet aperture." He laughed again. "Our Besa is also jammed, so let's hope the chaps in Tummar East and Point 90 don't resist too much."

"Let's hope not," Tulloch said, nodding to Hogg. "Or I'll have to send Private Hogg to sort them out."

Craig glanced at Hogg and gave a dramatic shiver. "As the Duke of Wellington said, 'I don't know what effect these men will have upon the enemy, but by God, they frighten me.'" He patted his tank. "I have an Italian officer with us to ease our way. Are you ready, Tulloch?"

"Ready," Tulloch said.

"Let's go then!" Craig lifted a hand and pointed eastward. "Drive on!"

Four Platoon formed up behind the Matilda and marched eastward. Innes tried to sing *Waltzing Matilda* but gave up as the tank's dust choked him, so they marched in silence except for the occasional grunt or muttered curse.

"Bugger this for a game of soldiers," Hogg said, bowing his head from the dust.

The Italian officer wore a splendid blue uniform and looked decidedly nervous as Craig made him stand under the loader's hatch with his head and shoulders clearly visible to the outside world.

"Your friends won't shoot at an Italian officer," Craig assured him.

"The Blackshirts might," Hardie grunted.

"Don't tell the Italian lad that," Tulloch advised.

"Here!" Craig thrust a white flag into the prisoner's hand. "Wave that. If nothing else, it will make the garrison look at you. They might think General O'Connor is surrendering to them."

"Extended order, lads," Tulloch shouted. He knew he'd lose the protection of the armour from machine gun fire, but if the

Italian artillery targeted the Matilda, he wanted his men well out of the way.

"Fix bayonets; I want a Bren gun on either flank and one in the centre. Smith, take position central left in case the Italians send out their tanks."

"Three Brens and a Boys against an entire Italian fort," Connington said.

"And a tank," Sergeant Drysdale reminded.

"Aye, a tank that can't fire."

Drysdale grinned. "The Italians don't know that," he said. "Bluff and deception can be as important as firepower in battle."

"Maybe, aye," Connington said, "and maybe no, but I'd prefer one with a gun that worked."

The Italians in Tummar East did not fire when the lone tank and its escort approached, and a handful of Italian officers emerged from the gate and approached the Matilda.

"Do your stuff," Craig called cheerily to the prisoner. "Ask your friends to surrender."

"Kneel, men," Tulloch ordered. "Smith, aim at the gate in case the Italians send out a tank. Bren gunners, concentrate on the walls."

The Italians spoke for a few moments, with their voices clear even above the low grumbling of the tank engine.

"Hardie! Do you know what they are saying?"

"Yes, sir," Hardie said. "The officer from the fort says he's willing to surrender, but not to somebody as junior as a second lieutenant. He suggests we withdraw, bombard the camp for a while without causing casualties, and return with a larger force. Then they'll surrender." He brushed away a fly. "Honour satisfied."

"Do they think this is some sort of game?" Tulloch asked.

"I don't think these lads want to fight, sir," Hardie said. "Most of them are Libyans anyway, not Italians, and they probably don't know what it's all about."[1]

"Was that it?" Hogg sounded disappointed.

"This is a strange situation," Craig said. "If you infantry fellows remain here, I'll return and see if I can organise some sort of barrage and round up a few higher-ranked officers."

"We'll stay here," Tulloch promised.

With his platoon well spread out and digging holes in the sand, Tulloch waited for results. After an hour, he heard the rumble of artillery, and the first salvo of British shells landed just outside Tummar East.

"That was bloody close to us!" Hogg exclaimed. "I hope the gunners know we're still here!"

Another ominous whistle announced the arrival of the next salvo, and the desert rose in a succession of explosions, with dust rising a hundred yards in front of Four Platoon's position.

"Keep your heads down, lads!" Tulloch warned as the artillery subjected the ground between Four Platoon and Tummar East to a relentless, if short-lived, bombardment without a single hit on the fort.

When the guns stopped, Tulloch saw a column of dust and a convoy of 15-hundredweight trucks heading his way.

"Is that our boys?" Sergeant Drysdale asked.

Rather than the Lothians, it was the 3/1 Punjab Regiment who trundled up. The Punjabis' commander greeted Tulloch with a grin and a wave.

"Waiting for us, are you, old man? Quite right! Let my Punjabis take over."

The Punjabis disembarked with professional nonchalance and filed inside the fort, rifles ready for any resistance. Tulloch led his men beside the Punjabis, wary of the ease with which the defenders surrendered.

"Keep your bayonets fixed and your mags charged," Tulloch warned. "The Italians outnumber us, and they may want to fight." He glanced at the Punjabis and knew he was in good company. They looked very efficient fighting men.

When they entered Tummar East, the Punjabis and Lothians stopped in surprise. The Italian garrison had formed up, rank after rank of smartly uniformed men on parade, with white flags flying in front of each unit.

"What the hell is this?" the Punjabi officer asked.

"I think we've just captured the camp," Tulloch said as the Italian officers saluted the Punjabis. Many Italians had their neatly packed kitbags and suitcases beside them to ensure they were comfortable in the Prisoner-of-War camps.

"I've never seen anything like this before," Sergeant Drysdale said.

"And probably never will again," Tulloch said, staring at the ranks of smiling prisoners. "So much for Mussolini's vaunted fascist army. They're as warlike as little girls in primary school. Is this normal behaviour, Hardie?"

"I would not know, sir," Hardie replied. "I've never heard the like before."

"Tulloch!" The Punjabis' colonel said. "Your Colonel Pringle wants you back with the Lothians. Take a couple of these Italian trucks; there are plenty."

Tulloch agreed. Behind the parading defenders stood rank after rank of trucks, shining under the sun.

"Come on, lads!" Tulloch shouted. "We're going back in style."

Four Platoon drove back towards Tummar West, where burning Italian ammunition lorries threw flames into the air, with dark, oily smoke pressing down on the carnage below. Loose mules wandered over the camp, harassed medical orderlies searched for the suffering wounded, and fitters and mechanics worked on abandoned and damaged vehicles.

We captured two enemy forts today, one with casualties and one without. That's two baby steps towards victory.

The Lothians camped between the forts and Sidi Barrani, the Italian base on the coast. They greeted Four Platoon with cheerful insults, yet Tulloch noted that Major Hume had ordered them to dig trenches and had set up Bren guns as anti-aircraft protection around the camp.

"Graziani is bound to retaliate," Hume said. "We can't relax until we've pushed the Italians back to Benghazi or even Tripoli. Until then, we can expect Graziani to send his aircraft over."

Colonel Pringle nodded his satisfaction. "Well done, Major. Sidi Barrani will be our next objective," he looked skyward. "If the Italians have any sense, they'll bomb us tonight, so ensure the men are dispersed."

"I will, sir," Hume said.

The Lothians spread blankets over their shelter trenches as camouflage and tried to get some sleep as the night-time chill descended. The sentries stared at the sky or patrolled the camp's perimeter in case the Italians sent out raiding parties. Tulloch checked his platoon, wrote a letter to his parents, and started another to Amanda while remembering the day's events.

Maybe the tide has turned, and we will start winning this blasted war.

Sometime in the early morning, the rumble of a distant bombardment woke Tulloch as the Royal Navy hammered Maktila. He looked up briefly, grunted, and fell back to sleep. The *Regio Aeronautica* did not attack the British camp that night.

"That was kind of them to leave us alone," Kinnear said.

"Maybe they don't realise we've captured half their fortified camps," Tulloch said.

"Or they don't want to bomb the camps in case they hit their own men," Kinnear replied.

"I can believe that," Tulloch remembered the compassionate Capitano Galuzzo.

"What was that other clattering sound I heard all night?" Kinnear asked.

"That was the fitters working on the tanks," Captain Kilner told him. "Between enemy fire and mechanical problems, we have thirty-five tanks unfit for action and a big battle looming. I doubt the Italians will abandon Sidi Barrani as easily as they did Tummar East."

Tulloch nodded. "I reckon not," he said.

"They've abandoned Makila, though," Kilner said. "Last night's naval bombardment was too much for them. The First Libyan Division has pulled out first thing this morning."

"They might reinforce the Sidi Barrani garrison," Tulloch said.

"Let's hope not," Kilner replied. "If so, the Little White-Haired Terrier will still sort them out."

Tulloch ignored Kinnear's cynical glance.

Despite all the fitters could do, twenty-four tanks remained out of action when Lieutenant-Colonel Roy Jerram led his 7th Royal Tank Regiment, ready for the day's battle.

"The 7th RTR only have eleven tanks!" Atkins said.

"So I see," Tulloch agreed.

"Will that be enough?"

"If one lone tank can capture Tummar East," Tulloch said. "Imagine what eleven can do." He walked away, leaving Atkins to ponder his words.

"We're attached to the 16th British Infantry Brigade for the assault," Pringle explained to his officers. "Our task is to help cut the road between Sidi Barrani and Buq Buq, hold it to prevent the Sidi garrison from escaping, and to stop any reinforcements coming through."

"Who's on our flanks, sir?" Captain Muirhead asked, taking notes in a small black book.

"The 2nd Leicesters," Pringle said. "We each have to capture a small, defended camp beside the road. The 2nd Argylls and the 2nd Queens block the road to the north, and the 11th Indian Infantry Brigade will ensure the roads out of Sidi to the south and southwest are safe."

"General O'Connor has things well in hand," Muirhead said. "When do we move against Sidi Barrani itself, sir?"

Pringle stuffed tobacco into his pipe before he replied. "We don't," he said quietly. "The general thinks we had sufficient fighting yesterday."

"We hardly fired a shot," Hume said, frowning.

The colonel scratched a match and puffed his pipe into life. "I know that. I suspect the general thinks Dunkirk impaired our effectiveness."

"That silly business on the beach!" Kinnear said, and Atkins looked away.

"That's nonsense!" Hume growled.

"That would be Brigadier Worthington spreading poison," Erskine suggested.

Tulloch looked up. "Does he think we're not fit?"

"Maybe," Pringle said. "I heard somebody say that the men defeated at Dunkirk had lost the will to fight."

"That's a bloody cheek!" Muirhead said. "We're the best there is!"

"We'll prove that as soon as possible," Colonel Pringle replied. "In the meantime, we'll obey orders and do our duty as General O'Connor demands." He removed the pipe from his mouth. "This Desert Army seems quite well balanced."

The officers nodded. After the victories of the previous day, they could all feel the renewed confidence surging through the Lothians and the British Army.

"We need some success after Dunkirk," Martin said. "We've taken a bit of a pounding so far, what with Norway, France, and British Somaliland. Maybe Egypt is the turning point."

"Maybe so," Tulloch agreed. "I think the Germans are the real enemy, not the Italians."

"Don't discount the Italians," Pringle said. "They can be as tough as the best Germans if they choose." He grinned without humour. "We're the Lothian Rifles, and we can cope with whatever Mussolini throws at us."

"Yes, sir," Kinnear said and lowered his voice. "I hope so."

Chapter Thirteen

WESTERN DESERT, DECEMBER 1940

The Lothians were quiet when they clambered into the backs of lorries, a mixture of fifteen hundredweight British and captured Italian vehicles, and motored northward.

"Innes, get the Bren set up in case of air attack," Tulloch ordered.

"Yes, sir," Innes said.

As always, they travelled within a cloud of dust, with men watching for Italian aircraft as they contemplated what lay ahead.

"Let's hope the Italians fight like the lads in Tummar East," Cummings said. "I like that kind of victory."

"Are you scared of fighting?" Connington sneered.

"I want to survive the war and get home," Cummings said quietly.

Hogg grunted. "The more we kill today, the less we have to fight next time."

When some of the men grunted approval, Tulloch nodded.

His platoon had not lost their will to fight, whatever Brigadier Worthington believed.

The trucks pulled up at seven in the morning, with the Lothians debussing onto the sand as the NCOs and officers gave sharp orders. Tulloch took command of Four Platoon, checked every man was present, and ensured they had their quota of ammunition and full water bottles.

"Smith, make sure the Boys is ready. Bryson, you're the number two for the Boys. Innes and Elliot, keep the Bren handy. Corporal Borthwick, you have the two-inch mortar." The men nodded, checking their personal weapons as the tension rose. A faint wind lifted surface dust from the ground, covering the men's boots and snapping at their bare legs.

"The Italian camp is just there," Tulloch nodded to the walls, half a mile away. Sunlight glinted on a ribbon of barbed wire, a reminder of the earlier war that was burned into the folk memory of every man present. Tulloch thought of the Great War poem, *Hanging on the Old Barbed Wire*.

If you want to find the private
I know where he is,
He's hanging on the old barbed wire.
I saw him, I saw him,
Hanging on the old barbed wire,
Hanging on the old barbed wire.

Tulloch shook away the words.

"Drummond, have you got the wire cutters?"

"Yes, sir," Drummond replied. An ex-fisherman, Tulloch expected Drummond to be out of his depth in the desert, but he had adapted as well as any landsman.

"Connington, you're number two with the cutters. If Drummond falls, you're responsible for looking after them."

Connington nodded, glanced at Drummond, and looked

away. The wind increased slightly, blowing sand in the Lothians' faces, so they half-closed their eyes and turned away.

"How big is this Italian fort, sir?" Sergeant Drysdale asked.

"It's maybe a quarter of the size of Tummar East, and we're not sure of the garrison," Tulloch said. "We'll ask them to surrender and hope they'll oblige."

Some of the men smiled; most licked dry lips with dry tongues. Despite their previous success in the Western Desert, they knew an attack on a defended position was hazardous. Somebody laughed, high-pitched and nervous. Hardie looked as calm as if walking along Edinburgh's Princes Street.

When Colonel Pringle lifted his hand, Tulloch took a deep breath of sand-laden air. "Right, lads, here we go, the best of luck to everybody. If anybody is hit, lie quietly and wait for the stretcher-bearers. Follow me." He stepped forward, feeling his heartbeat increase.

Once more into the breach.

The words of *Flowers of Edinburgh* ran through Tulloch's head as he regulated Four Platoon's pace, feeling his feet crunch on the sand. The pipers began to play, with the sound of the pipes hauntingly nostalgic in this alien environment.

The Lothians advanced in open order, with the Italian camp seen through a heat haze. There was no sign of military occupation as the Lothians drew closer, only the long plain walls behind the barbed wire curtain and the faint wind whipping loose sand into the infantrymen's faces.

"I think the Italians have left," Connington said. "Either that, or they're already lined up inside, ready to surrender."

"Extended order!" Colonel Pringle ordered, and the Lothians opened ranks. They marched slowly forward, bayonets gleaming in the sun, waiting for the Italians to open fire and hoping the garrison had deserted the fort.

The first shot sounded when the Lothians were a hundred yards from the wire. A volley followed, and then the terrible chatter of a machine gun.

"They're awake now!" Innes shouted, firing a short burst with his Bren.

"Push on!" Colonel Pringle ordered. "Increase the speed."

The Lothians advanced, zig-zagging as the Italian fire intensified. Men fell, dead or wounded, and some dived to the ground, seeking cover.

"Get up!" Sergeant Drysdale kicked one man, a young replacement. "Get up and get forward, Mitchell!"

A bullet smacked into the ground three inches from Tulloch's left foot. He saw the fountain of dust with little interest, although he knew the memory would haunt him later that day. He motioned Four Platoon forward, heard a long scream behind him, and fired his revolver at the defending wall without a hope of hitting anybody. Bullets whined and whistled around them, kicked up sand, and rattled from the barbed wire.

Three men from C Company broke away, charged forward, and reached the wire, but a burst of machine-gun fire scythed them down before they got further.

Hanging on the old barbed wire.

"Down!" Pringle ordered. "Get down!"

The Lothians flattened onto the sand, aiming and firing at the fort, furiously working the bolts of their Lee-Enfields. Tulloch saw the defenders bobbing around, with machine guns and rifles jabbing at the Lothians. He heard the crack of artillery and saw the mushroom rise of an exploding shell.

These Italian lads are not going to surrender tamely.

Hogg was on his face in a shallow depression, working the bolt of his rifle and firing like a man demented, while Hardie was aiming each shot, firing slowly and precisely. Tulloch watched him for a moment and realised he took a deep breath and released it slowly each time he squeezed the trigger.

As Tulloch watched, Hardie fired, muttered "four" and worked his bolt. One of the Italian defenders stiffened and fell backwards from the wall.

Four? Is that four defenders that Hardie has shot?

"Mortars!" Tulloch shouted, and Corporal Borthwick fired the two-inch mortar, sending its two pounds two-ounce high-explosive shell in its high arc over the Italian wall. Other platoons followed, subjecting the Italians to a counter-barrage. Tulloch saw one shell explode on top of the wall, knocking down a section of the stonework and scattering the defenders.

"I wish we had some tanks," Kinnear commented.

Tulloch ignored him. "Wire cutters!" he roared. "Where's Drummond with the wire cutters?"

"Here I am, sir!" Drummond shouted from behind the minimal shelter of a small rock.

"Bring them forward!" Tulloch ordered. "The rest of you, give us covering fire!" He heard the controlled hammer of the Bren as he weaved forward, with Drummond at his side and Italian bullets kicking up dust all around them. One bullet hit the wire, making it vibrate and sing.

One of C Company's wounded was still alive. Badly injured, he moaned, staring at Tulloch through wide, pain-racked eyes.

I can't help you, son, not yet.

"Get a hole in the wire!" Tulloch shouted. Holstering his revolver, he took hold of Drummond's rifle and fired at any Italian he saw on the wall. An Italian machine gun opened up, with the bullets hissing above his head. A bullet hit one of the dead Lothians on the wire, making his corpse twitch and swivel in an obscene parody of life. Tulloch saw Innes swing round the Bren, with Elliot handing over a fresh magazine.

"Hurry up, man!" Tulloch said.

"I'm going as fast as possible, sir," Drummond replied.

Tulloch heard the ping as the cutters sliced through another strand of wire and hugged the ground as the Italian machine gunner fired again. Something crashed against his helmet, making his ears ring.

Some bloody walkover!

Three more Lothians were frantically working with wire

cutters as the mortars fired their eight rounds a minute, so a constant stream of bombs fell on the Italian fort.

The wire pinged again, and then Drummond grunted and rolled aside. Tulloch saw the neat little hole in Drummond's helmet and the fist-sized exit wound where a mess of blood and brains spread across his shoulders.

"Connington!" Tulloch shouted.

Dropping the rifle and grabbing the wire cutters, Tulloch continued the work, wrestling with each strand of wire. He realised the cutters' handles were sticky with warm blood. He ducked as something buzzed past his head, realised the bullet had missed, and continued. Innes's Bren stammered and stopped, and Innes cursed.

"It's jammed!"

"Clear the bloody thing!" Sergeant Drysdale shouted.

Tulloch glanced over his shoulder. Connington was halfway towards him, pinned down by Italian fire.

"Smith! Try the Boys! Fire at the wall!"

Tulloch heard the Boys' ear-splitting crack. It was intended as an anti-tank rifle, but any sort of explosive might persuade the Italians to leave that section of the wall.

Another bullet burrowed into the sand at Tulloch's elbow. He jerked aside, cut another strand, and saw he had created a gap. He shoved aside the wire, swore at the sting as a barb sliced his hand open, half rose, and saw his platoon crowding towards him, still firing at the Italian camp.

"Come on, boys," Tulloch shouted, with his voice sounding distant. His head ached after the strike on his helmet.

The wall was a hundred yards ahead, with a shallow ditch in front and Italian infantrymen lining the defences. The machine gun concentrated on the gap Tulloch had made in the wire until Hardie fired a single shot that hit the gunner. When the machine gun stopped, Four Platoon rushed through, cheering in a mixture of elation, fear, and relief.

Innes tore off the empty magazine, cleared the jam, and

rammed in a new magazine. Levelling the Bren at the wall, he fired the entire magazine from the hip, with the bullets knocking chips and dust from the wall.

"Watch for mines!" Tulloch shouted as he loped forward. He dreaded the thought of stepping on a mine and having his legs shredded. The idea seemed much worse than a straightforward bullet wound to the upper body.

"This way, lads!" Hogg shouted, running at the wall with the sunlight glittering from his bayonet. Four Platoon followed, as Drysdale roared at them to keep in extended order and not give the enemy a perfect target.

Unlike the men from Tumar East, the Italians stood their ground and fought back as the Lothians roared up to the wall. The ditch was only a couple of feet deep and three feet wide, no obstacle to fit infantrymen, and then they were at the base of the wall.

"Innes! Hardie! Make them keep their heads down!" Tulloch ordered as he threw himself at the ten-foot-high wall. The others followed, clambering on each other's shoulders as they climbed. Tulloch heard yells and curses, obscene shouting, and cries of triumph as the Lothians reached the top to face the Italians.

Hogg was first over, snarling as he lunged at a defender with his bayonet. Tulloch was next, staggering as he landed on the firing platform.

These Italians are Blackshirts, Tulloch realised when he saw the black shirt and fez. *They are dedicated Fascists, not the usual reluctant conscripts or scared colonial infantry.*

An Italian soldier aimed a rifle at him, snarling as he pulled the trigger. Tulloch ducked, grabbing for his revolver, to see Hogg thrust his bayonet into the man's abdomen, twist and withdraw. As the Blackshirt screamed, Hogg swung the butt of his rifle and knocked him to the ground. More of the platoon were coming over the wall, with other Lothians further along.

We've breached the wall. Now, we must push on.

"Come on, Lothians! Come on, the Jocks!" Erskine had leapt

from the wall into the fort's interior, firing his revolver at any defender he saw. His platoon was a few steps behind, snarling as they advanced.

"Come on, Four Platoon!" Tulloch shouted. "Don't let Five Platoon get ahead!"

The camp was rectangular, with tents in the middle and what looked like deep dugouts on one side. The garrison had placed camouflage netting over a score of trucks inside one wall and a group of huts along the opposite side. Tulloch looked for tanks or armoured cars and sighed with relief when there were none.

"Keep pressing them back, lads!"

Atkins shouted, tripped over, and sprawled face-first on the ground. Ignoring him, his men surged onward.

An Italian officer ran forward, firing his pistol as the Blackshirts behind him roared their defiance against the British intruders.

"Innes! Where's your Bren?" Tulloch aimed and fired at this latest threat. All around him, the Lothians were pouring over the wall, advancing into the camp, firing at the enemy, and shouting in fear and fury.

The Italian officer ran directly towards Tulloch, with tight dark curls shining in the sun and his uniform pristine. Tulloch fired, missed, and saw the officer take deliberate aim at him. Tulloch swerved to one side as if he were running on the rugby pitch in Edinburgh, fired two quick shots, and saw the officer fall backward, dropping his pistol.

With their leader down, the Blackshirts hesitated.

"Go for them!" Tulloch shouted, reloading quickly. He fumbled a cartridge, saw it fall with the sunlight reflecting on the brass, and reached for another.

"Rummel them up!" Elliot roared, fired his rifle, worked the bolt, and fired again.

Hardie dropped into a crouch, aimed, and fired, dropping a Blackshirt NCO. He worked the bolt and fired again, seemingly as calm as if he were on the ranges in the Pentland Hills.

"Come on, Four Platoon!" Tulloch charged forward, hoping his men would follow. He heard shouting, screaming, and curses from all around, in Scots, Italian, and English.

"They're breaking!" Pringle shouted. "Tulloch, take your men along the north; Erskine, take the south; Atkins, Kinnear, Martin, you and I will take the centre. Come on!"

The Lothians advanced with bayonet, bullet, and rifle butt, driving the Blackshirts before them. Italian soldiers, brave a few moments earlier, began to surrender, and within twenty minutes, only a few pockets of resistance remained.

Tulloch stepped over the officer he had killed, stooped, and lifted the man's pistol. He looked at the dead man with little emotion. When Tulloch had killed his first man on the North-west Frontier, the memory had haunted him for months. He knew the Italian's face would occur in his dreams for a night or two and then fade away as new experiences overlaid the memory.

Perhaps I have a store of these memories deep inside me, waiting to erupt at some time in the future.

Hardie fired the last shot, turned a dead Blackshirt officer onto his back, and studied his face.

"Are you all right, Hardie?" Tulloch asked.

"Yes, sir," Hardie straightened up and reloaded his rifle.

Pringle holstered his revolver and looked around. "That'll do," he said calmly. "We hold the camp. Kilner, round up the prisoners. Kinnear, mop up those who want to fight. Tulloch, get your platoon on the walls and see if there are any escapees from Sidi Barrani."

Tulloch had been so preoccupied with capturing the camp he had nearly forgotten the action had only been the first stage of the operation.

"Come on, Four Platoon! After me."

Realising he still held the Italian pistol, Tulloch thrust it under his belt and raced up a flight of stone steps to the wall.

We've captured the fort. The Italians fought well, but we defeated them. That's a step forward for the Lothian Rifles.

FROM TULLOCH'S POSITION ON THE WALL, THE ROAD BETWEEN Sidi Barrani and Buq Buq was plain, half-covered with blown sand. On the opposite side, the 2nd Leicesters had also captured their objective, but a scatter of dead bodies in British khaki showed that the Italians had fought hard.

"Whoever said the Italians were cowards should come out here," Connington said soberly.

Innes nodded. "Some soft-arsed politician, probably, or an armchair warrior who has never heard a shot in anger."

Tulloch silently agreed. He watched a thin ribbon of smoke rise above the Leicester's fort and listened to the desultory shooting behind him as Kinnear mopped up the last pockets of Italian resistance. The joy of victory was wearing off now, and he felt his usual sensation of hopeless despair.

I know I chose soldiering as my career, but why do supposedly civilised nations sink so low as to solve disputes by killing each other? War is the most primitive, sordid affair imaginable, officially sanctioned murder on an industrial scale.

"Smith! Get the Boys ready in case any Italian vehicles try to escape from Sidi. Innes, where's Bryson? Has anybody seen Bryson?"

"He's dead, sir. An Italian machine gunner cut him in half!"

"Oh," Tulloch had hardly got to know Bryson. He knew he would mourn Drummond and Bryson's deaths later, but just now, his duty came first. "Cummings, you're now number two on the Boys. Mortar men, take a couple of ranging shots at the road."

Tulloch organised his men, spreading them along the wall. He felt tired and sick, as always, when the after-battle reaction set in.

The wind rose further, whipping up the dust so it enveloped the camp and restricted visibility on the road.

"How are we meant to see anything coming in this?" Cummings asked. "I can hardly see a hundred yards!"

"Listen for approaching engines," Tulloch said. "But don't fire until you're sure they're Italian and not ours." His head was still aching, making it difficult to concentrate. He removed his helmet, saw a large dent in the crown, and wondered if a piece of shrapnel or a flying stone had hit him.

I'll never know now.

The wind increased, blasting sand into the faces of the sentries and nearly obscuring the road.

"Nothing can drive in this, sir," Drysdale said.

"A desperate or a terrified man can drive in nearly any condition," Tulloch replied. "Listen!" He held up his hand.

Four Platoon stopped, trying to ignore the whine of the wind and the batter of the sand. Smith crouched with the Boys, peering into the storm of sand to search for enemy transport.

"That's artillery, not vehicles," Drysdale said. "Heavy stuff, I'd say."

"I think you're right," Tulloch agreed. "The Italians are putting up a fight."

The artillery fire continued for some time, with the flash of explosions visible even through the swirling yellow haze of the sandstorm. As the wind eased, Tulloch heard engines faintly from the east.

"Tanks, sir," Drysdale said.

"Theirs or ours?" Tulloch asked.

"Ours, sir," Drysdale said. "Definitely ours." He paused for a moment. "I think."

"Get the Boys ready, Smith," Tulloch ordered. "Point it northward, but don't fire until I say."

When the wind shifted, the sound of gunfire died away, leaving the Lothians to wonder what was happening in the battle for Sidi Barrani. They learned later that the sandstorm and heavy

Italian artillery stalled the advance until the Royal Tank Regiment's Matildas attacked the Italian artillery.

Tulloch could imagine the duel between the British tanks and the Italian guns, with bravery and sacrifice on both sides. With the advantage of thick armour, the tanks triumphed.

As the remaining Italians withdrew, the British advance continued, and the Queens and Argylls achieved their objectives. Meanwhile, the 11th Indian Infantry Brigade positioned themselves on the south and southwest of Sidi Barrani, effectively blockading the Italian garrison within the village.

General O'Connor had surrounded the town, and Sidi Barrani was ready to fall.

"Sir!" Hardie said. "Something's coming!"

Tulloch peered into the distance, where a rising ribbon of dust foretold an approaching vehicle. "Get ready with the Boys, Smith! It's coming fast." He focused his binoculars. "Don't fire! It's ours! A staff car!"

Smith lowered the Boys as the staff car roared into the fort, and a bevy of red-tabbed officers emerged. Colonel Pringle met them at the camp's entrance, and they spoke for five minutes before the staff officers returned to their car and drove away.

"That's the closest they lads have been to the front since the last war," Erskine said.

"I wonder what that was all about?" Atkins asked.

"We'll see in a minute," Tulloch said as Pringle summoned all his officers. "Take over here, Sergeant."

"Yes, sir," imperturbable as ever, Drysdale stepped up as Tulloch descended to the centre of the fort.

"Feed your men and replenish their ammunition," Pringle said curtly. "We're going to take Sidi Barrani this evening."

Tulloch thought of the wounded and the weary. "Are we going alone, sir?"

Pringle began to fill his pipe. "We're going in from the north at 16:15, together with the Cameron Highlanders and the

Rajputana Rifles. The Queens and Leicesters are attacking from the south. We'll all have artillery and armour in support."

The officers nodded, calculating routes, possible casualties, and who would support them.

Pringle struck a match and set it to his tobacco. "We're leaving one company here to hold the fort and care for the wounded. We'll send away our prisoners in case they decide to make trouble when the bulk of the regiment is away."

"How many men did we lose?" Tulloch asked.

"Six dead, seven wounded," Dr Mercer replied at once.

"Two dead and one wounded from my platoon," Tulloch said.

"I hope the general thinks we're fit to fight now," Kilner said, ignoring Dr Mercer's glare.

"It's not the general, sir," Erskine said. "It's his aide-de-camp, Brigadier Worthington."

"Quite so," Colonel Pringle agreed. "Quite so."

Chapter Fourteen

WESTERN DESERT, DECEMBER 1940

The Lothians left the camp by truck, motoring across the desert with the men tensing themselves for a renewal of the advance. Most were quiet, checking their rifles and ammunition, with a few in high spirits.

"This is where I'm going to die," Connington said. "I can feel it. This is my last day alive."

"Thank God for that," Hogg said unfeelingly. "Then we'll be rid of your constant bloody moaning."

Sergeant Drysdale tapped Connington's shoulder. "You obey orders, Connington, and do your duty. If death wants you, there's nothing you can do except know you've done your best."

"Yes, Sergeant," Connington said.

The Lothians drove on, with the choking dust and the knowledge of the forthcoming battle stifling conversation.

When the leading truck halted, the convoy followed.

"Out we get, men!"

They joined the Camerons and Rajputana Rifles in a patch of desert that looked no different to any other they had driven through. Tulloch organised Four Platoon while the regimental colonels and a portly staff major greeted each other with formal handshakes.

"What's the plan, gentlemen?" Pringle asked.

"We'll go first," the Cameron colonel said as they pored over a map on the ground. "When we reach this point," he tapped the map, "you can leapfrog us and advance as far as here. The Rajputs are on our flank."

The colonels prodded at features on the map that were just names but which Tulloch knew his men would soon remember as places where men suffered and died, places that would live in their memories for years.

"Are your men battle-worthy?" The staff major asked. "Brigadier Worthington mentioned they were suffering after Dunkirk."

Colonel Pringle stiffened. "My men captured an Italian fort this morning without artillery or armoured support," he said. "Did you do anything except shuffle paper, Major?"

"The Leicesters captured their fort in half the time and bagged two thousand prisoners," the staff major replied. "We're still not sure about the Lothians."

"We're not sure about staff officers who criticise men who do the actual fighting," Pringle retorted. "And who don't say sir when they talk to a senior officer."

"Sorry, sir," the major said.

"I'm sure you are a busy man," Pringle said. "Somebody must find a use for you. Dismissed." He watched as the major coloured and marched away.

"Good," the Cameron colonel said. "That's what I hoped to hear." Tapping his cromack[1] on the ground, he walked away, leaving Pringle glaring after the major.

"He didn't mean anything by it," the Rajputana colonel said. "He's a bit concerned about the battle's outcome, and Dunkirk must have been a horrendous experience."

"We survived," Colonel Pringle said curtly. "And we fought our way home."

"I am sure you did," the Rajputana colonel agreed.

The Camerons formed up first, with the men talking in low tones as they contemplated the road ahead, with the white walls of Sidi Barrani in the distance. At quarter past four, their colonel blew his whistle, and they moved on, with the Rajputana Rifles on the right and the Lothians as a second line.

Don't the staff officers trust us to lead an assault?

The Italian artillery had been waiting and greeted the British advance with a storm of shells, to which the British guns responded in kind. Tulloch looked up to visualise the shells arcing overhead, British and Italian crossing each other in the crisp blue sky.

"Keep in extended formation, Four Platoon! No bunching when we move!"

A unit of cruiser tanks formed up beside the Lothians, and the crews exchanged light-hearted banter as they prepared to advance.

"Hey, Jocks! Fresh haggis if you take the town!"

"Get back and find your father, you English bastard!"

Tulloch heard a whistle from ahead, and the Lothians moved forward.

"Come on, lads!" Tulloch said. "Let's show the Camerons that we're the best fighting regiment in the army."

We're fighting two battles here, one against the official enemy and the other against our own people. If we don't prove ourselves capable of fighting, we'll be stuck on garrison duty in some backwater for the duration, or worse, broken up, and our men will be used as replacements for other regiments.

The Lothians advanced at the double, with men skirting the blackened craters where Italian shells had landed and ducking when shells exploded nearby. The pipes started, sending their evocative wail across the battlefield, easily heard above the crash of exploding shells and the rattle-grumble of the tanks.

"Keep going, boys!" Tulloch shouted as they reached the Camerons' positions, and steel-helmeted Highlanders yelled encouragement at them. On their right, Tulloch saw the Rajputana Rifles rushing forward, ignoring the shells that burst among them.

Tulloch heard a Rajput shout his war cry: *"Bol Bajrang Bali Ki Jai!"*

Others joined in, with the shout rising from the Rajputs' ranks. *"Bol Bajrang Bali Ki Jai!"*

The Lothians spread out, moving from cover to cover as the Italians fired with artillery and machine guns. Tulloch saw a man stagger and fall, holding his leg. He was one of the replacements, and Tulloch knew him as a nervous, cheerful man. Four Platoon surged on, angry that another of their own had been hit.

"Keep moving!" Tulloch ordered as he saw movement ahead. The village was only half a mile in front, the shattered remains of white houses gleaming under the sun. He saw gun smoke drifting among the ruins and busy defenders bobbing up and down as they tried to repel the British and Indian attack.

Sidi Barrani is tiny, Tulloch thought. *I doubt there are two dozen houses here. The way Mussolini proclaimed the capture, I thought it was a large town rather than a minor fishing village.*

The British artillery fired again, with a salvo landing square on the village, sending stones and sand high into the air. Smoke obscured the buildings before an offshore breeze cleared it away.

God help the Italians under that lot, and God help the poor inhabitants caught up in a war they won't ever understand.

"Halt!" Colonel Pringle ordered. "Form a defensive line here. The Camerons and Rajputana Rifles are to have the honour of capturing the village from this side."

"Why not us, sir?" Hume asked.

Pringle did not reply.

"What do we do, sir?" Hume peered forward. "Are we permitted to fire on the Italians?"

"Yes," Pringle sounded irritable. "Use the mortars."

As the Lothians found cover in the sands and opened mortar fire on the Italian positions, the Camerons advanced through them, jogging forward with a nonchalance Tulloch found impressive.

"See you in *Sidi Barrani*, Lothians," the Camerons shouted as they headed for the shattered village.

"Leave us some vino!" Cummings shouted.

"And some women!" Elliot added.

Tulloch watched the Camerons and Rajputana Rifles advance, with the British artillery lifting their barrage a few moments before the British and Indians reached the defences. The Italians met them with artillery, rifle, and machine-gun fire. Tulloch saw the glitter of sunshine on extended bayonets and momentarily pitied the Italian defenders facing a combination of Highland and Rajput warriors.

"Right, gentlemen!" Colonel Pringle shouted and motioned the Lothians forward. "Time to move."

Tulloch rose with the rest, checked Four Platoon, ducked as an Italian shell exploded twenty yards away, and marched forward. He heard the cheers as the Camerons and Rajputanas reached the Italian outer defences and saw the khaki lines pressing on with hardly a pause. A few men lingered to round up Italian prisoners. On the south, the Queens and Leicesters burst through the defences and into the village, driving everything before them. The firing rose to a crescendo and died away to a few isolated shots.

"What the hell are we doing here?" Hogg asked. "We are just here to make up the numbers."

"We're like the unwanted gooseberry," Innes agreed.

"We're doing our duty," Sergeant Drysdale said. "Shut your mouths and keep moving."

"Forward!" Colonel Pringle ordered. "Round up any remaining stragglers, men!"

The Lothians marched on, past a handful of crumpled khaki corpses, and by the time they entered Sidi Barrani, the Italians had surrendered.

"Well, we had a nice wee walk anyway," Connington said as

they marched into the village. British and Indian soldiers guarded hundreds of Italian prisoners while captured artillery, military stores, and vehicles littered the streets.

"Aye, here come the Lothians," a skull-faced Cameron corporal jeered. "Like the coo's tail, always at the arse-end."

Tulloch looked around at the devastation. "Now we have experienced the devastation of defeat and the ecstasy of victory."

Erskine sat on a pile of rubble that had once been a house. "I prefer the latter," he said, lighting a cigarette with a steady hand and placing it delicately into his holder.

"So do I," Tulloch said quietly. "And we only lost one man."

Only one man. That man's family will suffer when they hear. There's not an 'only' for them.

The Lothians set up camp outside Sidi Barrani in a collection of now sadly battered tents, some strewn with camouflage netting and others sheltering in the lee of damaged British and Italian trucks. Leaving Four Platoon under Drysdale's stern control, Tulloch stepped inside the large tent used as the Officers' Mess, ignored the badly patched bullet holes in the roof, and captured a tumbler of whisky.

"A successful operation, Tulloch," Captain Muirhead said.

"Yes, sir," Tulloch replied.

"That's another step forward," Muirhead continued. "We're making progress but still have a long way to go."

"Indeed, we have," Tulloch agreed. "Let's hope that success breeds success."

Wavell's intention in Operation Compass was to send General Richard O'Connor and his thirty-six thousand men of the Western Desert Force on a short attack on Marshal Rodolfo Graziani's hundred and fifty thousand strong 10th Army. Wavell intended the entire raid to be accomplished in five days, with the Allies probing from Mersa Matruh against the Italian positions within Egypt.

Operation Compass was the British Army's first significant

offence of the North African campaign, and many were surprised at its success. When they took Sidi Barrani, the British also captured Generale Gallini, the Italian corps commander, and his entire staff.

"That's another in the bag," Kinnear said. "We're capturing more prisoners than we can hold."

"We'd be better off letting the senior officers go free," Tulloch replied. "Their tactics and leadership are so incompetent that they seem to be fighting on our side."

Kinnear laughed. "Maybe so." He sipped at his whisky and held the tumbler up. "Damn this place; there's even sand in the whisky." He shrugged and swallowed some more. "Anyway, that's three days of our five-day Compass raid completed. General O'Connor will probably pull us back to Mersa Matruh now."

"It's been good to have some success," Tulloch said.

"We've not been totally successful," Kinnear reminded. "The Italians escaped from Rabia and Sofafi, even though O'Connor sent the armour to stop them."

"The 8th Hussars were caught in a sandstorm," Muirhead said. "We caught the tail end, but they got the full blast. That's why the Italian garrisons got away. Don't forget that the Hussars chased them halfway to Libya in their toy tanks."

"The light Mark VIs?" Tulloch asked.

"That's the ones," Muirhead agreed and smiled. "At least when the Mark VIs break down, the driver can pick the thing up and put it in their pocket."

"They had to," Kilner said. "The 3rd Hussars were chasing hard when they ran smack into an area of salt marsh. Their wee tanks got stuck, and the Italian artillery made full use of these tempting targets and knocked out thirteen tanks inside ten minutes."

Tulloch pulled out his pipe. "That was a reminder not to take the Italians for granted. We've been victorious so far, but Graziani's men can fight when they want to." He paused momentarily, "and we've not fully proved ourselves yet. The Army still doesn't trust the Lothians."

"They'll learn," Kilner said.

"They'll have to," Muirhead agreed grimly. "Some of our lads had a turn-up with the Camerons last night. The Highlanders were shouting about that incident on the East Lothian beach, and two of our boys charged straight at them."

Atkins smiled. "That's not unusual, though, a Highland and a Lowland regiment knocking seven bells out of each other. We have a long history of animosity stretching back to the seventeenth century when we fought on opposite sides during the Jacobite Wars."

"We don't need a history lesson from a subaltern," Kinnear said coldly.

"The army's done not bad in O'Connor's Western Desert Force," Muirhead said. "I don't know how many Italians we killed, but we captured over thirty-eight thousand, plus hundreds of tanks and other vehicles."

"What was the cost?" Tulloch asked.

"We had about 630 casualties," Muirhead replied.

"That's not a bad score," Tulloch agreed, "and we're not finished yet. We still have two days left of Operation Compass. Maybe O'Connor wants to push the Italians right out of Egypt."

They looked up when Colonel Pringle entered the tent.

"Sorry to disturb the happy gathering, gentlemen, but General Wavell has decided to withdraw the 4th Indian Division from the Western Desert and send it to the Sudan."

"Sudan? What the hell for, sir?" Muir asked.

Pringle smiled faintly. "Best ask General Wavell that, for I'm sure I don't know."

The officers looked at each other in consternation. "We're just building up a little momentum here; why break up the party to send us from one desert to another?"

Erskine looked up quietly. "What country borders Sudan,

gentlemen? Ethiopia. I'll wager Wavell will boot the Italians out of Ethiopia next."

Colonel Pringle waited until the furore died down before he continued. "We're not going with the 4th Indian," he said quietly. "Wavell is attaching us to the 16th British Brigade and leaving us here."

"I wish he'd make his mind up," Tulloch said. "I was getting to like the Rajputana lads."

"If the 4th Division is going to Sudan, who is replacing them?" Hume asked. "Or are we meant to fight five times our numbers with even fewer men?"

"The 6th Australian will join us," Pringle replied. "If Wavell can muster up sufficient transport to ship them here."

Tulloch nodded. Changing a division in the middle of a successful campaign was unusual. "That may upset our momentum," he agreed.

"Let's ensure it doesn't," Pringle replied. "We're on the move again tomorrow." He lit a cigarette with a steady hand. "The 16th British Brigade is taking care of the Italian prisoners, so we're being motorised and following up the 7th Armoured Div."

"They don't know what to do with us, do they?" Tulloch asked.

"They don't trust us," Pringle said. "Break up this happy gathering and return to your men, gentlemen. We have a lot of work to do yet."

THREE HOURS LATER, LOADED INTO A MIXTURE OF BRITISH and captured Italian trucks, the Lothians moved off.

"Where are we going?" Connington asked.

"Wherever the general sends us," Drysdale told him.

Still weary, many men tried to sleep in the jolting, sand-laden trucks as they rattled and banged along the desert road.

"How far do you think we'll get, sir?" Atkins shared the cab with Tulloch.

"We'll chase them out of Egypt," Tulloch guessed. "We've only two more days of Operation Compass, and then O'Connor, or maybe Wavell, will call a halt. I can't see the Italians allowing us into Libya."

Atkins nodded. "Back to the status quo, then, sir. We sit in Egypt, Graziani in Libya, and we'll growl at each other across the Wire."

The desert stretched on either side in a monotony of dull sand and rock, with the vast abyss of the sky above. Twice, Tulloch saw small groups of Arabs watching them and wondered what these people thought about invaders fighting over the land they had inhabited for centuries.

"If I were in command of the Italians, I'd send my aircraft to attack us now," Atkins said, nodding towards the British convoy that stretched interminably along the road.

The lad's beginning to think like a soldier. "Don't give him ideas," Tulloch said. "I haven't seen any sign of RAF air cover for days."

"I don't think the RAF has the resources out here," Atkins said. "After their losses in the Battle of France, they'll need all they can to defend Britain."

Tulloch nodded. "Aye, I hear London's getting it bad now, with the Germans bombing it day and night." For a moment, he thought of Amanda, wondering where she was and what she was doing. He hoped she was safely miles from London and the Nazi Blitz. He fingered the letter she had sent, contemplated reading it for the twentieth time, and concentrated on the road ahead.

"Look!" The New Zealand driver pointed ahead, where a neat formation of black dots moved slowly across the sky.

"Italian aircraft," Tulloch said. "Savoia-Marchetti SM 79s, I think." He had learned the main types of enemy aircraft.

"We call them the Circus," the driver said. "They come, they observe, they drop their bombs, and they run."

"How accurate are they?" Tulloch asked.

The driver shrugged. "Sometimes they score a hit. More often, they only disturb the sand." He peered into the sky. "These aircraft look more dangerous than most. They're coming to have a look at us."

Tulloch did not know who gave the command, but the Lothian convoy scattered into the desert, using dispersal to present the enemy with a difficult target.

The men ran from their trucks, with NCOs bellowing orders.

Tulloch leapt from the driver's cab. "Atkins, look after your platoon! Innes! Set up the Bren!"

"Yes, sir!" many of the Bren gunners attempted to find positions to fire upward, but the enemy aircraft remained too high.

"Here they come!"

The aircraft circled, remaining in formation far out of the Bren's range, and released their bombs. Two less experienced Bren gunners opened speculative fire until their NCOs roared at them not to waste ammunition.

"Some poor seamen died to bring these bullets, you stupid bastards, and you're throwing it away without a hope of hitting a Wop!"

The Brens fell silent, with only the whistle of falling bombs breaking the tense silence. Tulloch thought they seemed to take a long time to descend, and suddenly, they landed with loud crumps and the blossom of orange fire, clouds of white smoke, and yellow sand. Duty done, the aircraft turned away and flew back towards Libya without breaking their formation.

"Casualties!" Muirhead demanded, and each platoon commander checked his men.

"None here!" Tulloch replied and listened as other officers said the same. The Lothians returned to their trucks, helped dig one vehicle out of soft sand, and continued their journey in the wake of the 7th Armoured Division.

"I wonder what report the leader of that Italian squadron will make," Atkins said.

Tulloch smiled. "He'll report that he destroyed a major British attack, blew up scores of lorries and endured a torrent of anti-aircraft fire."

The convoy trundled on, each mile pushing the Italians back towards the Libyan border, but each mile also extending the supply lines from Alexandria.

Tulloch looked forward, where the 7th Armoured Division was pressing forward somewhere in the dust clouds. "If we can finish this campaign quickly, we can use all these men to defend Britain against the Germans."

"This arena is important, too," Atkins seemed to grow in confidence by the hour. "We need to defend Suez, and we need the Middle Eastern oil."

"I am aware of that," Tulloch said.

"The Italians won't be back today," Atkins claimed. "It will be plain sailing all the way to the Libyan border now."

Tulloch unfolded his map of the Egyptian-Libyan border and placed it on the dashboard. "I hope you're right," he said.

"Here they come again!" the driver shouted as another formation of aircraft appeared ahead.

"These flying buggers are slowing us down," Sergeant Drysdale said as the Lothians' trucks dispersed, and the men ran into the desert once more.

"Fighters," Hardie said casually. "Fiat Freccia fighters."

"How do you know so much about the tallies?" Hogg asked. "Is your ma a tally or something?"

"I know enough to know these boys mean business," Hardie replied as the Freccias zoomed towards the Lothians in line astern.

"Brens!" Tulloch roared above the snarl of Fiat engines. "Dissuade these planes!" He saw Innes was already in position, with other Bren gunners raising their weapons to fire.

For what we are about to receive, may the Lord make us truly thankful.

"Fire!"

Chapter Fifteen

WESTERN DESERT, DECEMBER 1940

The first aircraft fired a ferocious volley that ripped up the sand between two trucks without doing any damage. Innes replied with a controlled burst that missed the aircraft but caused the second Freccia to veer slightly, sending his bullets well wide of any target.

"Well done, Innes!" Tulloch shouted.

The Freccias swooped in a steady stream, firing, levelling out and rising again, with the Lothian Bren gunners following them. Tulloch saw pieces fall off one aircraft's tail.

"Magazine!" Innes shouted. "Magazine!"

Elliot passed him a fresh magazine, then scrabbled for more. "Keep firing, Innes!"

"Shoot them down!" Hogg yelled, firing his rifle as most of the men hugged the sand, trying to burrow into the ground to escape the darting streams of bullets.

"Save your ammunition, Hogg!" Tulloch shouted, knowing a rifle bullet had little chance of hitting the aircraft.

A truck exploded in a ball of orange fire as a Freccia's bullets hit the fuel tank. The driver, sheltering beneath, died immediately, and a fitter fell as a burst of machine gun bullets sliced into him.

The attack ended as quickly as it had begun, with the aircraft returning to the west.

"I hit one of them," Innes said. "I saw bits falling off it." He removed the magazine from his Bren Gun, checked to see how many bullets remained, and replaced it.

"So did I," McAllister said. "We both hit it square on, Innes."

Tulloch allowed them a few moments to compare notes as the battalion straightened itself and readied for the next stage.

"Get back into the lorries, lads!"

The Lothians returned to the trucks, leaving one burning vehicle and two dead men behind. They moved on, slower now, leaving larger gaps between each truck and with each section's Bren gunner ready to retaliate.

The *Regia Aeronautica* did not return that day, but the Lothians heard shellfire ahead and the distant chatter of a heavy machine gun.

"The Italians are making a stand," Kinnear said.

Tulloch consulted his map. "Probably at the Halfaya Pass area," he said.

"The Hellfire Pass," Kinnear said, smiling at his attempted humour.

They passed some wrecked Italian vehicles, a few still smouldering, and one 11th Hussar armoured car, with its disconsolate crew sitting smoking in the shade while two fitters tried desperately to fix the engine.

"On you go, Lothians," one of the Hussars shouted. "We've done the hard fighting for you."

Hogg replied with a mouthful of oaths that should have curled the Hussars' hair. Instead, he laughed and prodded two fingers into the air in the habitual farewell of the British soldier.

"Up your kilt, Jock!"

The Lothians pushed on to the rear of the 7th Armoured

Division, where Italian shellfire made the Halfaya Pass dangerous.

"Hellfire Pass indeed," Tulloch said as an Italian shell exploded to the right and left of the convoy, spreading shrapnel over the Lothians' trucks.

The convoy accelerated to pass through the danger zone and parked on the far side, where a squadron of Hussars watched them curiously.

"The Italians are pulling back," a Hussar lieutenant told Tulloch. "I don't think there's much for you lads to do here." He grinned. "I suppose you can sit back and watch the professionals work."

"We can do that," Tulloch replied. "If we see any, we'll let you know."

The Hussar laughed, watched another Italian salvo explode on Hellfire Pass, and bit into an apple. "Best of British luck to you, mate."

The *Regia Aeronautica* was busy, buzzing overhead and occasionally dropping bombs or swooping down to machine-gun a column or an isolated truck, with the British retaliating with anti-aircraft fire. An occasional RAF fighter appeared to contest the skies. Simultaneously, the Royal Engineers checked the roads for mines and booby traps.

General O'Connor pushed his army on, taking control of Fort Capuzzo with the minimum of fighting and occupying the border village of Sollum. Graziani's army recoiled into Libya, licking its wounds after its abortive invasion.

"We've pushed the Italians out of Egypt," Captain Muirhead said. "So much for Mussolini's vaunted fascist army."

Tulloch stood on the border, with the old boundary fence at his feet and the harsh sand of the desert blowing in his face. The Lothians' previous incursions into Libya seemed a very long time ago.

"What next?"

Muirhead lit a cigarette and allowed the wind to blow out the match. "That's up to General O'Connor. We've already achieved more than we expected with Operation Compass. The question is, do we stay put and defend Egypt, or do we advance and push Mussolini out of North Africa?"

Tulloch glanced at his platoon. Sergeant Drysdale had posted sentries to watch for possible Italian incursions by land or air while the others were searching for shade, playing cards, or trying to sleep. Tulloch was constantly surprised by the British soldiers' ability to sleep under any conditions.

"Here comes the colonel," Muirhead drew on his cigarette. "He'll know more than us."

"Gather the men together," Colonel Pringle ordered quietly. "My words concern everybody."

"We've retaken Egypt," Pringle patted tobacco into his pipe as he addressed the Lothians. "General O'Connor has decided to push on and drive the Italians out of Bardia." He clamped his teeth on the stem of his pipe and smiled. "We are invading Libya, gentlemen, and *Il Duce* will see his African territories crumble."

Tulloch felt the Lothians' satisfaction. Some men cheered, while others looked thoughtful as the colonel continued.

"If we are fortunate, the Lothian Rifles will find an opportunity to prove we are as good as we already know we are," he puffed out smoke. "Our friends of the Fourth Indian Division have departed for the Sudan, and the Sixth Australian Division is coming to replace them. We all know the Australians' reputation from the last war, so I expect Six Div will be just as good."

The officers nodded as the men debated how good the raw Australians might be.

Hume asked the question that was in everybody's mind. "What's our part, sir?"

"We're the mobile reserve," Colonel Pringle replied.

"Do we know who commands the Italians at Bardia, sir?"

Pringle's smile was slow and genuine. "We do, Hume. Generale Annibale Bergonzoli commands the garrison."

Erskine looked up quickly. "Barba Elettrica?"

Pringle frowned. "What's that, Erskine?"

"Barba Elettrica, sir," Erskine repeated. "It means Electric Beard. He commanded the Littorio Division during the Spanish Civil War, and his men called him Barba Elettrica."

"You may be right," Pringle said, adding tobacco to his pipe. "Bergonzoli is a veteran commander, so we'd better be at our best." He paused momentarily, allowing his gaze to ease over his battalion. "Our intelligence people have intercepted a message from Il Duce to Bergonzoli. I'll read the entire text to you." The colonel removed a handwritten note from his breast pocket.

"Mussolini said this: 'I have given you a difficult task, but one suited to your courage and experience as an old and intrepid soldier; the task of defending the fortress of Bardia to the last. I am certain that Electric Beard and his brave soldiers will stand, at whatever cost, faithful to the last.'"

The Lothians' officers listened, wondering what Mussolini's exhortation meant for them.

"Do we know Bergonzoli's reply, sir?" Tulloch asked.

"We do," the colonel replied. "He said, and I quote word for word: 'I am aware of the honour and I have today repeated to my troops your message – simple and unequivocal. In Bardia, we are, and here we stay.' So now we know."

Captain Martin gave an obscene reaction to Bergonzoli's reply.

"How are we proceeding, sir?" Hume asked.

"We are at the end of a long and precarious supply chain," Pringle said, "and the Australians have not arrived yet, so we don't have our troubles to seek. The RAF has already dropped leaflets on Bardia suggesting that the Italian garrison surrenders, and we'll leave the road to Tobruk open to entice them to leave before we arrive." He waited for the murmur of comments to die down. "The port will be invaluable for resupply. That's more important than defeating Electric Whiskers and adding to our total of dead and captured Italians."

"Will the Italians surrender, sir?" Atkins asked.

"No." The Colonel shook his head. "I don't believe they will. We'll have to fight for Bardia."

Hume nodded. "When do we move, sir?"

"Tomorrow," Colonel Pringle said and raised his voice. "I know you will all do your best and make the people of Midlothian proud of you."

The Lothians joined the 16th British Brigade on the front line, supporting the 7th Armoured Division, which had already crossed the frontier and was probing around Bardia.

"Trust the 7th Armoured to push on," Kinnear said. "They're always eager to get to grips with the enemy."

"I've heard them called the Desert Rats," Atkins said cautiously.

"I'd call them the desert scouts," Kinnear replied.

The Libyan desert was more stony than sandy, with the men swearing as they dug shelter trenches and swearing again as night brought a savagely cold wind.

"I thought the desert was meant to be hot!" Hogg complained.

"Only if you're a bloody Eskimo!" Cummings said. "I've known hotter days in Bonnyrigg in December."

"Aye, bugger this for a game of soldiers," Hogg gave his habitual reply.

The miners in the Lothians' ranks proved to be the best diggers. They showed the others how to use a pick and shovel while laughing at the soft-handed townsmen who made up the bulk of the battalion.

"We're not sitting waiting for something to happen," Pringle said. "Erskine and Tulloch! You're our patrol experts. Go out and scout Bardia's defences. You may look for trouble, but don't bite off more than you can chew." He lowered his voice. "I don't want any more of these damned smug staff officers saying we're no longer fit to fight."

"Yes, sir," Tulloch understood.

"And bring back all my men," Pringle said. "We can't afford many casualties."

Tulloch led his three carriers out the following evening, with the men huddled into their greatcoats and the tracks grating over the harsh terrain.

"Where are we heading, sir?" Hardie asked.

"Due west in the usual pattern," Tulloch said. "We're investigating the enemy's defences, so when the attack goes in, we know what to expect."

"So, we're going close to Bardia, sir."

"As close as it's safe," Tulloch said. "And then a little closer."

Hardie grinned. "Yes, sir." He waited for a moment. "Have the Italians laid any mines?"

"I'll let you know if I hear a bang," Tulloch said with a wry grin.

"Thank you, sir," Hardie replied.

The three carriers moved in line astern, throwing up less dust than further east but with the sound of engines loud in the night. Tulloch could hear Erskine's patrol to the north, with the engine noises fading away as their courses diverged.

"I wonder if the Italians have any patrols out?" Innes asked.

"Listen for their engines," Tulloch said. "If it sounds like a truck, head for them, but if it's a tank, shift right and keep moving." He looked behind him, where Smith had his Boys anti-tank rifle in the second carrier. Corporal Borthwick lifted a hand in acknowledgment, and then clouds gathered above, cutting out the starlight.

"I don't know about their engines, sir, but ours is sounding a bit rough," Hardie said.

Tulloch grunted. "Keep an eye on it, Hardie. And an ear."

"I'll keep both ears open, sir," Hardie replied. "These vehicles were not designed for continual use in this type of terrain. They could all do with a thorough overhaul in a decent garage rather than just a patch-up by a fitter."

"I agree," Tulloch said. "However, our fitters are the best in the business. Let's hope these machines last until we've chased Mussolini out of Africa."

"Yes, sir."

"If the engine gets too rough, we'll abort the patrol and return to the battalion."

"I'll keep my ears open, sir."

They motored on with the three engines purring and the dust rising to the cold sky above. Tulloch had his map open before him and navigated by compass and the stars.

Desert driving is much like navigating a ship at sea. With few landmarks, we follow nature's course and live in hope. He glanced upwards at the clouded sky. *It's nearly Christmas; I wonder if the three wise men watched these same stars when they travelled to see the baby Jesus. No, they had the single great star to guide them, the lucky buggers.*

Checking his map, Tulloch steered a wide course to avoid the Italian garrisons of Fort Maddalena and Garn el Grein. He was here to observe and find Bardia's defences, not to exchange gunfire with a heavily defended fort.

Tulloch halted the carriers when they heard the low rumble of artillery to the north and saw the brilliant flashes of explosions on the horizon.

"Somebody's having a duffy," Innes murmured. They waited for a moment as the distant firefight faded away, heard the rattle of Italian machine guns and the controlled drilling of a Bren, and then silence.

"I wonder what that was all about," Innes said.

"I doubt we'll ever know," Tulloch replied. "Drive on."

The distant flashes had starred Tulloch's night vision and reminded him he was not the only predator in the dark. He checked his position by the stars and headed south and west, keeping to a fixed bearing. He had grown used to the carrier kicking up less dust on the stony terrain when the engine sound altered.

"We're driving over soft sand, sir," Hardie reported. "If we go this way, we'll be bogged down like the tankies."

Tulloch nodded. He did not want his carriers stuck in soft sand, an easy target for any prowling Italian aircraft. "Head south," he decided. "We'll find a way around." He signalled for his other carriers to follow.

The gunfire had restarted in the north, with the harsh bark of artillery a warning that the carriers only had thin armour and no protection from overhead bursts. Tulloch moved them south, probing into the area of soft sand and finding no safe route. He checked his watch and swore softly when he saw the time. The dark hours were slipping away, and he had achieved nothing. He was about to call a halt and abort the mission when Hardie lifted a hand.

"The ground's firmer here, sir."

"Drive slowly," Tulloch ordered. "Follow me." Dismounting, he stepped ahead of the carrier, probing at the sand with a bayonetted Lee-Enfield. He wished he carried a cromack like the colonels of Highland regiments, grinned at the image of a dignified Highland colonel thrusting his cromack into the sand, and walked on, hoping not to find a mine or soft sand that sucked him down.

The carriers followed with their engines purring through the night.

When the sand gave way to gravel, Tulloch climbed back on board. "Move on," he said, checked his map for the twentieth time that night, and gave directions that saw them heading northward.

The battle to the north and east flared up again and died down a second time.

"That must be around Fort Maddalena," Innes muttered.

Hardie and Tulloch heard the sound simultaneously.

"That's a tank, sir," Hardie said. "It sounds like an Italian Carro Armato L 6/40, one of their light tanks, sir."

"Any Italian tank is too big for us to handle," Tulloch said and ordered the carriers to cut their engines. He lifted his binoculars and peered around in the dark desert. "I can't see anything."

"Nor can I, sir," Hardie said, "but I hear them plain enough."

"Sound travels far in a desert night," Tulloch reminded him. "And if we heard them, they probably heard us." He saw the dark figure of Smith hunched over his Boys inside the second carrier.

The Lothians waited, listening as the Italian engines grumbled unseen in the night.

"Over there, sir," Hardie said. "I heard a rattle; they're coming closer."

Tulloch swivelled left, trying to focus in the dark. "You're right," he said. "I can see something moving."

The crack of a gun shook them. Tulloch saw the distant flash of a muzzle flare, but the shell landed three hundred yards away, raising dust and pebbles.

"They've seen us!" Innes traversed the Bren.

"Move left," Tulloch ordered. "Hold your fire, Innes." He headed his patrol at an angle, not directly away from the Italians but obliquely, towards the nearly impassable desert to the south. The Italian tanks fired again, with the shots coming closer but not sufficiently close to cause alarm.

"I think they're firing blind, sir," Hardie said.

Tulloch swivelled to watch the enemy, allowing Hardie to pick his best route over the desert. He saw five distinct flashes as the Italians fired and ordered another change of course. The shots all fell short, throwing up fountains of dust and stones more than a hundred yards to the patrol's left.

"Five of them," Tulloch said. "Stop here." He passed the binoculars to Hardie. "You're the expert, Hardie. Tell me what you think."

Hardie refocused the binoculars. "I'm not sure, sir. It's hard to see in the dark, but they may be L 6/40s. Not tankettes, for sure."

"Heavier than us?"

"Undoubtedly, sir," Hardie replied. "About seven tons, with a 20 mm gun and two machine guns."

Tulloch grunted. "Faster than us?"

"I don't think so, sir. They're heading towards us."

"Move away," Tulloch ordered. Playing cat and mouse with a handful of Italian tanks was hard on his nerves.

Hardie started the engine, grunted when it stuttered and finally drove away. He looked up. "Did you hear that, sir? The engine's cutting up rough again."

"Well, smooth it down!" Tulloch snarled without hiding his anxiety.

The Italian tanks fired again. When the shells exploded further away, Tulloch felt some relief. "Keep moving on this course," he ordered. The Italian engines seemed to dominate the desert. Any one of the tanks could destroy his little patrol.

If I were the Italian commander, I'd spread my tanks out to cover a wider search area.

After another ten minutes, Tulloch ordered the drivers to cut their engines and cover the carriers with camouflage netting.

"It's dark, sir," Elliot said.

"The netting will prevent any reflection if the moon comes out," Tulloch explained.

"Yes, sir."

The carriers were in a slight depression, with a slow-rising rocky ridge between them and the tanks.

"Keep quiet," Tulloch passed the order. "Hopefully, the Italians will pass us by."

The Lothians nodded while Smith held the Boys, ready to fire if the tanks appeared. The wind rose slightly, carrying intermittent noises, and Tulloch heard the tanks' engines slowly fading away.

"They've gone, sir," Innes whispered.

"Maybe. Wait a few moments," Tulloch replied. "They might be parked, listening for us."

The Lothians waited, listening to the wind stirring the sand. Tulloch looked up at the moon, wondered if Amanda was doing the same, wherever she was, and pushed the thought away. After another ten minutes, he left the carriers and mounted the ridge, sweeping the surrounding desert with his binoculars. When the wind shifted the clouds, cold moonlight gave the landscape a surreal, almost unearthly, appearance.

"All right lads. Start the engines and head back to the battalion. We'll abort this mission."

The three carriers started, with the sound startlingly loud after the recent silence. Tulloch led them south, moving slowly to conserve fuel.

The salvo of guns was unexpected, with the shells landing uncomfortably close to the rearmost carrier.

"God Almighty!" Corporal Borthwick's blasphemy carried clearly across to Tulloch.

Chapter Sixteen

Tulloch swore. *The Italians were waiting for our engines to start. We're up against a clever and patient man.* "Increase speed," he ordered, "and weave around."

"If I weave too much, she might pack in," Hardie said.

"If we steer a straight course, the Italians might pack us all in," Tulloch replied. The Italians fired again, and Tulloch saw their vehicles as darker smudges against the gloomy desert.

"We'll be visible to them soon," Tulloch said.

"Yes, sir," Hardie replied calmly. "What course should I drive?"

"Steer straight ahead for a hundred yards, and veer right," Tulloch said, "then head generally south for a mile."

"Yes, sir," Hardie replied.

Feeling very vulnerable with the tanks so close behind, Tulloch kept his nerve and drove on. He could hear the Italians' engines clearly now and longed for the dawn he once thought would be an enemy.

"Right," Tulloch looked at the fading stars, hoping he had judged his distances correctly. "Now steer eastward."

The carriers altered directions, with Tulloch's vehicle stuttering every few moments and Hardie struggling to keep it mobile.

"You're doing fine, Hardie," Tulloch encouraged.

"Maybe, sir, but the carrier's not."

Tulloch looked over his shoulder, judging distances and times. He hoped to be at the extreme edge of the Italian tanks' 20-mm gun range before the light strengthened, or even better, out of range completely.

"I hear them, sir," Hardie said.

Dawn rose with the beauty and suddenness Tulloch had come to expect in the desert, the sun rising in orange glory and putting the carriers in silhouette.

"That should tempt them," Tulloch said as he saw the Italian tanks as vague shapes across the desert. They halted to fire, with the muzzle flares vivid against the gloom, and Tulloch wondered if he had taken too many chances.

Hopefully, the sun will be in their eyes.

The explosions came almost immediately, rocking the first and second carriers and splattering them with sand and small stones.

That was too close. These lads are good shots.

The light strengthened rapidly, enabling Tulloch to see the Italian tanks only half a mile away. He motioned the carriers closer.

"Right, lads!" Tulloch said. "Spread out and run like hell. We'll meet up in two miles; don't lose sight of one another!" He saw the tanks creeping closer and knew they would be preparing to fire another salvo. "Move!"

The carriers were just in time before the tanks fired again, with all five shots landing close to the carriers. Tulloch saw the tanks moving, intending to cut the distance between them by heading straight forward rather than driving south and then east.

"Innes!" Tulloch snarled. "Give them a burst with the Bren!"

"It won't damage them, sir," Innes reminded.

"I'm aware of that, but it might distract them from the soft sand."

Hardie grinned as he realised Tulloch's plan. "You're a cunning man, sir."

"Only if it works," Tulloch replied.

If my idea doesn't work, I've probably led my men to their deaths.

Innes fired in five short bursts, aiming at each tank in succession as the carrier rocked, coughed, and rolled across the stony plain. Tulloch did not know if the Bren's bullets reached their target or even came close, but being attacked seemed to galvanise the Italians as they increased speed and powered forward.

"Come on, my beauties," Tulloch said.

The sound of gunfire had attracted the other carriers, and both had circled to support Tulloch, with Smith crouching hopefully over his Boys.

"Get away!" Tulloch roared. "Obey orders!"

He watched as Smith lifted the long Boys rifle and aimed at the oncoming tanks.

"The range is too long!" Tulloch shouted. Lifting his binoculars, he watched the Italian tanks plough into the sand, gradually slowing.

"Soft sand," Hardie said, smiling. "We circled that on our way out."

"Yes," Tulloch agreed. "Take us beside number two carrier. If Borthwick has forgotten how to obey orders, he can make himself useful."

Preoccupied with trying to escape from the soft sand, the Italian tanks did not fire as Tulloch gave orders to the carriers.

"Smith, you and Cummings come with me. Innes, I want you; bring your Bren. The rest, drive out of range and wait for us," he gave them map coordinates.

"What do you plan, sir?" Corporal Borthwick asked.

"I plan to kill these tanks," Tulloch said brutally. He waved the carriers away and headed into the soft sand with Innes, Smith, and Cummings behind him.

Tulloch found that even walking in the sand was hard, with his feet sinking ankle-deep with every step. He saw Smith struggling under the weight of the Boys and offered to carry the weapon for a while.

"Thank you, sir," Smith said, handing it over gratefully.

The Boys was heavier than Tulloch remembered, and he soon regretted his generous impulse.

No, I was right. Smith is our best Boys operator, and I need him to be as fresh as possible. I should have given the weapon to Cummings, though.

After a few minutes, the Italians noticed the advancing British soldiers, and the closest tank opened fire with a machine gun.

"Down, men!" Tulloch ordered as the bullets kicked up sand around them. "Innes, give them a burst!"

"Yes, sir!" Innes responded, targeting the tank that was firing at them. The tank replied, with bullets flying both ways.

"Cease fire now," Tulloch said.

Innes obeyed, and within a few moments, the Italian also stopped firing.

"Give it a moment and move forward again," Tulloch ordered. "Keep moving until we're in range of the Boys, but be quiet and try not to be seen."

The closer we get, the more dangerous it will be. The Italians have five 20-millimetre guns and five machine guns, to our one Boys and a single Bren.

Tulloch plainly heard the Italians talking to each other as they tried to dig their tanks out of the soft sand. He waited until they were all occupied with spades and gave the word to advance.

Keeping low, the Lothians ran fifty yards forward and sunk into the sand, watching the enemy constantly.

"They're too busy to notice us," Innes said.

"Either that or they don't think we're a threat," Cummings added.

"Another fifty yards," Tulloch ordered, wondering how long their luck would last.

They moved again, gasping for breath in the increasing heat, hoping the Italians were not luring them into a trap.

"Are we in range of the Boys yet, Smith?" Tulloch asked.

"Nearly, sir," Smith replied.

"How much further?"

"The effective range of the Boys is only a hundred yards, sir," Smith replied.

Tulloch swore. "All right, another advance."

Am I leading these men to their deaths? I never thought I'd be a death or glory boy!

They advanced in small rushes, keeping low and praying that the Italians were too busy digging to look around. As the sun grew hotter, sweat flowed from them, accompanied by the ubiquitous flies.

"That's close enough," Tulloch whispered. He could make out every detail of the Italian tanks and the expressions on the Italians' faces. They were working hard, shifting the sand with a feverish energy as they struggled to free their tanks. One man sat inside each vehicle, frantically gunning the engine.

"They're buggered," Innes said casually. "They'll need something to tow them out of this muck."

"Right, Smith," Tulloch said. "Choose a target and do your best."

The Lothians scraped shallow trenches, piled up sand around them for a measure of concealment, and Smith aimed the Boys. The gun was a clumsy weapon at best but had already proven its worth against thin-skinned vehicles and the smaller Italian tanks. Tulloch hoped a surprise attack would panic the enemy so they did not realise how small the attacking force was.

Tulloch plainly heard the Italians' voices, carried on a northerly breeze that also whipped sand into his face.

"When you're ready, Smith."

The deep boom of the Boys seemed to reverberate for minutes. With plenty of time to aim, Smith could hardly miss, and Tulloch saw the projectile smash into the closest tank, knocking the turret sideways and spreading shards of metal around like shrapnel. Two of the Italians fell back, yelling in pain and surprise as Cummings handed over a fresh projectile and Smith reloaded.

"Give them a burst with the Bren, Innes," Tulloch ordered.

Innes responded with a two-second burst aimed at the second tank. One man fell as the rest scattered, some diving behind the tank and others throwing themselves onto the ground.

"Take the furthest away tank!" Tulloch ordered. "Keep them guessing." He knew the Italians would soon realise where they were and would retaliate. Already, men were climbing into their vehicles.

"Yes, sir!" Smith wiped the sweat from his eyes, aimed the Boys and fired again. His second shot at extreme range was not quite as accurate and only hit the tracks of the fifth tank.

"That will immobilise it," Tulloch said. He heard the crisp voice of an officer giving orders and saw a small group of men begin to move away. "They're going to circle us," he said. "Innes, take those men."

"Yes, sir!" Innes's Bren hammered again, scattering the group and throwing spurts of sand and dust into the air. An Italian machine gun probed for the Lothians.

Smith fired again, with his third shot hitting another tank square and punching a hole through the armour, but the Italians had recovered, with three machine guns now searching the desert for the attackers.

Innes snapped in another magazine, swearing as bullets sprayed the ground in front of them.

"We're a bit close for comfort," Tulloch began to regret his impetuosity. "Can you get another tank, Smith?"

"I'll try, sir!" Smith ducked as machine gun fire ripped around them. "The Italians seem a little agitated!"

"One last shot, and then we're away," Tulloch ordered, watching the Italians move in a wide circling action. "Make them keep their heads down, Innes!"

"Sir!" Innes fired a series of short bursts, with his bullets clanging and ricocheting off the tanks' armour.

Smith fired again, blowing the track off a fourth tank without causing any visible casualties.

"Good shot, Smith. Now, pull back. We'll cover you."

"Sir!" Cummings pointed upwards, where three aircraft appeared.

The Italians might have radioed for air cover, or perhaps a patrol saw the smoke from the burning tanks.

"Pull out, boys. Innes, give them a last burst and move."

The Italians had also noticed the aircraft. Tulloch saw some looking upward, with one or two waving hopefully.

"Move!" Tulloch took advantage of the distraction the aircraft afforded. "Come on, Innes!" Taking the Boys from Smith, he led them at a loping run, more concerned with putting distance between his men and the tanks than with concealment. He heard the noise from the aircraft increase, glanced over his shoulder, and saw they were descending.

"They're ours!" Innes said. "Hurricanes!"

That's the first Hurricanes I've seen in Africa, and they could not come at a better time. "Keep moving and spread out!" Tulloch ordered. "I doubt they'll be able to differentiate between British and Italian from that height."

The aircraft roared overhead, banked, and returned. One fired a quick burst that did little damage but scattered the Italians.

"Thank God for the RAF!" Innes said.

"Keep moving," Tulloch said. "I doubt the Italians will follow us now." He handed the Boys to Cummings and checked his compass, working out their route to the rendezvous.

As the patrol moved, Tulloch realised how thirsty they were. The skirmish following the patrol had taken its toll on their strength, and men reached for their water bottles to find them nearly empty.

"We'll fill up when we reach the carriers," Tulloch said. The aircraft had long gone, but a thin column of smoke behind them marked the burning Italian tank.

We did well, Tulloch thought. *We destroyed one tank and damaged others. That soft sand was a Godsend.*

The desert seemed harsher now, with the wind rising again, blasting sand into their faces and bare legs.

"Whoever thought wearing shorts was a good idea?" Smith said. "All it means is desert sores and sunburn."

They moved on, with Tulloch keeping their pace up. They took turns carrying the heavy Boys, although Tulloch was tempted to jettison it to save their strength. Then he thought of the lack of resources in beleaguered Britain and the lives of the merchant seamen who carried weapons and supplies across the dangerous oceans.

"Keep going, boys. Only another mile."

"Is that all?" Innes asked. "We could do that on one leg."

The final mile seemed like twenty, with the men dragging their feet through the sand and draining every drop from their water bottles before Innes pointed ahead.

"There they are, sir!"

The carriers were parked fifty yards apart, each under camouflage netting.

"You're back, sir!" Hardie appeared first, smiling. "We were getting worried about you. We heard firing and aircraft."

"Get the engines running," Tulloch ordered tensely. "Fill our water bottles, and let's get home."

Hardie shook his head. "Our carrier's packed up, sir. There's no life in the engine at all."

Chapter Seventeen

LIBYA, DECEMBER 1940

Tulloch swore. "We can't hang about here," he said. "The Italians will be spitting blood after we wrecked their tanks. They'll send a patrol after us." He made a quick decision: "Abandon our number one carrier and move all the equipment into the other two. We'll mark its position on the map, and the fitters can pick it up later." He nodded to Hardie. "I want you to drive the number two carrier."

"Yes, sir," Hardie said.

The Lothians transferred the equipment, squeezed into the two remaining carriers, and headed eastward, watching the sky for Italian aircraft.

"I hear aircraft, sir," Hardie warned.

"So do I," Tulloch agreed.

"Ours or theirs?"

"They're coming from the west, so most likely theirs," Tulloch said.

Do we stop and camouflage the carriers or move and hope to evade them? Our dust is a giveaway, so they'll have seen us anyway.

"Spread out!" Tulloch ordered. "Bren gunners, get ready."

"We are, sir," Innes replied, peering at the sky. The little black dots looked innocuous from ground level, inconsequential to the battles and killing in the desert, yet every man knew how dangerous they were.

The aircraft flew over, circled, and returned. One descended to around a thousand feet, dropped a single bomb which exploded fifty yards away, and flew on.

"Was that it?" Elliot shouted. "You couldnae hit a bull's erse with a banjo."

Tulloch nodded. The Bren gunners relaxed without having fired. They scanned the now-empty sky.

"Back home, lads!" Tulloch said. "We should reach our lines in a couple of hours." He licked his parched lips with a dry tongue and lifted his water bottle.

"We don't appreciate how fortunate we are to have abundant water in Scotland," he said.

Ship me somewhere east of Suez,
Where the best is like the worst,
Where there ain't no Ten Commandments,
And a man can raise a thirst.

"We have much to be thankful for, sir," Hardie agreed.

Cummings shook his empty canteen and lifted the carrier's water container. "It's nearly empty, sir," he said. "That Italian bomb must have punctured it."

Tulloch swore and lifted the container. "It wasn't the bomb," he said. "It's just a badly made can." He lifted a second canister. "This one's as bad, leaking like a sieve."

The carrier's crew crowded around, their hot faces and cracked lips showing how much they needed water.

"Kipling was right," Hardie said. "But when it comes to slaughter,

You will do your work on water,

And you'll lick the bloomin' boots of 'im that's got it."

187

Tulloch nodded. "Kipling knew his stuff," he agreed, realising that Hardie and he had similar thoughts. "We could do with a Gunga Din out here with his water skin." He looked around the arid plain. "Well, we don't have one. Only us and what we have, which isn't much. Fill the canteens, lads, and we'll have to self-ration until we get back to base."

With the canteens quarter full and no more water available, the carriers drove on, with the sun hammering down on them and the metal burning to their touch.

"How long, sir?" Hardie asked. "The boys are dropping with thirst."

"We all are, Hardie," Tulloch said. He checked their position. *We're driving by grace and by God now.* "With luck, we'll get there in a couple of hours. Our diversions lengthened the patrol."

"We'll need water before then, sir. And petrol."

"I know," Tulloch said. *I hope we meet a British patrol soon.*

The map did not mention any oases, only great blanks between the Italian forts. We could head for the road and chance any prowling aircraft or Italian patrols. I can't think of another way of finding water or petrol.

Overloaded, the carriers moved sluggishly, using valuable fuel. Tulloch saw Innes drooping in his seat. *It's no use. We'll have to chance the road. We'll move faster there and might meet a British patrol.*

"Sir!" Hardie gestured ahead. "What's that?"

Before Tulloch could lift his binoculars, he saw the rising dust from a moving vehicle.

"Drive towards that dust," he ordered.

"It might be an Italian tank, sir," Hardie warned, "and we've no speed and precious little fuel."

Tulloch had considered the possibility. "We'll rely on bluff and aggression," he tried to sound more confident than he felt.

The two carriers closed on the vehicle, with Smith holding the Boys ready and the Bren gunners pushing for elbow room.

"It's a truck, sir," Hardie said. "Italian ten-tonner and moving fast."

"The poor devil must have got lost," Tulloch said. "Give him a burst with the Bren, but don't puncture his water supply, for God's sake."

Innes fired, with the bullets kicking up sand in front of the truck. The driver increased his speed, with one man in the rear of the vehicle firing a rifle at the carriers. The bullets kicked up dirt without coming close.

"Brave man," Tulloch said. "Do we have enough speed to catch him? We need him intact."

"No, sir," Hardie said. "He's faster than we are."

Tulloch swore. "Innes! Put a burst ahead of him. Make him slow down!"

"Yes, sir." Innes fired a short burst that kicked up sand twenty yards in front of the truck, which slammed on its brakes, veered to the right, and stopped. The driver and another man jumped clear, with the rifleman in the body of the truck falling onto the ground and dropping his rifle.

"Steer to the lorry!" Tulloch ordered. "Let the guard go."

Innes lifted his aim from the fallen rifleman.

Tulloch jumped out of the leading carrier as they converged on the stricken truck.

"Cover me!" he ordered and zig-zagged forward, revolver in hand.

The truck's engine was still running, and Tulloch switched it off. He ordered one of the carriers to move to a slight rise two hundred yards away and keep watch while he searched the vehicle for water.

"Here we are!" The Italians had supplied their truck with water, pastries, and half a dozen bottles of wine. For the first time in his experience, Tulloch saw British soldiers prefer water to alcohol.

"Hardie, can we drain the truck's petrol tank?"

"No, sir. It's diesel," Hardie replied.

"We'll have to make do with what we have," Tulloch hid his disappointment. "Grab all the water. Corporal Borthwick, you're in charge of distribution." He raked through the driver's cab, taking all the documents in case they could be useful. "Is the truck drivable?"

"No, sir. Some of Innes's bullets hit the front offside wheel. The tyre's shredded, and the axle is all to buggery."

"Pity; we could have captured it. Load up, and let's be off," Tulloch said.

"Yes, sir," Hardie replied happily.

***

"Halt!" The sound of British voices was reassuring. "Identify yourselves!"

"Lothian Rifles!" Tulloch replied.

The men appeared from rocks beside the road, and Tulloch saw a camouflaged two-pounder anti-tank gun fifty yards further back.

"Evening, lads," Tulloch said. "Which way are the Rifles?"

"A quarter of a mile due south, sir," a tired-looking corporal said. "Just turn right and drive straight ahead."

"I'll be glad to get back, sir," Hardie said.

"And me," Tulloch replied, wondering what Colonel Pringle would say about the abandoned carrier. *We did our best. I can't do more than that.*

***

Tulloch sat in the tented Officers' Mess with his eyes closed, listening to the hum of conversation without participating. Colonel Pringle had sent out fitters to reclaim the abandoned carrier and congratulated him on the mission's success.

"You're regaining my trust, Tulloch," Pringle said. "Keep it up."

"Thank you, sir," Tulloch saluted as he left the colonel's presence. Now, he heard Captain Muirhead talking quietly.

"The Australians are doing well so far," Muirhead said. "A squadron of the 6th Australian Cavalry sorted out the Italians at Fort Maddalena and Garn el Grein."

"They were bonny fighters in the last war," Kilner replied. "I'd be surprised if they were any different in this one."

"That was the 6th Aussies Cavalry's first action in this war," Muirhead told him, shaking his head. "Churchill made a right haggis of reporting it, though, when he claimed the Australians charged sword in hand."

"That man is still fighting at Omdurman," Kilner said sourly. "He'll be expecting us to form a square soon."

Muirhead grinned. "Maybe so, but I'm damned glad he's in Number Ten and nobody else."

Tulloch kept quiet. He thought Churchill was a remarkable politician with encouraging rhetoric but hardly a master strategist. *Churchill's idea of a ten-year rule cost us dearly in this war, with inferior equipment and a lack of preparedness.*

"It's too early to judge the Australians yet," Kilner said, "but if they're half as good as the Fourth Indian Division, they'll be a decided asset."

Tulloch agreed. He had a lot of time for the Indian soldiers.

"Let's ensure the Lothians are up to scratch," Muirhead said. "Let the Aussies take care of themselves."

"I'm sure they will," Kilner murmured.

As O'Connor's army gathered its forces for the next stage in the campaign, the war became less about battles and more about administration and supplies. The men, British, Australian, and Italian, required fuel, food, and water, which was limited in the desert. O'Connor used the recently captured port of Sollum to land supplies while fitters worked around the clock to repair the hundreds of vehicles damaged by desert conditions.

When not patrolling in front of the British lines, the Lothians took turns unloading the ships.

"Why are we here?" Rifleman McAllister looked around the dock at Sollum.

"We're here to help the Kiwis," Sergeant Drysdale told him.

The New Zealanders of the Four Reserve Motor Transport Company had been operating the dock at Sollum, unloading and organising the constant stream of supplies that General O'Connor demanded for the next stage in his plan.

"What do we do?" McAllister asked.

"The nice sailors carry the supplies across the sea to Sollum, and we help unload them onto this stone pier," Drysdale explained. "We help the porters, mostly Palestinians and Cypriots, carry the supplies from the pier into the lorries, and the Kiwis take them to various dumps ready to hand to different units."

"How come the New Zealanders get to use the lorries, and we have to humph the stuff?" McAllister asked.

"Can you drive?" Drysdale asked.

"No, Sergeant."

"That's why the New Zealanders use the lorries, and you have to humph the stuff," Drysdale explained and raised his voice to a roar. "Now get humphing!" He shook his head as Tulloch came close. "I don't know where we got this lot from, sir, but they're only good for carrying heavy loads a short distance in a straight line under constant supervision."

Tulloch hid his smile and nodded sagely. *I wish I had a shilling for every time I've heard an NCO quote that.* "We must do the best we can with what we have," he said. "Carry on, Sergeant."

Tulloch heard a loud whistle and the immediate crump of a falling shell as something exploded in the brilliant blue water, sending up an immense tower of water.

"What the hell was that?"

"Bardia Bill, mate," a laconic New Zealander said. "The Eyeties have a bugger of a gun in Bardia, and they fire it at us from time to time." He glanced upwards. "When they're not sending over planes to keep us occupied."

"The sooner we take Bardia, the better," Tulloch said.

"A big Amen to that, mate."

No sooner had the New Zealander spoken than a heavily bearded man emerged from a hut at the base of the narrow wharf, waving his hands and shouting. "Air raid!" he yelled. "Air raid!"

Before Tulloch could look upward, the porters dropped whatever they carried and fled inland, where a succession of caves provided some shelter from falling bombs.

The two Royal Navy gunboats in the bay immediately began to fire upwards, and Tulloch saw a flight of half a dozen aircraft seemingly ambling across the sky. Hogg reached for his rifle.

"Find cover, lads," Drysdale said, almost casually as the Lothians' fatigue party looked upwards. He put a heavy hand on Hogg's shoulder.

"They're too high. Don't waste ammunition."

Although the bombs whistled as they fell, Tulloch did not experience the same feeling of dread as he had when the Stukas bombed him in Belgium and France.

Am I getting more used to the experience? Or are the Italian aircraft less terrifying than the Stukas with their screaming whistle? He realised he had thrown himself prone on the wharf and was clutching his steel helmet to his head with both hands, although he could not recall having moved.

When the aircraft droned away, Tulloch, rather shamefacedly, stood up to realise that everybody else had also sought cover.

"That was just Mussolini saying hello," the New Zealander said, brushing dust from his knees.

Tulloch saw a newcomer marching along the quay.

"Are you Lieutenant Tulloch, sir?" The voice was crisp and educated.

Chapter Eighteen

LIBYA, DECEMBER 1940

"I am," Tulloch did not know the nervous young lieutenant who saluted with as much punctiliousness as any newly qualified Sandhurst graduate.

"Colonel Wingate requests your presence, sir," the subaltern said.

"Who?" Tulloch replied without thinking.

"Colonel Wingate, sir. He's waiting for you and your driver."

Tulloch blinked. "Why?"

"I don't know, sir," the subaltern replied. "Shall I take you to Colonel Wingate?"

Tulloch remembered hearing of an eccentric officer of that name who had worked in the Holy Land, but he had no idea why Wingate should wish to talk to him. It was also unusual for a colonel to ask for a private soldier. "You'd better take me to him," Tulloch said, indicating that Hardie should join him. "I have no idea what this is about, Hardie."

"We'll soon find out, sir," Hardie said.

The lieutenant led them outside the port to a large but travel-stained tent sitting under a ragged stretch of camouflage netting. Beside the tent, a battered fifteen-hundredweight truck stood in the sun, with a machine gun in the open back and a corporal outside, cleaning a rifle.

"Colonel Wingate is in here, sir," the lieutenant pulled back the flap and snapped to attention. "Lieutenant Tulloch, sir, and his driver." He did not refer to Hardie by name.

"In you come," a rich voice sounded inside the tent.

Tulloch stepped inside and stopped in surprise. The serious-faced man lounging on a chair was stark naked except for a large Wolseley-style pith helmet.[1]

"Tulloch!" The naked man stood up. "I am Wingate." He did not comment on his state of undress. "Sit down. You too, Rifleman. You are John Hardie, I presume?"

"Yes, sir," Hardie said.

Wingate eyed Hardie for a moment. "Yes, you look as I imagined."

Tulloch sat down while Hardie stood at attention at his side.

"Sit, Hardie!" Wingate ordered sharply, and Hardie obeyed, watching Wingate curiously.

Wingate pulled a small table towards him, dismissing the subaltern with a curt nod. "You'll be wondering why I summoned you both here."

"Yes, sir," Tulloch replied.

Wingate leaned across the table, nearly shaking with enthusiasm as he explained his ideas. His eyes were strange, almost mesmeric, as he spoke.

"We are going to take Ethiopia back from the Italians with the expenditure of only a minimum of manpower and resources," he said.

A flicker of emotion passed over Hardie's face, but Tulloch was unsure what it was.

"Yes, sir," Hardie said.

"We are organising a revolt against the Italians in the country, with Ras Tafari, or Haile Selassie, as you know him, as the figurehead. We are raising patriot groups and training them in

Khartoum. We will have fifty British officers and forty NCOs to lead them."

Tulloch hid his surprise. While many people believed Britain had been sitting back, reeling from one disaster after another, here was a man going from the defensive to the offensive. With O'Connor's successful advance in the Western Desert and now Wingate, Tulloch could see gleams of hope on the horizon.

"I call this force Gideon Force," Wingate said.

Tulloch remembered his Bible. *"When the angel of the Lord appeared to Gideon, he said, 'The Lord is with you, mighty warrior.'"*

"That's a good name, sir," Tulloch remarked.

Wingate nodded, although Tulloch suspected the colonel did not need encouragement. "I used similar methods—the Special Night Squads—in the Holy Land to fight against Arab terrorist gangs."

Tulloch had heard vague rumours about the clandestine operations in the British-mandated territory before the war started but had been too occupied on the Northwest Frontier to pay much attention. He looked at Wingate with new interest, for the troubles in the Holy Land had filled many newspaper columns. He remembered Wingate better now, a wild, unconventional soldier who operated on the fringes of civilization.

When Wingate spoke, Tulloch could ignore his state of undress and allow the words to weave a near-mesmeric spell around him. "You will be aware that many thousands of Ethiopians fled their homeland for Sudan and Kenya when Mussolini invaded their country. I am raising two refugee battalions from these men, and I'll add the Frontier Battalion of the Sudan Defence Force." Wingate seemed to hold Tulloch's attention without effort while including Hardie in the conversation. "I'll use the refugees and Ethiopians to recruit more men into the Patriot force, and we'll reinstate Haile Selassie on his throne."

"That's all very interesting, sir," Tulloch said slowly. "But why tell us? We're a regular infantry regiment in the middle of a campaign, and I have no knowledge of Ethiopia."

Wingate turned his entire attention to Tulloch. "You may have no knowledge of Ethiopia, Lieutenant, but Mr Hardie has, and your reputation as a patrol leader precedes you."

Tulloch grunted. "My reputation, sir? And Rifleman Hardie?"

How does Hardie know about Ethiopia? And how does Wingate know about Hardie and me?

"I'll answer your questions one at a time, Lieutenant." Wingate's eyes seemed almost mesmeric as he held Tulloch's gaze. "You worked in wild country on the Northwest frontier, Tulloch, and led successful patrols in Belgium and the Western Desert." His mouth twisted into a slight smile. "Colonel Campbell, Jock Campbell, mentioned you as a daring man most suitable for irregular exploits."

Tulloch shook his head. "I only met Colonel Campbell on a couple of occasions, sir."

"Those occasions made a big impression on the colonel," Wingate said. "He recommended you as a man suitable for irregular operations."

"I don't know why, sir."

"Are you arguing with a senior officer, Tulloch?"

"No, sir," Tulloch shut his mouth at a sudden memory. Wingate had a reputation for bouts of sudden anger and had been known to punch soldiers in the face. Tulloch did not know how he would react if a senior officer struck him but guessed he would retaliate in kind, leading to a court-martial, disgrace, and the end of his career.

"I have too many mediocre officers in Gideon Force," Wingate said, "and you seem to be a good officer in a mediocre regiment. It's time you put your talents to better use."

Tulloch felt his temper rise. "The Lothian Rifles is a good unit, sir."

"I've heard otherwise," Wingate dismissed Tulloch's protests. "I heard about cowardice on an East Lothian beach and sluggishness when attacking an Italian fort. Think about my proposition, Tulloch, and let me know by the end of the day." He turned to Hardie. "Now, you, Rifleman Hardie."

"Yes, sir," Hardie faced Wingate squarely, lifting his chin slightly.

"You were an officer in the King's African Rifles," Wingate said.

Hardie said nothing.

"You operated on the border between Kenya and Ethiopia, I believe."

"I did, sir," Hardie agreed.

"What did you do there?"

Hardie glanced at Tulloch before he replied. "I patrolled to stop slave and cattle raids from Ethiopia into British-protected territory."

"You must know the area and the people," Wingate said.

"I used to be familiar with both, sir," Hardie agreed.

"Why did you leave the KAR?"

Again, Hardie glanced at Tulloch before he replied. "I was asked to leave, sir."

"Why?" Wingate's questioning was relentless.

"I led a patrol inside Ethiopian territory to recover some people. There was a skirmish, and some people got killed."

"When was this, Hardie?"

"1936."

Tulloch noted that Hardie had dropped the "sir" from his answers.

"During the Italian invasion of the country," Wingate said.

"That's correct."

"You were cashiered," Wingate said calmly.

"That's correct," Hardie agreed again.

Tulloch listened with some interest. Wingate had confirmed that Hardie was more than an ordinary private soldier, and Tulloch guessed that more was being concealed than revealed.

"Then you fought in the Spanish Civil War," Wingate said.

"You've done your homework," Hardie said.

That's how Hardie knows so much about the Italian military. He met them in Spain and Ethiopia.

"You fought for the Republicans," Wingate said. "The Communists."

"That's correct," Hardie agreed, level-voiced.

"Are you a Communist?"

"I'm not any kind of -ist," Hardie replied.

Wingate nodded with what Tulloch thought could be the hint of a smile. "I want you as an officer in my Patriot force," he said. "You'll be working with Ethiopian forces fighting for Haile Selassie and against the same enemy you fought in Spain. You'd do more good there than as a Rifleman in a mediocre British infantry regiment."

Mediocre? I don't like you, Colonel Wingate.

"I am content where I am, sir," Hardie replied.

"I don't care how content you are, Hardie," Wingate snapped, and Tulloch sensed the latent violence in the man. "I only care how useful you can be. You've seen the Italian Blackshirts in action."

"Yes, sir," Hardie agreed.

"Mussolini has sent Blackshirt units to Eritrea and Ethiopia," Wingate said.

"Has he, sir?" Tulloch sensed Hardie's sudden interest.

"You may know the name Tenente Colonnello Lorenzo Rotunno," Wingate said.

Hardie took a deep breath. "I do, sir," he agreed, glancing at Tulloch.

"He is one of my main adversaries in Ethiopia," Wingate said. "I believe you've crossed swords with him before."

"Yes, sir," Hardie said.

"You'll want to join me now," Wingate said quietly.

Tulloch nodded slowly. "I'd have to clear it with the regiment, sir," he said, glancing at Tulloch.

Wingate nodded. "Leave that to me, Hardie. I can pull strings."

"I don't want to lose one of my best men, sir," Tulloch said. "Rifleman Hardie is an asset to my platoon."

"This is above your head, Lieutenant Tulloch," Wingate said, standing up. "I'll arrange your transfer, Hardie, and expect your reply by dawn tomorrow, Tulloch. If you have any sense, you'd accept my proposition and leave a failing battalion. Let Colonel Pringle know your decision in writing." Wingate nodded to the tent flap. "You'd better be about your business now, gentlemen."

Chapter Nineteen

Four Platoon missed Hardie when he left with Colonel Wingate. They had grown used to the quietly efficient, enigmatic man.

"Imagine Hardie with the KAR," Innes said.

"I always thought he was a bit strange," Connington said. "He was never one of the lads."

"He was all right," Hogg growled.

"All right!" Sergeant Drysdale loomed up. "Have you men nothing better to do? I can find work for you!"

The men drifted away. They knew men coming and going was part of army life, with bonds forged in battle ending suddenly and new friendships begun. They accepted change as readily as they expected hardship.

Tulloch heard them as he walked past, inspecting the standing patrols on his way to see the colonel. He did not expect Brigadier Worthington to be with Pringle.

"You are Lieutenant Tulloch, I presume," Worthington said sharply.

"That's correct, sir," Tulloch admitted.

201

"Colonel Pringle has something to say to you," Worthington stepped back as if giving the colonel permission to talk.

"You could have gained a promotion working with Wingate," Colonel Pringle told Tulloch with a wry smile.

"Perhaps, sir," Tulloch stood at ease before the colonel's desk. "But my place is here, with the battalion."

Pringle eyed him for a moment, cleaning out the bowl of his pipe. "I have some bad news for you, Tulloch. The RAF are claiming the tanks you destroyed." He spoke without visible emotion.

"The tanks you *claimed* to have destroyed on your last patrol," Brigadier Worthington interrupted. He shifted his position so the light gleamed on the red tabs on his uniform.

"Rifleman Smith hit at least three of them, sir," Tulloch defended his men. "One at least was irreparable, another severely damaged, and Smith blew the tracks off a third."

Worthington shook his head. "I am sure you speak in good faith, Lieutenant, but the RAF report from a wing commander speaks of five intact tanks until he attacked them and put three out of action." He smiled. "In the fog of battle, we all see things differently, and the pilot of an aircraft has a better view than men on the ground."

Tulloch felt his anger grow. "I know what we did, sir. Rifleman Smith is the best shot with a Boys I have ever known, and he's experienced fighting in France and Belgium."

"Ah, yes," Worthington said softly. "During the battalion's retreat to Dunkirk."

Tulloch retained his temper, saying nothing.

"We have already credited the RAF with the kills," Worthington said. "The matter is closed. Now, there is the carrier you abandoned in the desert and the Italian ten-ton truck you left on the road."

"The carrier was U/S, sir, and the truck was damaged and immobile."

"Our fitters managed to recover the carrier while the Italians retrieved their vehicle," Worthington said. "They will now be using it against us. You should have destroyed the truck and towed back the carrier rather than making spurious claims about fighting Italian tanks."

"We were a bit busy trying to return to the British lines, sir," Tulloch tried to control his temper. "And there was nothing spurious about our claims."

"Enough, Tulloch," Pringle said. "You'd better return to your platoon."

Tulloch restrained his desire to punch Worthington in the mouth. "Yes, sir," he said. He gave the colonel a punctilious salute, ignored the brigadier, and marched from the tent.

Bloody brigadiers, tied to a desk by their red tabs and think they know more about the war than the men who do the actual fighting. He kicked at the sand, swore when he raised a cloud of dust, and realised that two NCOs were watching him curiously.

"Haven't you men got anything better to do?"

"Yes, sir!" a tired-faced sergeant replied.

"Then get on with it!" Tulloch strode on, hating himself for venting his frustration on innocent men.

———

"I HEAR THE GERMANS HAVE STARTED BOMBING LONDON again," Atkins seemed to have access to a never-ending fund of information and rumours. "They're trying to level the city into the ground."

Tulloch nodded, thinking of Amanda sheltering under a wall of sandbags while the Luftwaffe dropped sticks of bombs. He remembered the Stukas screaming over the BEF in France and the fear as men hugged the ground.

"I hope the RAF shoots every one of the bastards down," Tulloch pictured Amanda face down in a shelter with her hands folded over her head as bombs exploded around her. "I hope the bastards burn."

Erskine raised languid eyebrows. "Now, now, Tulloch, one must not take these things personally. The Luftwaffe pilots are only serving their country, much as we are." He smiled, thrust his cigarette holder into his mouth, and waited for Tulloch's response.

"They're nothing like us," Tulloch snarled. "They're murdering hounds serving a regime of pure evil."

Erskine opened his mouth to speak, saw the expression in Tulloch's eyes, and wisely decided to remain silent. He blew a slow smoke ring and leaned back in his chair.

Captain Kilner raised his voice. "Quiet now, gentlemen. Here comes the colonel."

Colonel Pringle strode into the tent and stood before his officers, with a map spread on a tripod and his pipe in his hand.

"You'll all be aware that our next objective is Bardia," he jabbed the stem of his pipe at the map.

"There have been some changes since our last advance. As you know, the Lothians are now attached to the 6th Australians, and O'Connor's army has lost five RAF squadrons."

The officers voiced their dissatisfaction. They knew that General Wavell had sent a sizeable portion of their air cover to support the Greeks against Mussolini. They would miss the professionalism of the 4th Indians, while transferring the RAF squadrons weakened O'Connor's force even as it approached a strongly defended town.

"Now, we concentrate on Bardia," Pringle halted the murmurs of discontent as he jabbed his pipe at the Libyan coastal town. "It is a sizeable place, not just a village like Sidi Barrani, and the Italians have created formidable defences."

The officers studied the map, each man wondering what part the Lothians would play in the forthcoming battle.

We're back to set-piece battles rather than patrol work. Let's hope the Lothians can persuade Brigadier Worthington that we're a good fighting battalion.

Colonel Pringle circled his pipe stem around the town.

"According to the RAF reconnaissance, Bardia's defences are eleven miles long and five miles deep." He allowed the words to sink in. "The Italians have learned since Sidi Barrani and have the sea defending their back and a semi-circular defence, so we cannot thrust between their forts. They have erected a double curtain of deep barbed wire right around the landward side, plus an anti-tank ditch fifteen feet wide and up to ten feet deep."

The officers listened, taking notes.

The Italians are superb engineers and adapt their defences quickly.

Pringle circled areas on the map. "We have located mine-fields here, here, and here, and there may be more."

Tulloch frowned; he disliked minefields more than any other form of defence.

Pringle ran the stem of his pipe around Bardia's perimeter. "The Italians also have a double line of eighty fortified posts, with forty in front and the remainder between two hundred and five hundred feet behind, with an unknown number guarding the defence's weak points."

Pringle returned the pipe to his pocket. "We have already learned that the Italians are masters at building strong posts, with those in the south having a concrete trench with a diameter of forty yards, ten feet deep, and each holding one 47 mm anti-tank gun and three machine-gun nests."

The officers took notes, some glancing at their neighbours.

"This won't be an easy battle," Kinnear remarked. "If the Italians decide to fight, we'll be hard-pressed to penetrate these defences."

"We'll defeat them, Lieutenant," the colonel said quietly.

Kinnear looked away. "Yes, sir," he replied.

Pringle nodded and continued. "The Italians have fitted over-head cover to the larger posts to shelter them from bombs, added deeper trenches inside, and we believe there are underground shelters where the garrison sleeps."

"They've done a good job," Hume said, adding, "which makes

them very defensively minded." He glanced around at the officers. "We have to be offensively minded when we defeat them."

"How many men garrison each strongpoint, sir?" Tulloch asked.

Pringle shook his head. "We don't know that yet, Tulloch. I'd estimate a company, say seventy men, but that is only a guess."

"How large is the garrison of Bardia, sir?" Hume asked.

"We estimate around 25,000 men," Pringle paused before continuing. "Including the 1st and 2nd Blackshirt divisions."

Remembering his previous encounter with the Blackshirts, Tulloch drew in his breath. "What about artillery, sir?"

"Our intelligence experts reckon about three hundred medium and field guns, plus the usual light stuff, with perhaps a hundred and twenty-five tanks."

"Bloody hell!" Atkins said. "Sorry, sir."

"Now for the good news, gentlemen," Pringle said. "Most of the tanks are the light CV3/33s and are static rather than mobile. Mussolini is experiencing the same problems as we are with his mechanical devices; they break down in desert conditions. Only about ten or twelve are the heavier M13 tanks."

"Twelve M13s are enough for anybody," Captain Kilner murmured.

Erskine smiled, blew a smoke ring, and nodded. "The Italians will say the same about our Matildas," he murmured.

"Most of Bardia's artillery is on the south," Pringle said, "where they expect our attack to come. On the west, the perimeter is dug into flat ground, but the escarpment stretches eastward into the defences, where the ground is more rugged, with wadis and rough country that extends to the cliffs on the coast."

Tulloch drew a mental picture of the defences. "How high are the coastal cliffs, sir?"

"About six hundred feet high," Pringle said.

"We can't have a seaborne landing then," Muirhead said. "Mussolini has tied all the knots."

"Remember how Alexander disposed of the Gordian Knot, gentlemen," Colonel Pringle said. "He hacked it open with a sharp sword. Now, I have more good news. Bardia's garrison is isolated, with no reinforcements closer than Tobruk, some seventy-five miles away."

"Will we besiege them, sir?" Kinnear asked.

"I hope not," Pringle said. "That would be a supply nightmare. General O'Connor is not a man to do things by halves. We'll take Bardia by storm."

The officers were quiet for a moment, thinking of the deep defences.

"Are the Lothians going to be involved, sir?" Hume asked the question everybody was thinking.

"We are," Pringle said. "We're supporting the Australians."

"Only supporting, sir?" Hume asked.

"Unless the Australians run into difficulties," the colonel replied.

"When do we attack, sir?" Muirhead asked.

"The attack is scheduled to begin at 05:30 on Friday, the 3rd of January, gentlemen," Pringle said. "In the meantime, enjoy Hogmanay, except for the duty officer. Nineteen Forty was a difficult year, so let's hope for a better Nineteen Forty-one."

"Amen to that," Muirhead said. "Here's to success for the Lothian Rifles. Gin ye daur!"

"Gin ye daur!" the officers replied, more dutifully than with feeling, Tulloch thought.

Tulloch was the duty officer, so he did not indulge in the Lothians' habitual Hogmanay celebrations, where officers and men indulged in loud revelry. He paced the regiment's perimeter, spoke to the other unfortunates on duty, and glanced into the tent that housed the Officers' Mess to see what was happening. The music and laughter reinforced his slight sense of isolation, and he moved on.

I wonder how Amanda is celebrating Hogmanay. I hope she is safe from the bombing.

Although the Lothians were five miles behind the front lines, the sentries were still alert. The replacements acted like old soldiers, and the veterans now accepted them as part of the battalion. After sixteen months of war, the peacetime battalion was metamorphosing into a different entity.

The anti-aircraft Bren gunners were staring aloft when Tulloch arrived.

"You'll hear them before you see them," Tulloch advised, ignoring the smell of tobacco and hastily stubbed-out cigarettes. "Listen for the engines rather than wear yourselves out."

"Yes, sir," Corporal Borthwick replied.

"Happy New Year, lads," Tulloch said quietly.

"Happy New Year, sir," the men replied.

The Lothians had laboriously dug holes in the stony ground to create bomb shelters and relief from the wind-borne dust. With captured green-and-brown Italian groundsheets as cover, or corrugated iron when it was available, the resulting dug-outs were surprisingly comfortable.

Sergeant Drysdale was also on duty. "I heard we'll be joining the Aussies, sir."

"I heard that too, Sergeant," Tulloch said.

They stood in silence for a moment, listening to the whine of the wind around the tents.

"Good lads, the Aussies," Drysdale said. "I met a few in the last war. Hard buggers, but they knew their stuff."

"I'm sure they'll be every bit as good in this war," Tulloch guessed Drysdale's meaning.

"I'm sure they will. Our tankies did well at Sidi Omar," Drysdale said. "Did you hear about that, sir?"

"I heard they took the fort," Tulloch said cautiously. The NCOs seemed to have access to stores of knowledge denied to officers, while the Lothians' Sergeants' Mess would shame the cellar of any upmarket hotel.

"Our armour circled Sidi Omar like Indians around a wagon train in the flicks, sir," Drysdale said. "They were firing their guns until they saw a breach in the wall, then they charged in and captured the place."

"We're doing well in the desert," Tulloch said.

"Yes, sir," Drysdale agreed. "Once we sort out Mussolini, we can get back into Europe and have another round with Adolf."

"Amen to that, Sergeant," Tulloch said. "Happy New Year."

"Happy New Year, sir," Drysdale replied. "Let's hope for victory."

Sand continued to be a problem for O'Connor's men, seeping into engines and petrol tanks, food and hair, every body orifice, and the workings of rifles and machine guns. The men huddled from the sharp winds of the Libyan winter, swearing at an Africa that lacked the romance they had imagined and presented only hardship and short rations.

"Bugger this for a game of soldiers," Hogg gave his ubiquitous comment as he stood sentry with the wind blasting sand in his face.

Innes narrowed his eyes from the flying dust. "At least the wind will bother Mussolini's soldiers as well. That's one consolation."

Elliot shook his head. "It won't bother them at all," he said. "They'll be sitting snug in their billets, swigging wine, and cuddling up to some warm woman, the lucky buggers."

"I'd be happy snuggling up to a cold pint of McEwans in the Gorgie Arms," Hogg said. "After the Hearts have put three past the Hi-bees."

"A pint of McEwans?" Innes repeated. "I'd settle for a pint of water."

Despite the best efforts of the Royal Navy in escorting merchant vessels to supply the army, water was limited, so the men learned to cope with one gallon a day for all purposes. After a few weeks in the desert, even that reduced to only four pints. The officers shared the same hardships as the men.

"We're lucky in some ways," Lieutenant Kinnear said

gloomily. "The rationing in Blighty is getting ever more strict. We eat well compared to the civilians back home."

Tulloch nodded. "I'll remember not to complain," he said, thinking of Amanda in London and his parents doing what they could in Edinburgh. "This war affects everybody."

"Please, God, it ends soon," Kinnear said.

"Which God?" Muirhead asked. "The God we pray to, the God of peace, or the God the Nazis think is with them?"

"What God would be with the Nazis?" Atkins asked.

Muirhead shrugged. "The German belt buckles say *Gott mit uns*—God is with us, so they must believe God's on their side." He noticed Tulloch listening. "What do you think, Tulloch?"

"I think the Nazis are unadulterated evil," Tulloch said. "As soon as we put Mussolini's lot out of the game, we can concentrate on Hitler."

"You have no ambiguity, do you, Tulloch?" Muirhead said.

"Not our Tully," Erskine lay at full stretch across two camp chairs. "Our Tully sees things in black and white, don't you, Tully?"

"I do where good and evil are concerned," Tulloch replied. "The Nazis are evil."

"Then we must be on the side of good if we are fighting them," Erskine said. "Am I good?"

Tulloch began to fill his pipe. "There are always exceptions," he said.

"Touche," Erskine said.

Tulloch glanced at his watch. "Duty calls," he said. "I must check the sentries and change the guard."

"Quite right, Tully," Erskine said. "Ensure the Nazis, or the Devil, hasn't taken them away."

As he returned with the relieved sentries, Tulloch saw the Australians kneeling on the sand as the Roman Catholic priest held Mass.

"If any of you lads are RC, you are welcome to join them," Tulloch told his men. He saw Hogg grunt and look away. As a staunch Presbyterian and a member of the Orange Order, he had little time for the Roman Catholic Church.

"I'm RC," Innes said quietly.

"Do you want to join them?" Tulloch asked.

Innes nodded. "If I may, sir."

"Of course," Tulloch agreed at once.

Religion is a strange thing. It can be a force for good or a motivation for incredible wickedness. I am sure many of Hitler's adherents believed in their cause, while we know Nazism is evil. If Hitler succeeds, he will plunge all of Europe and perhaps most of the world into a dark age, and if prayer helps defeat that horror, then more power to your sermons, padre.

"I'm not a Catholic," Tulloch said on an impulse. "May I join you?"

"I'm sure the Good Lord won't object," the priest said with a smile.

Wondering what his devout Church of Scotland mother would think, Tulloch knelt between Innes and a brawny Australian sheep farmer.

The priest continued with the ceremony.

We need all the help we can get to win this war.

———

"WE ARE NO LONGER KNOWN AS THE WESTERN DESERT Force," Pringle said. "We are now XIII Corps."

The officers looked unimpressed. The significance of the unlucky number was not lost on the more superstitious among them.

"We are now officially attached to the 16th Australian Infantry Brigade, together with the 7th Royal Tank Regiment and their eighteen Matilda Mark Twos, A Squadron of the 6th Australian Cavalry, and a company of the Northumberland Fusiliers. The Australians are short of a brigade; hence, we make up the shortfall."

"Let's hope the acerbic Brigadier Worthington does not join us," Kinnear said.

"Let's hope some friendly Italian shoots him, or he steps on a mine." Although Erskine grinned when he spoke, Tulloch wondered if he meant every word.

On the second of January 1941, the Lothians marched to the start line as the Royal Navy monitor HMS *Terror* and the gunboats *Ladybird* and *Aphis* bombarded Bardia. The Lothians heard the rumble of heavy naval guns and saw the RAF flying overhead to soften the defences.

"It looks like we have RAF and naval support this time," Tulloch said.

"Aye," Kinnear said bitterly. "I wish we had that level of support in France."

Tulloch remembered the constant Luftwaffe attacks on the British, French, and Belgian armies the previous year and the many crashed and burning British aircraft. "The RAF did their best with outdated aircraft," he said. "They lost far too many good pilots who could be invaluable now."

Kinnear grunted. "I can't remember the Brylcreem Boys when the Stukas were attacking us."

"They were there," Tulloch said, "but we were too busy trying to bury ourselves into the ground!" He heard Erskine's bark of laughter and marched on at the head of his platoon.

"Pipey!" Colonel Pringle snapped. "Play us to the front!"

The pipe sergeant obliged, and the evocative wail of the pipes accompanied the Lothians as they marched to battle with the Australians nearby and the Italians waiting in their concrete fortifications. Tulloch thought of the battalion marching through Flanders only twenty-six years previously and their ancestors plodding to Tel-el-Kebir, Inkerman, and Waterloo. He envisioned a long, weary line of men fighting for causes they only vaguely understood, cementing the bones of history with their blood.

"I hope this is the last war we have to fight," Tulloch said. "At least we know we're on the side of the angels against evil."

Kinnear grunted. "I hope to God you are right," he said. "If we're on the wrong side, then we're wasting an awful lot of time."

Chilled and already tired, the Lothians were quiet as they reached the start line. The pipers had stopped playing, so only the whistle of the wind accompanied the soft words of command.

"Keep together, boys, no straggling. McAllister, your bootlace is coming loose; Elliot, keep your head up, son; Spalding, you'll lose your helmet; fasten the chin strap!"

With his platoon ready, Tulloch looked at the Australians as they filed into their positions. They did not look much different from British troops, except they carried themselves with more of a swagger and had more relaxed ideas about discipline.

More Australians passed in trucks, some singing, others laughing and joking with no apparent sign of nerves. They had nothing to prove because they knew they were good.

"These Aussie lads are cheerful enough," Captain Kilner said.

"It's their first action," Kinnear replied. "They have no idea what they're in for tomorrow."

Tulloch nodded. "Were we like that in France or on the Northwest Frontier?" It seemed impossible to believe that the Dunkirk campaign had been only a few months previously. He looked back at himself, wondering how he could have been so naïve.

The Australians waved to the Lothians as they marched to their penultimate positions, long greatcoats swinging and carrying their heavy packs with ease. They looked fit and capable.

The tanks grumbled up, and Tulloch saw them highlighted on the skyline. They appeared like steel monsters with fluttering gay pennants, the literal descendants of the horse cavalry of old, men who gave class to a battlefield that would otherwise be only an unseemly brawl. Or so they claimed.

As the last of the tanks arrived, night fell swiftly. The moon rose, shining on the endless rows of transport lorries that carried O'Connor's army and its equipment.

"Follow the tapes," the orders came from a hard-faced Military Policeman. "Follow the tapes."

The Lothians inched forward in the starlit night, with the chill deepening and a cold wind scouring their faces.

"I thought we were only supporting the Aussies," Elliot whispered.

"Change of plan," Sergeant Drysdale explained. "We're going in with the first wave."

"It's good to know what's happening," Elliot said, kicked a loose stone, and swore.

When they reached the jumping-off point, the Lothians slept while they could, aware that the following morning could be bloody. At two o'clock, they woke, ate, and drank a tot of rum that a thoughtful Australian quartermaster had provided for their Scottish guests.

"There you go, Scotties," a cheerful corporal said. "That'll put hairs on your haggis!"

Tulloch checked his platoon, ensuring every man had his equipment, rifle, and ammunition and nobody had got lost in the dark. He exchanged quiet words with the veterans, encouraged the nervous, assured the replacements that they were now old soldiers, and shivered in the cold.

Preparing for these operations is worse than the actual fighting.

At quarter past two, the Lothians and a battalion of Australian infantry moved silently forward to a single white tape. They moved slowly, with the NCOs rebuking any noise that might alert the enemy.

Tulloch stared forward, aware that nothing now lay between them and the waiting enemy.

If I don't get back, look after yourself, Amanda. Survive the war, find a good man, and settle down.

"When the order comes, follow me, lads." Tulloch led from the front, assuming a confident nonchalance at odds with the turmoil of mixed excitement and apprehension inside him.

The Lothians waited, shifting their feet on the hard sand, still tasting the sweet rum on their lips. They hoped the Italians did not push a patrol forward and waited for the battle to begin.

The artillery barrage began at five thirty that morning. Tulloch saw a long row of flashes in the dark, heard the scream of shells passing overhead, and heard the resulting explosions on the Italian positions.

"Poor buggers under that," Innes said quietly.

"The more the gunners kill, the less there are to kill us," Elliot replied softly.

Tulloch watched, listening to the hammer of the guns and watching the orange-yellow flashes of the explosions. He checked his watch, timing the twenty-five minutes the barrage was meant to last.

"Get ready, lads!" Tulloch shouted as the minute hand of his watch crept towards five-fifty-five. "Fix bayonets!"

Tulloch heard the sinister snicks as the Lothians fitted their eighteen-inch bayonets onto their rifles. The Bren gunners checked their magazines and nodded to their number twos, the Boys' men ensured their ammunition carriers were close by, and the officers loosened the revolvers in their holsters.

Tulloch took a deep breath and muttered Sir Jacob Astley's famous prayer. "Lord, you know I must be very busy this day. If I forget you, do not thou forget me."

"Forward, Lothians!" Colonel Pringle ordered and led his battalion towards Bardia.

Chapter Twenty

BARDIA, LIBYA, JANUARY 1941

The sound of British artillery drowned most noise, but in the small gaps between firing, Tulloch heard the Australians shouting encouragement to one another as they advanced. Their nasal voices were strange after the rounded accents of the Lothians and the various Indian languages.

Good luck, boys, Tulloch said to himself and concentrated entirely on Four Platoon. They walked slowly, hoping the scouts had not missed any minefields, keeping behind the barrage as they sought to cover the killing ground leading to the outermost defences. As the infantry advanced, the artillery kept the Italians under cover.

At 05:55, the barrage stopped, with the Australians and Lothians only a hundred yards from the outer belt of barbed wire. The sudden silence seemed deafening, and then Tulloch heard the Lothians and neighbouring Australians encouraging each other.

"Don't bunch, lads!" Sergeant Drysdale snarled. "Keep up, Elliot; you're lagging!"

"Not far now, boys!" Tulloch shouted. "Follow me!"

"Engineers!" Major Hume roared, and the engineers dashed forward with the twelve-foot-long Bangalore torpedoes with their deadly ammonal load. Tulloch did not envy the engineers their job, working in front of the infantry and in full view of the Italian defenders.

The Italians recovered quickly, and their artillery crashed out, landing shells among the advancing infantry. Tulloch winced as one shell exploded in the centre of a group of engineers. Four men died immediately, and others fell, wounded and screaming as the Italians continued to fire.

Kinnaird ducked as a shell exploded nearby, scattering shrapnel. "Hurry up, for God's sake! We're like fairground targets here!"

The surviving engineers shoved their Bangalore torpedoes into the wire and blew them up, dashing through the resulting gaps in advance of the infantry. As engineers widened the spaces with wire cutters, infantry carried their bayonets forward, probing for the Italian defensive positions.

Tulloch flinched as something whined over his head. He heard one of his men firing and knew without looking who it was.

"Save your ammunition until you see a target, Hogg!"

A morning mist slithered over the ground, making the supporting tanks appear like some monsters from a mythical past. They halted at the lip of the anti-tank ditch, firing at the Italian defences. The engineers ran over, wielding picks and shovels.

"Fill these ditches in!" A calm-voiced engineer captain ordered, striding to the side of the barrier. The tanks sought to protect the engineers by using a combination of sweeping machine guns and firing their two-pounders.

As soon as the Italians realised what was happening, their artillery began to probe for the engineers, with the machine guns soon joining them, involving the British armour in a battle within a battle.

Tulloch scrambled through a gap in the wire, stepping over the crumpled body of an Australian engineer.

A machine gun began its mad chatter, with bullets kicking up dust and rattling from the wire until one of the Matildas targeted it with a two-pounder shell.

"Come on, lads!" Tulloch shouted.

The infantry, Australian and Lothians, moved against the forward Italian posts, with most defenders still dazed from the bombardment. The Lothians' pipers began their encouraging music, pushing the men forward through the mist and smoke towards Bardia.

When the first Italian strongpoint loomed ahead, Tulloch raised his hand and ordered his platoon to the rear.

"This way, Four Platoon! The Australians are attacking the front!"

Hogg was at his side, with Sergeant Drysdale organising the remainder of the men. Tulloch heard Italian voices and the quick rattle of a machine gun; he saw the glint of Australian bayonets and a group of defenders running to a 75 mm anti-tank gun.

The gun fired once, with the shell arcing over the attackers, and then the Lothians and Australians closed in.

Tulloch leapt over a stone wall, revolver in hand and Hogg at his side, yelling, "The Gorgie boys are here!"

Tulloch saw a startled Italian face as a private soldier dropped his rifle and threw up his hands in surrender. Hogg plunged his bayonet into a gesticulating Italian officer, an Australian sergeant gestured with his rifle, and the remainder of the defenders decided to surrender.

"Good day, Scotties," the Australian sergeant said as the Lothians fanned out, bayonets ready.

The Australians were grinning, with their long coats flapping and their packs making them look unwieldy.

"That didn't take long," Drysdale said, sharing a cigarette with the Australian sergeant.

"Let's hope the rest are as easy," the Australian replied.

Tulloch glanced around. *That's one strongpoint taken. God knows how many more there are, and the Italians will be recovering now.*

"Come on, lads!" Tulloch ordered. "Move on before the Italians realise what's happening."

Four Platoon followed Tulloch out the rear entrance and onward toward Bardia. A British tank rattled past, firing its gun at an Italian weapon pit. Tulloch saw an Italian 75-millimetre gun respond, with the shell striking the tank head-on but failing to explode. The tank swivelled its turret and returned fire, with a section of Australians following up with the bayonet, yelling ferociously.

We needn't have worried about the Australians. They're proving themselves every day.

"Don't stop!" Tulloch waved his platoon on, seeing the Australians running forward, cheering, with their bayonetted rifles ready for action. He saw Captain Kilner on his left, a wraith-like figure with tendrils of mist wrapped around his legs. More Lothians were beside Kilner, alternatively appearing and disappearing in the smoky murk. Tulloch heard Atkins' voice, high-pitched as he encouraged his men.

An Italian M11 medium tank appeared behind a pile of rubble that had once been a building. It fired its 37-millimetre gun at a British Matilda and sprayed the ground with a machine gun, then backed off with the undamaged British tank in pursuit.

These Matildas are some machines!

Tulloch heard the crump of grenades and the rattle of small arms fire as a unit of Blackshirts held their position.

"Four Platoon!" Tulloch yelled. "We'll take these men on the flank!"

The morning mist was clearing, but battle smoke and dust took its place, drifting across the ravaged landscape as Italians, Australians, tanks, and the Lothians battled for supremacy around the North African town. Above them, an uncaring sun rose as it had done over other invaders, Romans, Arabs, and Carthaginians.

"The Italians are singing!" Innes said. "Listen!"

Tulloch heard the words floating above the battle clamour.

"La legge nostra è schiavitù d'amore,
il nostro motto è Libertà e Dovere,
vendicheremo noi Camicie Nere,
Gli eroi caduti liberando te!"

The Blackshirts held their position, firing continuously at the Australian and British infantry. Tulloch saw one Australian fall, holding his leg, and another duck behind a smoking Italian truck. An Italian officer rose amidst his men, shouting orders and firing a pistol at the Australians.

"These lads don't want to surrender," Connington said.

"Let's make them," Elliot snarled. "Rummel the bastards up!"

Innes threw himself down, holding his Bren. He fired a short burst that raised dust around the Italians and swore when the Blackshirts responded with an array of weapons.

"They're worse than the bloody Germans!"

An Australian threw a grenade, which exploded in a fountain of dust and flames, but the Blackshirts continued to fire with the officer at the forefront.

"Fire at that machine gunner!" Tulloch ordered. He did not want one strongpoint to slow the impetus of the attack. The longer the advance took, the more time the Italians had to recover and reorganise themselves, and they still outnumbered and outgunned the attackers.

"They're holding us back!" Captain Kilner shouted from the left. "See if you can shake them, Tulloch!"

"I'll try, sir."

An Italian 47-millimetre anti-tank gun opened fire on the Lothians, sending men diving for cover.

"Why don't these lads surrender?" Innes asked.

"They're Blackshirts," Sergeant Drysdale said. "Dedicated fascists."

Hogg lay on his face, aimed, and fired. "That's one dedicated fascist less," he said, working his rifle bolt.

Tulloch looked around. The Australians had thrust a great wedge into Bardia's defences, but the Italians seemed determined to hold them.

"Stay put, Tulloch," Kilner countermanded his earlier order. "We might have to consolidate here."

"Where are we?" Tulloch unfolded his map of the defences. "Post Number Eleven." He ducked as a battery of 47 millimetres fired, with the explosions landing in a group a hundred yards from the Lothians' position.

"Who said the Italians could not fight?" Kinnear asked, holding his helmet in place.

"Somebody who had never met them," Tulloch told him.

"Who's on our flank?"

"The 2/6th Australians," Tulloch replied.

"Are they any good?"

"They've done well so far. They're Australian," Tulloch said as if that was a sufficiently detailed reply.

Dense coils of barbed wire surrounded Defence Post Eleven, with interlocking machine gun nests and an untouched anti-tank ditch in front. Tulloch saw a unit of engineers approach the wire, only for the defenders to subject them to a torrent of machine gun fire supported by some accurate artillery. The engineers withdrew hurriedly, taking a wounded man with them and leaving the wire undamaged. The defenders cheered, with some singing the same stirring song.

"La legge nostra è schiavitù d'amore
il nostro motto è Libertà e Dovere
vendicheremo noi Camicie Nere
Gli eroi caduti liberando te!"

"What are they singing?" Kinnear asked.

Tulloch shook his head. "How the hell should I know? I don't speak Italian!"

"Two Platoon!" That was Colonel Pringle's voice. "Support the Australians!"

Mortars gave covering fire as a company of Australians rushed forward, bayonets gleaming in the sun. Lieutenant Kinnear led Two Platoon in support as the Lothians fired at Defence Post Eleven.

The Australians leapt the anti-tank ditch, losing men to the defenders' fire, and hacked through the barbed wire, shouting madly.

"Four Platoon!" Pringle shouted. "Give covering fire!"

"Keep the Italians occupied!" Tulloch ordered as Innes fired magazine after magazine at the defenders, with Elliot rounding up as much ammunition as possible.

Kinnear's Two Platoon joined the Australians inside the outer defences, firing from the hip, tackling machine gun nests with grenades and bayonets, and kneeling to fire their Lee-Enfields. Kinnear fired his revolver into a rifle pit, with two of his men dropping in grenades and following through with stabbing bayonets.

"Keep firing, lads!" Tulloch shouted as the Italians responded with machine gun and rifle fire, forcing the attackers back. Kinnear was the last to leave, helping a wounded man as he fired his revolver at the Blackshirts. Tulloch saw Lothian and Australian casualties inside the perimeter as the defenders sang that same victory song.

"La legge nostra è schiavitù d'amore
il nostro motto è Libertà e Dovere
vendicheremo noi Camicie Nere
Gli eroi caduti liberando te!"

Two Platoon staggered back, swearing and frustrated at

being repulsed. Kinnear immediately reported to Colonel Pringle, while Tulloch ordered Four Platoon to cease fire.

"Save your ammunition, men," Tulloch said. "We'll need it later." He watched as Pringle and the Australian colonel conferred, nodding towards the Italian defence post. The firing died down as both sides waited for the other to make the next move.

"We're stuck here until we take Defence Post Eleven," Colonel Pringle told his officers. "The Aussies will take the front and right flank; we'll take the left flank." He glanced at his watch. "Keep them occupied, gentlemen."

The Lothians found cover and opened a hot fire on the defenders, with the 2/6th Australians on the right doing the same and the Italians responding in kind.

"We're making little progress here," Major Hume said as an Italian shell exploded behind the Lothians' position, spreading dust, stones, and shrapnel into the air. "Contact the Aussies! Formulate another attack! We'll have to get back inside their defences."

Atkins pointed across the battlefield. "Sir! Look to the left!"

Two British tanks appeared, bypassed the beleaguered Defence Post Eleven, and thrust deeper into Bardia's defences.

"Put a few shots into Post Eleven!" Captain Kilner shouted hopefully. The tanks did not respond.

An Australian dispatch rider approached Colonel Pringle, passed a message, and sped away on his motorcycle, with his curtain of dust half hiding him.

"General O'Connor has given us orders to contain the Italians here," the colonel passed the message on to his officers. "Hold firm and advance when possible."

"We could storm the place," Hume said.

"Not until I give the order," Pringle replied.

As the Lothians seethed and exchanged fire with Defence Post Eleven, the Australians bypassed the position, broke the Italian defence line on the west, and pushed to the edges of

Bardia. The situation in the south was more complicated, with some units more advanced than others and the Italians holding firm in various strong points.

"We're winning," Tulloch said, "but it's not a walkover."

"We're not winning until we take Post Eleven," Major Hume said. "As far as I'm concerned, this battle is as much about the battalion regaining its reputation and its soul as it is about capturing Bardia."

"Tanks!" Sergeant Drysdale warned. "We need your Boys, Smith!"

"I see them!" Smith replied.

Three Italian tankettes powered forward in an attempted counterattack, but the Australians and Lothians responded with Boys and mortar fire that destroyed one and sent the others scurrying back.

"These wee things are useless," Atkins said. "Imagine sending men out to fight in them."

"They're brave men even to try," Tulloch replied. He glanced up. "It's nearly evening," he wondered. "What happened to the day?"

"Time always passes quickly when you're fighting," Atkins replied.

"Consolidate where you are," Colonel Pringle ordered. "Hold the line, and we'll push on in the morning."

Four Platoon scraped holes in the sand and waited as darkness fell. Tulloch changed the sentries every hour, knowing his veterans would remain alert. He grabbed an hour's sleep before dawn, woke after twenty minutes, and checked the sentries.

"The lads are all awake, sir," Sergeant Drysdale reported quietly. "I heard movement a few moments ago, but nothing's come against us."

Tulloch scanned Defence Post Eleven through his binoculars. "I think something's moving out there. Fire a Very, Sergeant."

The flare soared upward, harshly bright and somehow

reminding Tulloch of the stories he had heard about the First World War trenches.

"They're leaving, sir," Drysdale reported. "The Blackshirts are abandoning Point Eleven."

"What's that, Sergeant?" Colonel Pringle arrived, freshly shaved and looking as fresh as if he had enjoyed eight hours of uninterrupted sleep. "Erskine! Take a patrol forward and see what's happening!"

"Yes, sir," Erskine said.

Erskine returned within twenty minutes. "They've all gone, sir. The Italians have withdrawn from Defence Post Eleven."

"Push on," Colonel Pringle ordered.

The Australians and Lothians continued the advance, pressing the Italians back, surrounding and capturing the defence posts as they thrust towards Bardia. Four Platoon was in the second line that day, acting as a mobile reserve for Captain Kilner's B Company.

None of the remaining Italian defence posts proved as stubborn as Post Eleven, and when the 16th Brigade pushed through to the coast on either side of Bardia, the garrison began to lose heart.

"They're broken," Major Hume stated. "Press them harder, Lothians. Go for the throat!"

"Keep in line with the Australians," Colonel Pringle countermanded Hume's order.

Tulloch sensed Hume's frustration as Pringle pulled the Lothians back. They continued the remorseless advance, consolidating every small step.

Tulloch heard the Australians shouting at the now demoralised defenders. "Lashay lay army," which was Australian for *Lasce le armi* or lay down your arms. With their lines pierced and Australian infantry in the ascendancy, the Italians proved eager to obey. They surrendered in dozens and scores, raising their hands in surrender even before the Australians and Lothians arrived.

When the Australians ended the Italian resistance in the south, Bardia, which the Italians had believed to be impregnable, had fallen.

"They've jacked in," Captain Muirhead said, and the Lothians stood back and watched as the Australians herded the prisoners out of Bardia.

"Poor looking lot, aren't they?" Atkins said.

Tulloch agreed. The Italian private soldiers were mostly clad in ill-fitting and cheap uniforms that provided little protection from the cold Libyan nights, while many senior officers looked to Tulloch like figures from an opera. Immaculate in grey uniforms, complete with long swords and pith helmets, they marched at the head of their men as if they were proud of capitulating to a lesser number of Australians.

"Hey! Scotties!" a stocky Australian corporal shouted to the Lothians. "We've found Graziani's caravan! Have a look at how the other half lives!"

With the fighting over and Sergeant Drysdale in charge of Four Platoon, Tulloch wandered across to look. The trailer was the image of luxury, with silken sheets and bottles of perfume, a stock of wine, and a dozen changes of clothes.

"Better than the tucker at the Rocks," the corporal said with a grin. [1]

"Better than our Officers' Mess, too," Tulloch agreed. "Well done, Aussie!"

More important than Graziani's caravan was the freshwater supply in Bardia and the facilities in the port.

"Didn't the Italians try to destroy the port?" Kinnear asked.

"It seems not," Kilner replied. "They were in too much of a hurry to surrender."

Tulloch lifted his head as the sound of artillery came from the southeast. "Some of them are still fighting," he said.

"We're not involved in that," Kilner said. "Higher command wants us to consolidate in Bardia."

"That's our fighting done for the day, then." Kinnear sounded happy.

"Tulloch: help the Australians with the Italian prisoners," Major Hume ordered.

Tulloch did not like prisoner escort duty, herding disconsolate men into trucks for onward transport to Prisoner-of-War cages. He organised his platoon with the more aggressive men as guards and the quieter dealing face-to-face with the Italians. Tulloch knew some of his men would have looted bottles of wine from the prisoners and expected some raucous behaviour later. It was impossible to stop British soldiers from finding something alcoholic, so it was much better to limit the damage and turn a Nelsonian blind eye to minor breaches of discipline. Tulloch hid his smile. *If Aitken had been with Four Platoon rather than recovering from a wound in hospital, he would have taken Graziani's caravan, including its contents, and hidden it in his kitbag.*

"Taking Bardia was easier than I expected," Captain Kilner said as the battalion settled in for the evening.

"The Australians blooded themselves well," Tulloch said.

"We're lucky in the troops we have in the Desert Army," Kilner said, using the original name for O'Connor's force. "The 4th Indian were superb, and the 6th Australian are their equals." He saluted when the colonel strode up. "Where to now, sir?"

"I am summoned to the brigadier," Pringle said. "I have no doubt he will tell us."

"No doubt," Kilner said.

"Here he is now, sir," Tulloch said quietly.

Brigadier Worthington stepped towards them, looking around at the gathered officers. "One of your men challenged me," he barked. "Teach them to recognise a superior officer."

"He was doing his duty, sir," Pringle replied.

"His duty is to fight the enemy, not delay me." Worthington touched his badges of rank. "Lax, I call that."

Pringle stiffened. "My men are trained to challenge everybody, sir. In France, there were stories of Germans in disguise, and I am sure there are similar Italian agents in Bardia."

"Your men should recognise me, Pringle." Brigadier removed a pipe from his breast pocket and thrust it between his teeth.

Tulloch stood aside. Nobody could mistake the elegant, bristling, sandy-haired Brigadier for anything other than a British officer, but Tulloch inwardly thanked the sentry for doing his duty.

"Don't argue, Pringle. Put the man on a charge!"

"What was his name, sir?"

"How the devil should I know? He was a middle-sized man with a scowl and black hair."

That sounds like Hogg. He's on stag this evening. Tulloch hid his smile. He could imagine the truculent Hogg challenging a brusque brigadier.

"I'll look into it, sir," Pringle promised, ushering Worthington through the open flap of his tent.

Worthington looked around at the array of maps and administrative documents. "I hear your Lothians failed at Post Eleven," he said. "You still haven't recovered your fighting spirit," he sucked on his empty pipe. "Perhaps I could rephrase that, Pringle. Your regiment lost its soul at Dunkirk and hasn't regained it yet."

That's twice I've heard that phrase used against us.

Tulloch saw Pringle stiffen. "The Lothian Rifles are as good as any regiment in the army," he said, with steel behind his soft tone.

"I have yet to see you prove that," Worthington said.

"We've been fighting since before the Italians invaded Egypt, sir, and in Belgium and France earlier in the year."

"I am aware of that, Colonel." The brigadier moderated his tone. "I think the Lothian Rifles have been in action for too long, Pringle, and all the fight has been knocked out of you. If we weren't so short of men, I'd recommend you be transferred to the rear, maybe to load supplies at Alexandria or guard the Suez Canal."

Tulloch saw the pain in Pringle's face.

"Pull up your socks, Pringle. You're letting the side down." Worthington turned and stalked away, brushing past Tulloch without a word.

We might be defeating the Italians, but the Lothians are not making friends in the staff.

Chapter Twenty-One

LIBYA JANUARY 1941

"The question is, do we stop in Bardia and consolidate or drive on while we have the impetus," Kinnear mused.

"Supplies are the difficulty," Tulloch replied. "The extent of O'Connor's success is causing us problems. We already have around a hundred thousand Italian and Colonial prisoners to feed and water as well as our own men, and we need to find prisoner-of-war guards for the Italians. Every success weakens our army."

Kinnear nodded. "And every gallon of water and petrol and scrap of food has to be transported from Egypt or carried by sea, with Italian submarines lurking and Italian aircraft vastly outnumbering our own."

Tulloch watched as a Scammell R100 artillery tractor towed a broken-down tank along the road. "There's another problem. We're running short of tanks. They were not designed for continual use in desert conditions."

Kinnear agreed. "Maybe we'd best stop here at Bardia, reinforce the town and wait for the inevitable Italian counterattack."

"General O'Connor won't stop here," Tulloch said. He had met O'Connor a couple of times on the battlefield as the general had driven from place to place in his staff car. Although O'Connor appeared quiet, even pensive behind the lines, when the battle began, he was all action, giving orders to his forward commanders and darting from trouble spot to trouble spot to direct operations.

Kinnear glanced to the west, deeper into Libya. "Do you think O'Connor will push further?"

Tulloch nodded. "I think he'll want to push the Italians right out of Africa," he said, "and I wouldn't be surprised if he didn't invade Italy as well."

Kinnear laughed without humour. "With our little army? We've only got around 30,000 men."

"Why not?" Tulloch asked. "We've done wonders so far. Why not continue?"

"I have one word to answer that," Captain Kilner had padded silently across the sand. "Churchill."

"Winston Churchill?" Tulloch probed for more information.

"Churchill's more interested in Greece than Libya," Kilner said. "He's already had Wavell transfer RAF squadrons from Africa, and I think he wants more aircraft and maybe part of O'Connor's army as well."

"We're already undermanned here," Tulloch said. "I hope you're wrong."

"So do I," Kilner said. "So do I. We're operating on fresh air and prayers, with fighting units getting little time to recover between battles." He lifted his head to listen to distant aircraft engines, decided they were no threat, and continued. "If Churchill strips O'Connor of any formations, we'll be hard-pressed to continue."

"Are we continuing, sir?" Kinnear asked.

"The colonel will answer that tonight," Kilner replied, "at nineteen hundred hours sharp."

Tulloch glanced at Kinnear as Kilner strode away. "Nineteen hundred hours," he repeated. "Sharp."

Tulloch checked his sentries before arriving at the colonel's headquarters a few moments before seven. He was one of the last to arrive, with pipe smoke already thick in the tent.

"Tobruk," Pringle told them quietly. "Our next objective is Tobruk."

Tulloch glanced at the map behind the colonel, calculating the distance between Bardia and Tobruk.

"It's only fifty miles along the coast," Pringle informed them. "It would be an easy drive if the Italians were not in the way. Tobruk is another defended town, but we've already got the measure of the Italian defences, and the Italians will expect us to win." The colonel paused to draw on his pipe. "I suspect the garrison will already be looking over their shoulders at the road to Benghazi."

The officers nodded, some smiled, and others remembered Brigadier Worthington's harsh words and wondered how to prove themselves again. Tulloch glanced across to Kinnear, who gave a strained smile. Atkins leaned back in his chair, acting like a veteran.

Pringle continued. "General Pitassi Mannella commands the town with twenty-five thousand men of the 22nd Corps and more than two hundred pieces of artillery." He puffed smoke into the room. "That means the garrison is nearly as strong as O'Connor's entire army."

Although Operation Compass had been successful so far, Tulloch knew the Italian gunners were brave men and would fight until their cause looked hopeless. He did not expect an easy conquest.

The Italian numbers sobered the Lothians as they contemplated advancing over the open desert against intense shell fire.

Kinnear glanced at Tulloch and raised his eyebrows. "That's a large garrison," he murmured.

"Quality will defeat quantity every time," Tulloch responded.

Kinnear nodded. "Let's hope we have the quality," he said.

"Here are some details, gentlemen," Pringle continued. "The Italians have the 61st Sirte Division, backed by light and medium tanks, a couple of infantry battalions and perhaps seven thousand ordinary garrison soldiers."

Tulloch was glad there were no Blackshirts in the garrison. He noted the units and numbers as Pringle jabbed the stem of his pipe at the map. "As you see, we have two roads from Bardia to Tobruk. We have the coast road and a rough route known as the Capuzzo Track about ten miles inland. The Capuzzo Track stretches along the top of the escarpment to El Adem airfield."

The officers knew the geography of coastal North Africa, with its narrow coastal strip along which nearly all traffic passed, the sharp rise of the escarpment, and the great waste inland where only specialists such as the Long Range Desert Group could operate.

"General O'Connor has already begun operations towards Tobruk," Pringle said. "He has sent some light armour westward, with the 19th Australian Brigade following up."

"What's our part, sir?" Hume asked.

"We're still attached to the 6th Australian Division," Pringle said. "We're going along the coast road while the 7th Armoured Division uses the Capuzzo Track."

"When do we leave, sir?"

Colonel Pringle consulted his watch. "In four hours, Major. Make sure your men are ready."

The Lothians moved out later that day, boarding the now familiar column of mixed British and Italian trucks to motor westward.

"Innes!" Tulloch said. "Keep an eye on the sky. Have your Bren ready."

"Here we go again!" Innes shouted. "All aboard, who's coming aboard!"

"Bugger this for a game of soldiers," Hogg grumbled. "If we keep driving west, we'll end up back in Edinburgh."

As they moved beside the coast, dust rose around them, the sea was a brilliant blue to the north, and the *Regia Aeronautica* did not appear. The British drove at a steady fifteen miles an hour, eating up the miles.

"This is the easiest advance so far," Corporal Borthwick said. "Where are Mussolini's boys?"

"Maybe they've packed it in," McAllister suggested.

"Maybe we'll drive all the way to Benghazi," Borthwick said as he watched the sea break silver-white on the sand.

"Or Rome," McAllister said. "Shake Mussolini's greasy fat paw."

The convoy continued, roaring along the coast road. The Italians did not resist the Lothians' advance, and by the 9th of January, the British and Australian forces were thinly stretched around Tobruk's thirty-mile-long defensive perimeter.

"Another town, another battle, and another victory coming up," Tulloch said. "We're doing well so far. O'Connor has Graziani's measure."

"Maybe Graziani will send men to break the siege this time," Kinnear said. "He's got the 60th Sabratha Division at Derna, General Babini's armoured brigade at Mechili, and the 17th Pavia Division at Benghazi. This may be the battle where the Italians turn things around."

"You're a right ray of sunshine, you," Tulloch replied. "Have faith in the little white-haired terrier."

"After Dunkirk," Kinnear said. "I've no faith in any general."

"Then have faith in your own men," Tulloch replied quietly. He thought of Hogg and Innes. "Our lads are as good as any soldiers in the world."

"The Germans chased us out of Norway, Belgium, and France quickly enough," Kinnear said.

"And we'll be back to get them," Tulloch grated. "Buck up, man!"

The British quickly captured the airfield at El Adem,

relieving the worry of attack by Italian aircraft, and Tulloch took his carrier to the desert plateau overlooking Tobruk.

"That's the prettiest town I've seen since we arrived here, sir." Carnie, Tulloch's new driver, said.

Tulloch agreed. Tobruk spread over a rocky peninsula with the startling blue of the Mediterranean on three sides and a sheltered harbour able to accommodate sizeable ships. An Italian cruiser, *San Giorgio*, was aground in Tobruk harbour, unable to sail but with a battery of guns that would be a formidable addition to the town's firepower. "It will be a tough nut to crack," he said.

"The Terrier will find a way, sir," Carnie, an auburn-haired, cheerful man, said.

"I think you're right, Carnie," Tulloch agreed.

Once again, the capable Italian engineers had created formidable defences. The barbed wire ring was throat-high and augmented by two circles of concrete defence posts, with the outer around 700 yards and the inner 500 yards apart, each holding twenty men.

"Even if they fight like the Bardia Blackshirts, we'll still defeat them, sir," Carnie said. "Anyway, the Italian engineers haven't completed their anti-tank ditch, so the Mats will smash right through."

"The Mats?" Tulloch asked.

"The Matildas, sir," Carnie explained.

"Of course. Thank you, Carnie."

Tulloch sketched Tobruk's defences, concentrating on the sector the Lothians would be attacking. He brought back the information to the intelligence officer, who passed it to Colonel Pringle.

"Even incomplete, the ditch is still a formidable barrier for tanks," Pringle pointed to the ditch on his map as the assembled officers listened. "Especially since we must rely partly on captured Italian M11 and M13 medium tanks."

"How will we know which tanks are friendly, sir?" Tulloch asked. "Our anti-tank men will blast anything that looks Italian."

"The Aussie 6th Cavalry has sixteen Italian tanks," Pringle said. "We'll know them because the Australians have painted white kangaroos on them."

Tulloch nodded. "Let's hope our boys see them in time. I hope they are large kangaroos."

With most of his units surrounding Tobruk, O'Connor continued to build up his strike force for the assault. Until he was ready, he sent the engineers to mine the exit roads to the south to prevent the garrison from escaping or reinforcements from arriving.

"The Terrier doesn't take any chances," Kilner said. "The Italians must feel isolated unless Graziani sends out a relieving force."

"Graziani doesn't seem capable of doing that," Tulloch replied. "The Italians seem very defensively minded."

"Unlike General O'Connor," Kilner said. "He's called for offensive patrols around Tobruk. Some of the Australians have met severe resistance with trip wires, mines, and accurate machine gunning, so be careful when you go out."

"Am I going on patrol?" Tulloch asked.

"You are," Kilner told him. "You're taking three carriers."

Still angry at Brigadier Worthington's rebuke, the Lothians' officers were eager to prove themselves, volunteering to lead offensive patrols. Only Kinnear was quiet, claiming a bad dose of Gyppy Tummy.

"Don't take unnecessary risks," Pringle reminded. "The Italians still outnumber us, and every loss makes us weaker."

Tulloch led his three-carrier patrol that night, easing close to the escarpment before heading towards Tobruk's outer perimeter. He watched a unit of the 7th Armoured Division ascending the escarpment, with artillery gun tractors hauling some of the Matildas up the slope while others raced up with roaring engines and clouds of sand.

"You bloody fools!" A red-faced major shouted. "We're trying to save the tanks' engines, not wear the bloody things out!"

Hiding his smile, Tulloch turned away. He could appreciate the tank commander's impatience to move under their own power, but the major was correct. The shortage of tanks would only become more acute the further into Libya O'Connor pushed, and every vehicle was valuable.

"What's the plan, sir?" Carnie asked.

"We move forward in a vee formation," Tulloch missed Hardie's silent understanding of his techniques. "Chart the ground as we go; mark any enemy machine gun nests, possible minefields or other defensive features."

"Just a routine patrol, then," Carnie said.

"Exactly so," Tulloch agreed.

They moved forward into the gathering gloom, with the carriers' engines loud in the desert silence. Tulloch checked his watch.

Seven in the evening on the 10th of January 1941. I wonder what Amanda is doing now? I hope the Germans haven't bombed her out of wherever she is. I feel so useless away out here when Hitler and the Germans are the real threat. He called for a minor adjustment to their course. *The sooner we defeat the Italians in Africa, the quicker we can get at the Germans and to hell with Brigadier bloody Worthington.*

The landscape was featureless under the brilliant stars, with an occasional burst of machine gun fire or starshell to break the monotony. The wind whistled through the Italian barbed **wire**, a strangely melancholic sound that brought thoughts of the 1914-18 War to Tulloch's mind.

"Stop here," Tulloch ordered, holding up his hand to signal the following carriers. "We'll leave the drivers with the carriers and go forward on foot."

The men dismounted, allowing the sand to settle as they checked their weapons and readied themselves for the ordeal ahead. By now, the Lothians were well-versed in foot patrols in the desert.

They wore pullovers, shorts, and sandshoes for ease of movement. Tulloch had ensured each carrier held a bucket of mud to darken their faces and hands, for white skin gleamed in the dark. They carried no equipment that could catch or rattle, only their personal weapons and a handful of spare rounds stuffed into their shirt pockets. Tulloch led an intelligence-gathering patrol; he neither expected nor desired a prolonged firefight; any encounters with the Italians would be brief. The Lothians discarded their steel helmets in favour of woollen cap-comforters, partly because helmets could be conspicuous and reflect the light, but mainly because the wind could whistle on the overhanging helmet brim. Close to the Italian lines, the men depended on their hearing even more than sight.

Giving orders with silent hand signals, Tulloch led his men forward, watching for mines, hidden machine gun nests, and any Italian patrols. He moved slowly, careful of every step in case he triggered a booby trap, and with his compass in his hand to keep on course. They moved for thirty yards and stopped, lying in a circle, facing outward, and listening for the enemy for a quarter of an hour before moving again. Even the replacements were experts now, knowing that sound travelled far in the nighttime desert. Any human sound, the chink of metal equipment, a subdued cough, or a muttered command in Italian or English, would warn of a predatory patrol, Italian, Australian, or British. Tulloch checked his men for the stress of prolonged patrolling induced sleep, and these listening periods were dangerous for over-stretched men.

The patrol was intact, meeting Tulloch's gaze as he ordered them forward. They moved off again, carefully, for Tulloch knew the Italians had laid a minefield nearby. He dropped to a crawl, feeling the ground with his hands. The sand felt different here; it was more disturbed, as if somebody had been digging.

Holding up his hand, Tulloch stopped the patrol and made

the signal for mines. The men halted, and they began to probe the ground. Tulloch could sense the unease, for everybody was nervous about the unpredictability of anti-personnel mines.

"Sir!" Innes said. "Something's here. Anti-tank mine."

Anti-tank mines were triggered by the weight of a tank and, therefore, no danger to a foot patrol, but Tulloch was wary in case the Italian engineers had placed anti-personnel mines among the anti-tanks.

"Follow the edge of the minefield," he said, marking the position of the mines on his map. The men crawled across the ground, feeling in the sand with their bayonets, probing carefully and signalling to Tulloch whenever they found anything.

The cold wind lifted surface sand, stinging the men's faces and covering their tracks. Tulloch looked around the dark, featureless terrain, constantly checking his compass bearing to ensure he could return.

After an hour of careful searching and mapping, they reached an area of clear sand. *That's the edge of the minefield,* Tulloch decided, and thankfully stood up, stretching cramped muscles. He led them forward for another twenty yards, still probing the ground for mines.

The machine gun fire was close by, sudden and unexpected. Tulloch fell to the ground, with his men already there, automatically forming a defensive circle.

"Where?" Tulloch asked.

Elliot gestured with a nod, and Tulloch lifted his binoculars to scan the area. He saw the renewed muzzle flashes of a machine gun and then supporting barks of Italian rifles. None of the bullets came in the Lothians' direction.

"The Italians have seen a patrol," Tulloch murmured. "It's not us, though." He watched for a moment until he heard answering fire and saw the scattered flash of rifles. A Bren fired with its distinctive regular hammer.

There are no Lothians in that direction. An Australian patrol must have bumped the Italians.

"Come on, boys," Tulloch said, "we'll give the Aussies a hand." He crawled forward, keeping low in the gaps between the firing and moving when the gunfire covered them.

When he was within two hundred yards of the Italians, Tulloch raised his hand to halt his men. He lay still, counting the Italian defenders by their muzzle flashes.

"I see fifteen men," Tulloch whispered.

"I got eighteen," Innes said.

Tulloch nodded. "Form a circle for all-round defence. Innes, come to the front with your Bren, and Smith, I want you with the Boys as well. Elliot, bring spare ammunition for both."

Innes, Elliot, and Smith crawled to the front of the circle while the other men altered their positions to cover the resulting gaps.

A star shell zoomed above, exploding in a brilliant white flash, temporarily blinding Tulloch. He looked away, blinking, as the light slowly descended.

The firing began again, Australians and Italians fighting over a patch of African desert.

"Innes! Open fire!"

"I cannae see a bloody thing, sir!"

"I don't care! Fire towards the enemy! Aim for the noise!"

Innes's Bren fired with its regular hammer, reassuring in the eerie light. With his night vision destroyed, Tulloch hoped Innes's shots were damaging the Italians' position, not the Australians.

Caught in the flank, the Italians did not immediately respond, and Innes emptied an entire magazine without reply.

"Riflemen, keep them busy!" Tulloch ordered. He wished he had brought more ammunition but had not expected a prolonged battle with a machine gun nest. "Five rounds rapid!" The Lothians' riflemen fired, worked the bolts, and fired again, hopefully keeping the Italian machine gunner occupied within his concrete emplacement.

The Italian fire faltered and ended. When the Lothians

ceased fire, the silence seemed louder than the preceding gunfire.

"Who's that?" the Australian voice floated from the flank.

"Lothian Rifles!" Tulloch shouted back.

"Give us flanking fire!" The Australian roared, and moments later, Tulloch heard a prolonged cheer.

"Fire, lads!" Tulloch ordered, and the Bren and rifles opened up. "The Aussies are going in."

He heard renewed shouting, and the crump of a grenade, stood up, and charged forward. "Come on, Lothians! Support the Australians!"

By the time the Lothians reached the strongpoint, the fighting was over, with the Australians in control and the defenders either dead, fled, or prisoners.

"Thanks for your help, Scotties," a long-faced Australian captain said. He pushed back his bush hat with a thumb, eyeing Tulloch up and down.

"Our pleasure, Aussie," Tulloch replied. "Do you want a hand with the prisoners?"

"No, we can manage," the captain said. He looked up as an Italian machine gun in the second line of defence fired, spraying the perimeter with bullets. "We'd best get them back now. The Eyeties seem agitated tonight."

Artillery joined the machine gun, with shells exploding between the patrols and the British positions.

"They do seem agitated, don't they?" Tulloch tried to sound as nonchalant as the Australian.

A shell exploded thirty yards away, and when the smoke cleared, the Australians had gone.

"Good night, Aussies," Tulloch said and led his men back to the carriers.

"We heard shooting, sir," Carnie said.

"A skirmish with an outpost," Tulloch explained. "The Australians captured it."

Carnie grinned. "I'm glad the Aussies are on our side."

Tulloch thought of the laconic captain. "So am I," he admitted. "Take us home, Carnie."

That's another skirmish, a few more of the enemy out of the war and a tiny step closer to victory.

COLONEL PRINGLE LOOKED WEARY AS HE ADDRESSED HIS officers. "Here is the plan of attack, gentlemen," he said. "The 7th Armoured Division will create a diversion and contain the Italians in the west and south while the 6th Australian Division attacks the southeastern sector." He paused for a moment. "The 6th Australians will assault on a front of 800 yards; on the area our patrols have been probing and mapping the minefields."

"That's a very narrow front, sir," Hume said.

"It should mean strength in depth for the attacker," Pringle replied. "The 16th Australian Brigade will make the first assault, while the 17th Australian will demonstrate as a decoy by firing on the east. Once the 16th succeeds in the initial penetration, the 19th Australian Brigade and the tanks go in to deepen the assault."

"Where are we, sir?" Tulloch asked the question on everybody's mind.

"We go in with the 16th," Pringle said. "I want the minimum of casualties, so ensure everybody backs his colleagues." When the colonel looked over his officers, Tulloch knew he was wondering how many would still be alive the following night. "The best of luck to us all, gentlemen."

Chapter Twenty-Two

TOBRUK, LIBYA, JANUARY 1941

As January was the Khamsin month in Libya when the dust storms were nearly inevitable, nobody was surprised when the wind rose again on the 15th of the month. The Lothians wrapped towels around their faces, ducked their heads, and endured four days of sand-blasted torture when they could hardly see five yards.

"Come to sunny Africa," Kinnear said. "See the exotic wildlife of flies and scorpions, view the pyramids of sandbags around machine gun nests, and get blinded by the bloody dust."

Tulloch grunted. "It will pass. In time, everything passes."

"I wish this bloody sandstorm would bloody pass," Atkins said. "I used to think Portobello beach was bad on a windy day."

After four days of torment, the wind eased, and preparations for the attack continued. The RAF appeared, with Blenheims and Wellingtons roaring overhead to drop twenty tons of bombs by night and more by day. The Italian anti-aircraft gunners fired madly into the sky, hitting nothing as the Lothians watched the display from afar.

"Aye," Hogg said. "You couldnae hit a bull's erse with a banjo."

Nobody smiled at the worn-out joke. The men only hoped the bombs softened the Italian defences.

While the RAF controlled the sky, the Royal Navy added its quota of mayhem by sea. The monitor HMS *Terror* fired her fifteen-inch guns against the Italian positions, with gunboats coming closer inshore to hammer at the garrison and further lower their morale.

"Everybody's having a go at the Eyeties," Atkins said. "Poor old Mussolini must be wondering what's happening to his empire."

Erskine chuckled and lit a cigarette. "Don't you worry about him," he said. "Mussolini got the trains to run on time. The papers said so, so it must be true."

"Tobruk's garrison must be wishing there was a train to take them to Benghazi," Tulloch replied.

On the night of the 20th, as the RAF and Royal Navy continued to pound Tobruk, the Lothians moved forward to the start lines, where the 16th Australian Brigade was already in position. Tulloch felt the same subdued tension mixed with excitement and apprehension, yet something was different. He looked around Four Platoon, realising the men anticipated victory. They had accepted that O'Connor led them to success after success and trusted in the professionalism of his army.

"Here we are again," Atkins said.

"Once more into the breach," Tulloch agreed. He heard Sergeant Drysdale, an old soldier and a veteran of the Great War, muttering a refrain from that conflict.

"We're here because we're here, because we're here, because we're here." Drysdale glanced over the platoon and altered his chant. "We had a barney at Sidi Barrani, and here we are again!"

Hogg stamped his feet, spat on the ground, and glared forward while Elliot checked his spare Bren Gun magazines, and Innes intoned a quiet prayer.

The minute hand moved around the face of Tulloch's watch, remorselessly marking down the last few moments before the assault. 05:38. 05:39, and then the final jerking movement.

"05:40, boys!" Tulloch raised his voice. "Here we go!"

The Australians and Lothians moved forward in tandem, with supporting artillery firing overhead and the outer defences revealed by the bright, intermittent flashes of bursting shells.

Tulloch checked his platoon. "Don't bunch!" he snapped. "McAllister, get your bayonet on! Keep your distance and follow me!"

He stepped forward, with the surge of adrenaline conquering his fear, hearing his men padding behind him. An Italian shell burst nearby, with the momentary flash of flame and smoke lifting a fountain of sand, and then he was moving faster, trying not to run so his men remained together.

We have five hundred yards to the barbed wire. I hope the artillery keeps the Italian machine gunners under cover.

Australian engineers worked at the wire with Bangalore torpedoes and wire cutters. They scurried back as an Australian officer fired a red Very light, which soared upward, exploded in the air, and drifted slowly downwards. The harsh light reflected from coiled barbed wire and threw the landscape into sharp focus. Tulloch saw a thin scatter of khaki-clad officers marching in front of bayonet-wielding infantrymen.

The engineers lit the fuses of the Bangalores and hurriedly withdrew. Tulloch saw the fuses spluttering, and then the Bangalores exploded in red and white fury, ripping the wire apart.

"Come on, lads!" Tulloch sped up progress, running for the newly created gaps in the wire before the Italian machine gunners realised what was happening. Four Platoon followed, some men gasping with nerves or effort, others silent except for the pad of boots on the sand.

On the left, where the 16th Australian Brigade was advancing, somebody tripped a wire, and the resulting explosion decimated a platoon, leaving dead and dying men on the blood-soaked sand. Badly wounded men squealed, and others writhed in soundless agony.

"Push on, you bastards!" An Australian officer ordered. "The medical orderlies will care for them."

An Italian heavy machine gun rattled ahead, and spurts of sand showed where the bullets ploughed into the ground. An Italian bugle blared brassily, and somewhere, a man was screaming high-pitched, but whether Australian, Italian, or Scottish, Tulloch did not know. The Lothians' pipers began their battle music, with *Flowers of Edinburgh* sounding above the mayhem.

The Lothians eased through the cut wire as the British barrage crept forward, concentrating on the forward Italian positions as the Australians and Lothians approached. Tulloch emerged from the wire and saw a group of Australians on his right. During the battle for Bardia, the Australians had advanced with full equipment, including a long greatcoat and fifty pounds of sundries. Now, like the Lothians, they were more lightly laden with only leather jerkins over their uniforms, a haversack, and personal weapons. They loped forward, looking very professional as they covered the ground.

Well done, Aussies. You've learned fast.

The Australians and Lothians ran forward, spreading out when they breached the wire.

"Come on, you bastards!" An Australian sergeant shouted.

"Gin ye daur!" Captain Kilner shouted.

"The Gorgie boys are here!" Hogg added his unique contribution to the noise.

Confused by the bombardment and the speed of the advance, the Italians in the forward defence posts offered little resistance. A 12.7-millimetre heavy machine gun fired for a few seconds until Sergeant Drysdale threw a grenade that exploded a few feet away. Tulloch heard screams. Hogg scrambled into the machine gun nest, and the screams ended.

Tulloch leapt over the concrete wall of the nearest gun pit

with half his platoon at his back. Three Italian gunners rushed to the 47 mm M35 anti-tank gun; one reached for a pistol as the other two stared in horror at the bayonet-wielding Lothians.

"Aye, would you?" Hogg thrust his bayonet at the man with the pistol, forcing him to raise his hands. The other two Italians followed, and within a minute, Four Platoon had a score of prisoners and control of the gun pit.

"McAllister!" Tulloch said. "Escort these men back and rejoin the platoon." He moved on, knowing he could not afford to send many men back with the prisoners.

The loss of even a single man diminishes us as a fighting unit.

"Press on, boys!" Tulloch said. He heard machine guns and a strange rattling from the Lothians' left flank. "What the hell is that?" He looked over his shoulder, half expecting some devilish new Italian invention.

"It's our armour creating a diversion," Major Hume shouted. "They're beating up the Italians all along the perimeter and dragging hundreds of tin cans to make as much noise as possible."

Tulloch grinned with relief. "I don't know if they're confusing the Italians, but they're certainly confusing me!"

An Italian shell exploded behind the Lothians and another in front, sending up fountains of dust and small stones. Kinnear threw himself down, lay on the ground for a few moments, and rose when the shelling stopped.

"Push on!" Hume ordered. "Push on, Lothians, Gin ye daur!"

The Australians made good progress, advancing with an élan that Tulloch admired.

An hour after the initial assault, the attackers had captured five of the Italian strongpoints and thrust a wedge deep into Tobruk's defences. The supporting tanks followed, together with the supporting 2/1st Australians.

"Here comes the armour!" Pringle shouted. "Stand clear, Lothian Rifles!"

Small parties of engineers ran in front of the tanks, lifting the anti-tank mines that Australian and Lothian patrols had discovered. More engineers feverishly filled in the anti-tank ditches, and the Lothians stood back as the tanks came through their ranks.

One engineer ran ahead, shovel in hand, searching for the anti-tank ditch.

"Where is the bloody ditch? I can't see a thing in the dark!" The engineer's voice ended in a sharp yell. "Found it! Can some bastard help me out of this bloody ditch?"

The noise of the tanks, easily heard in the dark, attracted Italian attention, and the Lothians ducked as machine gun bullets and an occasional anti-tank shell kicked up sand around them.

"Get these tanks away from here!" Colonel Pringle yelled as Italian artillery joined the fire. "You're endangering my men!"

The tank commander stared at Pringle, ducked as a shell exploded twenty yards away, and nodded. "We're moving! We can't advance until the engineers fill the ditch!" He yelled instructions. "Driver! Left, left, left!" The Matilda slowly swung round, with shells creeping gradually closer. When the Matilda faced the direction it had come, Tulloch expected the tank to drive back towards the baseline, but instead, the commander continued with the same orders.

"What the hell are you doing?" Colonel Pringle asked. "Get your blasted tank away from my men!"

"If I go back," the tank commander explained, "the Aussies will think I'm Italian, and our own tanks will fire at me. It's safer out there!" He gestured towards Tobruk.

"Well, go then!" Colonel Pringle said. He stood erect as a shell exploded twenty yards away.

Tulloch watched as the tank completed a full circle. "Driver, advance!" the commander said and rattled on, away from the Lothians as it powered towards the Italian positions.

"I hope you fall in a ditch!" Elliot shouted.

"More tanks, sir!" Atkins reported, and the Lothians kept out of the way as another sixteen British tanks pushed through the gaps in the wire and headed right and left. Italian shells and machine guns probed for the armour, blasting at the weary sand.

"Push through!" Colonel Pringle ordered. "On to Tobruk!"

The Lothians helped clear the inner ring of defences with Bren guns, grenades, and the bayonet. One defence post held back the Australians for twenty minutes, only capitulating when the attackers poured in oil and kerosene and set it ablaze. The shocked survivors surrendered, and the Australian advance continued.

"These Aussies know how to fight," Major Hume approved.

The Italians fought well, defending their posts against tanks, Australians, and artillery, but the attackers overcame the defensive positions one by one. By the end of that first long day, the Australians and Lothians had regrouped inside the Italian lines, with British tanks and artillery hammering at the Italians in the town of Tobruk.

Tulloch saw his men sink onto the sand, all exhausted, one or two with minor wounds, all filthy with gunsmoke, sweat, and sand.

"Any casualties?" Tulloch counted his men. "Where's Brodie?"

"He copped a wound, sir," Sergeant Drysdale replied. "Shrapnel from an artillery shell."

Tulloch grunted. "Is it serious?"

"I'm not sure, sir," Drysdale said. "There was a lot of blood on his tunic."

I'll check on him later. Rifleman Brodie had survived the fighting in Belgium and the retreat to Dunkirk. Tulloch hoped he was not seriously hurt.

When night fell, the attackers consolidated their gains while officers consulted their maps, hurriedly marking the positions of each unit in preparation for the following days' action.

"How many men did we lose?" Colonel Pringle asked.

"Two killed, three wounded, one dangerously," Muirhead replied. "A small price for such gains."

"A big price for the casualties and their families," Pringle said.

He began to fill his pipe. "I hope the garrison surrenders without any more fighting."

Tobruk shuddered under the British shellfire, with the orange-yellow flare of explosions making the night hideous. Tulloch thought of Amanda in London as German bombs fell.

Keep safe, Amanda, please God, keep her safe.

Tulloch checked Four Platoon, ensuring they were fed, watered, and had sufficient ammunition. "Keep alert, boys," he said. "The Italians might send out patrols tonight."

Innes nodded while Hogg sharpened his already sharp bayonet.

"Sergeant Drysdale," Tulloch said. "Put four men on stag."

"Yes, sir," Drysdale replied without emotion. *He knows his job without me telling him.*

Only a few hundred yards in front of the Australians and Lothians, yet hidden by the dark, the Italians waited within the inner defences. Tobruk was the prize, and the two armies rested for the next round. While the Italians were punch drunk and with failing morale, O'Connor's thirty thousand were elated with a string of victories but with stretched supply lines and a growing casualty list in men and vehicles.

Tulloch slept fitfully, started a letter to Amanda, found he could not concentrate, and checked his platoon. Most of the men were asleep, with the sentries watchful, holding their bayo-netted rifles and waiting for the dawn.

Tulloch reread the last letter Amanda had sent and thought again of the German bombing of London. He imagined the horror of being a civilian under a rain of bombs, of the screams and agony and terror, and wished he were closer to her.

Not that I could help any, but being thousands of miles away, on different continents, makes things worse. Wars should not involve civil-ians. Only professional soldiers should fight when politicians make a mess of their jobs. Or better, let the politicians fight it out. Tulloch shook his head. *We cannot lose this war. We are a force for good, and we're facing the dark hordes of evil. We must win this war.*

Tulloch stared into the darkness towards Tobruk. *If we take Tobruk and push the Italians to Benghazi, that's a good start. We must win tomorrow.* He clutched Amanda's letter in his hand, picturing her face and knew he was fighting for her as much as for any idea of democracy or national pride.

Chapter Twenty-Three

The dawn of the 22nd of January broke with a vivid red band across the eastern horizon. Tulloch drew on his pipe, lifted his binoculars, and studied the town of Tobruk with its neat white buildings. The vivid flash of an explosion destroyed the fragile placidity of the scene.

"Something's happening over there."

Captain Kilner nodded. "I can hear gunfire from the left and on the west."

"We're only in support, gentlemen," Pringle reminded. "We wait for orders."

"I can't see what's happening," Tulloch said, turning his binoculars left and right. He saw a few explosions and columns of rising dust and smoke.

"That will be the 7th Armoured Division hammering at the western defences of Tobruk," Pringle said.

"Knowing 7th Armoured, they'll kick the gate down without handing the butler a calling card," Tulloch said grimly.

Pringle smiled. "You may be correct, Lieutenant. We can rely on Seven Div. to do their duty."

The Lothians waited in frustration as the British tanks smashed through Tobruk's western perimeter defences and poured towards the centre of the town.

"We're the gooseberry again," Erskine said. "Always the bridesmaid and never the bride."

Tulloch stood on top of a Bren carrier and focused on Tobruk, trying to follow the armour's progress by the smoke and explosions. "If Seven Div. carries on like that, they'll capture Tobruk on their own."

"Sir!" the battalion signaller ran to the colonel. "There's a message for you, sir!"

Colonel Pringle followed as quickly as his dignity permitted. He returned a few moments later.

"We're moving, gentlemen! Our orders are to advance in support of the Sixteenth Australian Brigade."

The officers scattered to their respective companies and platoons, happy to be doing something worthwhile.

The Sixteenth Australian Brigade pushed through Tobruk's inner defences to the northwest, with the Lothians a few hundred yards behind. Tulloch and the officers marched before their men, waiting to support the Australians if they met serious resistance.

An Italian 75/27 gun opened up, sending shells towards the Australian infantry, which immediately spread out and attacked on both flanks. After ten minutes, the Australians had rounded up the gunners and moved on, with the Lothians not involved.

"Always the bridesmaid," Erskine repeated his earlier words.

"Maybe later," Atkins said. "The bride must throw her bouquet over her shoulder, remember, and we're here to catch it."

"Very good, Atkins," Erskine said, with his cigarette holder thrust elegantly into his mouth. "If you don't manage to make a soldier, you can start a career as a comedian."

The advance continued, with the Australian 2/4th Battalion

and a troop of Matilda tanks thrusting into the centre of Tobruk and the Lothians at the rear without seeing any action.

"Press on!" Tulloch ordered Four Platoon as the Italians withdrew or surrendered to the Australian infantry and British armour. The less stubborn defenders emerged from hiding places, seemingly happy to give themselves up, abandoning strong positions and handing over their weapons.

Six hours after dawn, the Lothians entered the centre of Tobruk without firing a shot. Everywhere they looked, small parties of Australians probed into houses searching for stray Italians, and British tanks roared around bearing large Italian flags they had captured. Dense black smoke rose from oil tanks that the Italians had set on fire to deny the contents to the victors. In the harbour, the damaged cruiser *San Giorgio* was ablaze, alongside a couple of merchant ships and a stranded Italian submarine.

"Well, that was easy," Captain Kilner said, replacing his unused revolver in its holster.

"General O'Connor's winning this war," Tulloch said. "With the Australians."

We can defeat the Italians, but are we ready to face the Germans yet?

Columns of Italian prisoners marched cheerfully into captivity, with an Italian admiral in white gloves smoking a cigar and with his suitcases ready packed for the POW cage. In front of the naval barracks, a group of Australian soldiers dragged down the Italian flag and, lacking an Australian flag, hauled up a bush hat instead.

"It seems that Australia has taken over Tobruk," Kilner said quietly.

"It seems so," Tulloch agreed. "Will O'Connor stop here, do you think?"

Kilner shook his head. "No. O'Connor is a wee terrier. He'll push on until no more Italians are in North Africa."

And every mile stretches our supply lines and gives us more territory to patrol and defend with diminishing forces.

"He'd better get his foot on the accelerator then," Erskine said. "I heard a whisper that Churchill wants to send more men and aircraft to help the Greeks."

"Where are we going to get them from?" Tulloch asked. "Make them out of sand? We're already outnumbered and over-stretched."

"Maybe so," Erskine replied, nodding towards the west. "Maybe our Winnie thinks we've already won this campaign."

"There's a long way to go yet," Tulloch replied. "If we push Mussolini too far, Hitler is bound to interfere, and we know what his army is capable of."

"We outfought him in France," Kilner said. "If the French had held, we'd have won that campaign, and we'd be fighting in Germany now unless Hitler had already thrown in the towel."

"Maybe," Tulloch said. "Maybe." He remembered the nerve-shattering scream of the Stukas and the way the Germans had outmanoeuvred the allies, the murderous brutality of the SS and the terrified columns of civilian refugees.

Kilner eyed him curiously. "Do you think the Germans are better soldiers than us?"

Tulloch considered the question. "No. I do think they're more single-minded and better prepared for modern war. Too many of our senior officers believed they were fighting the last war and didn't allow for the mobility and speed armies are capable of now."

Kilner lit a cigarette and pushed back his steel helmet. "O'Connor doesn't seem to be one of them," he said.

Tulloch nodded. "Amen to that." Both men looked up when an excited Corporal Borthwick ran to them, hastily saluted, and spoke to Tulloch.

"Sir!" the corporal shouted. "Look what we've found!"

A lorry lurched around the corner with Corporal Borthwick at the wheel. It pulled up in front of Tulloch, and a grinning Elliot hauled back the cover.

"What do you think of this as a prize of war, sir?" Elliot

asked.

Half a dozen women looked out at the gathered Lothian infantrymen.

"What the hell?" Tulloch asked.

"Women, sir," Elliot said. "Do we get to keep them?"

"I can see they're women," Tulloch snapped. "No, we don't get to keep them. What the hell have they got to do with us?"

"We captured them, sir," Elliot explained, grinning. "They're Italian women, something to do with the garrison."

"And nothing to do with us," Tulloch said. "Let them go."

"We can't, sir," Elliot said. "The town's in an uproar with all the Arabs and whatnots looting the Italian houses and unexploded bombs and shells littering the place. These poor ladies would be in danger."

Tulloch sighed. There was a lot of truth in Elliot's words, for many of the Italian and some of the British shells had failed to explode, so until the engineers rendered them safe, they posed a threat to anybody who came close.

"What the hell do you expect me to do with these women?" Tulloch asked.

"We'll take care of them, sir," Elliot promised. "They'll be safe with us."

Tulloch glanced at the women. They were laughing with the British soldiers, seeming not in the least upset by the change in men. "No," he decided. "They'll be anything but safe with you." He thought of the various sexual diseases such women might carry and his men ending up in the base hospital. "Corporal!"

Corporal Borthwick slammed to attention. "Sir!"

"Take these women to the Provost Sergeant and let him deal with them. We can't have them wandering around Tobruk unescorted, and we can't care for them."[1]

"Very good, sir!" Borthwick hid his evident disappointment.

"Elliot, you think you know about women. Go with the corporal and ensure they behave themselves."

"Yes, sir," Elliot saluted and jumped in the back of the truck. "Now, then, you lucky ladies. I'll look after you."

Kilner drew on his cigarette as the lorry drove away, with the women on the back waving and shouting comments to every soldier they passed. "Now there's a load of trouble. You made the correct choice, Tulloch; the sooner the navy evacuates that lot, the better for everybody's peace of mind."

"I hope the Provost Sergeant knows what to do with them," Tulloch said, smiling.

"He can do whatever he likes as long as the women are not near us," Kilner replied.

Corporal Borthwick had hardly left when Tulloch heard a screech of brakes and angry, upraised voices.

"What the hell is it now?" Tulloch asked.

"You'd best go and sort it out," Kilner said, smiling.

Tulloch nodded and strode towards the noise. As he turned a corner, he saw a group of Australians surrounding the lorry. Elliot, with his chin thrust out, challenged them as he defended his prize.

"One Scottie doesn't need all these Sheilas," a lanky Australian said. "Share them with us."

"Two Scotties," the corporal joined Elliot. "Get out of our way, or we'll drive right through you."

"There's more of us than you, mate," the lanky Australian said.

"Aye, but we're the Lothians," Elliot said. "Get out of our road!"

"What's all this?" Tulloch knew he could not depend on his rank to overawe Australians.

"These Aussies want our women, sir," Elliot reported.

Tulloch counted seven Australians, all mature, tough-looking men. "We are taking the women to the Provost Sergeant," he explained. "Now stand aside and let us be on our way."

In reply, the lanky Australian threw a punch that Tulloch only blocked with difficulty. Although it was against all the rules, instinct took over, and he retaliated with a right cross that landed squarely on the Australian's jaw.

Within a second, the other Australians joined in, and Elliot and Corporal Borthwick leapt from the truck to complete the riot.

"Gin ye daur!" Borthwick yelled as he kicked with his heavy boots.

Tulloch heard the women squealing encouragement, although he did not know which side, if any, they supported. Outnumbered two-to-one, things might have gone badly for the Lothians if a staff car had not roared, pennants fluttering, down the street.

Tulloch had time for one glance, saw Brigadier Worthington's startled face in the back of the car and realised he faced a court-martial and instant dismissal if he was caught brawling.

"Into the lorry, boys, and drive like the wind!"

Borthwick landed a final kick at an Australian and jumped into the driver's seat while Elliot and Tulloch clambered into the back of the truck.

As the lorry lurched off, Tulloch saw the Australians surrounding the staff car. He decided it could not have happened to a better brigadier, so he lay back and closed his eyes.

What the hell was I thinking, punching a private soldier? I'll lose my commission, and Worthington will have another excuse to dislike the Lothians.

Tulloch realised that his head was resting on the smooth thighs of a chattering woman, and his legs were across the plump breasts of another. He struggled up, saw Elliot was watching him through curious eyes, and straightened his cap, which had miraculously remained on his head.

"Corporal!" Tulloch moved to the front of the truck and leaned over. "Take us to the Provost Sergeant as quickly as you can."

"Right away, sir," Borthwick said. He glanced over his

shoulder at Tulloch. "That was a beautiful punch, sir. Were you ever a boxer?"

"Go to the Provost Sergeant, Borthwick, and don't ask foolish questions."

"Yes, sir," Borthwick said, concentrating on driving, yet Tulloch saw his eyes watching, wondering who his officer might be.

What the hell have I done?

———

"IT's NOW SIX WEEKS SINCE WE BEGAN THIS OFFENSIVE," Colonel Pringle said. "In that time, we have pushed the Italians out of Egypt, penetrated deep into Libya, and won three significant victories."

The officers nodded, waiting for the long-winded colonel to reach the point.

"The Lothians have played their part nobly and with honour," Pringle continued. "But General O'Connor is not yet finished. Tobruk is not our final destination but only a launch pad for the next stage in our advance."

"What's next, sir?" Hume asked, the crucial question so often that Tulloch believed the colonel had primed him in advance.

"General O'Connor plans a double advance for the next stage," Pringle said. "The 6th Australian Division will move along the coast road towards Derna, and the 7th Armoured Division will trek across country to Mechili."

"Are we still with the Australians, sir?" Hume asked.

"We are," Pringle said.

"Is there any news of reinforcements for the army yet, sir?" Captain Kilner asked.

"Not a whisper," Pringle replied. "I have only heard hearsay reports of some of our force being transferred to Greece and Germans arriving in Libya to stiffen the Italians." All the officers had heard similar rumours, but when the colonel's words put substance into the stories, Tulloch saw men stirring uneasily at the prospect of O'Connor's army bleeding more men while the enemy reinforced.

"There we have it, gentlemen," Pringle said quietly. "The sooner we kick Mussolini out of Africa, the quicker we can form true defensive positions to defeat Hitler's fresh troops."

"O'Connor isn't afraid to take risks," Major Hume approved. "It looks like he's heading for Benghazi."

Tulloch agreed as Colonel Pringle ended the meeting, and the officers returned to their duties.

"We're in a race," Tulloch said to Kinnear. "We must eject the Italians before the Germans arrive. If we control the entire Egyptian and Libyan coast, the Germans won't have a decent harbour to land their men."

"As long as we have the manpower to stop them," Kinnear added. "If Churchill strips us of men for Greece, we can't defeat Mussolini's boys and defend such a long coast."

"We'll have to move fast, then," Tulloch said.

"We will," Kinnear agreed and shrugged. "Unless the Germans land in Vichy French-controlled Tunisia or Algeria, of course."

"Of course," Tulloch agreed. "I doubt even the Little White-Haired Terrier could stretch thirty thousand men to control the entire North African coast."

As always, O'Connor's advance began with administrative confusion as the different units were resupplied and given their objectives. The 19th Australian Brigade was pulled out of Tobruk, with the Lothians again in a supporting role.

"We're eating Australian dust again," Hogg said as the convoy of mixed British and captured Italian trucks grumbled along the coastal road with the Mediterranean brilliant blue to the north. Innes was on guard with the Bren gun, watching for enemy aircraft.

"Good," Elliot said. "Let the Aussies do the fighting, and we'll have the wine and women."

Corporal Borthwick grunted. "Have you not had enough of women, Elliot? All they bring is trouble."

"I can never get enough women," Elliot said, "and they can never get enough of me."

Hogg favoured Elliot with a malevolent glare. "Bugger that," he said, without explaining to whom or what he referred.

The Lothians reached Martuba, passing a couple of broken-down tanks with fitters working furiously on repairs. Tulloch stared over the seemingly limitless landscape and wondered how to find sufficient fuel for all the vehicles.

"I hear we've less than fifty cruiser tanks left," Kinnear said, "and less than a hundred lights. O'Connor's having to reorganise 7th Armoured to spread them around."

"Seventh Armour will keep going," Tulloch said. "They'll bash on even if they have to lift the tanks and carry them on their backs."

Kinnear looked away. "Our lines are already too extended," he said. "We should stop now and consolidate, especially if the rumours about the Germans are correct."

"I don't agree," Tulloch said. "If we stop, we'll give the enemy time to regroup."

The Australians continued their advance, with the Lothians following deeper into Libya. On the 22nd of January 1941, the 7th Armoured Brigade encountered Italian artillery outside Martuba. They were on the main coast road west, and strong infantry forces supported the Italian guns. After an initial skirmish, the tanks withdrew to pass on the information.

"We're moving forward, gentlemen!" Colonel Pringle announced with some satisfaction. "Seventh Armour has bumped into the enemy at Martuba, and we're ordered to clear the way."

The 6th Australian Division motored on, with medium

machine gunners, artillery, and engineers, backing A Squadron of the 6th Cavalry. The Lothians were in support, ready to exploit any breakthrough. Tulloch glanced over his platoon as they sat in the back of fifteen-hundredweight trucks with Bren guns prepared for any Italian aircraft. They looked professional, hard-faced veterans.

"Are we the only infantry support?" Kinnear asked as the Lothians eased across the desert with its camel scrub and stinging sand.

"No, the 19th Brigade is close behind," Muirhead replied. He grinned. "We're going to take Derna."

"That's a bit ambitious," Kinnear glanced at the map.

"Not for O'Connor," Muirhead said. "We've found ourselves a thrusting general, gentlemen. Mussolini and Hitler had better watch out!"

While the armour powered across the interior, the Australians and Lothians followed the coast road, passing through Gazala and Martuba. They advanced on Derna and gradually pushed back Italian resistance as they probed the town's outer defences.

"We're still in reserve," Hume said. "The Australians are having all the fun!"

"It's a team effort," Colonel Pringle rebuked him mildly. "We'll get our chance, never fear."

"This campaign is moving so quickly, sir, that I wonder if we will," Hume said.

While the Lothians fretted in frustration behind the Australians, the 7th Armoured Brigade skirmished with the Italians, advancing to within ten miles of Derna. The news came in daily and almost hourly as the 6th Australian cavalry grabbed Martuba airfield without much difficulty. The 6th Cavalry advance was so rapid that an Italian aircraft landed, thinking their countrymen still controlled the airfield, only for the crew to find themselves prisoners of war.

"Are we part of this war?" Atkins asked as the Lothians trailed in the Australians' wake.

"Only marginally, it seems," Tulloch replied. "Brigadier Worthington, or somebody on the staff, doesn't seem to trust us much."

"Our turn will come," Colonel Pringle said. "Bide your time, gentlemen."

Hume exchanged glances with Muirhead and said nothing.

The Lothians bivouacked in the lee of a rocky ridge and listened as the 1st Royal Tanks, backed by field guns, attacked an Italian position at Siret el Chrieba. Tulloch and Atkins clambered to the top of the ridge and watched the action through their binoculars.

The Italians held an impressive blockhouse near an airfield, greeting the British tanks with artillery and machine guns.

"I'll be an old man before we get into action," Atkins grumbled.

Tulloch grunted. "O'Connor will need us before this war is finished," he said. "Not even Australians can fight forever."

When the Royal Tanks captured the blockhouse and hammered the airfield, sending many Italians into retreat, the Australians took over the fighting. No sooner had the smoke from the initial battle cleared than a couple of Australian carrier groups drove around the airfield.

The Italian artillery must have been waiting, for as soon as the carriers appeared, they opened accurate fire, forcing them to withdraw and leaving one carrier a burning wreck.

"They might need us at Siret el Chrieba," Atkins said hopefully.

"We'd best return to the battalion," Tulloch replied.

When they reached the camp, the battalion was preparing to leave. The Lothians boarded their trucks, checked their ammunition, and prepared to move to the front.

"Ready, Four Platoon?" Tulloch asked. He felt a sense of anticipation mingled with natural trepidation.

"We're ready, sir," Sergeant Drysdale replied. "Here's the adjutant now."

"Debus, lads," Muirhead ordered quietly. "We're not needed."

Or not wanted, Tulloch thought.

The Lothians left the trucks as the 19th Australian Brigade motored past, giving raucous comments. Within an hour, Tulloch heard the rattle of rifles and the sinister brr of machine guns as the Australians and Italians fought for control of the airfield.

"We could move forward and help the Australians, sir," Tulloch suggested as the firing continued.

Colonel Pringle bit deeply onto the stem of his pipe. "No, Tulloch. We obey orders. We might get ourselves involved in a firefight and take casualties, then be ordered to another sector of the front."

"Yes, sir." Tulloch listened as the firing rose to a crescendo and died away. He knew the Australians had overcome the Italian resistance to take over the airfield.

The Lothians waited in increasing frustration as the Australians advanced, overcoming strongpoint after strongpoint with battalions leapfrogging each other, and the Italians retaliating with accurate artillery fire. Some older veterans accepted the situation philosophically, playing cards during the halts and enjoying the peace.

"Relax, lads," Innes said. "Every day that passes, we're pushing Mussolini back, so every day we're nearer the end of the war."

"Roll on demob," Elliot said.

The Lothians halted on a ridge overlooking Derna, where an artillery Forward Observation Officer (FOO) lay among rocks, scanning the town for military targets. The men left the lorries and prepared the ground, with officers and NCOs ordering defensive positions, latrines, and cookhouses.

"Sir!" The Lothian's radio operator shouted to the colonel. "The brigadier's on the radio for you."

Pringle nearly ran to the radio and spoke for five minutes as the FOO gave instructions that saw shells explode around Derna's defences.

"Don't get too settled, gentlemen!" Pringle said when he returned. "We're going forward in an hour!"

"At last!" Hume said and issued a string of orders that had the men folding up camouflage nets and filing back into the trucks.

"Bugger this for a game of soldiers!" Hogg said. "Do these officers know what they're doing?"

After days of enforced idleness while the Australians fought on, the Lothians checked their rifles, stamped their boots, and readied for battle.

Tulloch walked with Muirhead to check his men, knowing they were all desert-hardened veterans and needed little supervision. As he neared Four Platoon, he heard Elliot's voice raised in argument.

"I was there in Tobruk, and Tullie was like a fighting fury, I tell you," Elliot said. "This massive great Aussie, six foot six if he was an inch and built like the side of a barn, stormed up to Tullie, shouting the odds. 'I'm taking all the women,' the Aussie says. 'No, you arenae,' Tulley replied. 'They're oor women,' and he belts the Aussie one right in the kisser."

"What happened then?" Hogg asked.

"We all piled in until some red-tabbed bigwig rolled up in his fancy car, and we pulled out, sharpish, with the Aussies lying on the road and Tullie cuddling half the women in Africa."

Tulloch heard the garbled account of his encounter in Tobruk with some dismay.

"It's all right, Tulloch," Muirhead sounded amused. "The Jocks like their officers to have some personality, and you've certainly achieved that." He grinned. "Well done; you'll be a regimental legend if you live to survive the war."

"I don't want to be a legend," Tulloch said.

Muirhead laughed. "Too late, old man. You've already taken the first step."

29th OF JANUARY 1941

Tulloch felt the old familiar mixture of dread and excitement as the column of trucks roared toward Derna. He saw smoke rising from around the town and heard the irregular crashing of exploding shells.

Here we go again, he told himself and began to hum his old school song, wondering if he was committing treason by repeating the old Latin phrases while fighting an Italian enemy.

"Vivas Schola Edinensis,
Schola Regia venerabilis,"

The Italians seemed determined to hold Derna, shelling the advancing troops with medium and heavy artillery.

"We're going to have to fight our way in!" Major Hume shouted as the Lothians left their vehicles and spread out in the surprisingly fertile countryside. Italian shells exploded around the palm-tree-lined road, blowing smoke and sand into the Lothians' faces. They advanced steadily in extended order with bayonets fitted, listening to the chatter of a British Vickers machine gun as the Northumberland Fusiliers put down covering fire.

Colonel Pringle led from the front, a slim, elegant figure looking more like an Edwardian gentleman than a fighting soldier as he clenched his pipe firmly between his teeth.

An Italian machine gun chattered, kicking up dust and knocking a Rifleman to the ground. The battalion took cover behind a sangar wall and returned fire with rifles and Bren guns.

"Musso must like this place," Innes said, clipping a fresh magazine in place. "He's fighting hard."

"He's got his wine store here," Connington said. "He knows what a bunch of thieving buggers the Lothians are and wants to keep us out."

"It's no' his wine," Elliot said predictably. "It's his women. Mussolini's got a harem here."

"You hope so!" Innes replied, firing a short burst at the Italian machine gun.

One Italian defence post proved stubborn, but Erskine led a section forward and disposed of the defenders with grenades and bayonets. The Lothians advanced further, moving from house to house. It was a style of fighting that seemed novel after the great spaces of the desert.

"Look here, lads!" Connington pointed to a poster of Mussolini that decorated a house wall. "Here's el Ducky."

"My ma would have liked that in her kitchen," Hogg said. "If she was alive."

As evening fell, the Australians and British pushed into Derna's suburbs, found shelter, and waited.

"Shall I take a patrol forward, sir?" Tulloch asked.

"No. Sit still. Watch for Italian raids; they know the town better than we do."

The Lothians heard heavy engine noises during the night and prepared for an Italian counter-attack, but dawn revealed an empty town.

"They've bugged out!" Erskine announced when he returned from a patrol. "We've taken Derna!"

That's another step towards defeating Hitler, Tulloch thought. *And I never fired a shot.*

COMPARED TO THE GRIM DESERTS OF THE PAST MONTH, DERNA was a fertile oasis. The Italian colonists had greatly improved the town, with lovely houses within watered green gardens, palm-tree-lined streets, and fresh vegetables thrusting from well-cared-for lawns.

The Lothians looked around appreciatively.

"This is all right," Innes said. "I could do with a bit of this for a while."

Hogg pointed to a poster of Mussolini that decorated a wall. "There's another portrait of El Duckie," he said. "That man gets everywhere."

"Il Duce," Cummings corrected Hogg's pronunciation.

"He's a daisy, he's a duckie, he's a lamb," Hogg quoted Kipling. "If I want to call him a duckie, I'll call him a bloody duckie." He glowered at Cummings.

"I've always thought Mussolini was a duckie," Elliot said. "Or something like that."

Hogg's more obscene interpretation caused his colleagues to smile and add insults that Mussolini would not have appreciated.

With the Italians removed from Derna, the local Arab population believed they could happily loot the houses. The Lothians found themselves policing the streets that night, chasing away bands of young men and women who emerged from houses to load furniture and food onto bare-ribbed donkeys.

"If I'd wanted to be a policeman, I'd have joined the bloody Polis," Hogg growled, waving his bayonet at a group of teenagers. "Poor wee buggers; they look half starved."

"Who? The looters?" Elliot asked.

"Looters be buggered! I meant the donkeys!"

Tulloch nodded, seeing a new compassionate side to Hogg. He kept Four Platoon on Derna's streets until Two Platoon came to relieve them. Kinnear looked weary when he approached.

"What next?" Kinnear asked.

"Ask General O'Connor," Tulloch replied. "Let's hope we chase the Italians out of Libya before the Germans arrive." He looked westward. "We've got quite a bit to travel yet."

"God help us," Kinnear replied. "Are we fit to fight the Germans? Our replacements are more used to battle and death now, but the Germans are a more ruthless enemy with more powerful equipment and better tactics. Are the Lothians ready for such a challenge?"

"I think so," Tulloch replied.

"We'll soon find out," Kinnear said. "We're heading out tomorrow. The Australian engineers are working like Trojans to repair the road to the west. General O'Connor is not a man to allow us to sit on our thumbs."

"There's no rest for the wicked," Tulloch said and raised his voice. "Come on, Four Platoon! Form up!"

Chapter Twenty-Four

LIBYA JANUARY 1941

"Where are we headed?" Atkins asked.

The Lothian Rifles debussed after a gruelling six-hour drive, with men looking around them and the sun pitiless above.

"Benghazi," Erskine told him. "I doubt Dicky the Terrier will stop until he reaches Benghazi itself."

"Graziani is running like a hare," Colonel Pringle said, "and we're the hounds coursing him. The RAF has seen huge columns of Italian trucks heading south from Benghazi, so we're trying to determine what Graziani plans."

"It sounds like he's abandoning Cyrenaica," Tulloch suggested. Cyrenaica was the eastern section of Libya, a large area of territory for the British to occupy with so few men.

"If he is, then we should chase him," Major Muir said. "Go hell for leather across the desert and kick Graziani's arse back to Italy."

"General O'Connor agrees," Pringle said quietly. "He believes Graziani is withdrawing his men, horses, guns, and all, back to Tripoli."

Tulloch saw Muir's slow smile of satisfaction. "Then we've got him," he said. "Let's go hell for leather and finish him off."

"That's one option," the more cautious Pringle said. "General O'Connor intends to throw the armour across the desert here," he scraped his pointer across the map, "cutting off the Italian retreat. The Australian infantry, with the bulk of the artillery, and the Lothians will follow and block any return. O'Connor wants to put Graziani's entire army in the bag."

Tulloch drew in his breath at the boldness of the plan. "Has anything like that been done before?"

"I doubt it," Hume said, "but O'Connor has the rights of it. We've been pussy-footing around for too long in this bloody war. Let's finish this African nonsense and get stuck into Hitler in Europe. That's our real enemy, not the Italians."

Pringle frowned without replying. "We're short of men and material," he said, "and Winnie is still pressing General Wavell to send thousands of men and half our tanks to reinforce the Greeks."

"Then the sooner we finish off Mussolini, the better, sir," Hume said. "You'll have noticed the increased traffic coming into Derna."

The officers nodded. The town had been busy with every variety of vehicle pouring in, from the ubiquitous fifteen-hundredweight British lorries to battered Italian trucks and dusty British ten-tonners with laconic New Zealand drivers. O'Connor had ensured he commandeered every available transport to supply his small army. At sea, Admiral Cunningham ensured supplies arrived for the land forces despite the attention of Italian submarines and aircraft.

"We're moving soon with whatever we have," Pringle informed his officers. "Moving without thorough preparation goes against all my theories of war, but the general seems to know what he's about."

"He's giving Mussolini a series of bloody noses," Hume agreed. "We can't fault O'Connor for that."

When Pringle sighed, he suddenly looked old and very tired. "No," he said, "but I prefer to build up reinforcements and supplies before we advance. This fighting on a shoestring at the end of a long and vulnerable supply line is a precarious way to fight a war." Maybe realising he had given too much away, Pringle closed his mouth. "Any comments, gentlemen?"

"None, sir," Hume said. "We obey orders, as always."

"Then get your men ready," Pringle ordered. "Gather all the spare ammunition and food you can, gentlemen. Captain Martin, you are the Motor Supply Officer. Find us some decent transport. Beg, borrow, steal or employ whatever magic you usually employ. I want all our men to travel on wheels and arrive in the best health for fighting."

"I'll do what I can, sir," Martin promised. His job was never easy, with every Australian unit also scrabbling for transport.

As the 7th Armoured Division raced across the desert from Mechili, raising vast clouds of sand and hoping the *Regia Aeronautica* was too busy elsewhere to notice them, the Lothians and Australians pushed along the coast road. Captain Martin had worked wonders to find sufficient transport to carry the entire battalion, although some of the requisitioned Italian vehicles were perforated with ominous holes.

"Do you think the Italians will fight?" Kinnear's eyes never strayed from the brilliant blue sky.

"Maybe once more," Tulloch replied. "I doubt they could stand any more than that. Their morale will be rock bottom after such a succession of defeats." He watched a distant shape in the desert, realised it was a Bedouin on a camel and lost interest. "However, Mussolini must be spitting blood and feathers to have his army shown up so badly after all his bombast."

"One last fight, and then we'll have won the Desert War," Kinnear said hopefully.

"That depends on Churchill and Hitler," Tulloch replied. "If Churchill still demands that Wavell sends half the army to help the Greeks, rather than having a single efficient fighting force, we'll have two weak bodies of men. In North Africa, we'll have a small force at the end of an overstretched supply line and virtually no air cover. On the other side of the Mediterranean, the poor lads who help the Greeks will be in an unfamiliar environment, encouraging the Germans to intervene on Mussolini's side."

"Do you think the Germans will intervene?" Kinnear asked.

"Yes," Tulloch said. "If our lads push the Italians out of Albania, they'll be poised on Italy's border. O'Connor could double the threat if he finishes this campaign with us sitting on the north coast of Africa opposite Sicily."

"A two-pronged attack on Italy?" Kinnear said. "How about the Italian navy?"

"Admiral Cunningham has them in his pocket," Tulloch said. "His victory at Taranto must have shaken them. I know they have more ships and aircraft than us in the Med, but we have Cunningham."

Kinnear smiled. "Cunningham is keeping Nelson's flag flying. Can we defeat Italy?"

"I think we can," Tulloch said. "And that would leave us clear to fight Germany without distractions and without Italy's air force and navy menacing our Mediterranean flank."

They relapsed into silence as the convoy jolted along the coast road, with B Squadron of the 11th Hussars as escort. They heard the occasional piece of news from the 7th Armoured Division. With Churchill ordering much of the RAF to support the Greeks, a handful of Hurricanes and a squadron of slow Lysanders comprised the convoy's entire air cover. They pushed on, nevertheless, with the bulk of the 11th Hussars acting as advance guard across the rough tracks, limited tracks, and no tracks of the desert.

"Drive on!" O'Connor ordered, and his small British and Australian army growled westward into the heart of Italian Libya. The infantry, travelling the long coastal route, passed through the once-Italian villages of Giovanni Berta, Cyrene, Barce, and El Abiar, with crowds gathered to watch them.

"I wish we had time to linger," Kinnear said. "Some of these towns look interesting."

"We might be stationed here later," Tulloch replied.

As the infantry travelled the coast road, the armour met resistance inland at the fort of Msus. The colonial garrison opened fire on the approaching tanks until the British armour threatened a pincer movement. Rather than staying to fight, the garrison fled, and the British armour occupied the fort.

The Lothians heard the news from the advancing armour with mixed feelings.

"The tankies have won another battle without us," Innes grumbled. "We're only here to look pretty and eat the Aussies' dust while the armour sends Graziani back to Italy."

"When did you ever look pretty?" Elliot scoffed. He ran a hand over his dusty, rugged face. "I'm the handsome one here; ask any of the dusky beauties of Africa."

The Australian advance along the coast continued, with the major town of Benghazi falling on the night of February 6th after a period of heavy rain.

"The Italians hardly defended their prize town," Kinnear commented as the Lothians drove through the sodden town. "They've lost heart."

"The papers will be full of our success," Erskine said. "They'll proclaim that we'll be in Rome within a fortnight and Berlin by Christmas."

"The papers are good at winning wars," Muirhead said. "Unfortunately, it's us that have to fight the damned things, not the journalists." He paused as the colonel walked from truck to truck.

"We're stopping here," Colonel Pringle announced. "Debus, gentlemen. We're going no further than Benghazi."

"Has O'Connor called a halt to the operation?" Major Hume asked.

"No," the colonel said. "The armour and the Australians are pushing on. Brigadier Worthington has ordered us to garrison Benghazi until further orders. The Australians will take our transport to replace breakdowns."

Although Pringle spoke without emotion, Tulloch could see the pain in his face as his battalion was removed from the front.

"Major Hume," the colonel said. "We are responsible for internal security on the eastern flank of Benghazi. Please make the arrangements. I must meet Brigadier Worthington."

"Yes, sir," Hume replied and began to organise the Lothians for their new responsibilities.

As soon as news of one victory reached the Lothians, another followed. "The armour has won another battle," Captain Muirhead announced. "Colonel Combe and two thousand men with twenty guns defeated about twenty thousand Italians at Sidi Salem, and then the Rifle Brigade and the Royal Horse Artillery with the 7th Hussars and Royal Tanks finished the job at Beda Fomm."

"The armour is running riot out there," Muirhead said. "They're winning the desert war without our help."

The officers nodded, glad to hear of another British victory yet frustrated they were not included.

"What happened?" Tulloch asked.

"The Italians were running to Tripoli and believed we were a hundred and fifty miles away," Muirhead said. "Imagine how they felt when they met the 11th Hussars and the Rifle Brigade waiting for them."

"They must be the most badly led troops in Europe," Tulloch said.

Muirhead grunted. "Perhaps. They tried their best with poor-quality equipment. The Italians had no idea how few guns Combe's force had, but they attacked anyway. They charged forward any old how, and the Hussars and Rifle Brigade hammered them. The Rifle Brigade had 37 mm Bofors guns mounted on the back of fifteen-hundredweight trucks, the tanks had their usual guns, and we had the advantage of surprise."

"The tanks must have been short of fuel," Tulloch said.

"They were short of everything except nerve," Muirhead said. "The Italians launched a few attacks, but our armour and the Rifle Brigade repelled them every time, and eventually, the Italians admitted defeat. Some escaped into the night, but we captured most."

"The battle of Beda Fomm," Tulloch shook his head. "I wonder if future generations will speak of it as they do Waterloo or Blenheim."

"We'll see," Muirhead said. "I admit that the Lothians not being involved is frustrating, but the war isn't over, and things could change." He looked up as a staff car entered the street and parked outside the colonel's quarters. Brigadier Worthington emerged, tapped a swagger stick against the side of his leg, and strode inside.

"There's our nemesis now," Captain Muirhead said.

"Why does that man dislike us?" Tulloch asked.

Muirhead pulled a pipe from his pocket and examined the bowl. "I'm not entirely sure, Tulloch, but I've heard rumours that it started at Sandhurst. Our colonel and Worthington were rivals for a competition or a woman, I'm not sure which, and Colonel Pringle won." Muirhead began to fill his pipe. "Something like that. They haven't been friends since."

"That's hardly the actions of a professional soldier," Tulloch said. "Brigadier Worthington is bad news."

Muirhead shrugged. "Like any major organisation, the army is full of petty jealousies." He thumbed in the last of his tobacco. "Worthington is not my favourite brigadier," he agreed.

"No, sir."

"Wait outside the colonel's quarters," Muirhead said. "Look circumspect, and I'll expect a full report of everything they say." He grinned. "I am the adjutant, remember, and should know everything that's happening in the battalion."

"Yes, sir," Tulloch agreed.

"That's an order, Tulloch," Muirhead said cheerfully and departed, whistling, with pipe smoke forming a cloud around his head.

Torn between a dislike of eavesdropping and a desire to hear more, Tulloch stood outside the open door of the whitewashed building, listening to raised voices from the interior.

"No, Colonel," Brigadier Worthington snapped. "When the Germans come to Africa, and they will come, I want units I can rely on. I do not have that trust in the Lothian Rifles." He pressed his fingers together and viewed Pringle across an ornate table. "There was that affair in Scotland when half your men ran from a British mine and the brawl in Tobruk, over women, I believe, and with a British officer involved." Worthington shook his head. "No, Colonel. I think your regiment is best suited for garrison duty or, at best, fighting the Italians rather than the Germans."

"I don't agree, sir," Pringle said, tight-lipped. "The Lothians are as good as any regiment."

"You may disagree all you wish, Colonel, but I have made up my mind. I am recommending the Lothians should be transferred to Eritrea, where you can try and regain your reputation fighting the Italians. I believe you know the Fourth Indian Division?"

"I do, sir," Pringle said stiffly. "The Fourth Indian is as fine a division as any in the army."

"I shall recommend you are transferred back to them."

"If that is what you wish, sir," Pringle said stiffly, "of course, I shall obey orders, although I protest strongly at your suggestion we are not up to scratch."

Worthington smiled. "You may lodge your protest verbally or in writing, Colonel, but I have made my decision. Perhaps you will have an opportunity to redeem your battalion's reputation in Eritrea."

Pringle straightened his back. "Thank you, Brigadier. I am

sure the Lothian Rifles will further enhance our reputation in Eritrea."

"If that's how you wish to view the situation, Colonel," Worthington replied.

"That is the truth of the situation," Colonel Pringle countered.

"As you see it, Colonel. I expect the Lothians to embark for Eritrea within the week."

"I am sure you will make the arrangements, sir," Pringle replied. "After all, the staff has to do something to justify its existence."

Chapter Twenty-Five

After the exertions of Operation Compass, Wavell allowed the Lothian Rifles a few days' leave before departing for Eritrea. Confused but compliant, the battalion waited in a transit camp on the outskirts of Cairo, harassed by flies and uncertainty about what awaited them in this new campaign.

"Tulloch," Colonel Pringle looked drawn and grey as he issued orders. "You're duty officer on Friday. Report back to the battalion on Thursday night."

"Yes, sir," Tulloch said.

Pringle puffed smoke from his pipe. "Enjoy the fleshpots of Egypt, Tulloch. We don't know what challenges Eritrea will provide."

"I will, sir," Tulloch said, suddenly desperate to escape from the army, if only for a few days.

"And Tulloch," Pringle said quietly. "Avoid Italian women. I heard what happened in Tobruk."

"I will, sir," Tulloch left the office.

Three days in Cairo. Tulloch felt the pressures of command

279

ease away as he walked the streets of the ancient city, savouring the bustle and noise after the vast spaces and savage encounters of the desert. He looked around at the different people, from the smart Egyptian soldiers who manned the anti-aircraft defences to the red-tabbed officers who would never visit the front. There were civilians here, too, men not in uniform, and not all of them were Egyptian. British and Europeans walked in smart civilian clothes, making money for their companies and themselves, while others suffered and died to ensure they lived their safe, comfortable lives.

How do I feel about civilians profiteering while my men suffer and die? Tulloch pondered the question as he avoided a group of singing British seamen. *I chose the army as a career, so I have no complaints. If these men can live with their conscience, that's fine.*

"Douglas! Is that you?"

The sound of the familiar voice made Tulloch start. At first, he thought it was a dream, one of the desert mirages that had followed him from the Blue. He turned around as the mirage persisted.

"Douglas!"

Tulloch stepped back. "Amanda?" She was like a vision, standing amidst the bustle of the street a hundred yards from the bazaar, wearing an army uniform and with an uncertain smile on her face.

"You haven't forgotten me, then?" Amanda's smile broadened.

Tulloch shook his head, struggling for words. "What the hell are you doing here?"

"It's good to see you too, Douglas," Amanda replied.

Suddenly flustered, Tulloch felt the blood rush to his face. "I mean, how did you get here? I thought you were in London."

"I was in London, and now I am in Cairo," Amanda explained with a slow smile. Her eyes drifted from Tulloch's face to his feet and back.

"Why?" Tulloch tried to collect himself. He found himself tongue-tied, with his heartbeat increasing.

"Why do you think?" Amanda asked, raising her eyebrows.

Tulloch could not think. He only wanted to stare at her, unable to believe she was there. "I don't know," he said.

"Where are you staying?" Amanda changed the subject.

"The Union Jack Club," Tulloch said. "I tried to get into Shepheards Hotel, but it was full of senior staff officers. There was no room at the inn for a lowly infantry lieutenant."

Amanda stepped closer. "Of course not. Stables and tents are good enough for the likes of you." Her eyes stopped roaming and fixed on Tulloch's face.

"Yes," Tulloch tried to order his thoughts. "Where are you staying, Amanda?"

"Government barracks," Amanda told him. "You've lost weight." She touched his arm. "Quite a lot of weight."

"Have I?" When a beggar approached, Tulloch fished in his pocket for a coin, but Amanda was quicker. She spoke to the boy in a flurry of Arabic and pressed something into his grubby hand.

"I didn't know you spoke Arabic," Tulloch said.

"A few words," Amanda said carelessly, raising her voice to be heard above the hubbub. "Let's walk, Douglas, or we'll attract the attention of every mendicant in Egypt."

They walked side by side, their hips nearly touching and hands occasionally brushing together. "We must find somewhere to talk," Amanda said. "Cairo is such a noisy city."

"I was worried about you in London," Tulloch told her. "With the bombing."

"I was worried about you in the desert," she countered. "With the fighting."

"Did you know where I was?" Tulloch asked.

"Yes," Amanda said no more, and Tulloch realised why she had come to Cairo. He glanced at her.

"Thank you," Tulloch said.

"For what?" She looked at him, laughed, shook her head, and looked away.

When he inched closer, her hand slid into his, and she smiled again at his start.

"You're a big, strong soldier now," Amanda said. "You shouldn't be shy of a mere woman."

"You're no mere woman," Tulloch said. After being in exclusively male company for months, he was unsure what to say or how to act with a woman. He hoped Amanda would do most of the talking.

"Why, thank you, kind sir," Amanda gave a little curtsey. She squeezed his hand. "What was it like out there?"

"Out in the Blue," Tulloch said.

"The Blue?"

"That's what we call it," Tulloch said. "The blue sky dominates everything. The desert is largely featureless and stretches forever, with the blue sky above." He struggled for words. "At night, there is nothing but the stars and the feeling of infinite space. It's as if one is alone with the world or with God." He was quiet for a few moments. "I often thought of you then and wondered if you were watching the same moon."

"I was," Amanda said quietly. "I once saw a German bomber against the moon, and all the anti-aircraft guns in London seemed unable to find it. I thought you might be looking up at the moon then."

Tulloch nodded. "I might have been," he said. "London must have been hell. Much worse than anything I went through."

"Fighting a battle must have been hell," Amanda replied. "Much worse than anything I went through."

"I doubt it," Tulloch said.

"Tell me about your life," Amanda said, with her eyes wide and soft. Tulloch could feel himself falling into her gaze.

"What do you want to know?" Their shared images of the moon had created an immediate bond.

"Everything," Amanda said simply. "I want to get inside your head and see things as you see them. Tell me about your childhood."

"It was no different to anybody else's," Tulloch said.

"Tell me anyway," Amanda demanded. Her sudden smile was irresistible. "I've travelled thousands of miles to see you, after all."

With his initial shyness dissipated, Tulloch found the words tumbling from his mouth in a torrent he seemed unable to stem. He knew Amanda was watching him, smiling through her expressive eyes, and wondered if she was laughing at him. Suddenly embarrassed, he stopped, and she put a single finger on his sleeve.

"Don't stop," Amanda said. "I'm listening."

"I must be boring you," Tulloch said.

"Not a bit of it," Amanda assured him.

"You didn't tell me what you do," Tulloch tried to steer the conversation around.

"Oh, this and that," Amanda replied.

"You're in the same sort of job as you did in India," Tulloch said.

She held his gaze. "That's correct," she agreed. "The same sort of job I did in India, so best keep your voice down."

Tulloch realised he could be putting Amanda in danger. "Yes, of course," he said.

Amanda had worked for her father, an intelligence officer, in India. Tulloch was unsure exactly what she did but knew she must deal with sensitive information.

"Can you tell me anything about your work?" Tulloch asked.

"That would be immensely boring," Amanda replied.

"Tell me about your life, then."

Amanda thought for a moment before replying. "My father is an officer, as you know, and I've been following the drum all my life, moving from one station to another, seldom putting down roots."

"Where have you been?"

"The usual suspects, UK, India, Malta, India, UK again and now Egypt." Amanda smiled.

"And now Egypt," Tulloch agreed. "With me."

"Let's go for a camel ride," Amanda suggested. "Let's forget the war for a while."

Tulloch agreed, smiling as he tried to push away the horrors of the desert war and enjoy Amanda's company.

Amanda proved adept at balancing cross-legged on a camel, with Tulloch less sure but eager to learn. "We don't have many camels on the streets in Edinburgh," he said.

"No," Amanda said solemnly. "They don't like the cold."

"Or the rain," Tulloch said.

They rode side by side with the Egyptian camel owner giving them advice and balancing a fez on Amanda's head.

"You look cute like that," Tulloch told her, and Amanda laughed.

"Nobody's ever called me cute before," she said. "I heard something about a brawl in Tobruk. Something about Italian ladies of the night. Were you involved?"

Tulloch started, so his camel nearly took fright, and the owner had to calm it down.

"I heard about that," Tulloch said.

"Only heard?" Amanda was smiling, riding her camel with a skill Tulloch could only admire. "Were you not involved?"

"Only marginally," Tulloch said.

"I heard the officer fought to defend his men," Amanda told him. "I rather liked that."

They rode as far as the pyramids as many thousands of tourists had before, and posed for their photographs.

"Come on, Douglas! Race you to the top!" Amanda lifted her skirt above her knees and bounded up, with Tulloch trying to resist the temptation to admire her legs. She glanced down, caught the direction of his gaze, laughed and continued.

"Come on, slowcoach!"

"It's lovely here," Amanda said as they sat, gasping and perspiring, near the summit.

"It gives one a sense of history," Tulloch fought to catch his breath. "It's strange to think that these things were thousands of years old before Scotland was even created."

"The rivers of history run long," Amanda said, "and don't ask me what that even means because I don't know. It just sounded nice."

"I was impressed," Tulloch told her solemnly. He realised he did not have to impress Amanda and did not care what she said, provided she said it to him. He looked at her as she sat on the ancient stone, with a thin trickle of perspiration running down her forehead and her grey eyes laughing one minute and pensive the next. He did not want to be anywhere else or with anybody else.

Amanda looked around. "Me too," she said in sudden understanding. "Me too."

They sat for a while, holding hands and with their legs pressed together, saying nothing. There was no need to talk and no desire to disturb the companionable silence.

"How long do you have?" Amanda asked at last.

"I'm due to report back tomorrow evening," Tulloch told her.

"We have tomorrow, then," Amanda said. "And tonight."

"Tonight?" Tulloch repeated the word.

Amanda nodded, suddenly serious. "Do you want a tonight with me?"

Tulloch read Amanda's concern. "I'd like nothing better," he said and saw the relief. "Except I'd like lots of tonights."

Amanda's smile teased him. "One at a time," she said. "One night at a time."

"One night at a time sounds perfect," Tulloch replied.

Chapter Twenty-Six

T he escorting destroyer seemed like Samuel Coleridge's painted ship upon a painted ocean as the small convoy eased down the Red Sea.

The transport SS *Cape Province,* which carried the Lothian Rifles, had seen better times. Patches of rust showed through the peeling paint, and the engine wheezed while the funnel emitted dirty black smoke to foul the pristine sky.

Tulloch left the weather side of the deck to return below. He took a last look at the glorious surroundings and the Royal Naval seamen who manned the two Bofors guns, the ship's only anti-aircraft protection.

While the other ranks crammed every inch of the accommodation, the Lothians' officers existed in relative comfort in the aft section of the ship, coughing when the breeze blew the funnel smoke in their direction and watching the coast slip past.

"What do you know about Eritrea, gentlemen?" Colonel Pringle addressed his officers, who crowded into a small cabin right aft.

"Not much more than bugger all, sir," Major Hume replied for them all.

"Well, listen, and I'll educate you," Pringle said, jamming his pipe between his teeth. He glanced around the cabin before he began.

"During the mad scramble for colonies in the last century, Italy grabbed Eritrea, and a few years later failed in an invasion of Ethiopia. In 1935, Mussolini tried again and defeated the Abyssinians, with the help of tanks, aircraft, and poison gas."

The Lothians listened grimly, with Kinnear openly wondering if the Italians would use gas against them.

"If they wanted to," Pringle said, "they'd have done so by now."

"Yes, sir," Kinnear agreed as the colonel continued his lesson.

"Mussolini combined Eritrea and Somaliland into one colony, which he named Italian East Africa." Pringle said, "and when he joined Hitler's War, he used the area as a base to attack British Somaliland and Sudan." He fiddled with his pipe. "Now we've turned the tables, we've invaded, and we're taking Mussolini's African prize from him."

The officers nodded in satisfaction. After the bad start to the war in Norway and France, any success against the Axis powers was good news. O'Connor's Operation Compass had restored some pride, but the British would welcome more victories.

"We scraped together two divisions from somewhere and stationed them in the Sudan, and three more in Kenya," Pringle continued. "Most of the units are Indian, with some Africans, British colonial, and British as well."

"And now us," Hume said.

"And now us," Pringle confirmed. "I'll keep this simple, gentlemen. We moved against the Italian positions in Eritrea from Sudan. We moved south from Karora and east from Kassala. We defeated the Italians at Agordat after tough fighting when our old friends, the Fourth Indian Division, were in the thick of things."

"Of course," Hume murmured. "Here's to the Red Eagles."

Tulloch smiled, for the Fourth Indian Division was proud of their symbol.

"We'll be attached to the Red Eagles," Pringle said.

"One of the finest fighting divisions in the world," Hume murmured. "The Fourth and Fifth Indian Divisions are the northern section of a huge pincer movement that skelped the Italians. At Agordat, the Cameron Highlanders and Rajputana Rifles, plus the Sikhs, excelled themselves," Pringle said. "We took about a thousand prisoners, and the Italians retreated to a place called Keren, where they still stand at bay, fighting well."

"Is that where we're headed, sir?" Once again, Hume asked the question on everybody's mind.

"That's where we're headed," Colonel Pringle confirmed.

"What's Keren like, sir?" Hume asked.

"Keren is a busy town that in itself is not fortified," Pringle said, "but it has a naturally strong position. Italian artillery can dominate the area from the surrounding high ridges and peaks. The Italians can see any attack before it develops, break it up with artillery, or move their forces to block us."

The officers listened. Used to desert warfare, they tried to visualise fighting in the Eritrean mountains. When Pringle unrolled a map and pinned it on the wall behind him, Tulloch saw a confusion of hills and mountains with steep gorges between.

"This pass is known as the Dongolaas Gorge, and the road and railway from Agordat to Keren run this way. As you see, this hill, Mount Zeban, and this one, Mount Falestoh, controls the pass on the southeast. The Italians built Fort Dologorodoc on Falestoh to make things more interesting."

"The Italians are excellent at building defensive forts," Hume murmured. "Their engineering skills are second to none."

"If only they had the fortitude to hold them," Erskine said, blowing a smoke ring into the air.

Colonel Pringle did not respond. "On the opposite side of

the Dongolaas Gorge, we have Mount Sanchil and its associated hills, Hog's Back, Flat Top, and Brig's Peak, all leading to Mount Sammana in the northwest." Pringle tapped one feature on the map with the stem of his pipe. "This ridge, which we call feature 1616, could be the key to the whole area, as it overlooks the railway line and the Ascidera Valley. As you see, it's in front of Mount Sanchil."

The officers took notes, with the enormity of the task becoming apparent.

"That ridge looks difficult to capture, sir," Muirhead observed.

"I agree. It will be difficult to capture and impossible to hold as long as the enemy occupies this spur we know as the Spike." Again, Pringle tapped the map with his pipe.

Even on the map, the Spike looked formidable, with contour lines so close together that they were nearly touching on two sides and what appeared to be a cliff face on the rear.

"As long as the Italians occupy the Spike, they can control Feature 1616, and as long as they have 1616, they can hold Keren."

Tulloch studied the map, wondering how the Lothians would cope with mountain warfare after months in the desert.

"Who defends Keren, sir?" Hume asked.

"Good quality Italian troops," Pringle said. "The 5th and 44th Colonial Brigades, with the 42nd Brigade, which fought well at Agordat, as did the 2nd Brigade. There is the 11th Regiment of Savoy Grenadiers, the Alpini Battalion of the 10th Savoy Grenadiers, the 6th and 11th Colonial Brigade, and a plethora of artillery." He paused for a moment. "And at least one regiment of Blackshirts."

"Some of these are elite troops," Kinnear said. "How many men do the Italians have in total, sir?" Kinnear asked.

"We estimate around 23,000," Pringle said.

289

"How many do we have, sir?"

"General Platt has around 13,000 men," the colonel replied.

"We have to defeat a far larger force in an impossible defensive position," Kinnear nearly whispered.

"That's correct, Lieutenant." Colonel Pringle stepped back. "Unless General Platt captures Keren before the Lothians arrive, gentlemen, that will be our next battlefield."

SS *Cape Province* unloaded her passengers and stood back out to sea, with her crew keeping a wary eye open for Italian aircraft and the Italian Navy. The Lothian Rifles boarded a train, chugged southwards from Port Sudan to Kassala, then travelled by a succession of trucks eastwards towards Keren.

"I thought Africa was full of lions and jungle," Connington said. "I haven't seen a single lion yet, and no jungle either."

"They were lying to you," Elliot replied. "There are no lions in Africa and no jungles, just camels, deserts, and bloody great mountains."

They stood on the main street at Agordat with heavy clouds overhead, and the NCOs checking their baggage as Muirhead and Kilner shouted over the radio to locate the promised transport.

Tulloch barely glanced at the officer who marched towards him. "Good morning, sir." The second lieutenant's uniform nearly shone with newness, while the gloss on his boots would have brought a smile to the RSM of the Scots Guards.

"Good morning," Tulloch replied absently and stared again. "Good God! Hardie! Is that you?"

"Yes, sir," Hardie threw a smart salute that did not hide his smile.

"When did you get your commission?" Tulloch frowned. "You were an officer before, weren't you? In the King's African Rifles?"

"Yes, sir. Colonel Wingate pulled some strings – he knows General Wavell, I think, and my commission was reinstated, but at a lesser rank."

"It's good to have you back in the Lothians," Tulloch said, checking Hardie's regimental insignia.

"It's good to be back, sir," Hardie replied.

"Have you seen the colonel?"

"Yes, sir. He's going to assign me to Six Platoon."

Tulloch nodded. "You'll fit in there," he said. "We always need good officers. How was Ethiopia?"

"A bit hectic, sir," Hardie said after a pause.

"Did you meet your Blackshirts? Tenente Colonnello Lorenzo Rotunno, if I recall." Tulloch held Hardie's gaze.

"No, sir," Hardie said. "I didn't meet Rotunno or any Black-shirts in Ethiopia."

"Why did you want to?" Tulloch asked. "We're both officers now, Hardie, equal in social status and nearly equal in rank. You have no reason to be reticent."

Hardie hesitated before he replied. "He led a unit that was responsible for some murders, sir."

"In Spain?"

Hardie shook his head. "No, sir, before that. In Ethiopia."

Tulloch nodded. "Did you know the people whom he murdered?"

"Yes, sir." Hardie closed his mouth.

"Were they close to you?" Tulloch felt he was holding a police interrogation rather than speaking to a fellow officer.

"Yes, sir," Hardie said. "Some of them were people the King's African Rifles had freed from Ethiopian slavers in the twenties."

"Were you involved in that?" Tulloch smiled to sweeten his questions.

Hardie replied immediately. "Yes, sir. I led regular anti-slavery patrols along the border between Kenya and Ethiopia. I helped free some people, and they elected to live in Ethiopia."

"I see," Tulloch had not known about the anti-slavery

patrols. *Another burden of Empire, patrolling huge borders in uncivilised lands.*

"I hear that Rotunno is in Eritrea with his Blackshirts now," Hardie said.

Tulloch nodded. "The colonel told us there are some Black-shirts at Keren. If so, there's a chance we might meet him."

"I hope so," Hardie said. His eyes were years away, fighting a different war. When he returned to the present, Tulloch saw something savage inside him and wondered what had not been said.

"Here come the trucks!" Captain Muirhead shouted. "Get loaded up, men!"

Here we go again, once more into the breach.

ERITREA. TULLOCH LOOKED AROUND. WHILE MOST OF THE fighting in the Western Desert had been on a level plain, Eritrea seemed to be composed of ragged, rocky hills, deep valleys, and patches of dense forests.

"If this is Africa, you can keep it," Innes said. "Why would anybody want to come here? We should tell Mussolini he can have Eritrea, Libya, and Ethiopia and throw in a poke of chips into the bargain."

"Aye," Hogg agreed. "Bugger this for a game of soldiers."

Tulloch tended to agree with Hogg. While the Germans were menacing Great Britain and thrusting through Europe, conquering country after country, the Lothians and a sizeable chunk of the British Army were moving ever further away.

"Where are we going, sir?" Innes asked.

"Inland and upwards," Tulloch replied. "The Italians have made a stand at a place called Keren, and we're going to kick them out."

Innes grunted. "Why, sir? Why not make a deal with them? If

they leave Egypt and Suez alone, they can keep their bits of Africa, and we can all go home."

Tulloch shook his head. "Wars don't work that way, Innes. If the Italians remained in Eritrea and Somaliland, they could threaten the ships in the Red Sea. We have a lot of trade sailing through the Red Sea, so we must keep it safe."

"Yes, sir," Innes said.

The Lothians climbed slowly, sliding on the ragged rocks as the sun hammered down on them. A predatory Rüppell's vulture circled above, watching the toiling men, hoping to find fresh meat. The men ignored it, concentrating on putting one foot in front of the other without falling.

Colonel Pringle stopped on a small hillock on the path, with the ground falling vertically on three sides to a deep rocky ravine and a view of savage hills all around.

"That's the Spike," Colonel Pringle pointed to a spur of the central massif, with a single narrow ridge the only access. The Spike ascended in a series of terraces, each of which the Italians had strengthened with stone sangars. When Tulloch focused his binoculars, he could see the snouts of artillery protruding from each sangar.

"Bloody hell's teeth!" Kinnear breathed. "How can anybody take that?"

"So far," Pringle replied. "We don't know. We've tried aerial assault and artillery without success. The Blackshirts and Savoy Grenadiers hold it and have repulsed every attempt we've made to capture it by assault."

Tulloch looked upwards. The terrain seemed designed for defence, with jumbled boulders providing shelter above the killing ground of open spaces. Through his binoculars, he could see a scatter of dead khaki-clad bodies where British, Indian, and African soldiers had died trying frontal assaults. A large Italian flag flew from the summit of the peak, with the sun reflecting from artillery and anti-aircraft guns.

"How do we get there, sir?" Tulloch asked. "I can only see one way up, and the Italians will have that well covered."

"Along Cameron Ridge and straight up," Pringle replied. "There is no other way. The rear of the Spike is a sheer cliff. Perhaps a mountain goat could make it up, but not a human being."

"Cameron Ridge, sir? You didn't mention that in your lecture!"

"It was called Feature 1616 then," Pringle said. "The Cameron Highlanders captured it recently."

Tulloch ran an experienced eye up the ridge and onto the Spike. "The Italians have chosen an excellent defensive spot," he said.

"Can't the RAF bomb them?" Kinnear asked.

"They've tried," the colonel replied. "The bombers have only a small target from above, and when they try, as many bombs fall on our positions as on the Italians. When the fighters come low to strafe, the Italian anti-aircraft fire is deadly." He pointed to the wreckage of three British aircraft on the slopes. "We can see three; there are others."

"How about artillery?" Kinnear sounded strained.

"We'll have a preliminary bombardment," Pringle said. "But we find the shells only break the rocks up worse, giving the Italians even more cover." He sighed. "It's all up to guts, boots, and bayonets, gentlemen." He shook his head. "I hoped to avoid casualties, but it seems there's no help for it." Pringle glanced over the Lothians and up the narrow spur to the Spike. "My poor boys, my poor, poor boys."

"Cameron Ridge," Innes grunted. "Why the hell would any sensible Cameron come here?"

"The Cameron Highlanders took it from Mussolini's men," Elliot replied. "And anyway, who ever said the Camerons had any sense?"

Tulloch looked up at the jumble of rocks, scrub vegetation,

and the ridges where the cream of Italy's army held out against General Platt's force.

"I'd love to meet the man who said the Italians were cowards who could not fight. Bring him here for one day."

"If he survives one day," Atkins said.

Tulloch gave a wry smile. "Aye, if he survives one day."

"Keren, is it? More like Hell," Kinnear said and laughed bitterly at his attempted humour. "Brigadier Worthington must hate us, sending us here."

Kilner glanced at Kinnear, raised his eyebrows, and looked away without speaking.

"Here we are, gentlemen," Colonel Pringle indicated a patch of relatively level ground spread with tents. "This is our home for the present. The cooks will rustle something up, and we'll see what tomorrow brings." He took his pipe from his pocket. "I'll find General Platt."

Chapter Twenty-Seven

KEREN, ERITREA, MARCH 1941

At five in the morning, the British artillery began another bombardment to spread dismay among the Italians on the peaks and persuade them to surrender. Already awake and standing by in case the Italians sent a raiding party, the Lothians listened to the thunder of the barrage and were glad they were not on the receiving end. Tulloch saw the bright petals of bursting shells through the dark and wondered if any were hitting their mark. The shells arced overhead, unseen, but the Lothians could hear the whisper of their passage.

When dawn rose, the bombardment continued, hammering at the Italian defences, shell after shell bursting on the slopes. The Italian artillery retaliated, concentrating on the British guns, Cameron Ridge, and the roads leading to the front. Tulloch saw the multiplicity of explosions on the Spike and wondered how the Lothians could succeed when other equally good battalions had failed.

"Ready, lads?" As Colonel Pringle looked at his battalion, Tulloch wondered if his mind was here in Africa, on the blood-saturated mud of Flanders or the screaming hell of the Dunkirk evacuation. He would see the faces of long-dead men and know this assault would add more to the already far too long lists in the Scottish National War Memorial in Edinburgh Castle.

"Ready, sir," Muir said.

The Lothians stood up. Some men prayed; Innes fingered the crucifix around his neck; others extinguished their cigarettes, knowing even that tiny glow could be a mark for an Italian sniper. They stamped their feet on the stony ground, coughed, grunted, and hitched up their trousers. Hogg tested the edge of his bayonet, hawked, coughed, and muttered, "Bugger this for a game of soldiers."

"We're going in light," Captain Kilner told B Company. "Steel helmets, personal weapons, ammunition, water bottles, one biscuit, and nothing else."

The men nodded; they knew what lay ahead of them. One man took a deep, shuddering breath to hide his fear. Others whistled, remained quiet, or cracked black humour. They were British soldiers of a Scottish regiment going into battle. They were ordinary men facing an extraordinary situation.

"Remember, we're the Lothian Rifles," Colonel Pringle said.

"How can we bloody forget?" An anonymous voice muttered from the ranks.

"Fix bayonets," Pringle looked upward, where the Blackshirts and Savoy Grenadiers, the pride of the Italian Army, waited for them. At that minute, he saw only the spitting fury of artillery muzzles behind the smoke.

Tulloch felt a shiver run down him as he heard the sinister click of determined men fitting the eighteen-inch bayonets onto the muzzles of their Lee-Enfield rifles. He ran his gaze along the faces of Four Platoon, knowing each man and wondering how many would still be alive when the sun set that night.

"Keep your heads down, lads," Tulloch said quietly. "The stretcher bearers will look after the wounded. Cover each other, follow orders, and we'll sort out these Italians. Gin ye daur! Follow me."

Tulloch stepped in front, aware that every Savoy Grenadier sniper would target the officers. He raised his voice. "Come on, the Lothians! Gin ye daur!"

The men followed, with their heavy, nailed boots crunching on the hard ground. Some muttered curses, but most were silent, intent only on finishing the job and surviving the day. There was no hatred for the Italians, no genuine desire to kill; they were professional soldiers doing their job.

The Italians fired a single shot, with the sound of the bullet strangely loud against the backdrop of deeper artillery. Trained on India's Northwest Frontier, Tulloch saw a faint movement ahead and knew the marksman had shifted to view the result of his shot.

Young Tam Fairbairn, not yet nineteen years old and fast becoming a decent soldier, stiffened and gave a slight grunt before he crumpled to the ground. He lay still, immediately dead.

Ferguson had a girlfriend in Loanhead. She will be crying when the telegram arrives.

The Lowland pipes began to wail, encouraging the Lothians to advance. Corporal Borthwick stopped for a second to view Fairbairn's body, stepped over it, and pushed on, face set in determination. Sunlight glittered on hundreds of bayonets, a promise of slaughter if the Lothians ever closed with the Italian defenders, a threat of revenge for the death of young Tam.

The British artillery began the creeping barrage intended to shelter the infantry, although Tulloch knew it was hard for the gunners to estimate the Lothians' position in this broken terrain. Inevitably, some shells would fall short, and men from Edinburgh, Penicuik, and the small mining towns of Midlothian would die under British artillery.

War is like that, Tulloch thought absently as he began to scramble uphill, with the slopes of the Spike before him, broken rocks scattered with broken bodies and smoke lurking in dark corners. *There is so much human wastage; so many good men killed and maimed for minimal gain.*

The Italian artillery replied, aiming at the advancing infantry. Tulloch heard the terrifying crump of shells landing among the Lothians and a long, drawn-out scream as shrapnel shredded a fragile human body. Shells flew in both directions, with the Italians better able to shelter in their deep dugouts while the Lothians were more exposed on the open ground.

"Push on!" the officers ordered. "Don't stop!"

Jesus, this is hot. Tulloch glanced over his shoulder. Four Platoon was following well, keeping formation, ready to break into a charge or dive for cover as soon as he gave the order.

"Gin ye daur!" Tulloch shouted the regimental slogan, knowing the hellish din of battle would blanket his words.

"The Gorgie boys are here!" Hogg roared, and then there was only the sound of artillery and the sustained rattle of heavy Italian machine guns.

Lieutenant Parker was down, writhing on the ground with half his chest blown away, white shattered ribs, and a lung exposed.

"Keep on!" Tulloch shouted. "The closer we are, the less their guns can hit us!" He knew the Lothians could not advance too quickly, or they would be within the curtain of their own artillery. By necessity, their progress must be steady and deliberate. More men were down. Three in one section, when an Italian shell burst at ground level, spreading deadly shrapnel. One lay still, the others squealing with shattered legs. McAndrew had been a promising footballer, Tulloch remembered, who played for Newtongrange Star and hoped to turn professional after the war. The Italian machine guns found their range, hammering A Company, who replied with Bren gun fire from the hip. More casualties, more screaming, broken men, more blood, agony, and death.

"Push on!"

Dear God, when will this nightmare end?

Something tugged at Tulloch's sleeve. He glanced down and saw a rip in his shirt where a bullet had passed close to him.

A quarter of an inch to the left and I'd be on the ground, able to escape this hell.

"They're firing at us!" Elliot said.

"So they are," Tulloch replied. He had hardly noticed the Italian riflemen were firing, with spurts of dust and chips of rock showing where the bullets landed. More men fell. Cummings staggered, looked down at the spreading blood on his shirt, and coughed.

"They've got me," he said in amazement. "They've shot me." He fell to his knees, still holding his rifle, still looking to his front.

"Push on!" Tulloch ordered. His arm was throbbing but usable.

The Lothians entered an area of broken ground where rocks provided cover from the machine guns but little from the shells as the explosions made vicious missiles from sharp shards of stone. Some men took advantage of the rocks to halt and fire at the near-invisible Blackshirts and Grenadiers on the upper slopes. Others lingered, hugging the lee side of the rocks for protection. Sergeant Drysdale landed a savage kick on Elliot's backside. "Move, you bastard! Pretend the Eyeties are women. Go for them!"

The British artillery was firing only thirty yards ahead, with some shells landing dangerously short. Tulloch saw an Italian machine gun nest among the rocks, with the gun and all the men sprawled in death, but whether from a direct British hit or an Italian shell falling short, he could not tell.

We've reached the Italian outer defences. That's further than anybody else.

"Come on, Four Platoon!" Tulloch shouted.

Seven Platoon was struggling, with Italian machine gun fire pinning them down. Tulloch saw Sergeant O'Brien lead a charge out and immediately fall. His men retired, seeking shelter among the rocks.

Where's their officer? Oh, yes, Parker is down.

The British artillery was forty yards ahead now and progressing slowly to the main Italian positions. Tulloch looked up the quickly steepening slope, now speckled with muzzle flashes as the Blackshirts and Grenadiers fired at the advancing British soldiers.

"We're falling behind!" Colonel Pringle shouted. "Come on, the Lothians! Keep level with our gunnery!"

Tulloch saw Captain Martin of C Company dash forward to encourage his men. He was laughing, with his eyes bright blue. "After me, lads!"

The bullets ripped into him, knocking his legs away, so he fell awkwardly.

Martin played rugger for Heriots and was in line for a Scotland cap. Not anymore. That's another good man wasted.

"Martin!" Pringle dashed to Martin's side. "My poor boy!"

As the colonel stooped beside Captain Martin, the Italian machine gunner fired again, with five bullets hitting Pringle. Tulloch saw the force of the shots lift the colonel from his feet and throw him backward. Three had hit him in the chest and two in the abdomen, nearly cutting him in half.

"Colonel!" Tulloch watched in shock. Pringle had been a father figure to the battalion, a man who had led them on campaign on the Northwest Frontier, in France, and through the Western Desert. Now, he was dead, killed by Italian bullets on a rocky mountain in Eritrea.

"Stand back, Tulloch!" Major Hume roared. "You can do nothing for him."

Tulloch nodded. He saw more Italian bullets kicking up the ground as two machine gun nests sprayed the ground in front of the Lothians. At that minute, the British artillery barrage intensified, covering the Spike with exploding shells.

If I die and go to Hell, I'll feel at home, for I am already here

301

"Pipers! Play *Johnny Cope!*" Major Hume roared. "Charge! Charge!"

With the pipers playing *Hey Johnny Cope*, a stirring tune commemorating the Highlanders' victory at the Battle of Prestonpans, Hume leapt towards the maelstrom of bursting shells that marked the Italian forward position.

"Come on, Four Platoon!" Tulloch felt a streak of madness as he followed the major, with his men behind him, yelling semi-coherent slogans, cursing, and shouting.

"The Gorgie boys are here!" Hogg roared, with his bayonet thrust before him.

"The Lothians are coming!" Innes shouted, firing his Bren from the hip.

"Remember the Colonel!" Despite the close battle, Smith carried his cumbersome Boys and staggered behind Innes.

"Gin ye daur!" Sergeant Drysdale yelled, and others joined in with the regimental slogan. "Gin ye daur!"

Tulloch heard the sudden silence as the British bombardment stopped, with dust and smoke drifting across the ground.

Dear God, we should be at the Italian forward defences now. The enemy has a clear shot at us.

"Push on!" Tulloch roared. He knew the quicker they covered the remaining open ground, the fewer casualties the Italian machine guns could cause. The ground was steeper now, slowing down the charge. Men had to scramble up, some using hands as well as feet, as the Blackshirts and Grenadiers fired continuously.

"Don't bunch!" Sergeant Drysdale shouted.

Tulloch saw the vicious sparkle of the light machine gun, and then Drysdale threw a grenade. The bomb landed inside the machine gun nest with a loud crump, followed by frantic screaming. Drysdale leapt the wall with Hogg and Elliot at his back. The screaming ended.

"Cleared," Drysdale shouted laconically as Hogg emerged with blood dripping from his bayonet.

Another machine gun opened up, and a third, with the bullets crashing and hammering all around the Lothians. Tulloch looked around, saw a group of Italians forty yards away, and cursed as something nipped his side. He gasped, looked down, and forgot the momentary pain as he concentrated on the enemy.

"Over there!" Tulloch fired his revolver at a machine gun nest and jumped behind a rock as the Italians aimed directly at him.

Bullets chewed at the rock, raising splinters and humming around Tulloch's head. He ducked, swearing, and feverishly thrust cartridges into his revolver.

"At them, Lothians," Hume shouted. "Take the bastards!"

Another man fell, clutching his leg, and an entire section disintegrated as the machine gun sprayed them.

We're losing too many men here and making no progress.

Hume dropped, rolled, wrestled the pin from a grenade, and threw it from his prone position. As the grenade exploded above the machine gun nest, he rose, shouting. Tulloch and Four Platoon followed, with Hogg overtaking Hume as he reached the lip of the nest.

Tulloch fired, hitting the machine gun loader, saw Hogg throw a man over his shoulder, gouge out an Italian eye, and thrust a straight-fingered jab into the throat of a third. Major Hume grunted approval, and then Tulloch swept past. He saw frightened Italian faces before him and a section of Grenadiers launching a counterattack.

These are the most determined Italians we've met. Thank God there weren't many like this in Libya.

Tulloch saw another officer on his right as Hardie led his platoon up the slope.

"Kill the murdering bastards!" Hardie shouted, adding some choice Italian oaths to strengthen his words.

Tulloch saw Hogg and Drysdale face the Italian counterattack head-on, bayonet to bayonet, with Hume a few steps behind and Hardie bringing his platoon towards the Italian flank.

"The Gorgie boys are here!" Hogg roared.

"Come on, Four Platoon!" Tulloch shouted with the fighting madness on him. He jumped over a man wriggling and screaming on the ground without noticing if he was Italian or British and charged the advancing Italians, firing his revolver until the hammer clicked on an empty chamber.

Tulloch expected the Italians to break when the British charged, but they held firm, and both sides met in a brutal, near-medieval clash of bayonets and rifle butts. Hogg was in his element, thrusting, ducking, slashing with his bayonet as Lieutenant Hardie threw himself on a Blackshirt, swearing. A tall Italian Grenadier dodged a Lothian's thrust and stabbed him in the stomach, shouting a slogan.

"Send them back!" Muir shouted, shooting a man.

"Watch the flanks!" Hardie warned as more Grenadiers emerged from above.

Tulloch glanced to the left and right. The Blackshirts were pouring from the cover of ragged rocks, firing into the Lothians' flanks and rear, with Grenadiers directly ahead.

The Lothian attack stalled, with some men turning back. The Italian counterattack ended as they returned to cover.

"Four Platoon!" Tulloch shouted as the Lothians' attack wavered. "Press on!"

Hogg and Innes struggled forward together until a burst of machine gun fire raised splinters of rock from the ground at their feet.

"There are thousands of them!" Kinnear shouted. "Retire!"

"Retire!" somebody echoed, and men began to fall back, still firing, still facing the enemy but stepping backward, granting victory to the Italians.

"No!" Hume ordered, but he was too late. Once the retiral started, men thought of safety and stepped back, sliding down the slope in their sudden quest for security.

A squat Blackshirt officer stood on a rock, encouraging his men.

I've seen that man before. He repulsed us in Libya.

"That's Rotunno!" Hardie shouted, pushing forward.

"Get back, Hardie!" Tulloch snarled. "You'll only be a target!"

"That's Rotunno!" the normally taciturn Hardie was red-faced with fury.

"Get back!" Tulloch grabbed Hardie's sleeve. "Come on, Hardie!"

"I want Rotunno!"

"He'll have to wait!" Tulloch saw Rotunno glaring at Hardie and wondered whose dislike was the greater. "Come on, Hardie!"

Chapter Twenty-Eight

KEREN, ERITREA, MARCH 1941

They stood alone between the Italian infantry and the retiring Lothians. Rotunno shouted another order, and the Blackshirts advanced from the left flank and the Grenadiers from the right.

Rotunno has organised a neat pincer movement, using his knowledge of the terrain to lure us British into an ambush.

"I want to kill him," Hardie said, careless of danger as he gestured towards Rotunno.

"Not today," Tulloch replied. "If we stay here, the Italians will kill us both." He saw the madness fade from Hardie's eyes.

"No, not today," Hardie replied, suddenly sane.

"Come on!" Tulloch pushed Hardie towards the withdrawing Lothians. Spurts of dust around their legs showed where Italian bullets landed. Fortunately, the Italian riflemen could not fire without hitting their own men.

Tulloch and Hardie moved together, with Sergeant Drysdale organising Four Platoon to cover their withdrawal, and Hogg a few steps in advance of the others.

Innes held the Bren at waist height, firing short bursts at the enemy. "No, you don't, you blackshirted bastards!"

"Keep them back, Innes," Tulloch said.

"I'll do my best, sir," Innes shouted.

The Lothians withdrew, step by step, over the khaki-clad bodies until they reached a ridge that provided some natural cover from above.

"That's far enough," Hume ordered. "No more, Lothians."

Most of the men stopped, with only two continuing to run downhill until loud-voiced Corporal Borthwick roared them back.

"The Blackshirts are coming!" Erskine shouted.

The Blackshirts had followed the Lothians, trying to push them to the bottom of the Spike.

"Send them back!" Hume ordered, and the Lothians slid into cover and fired uphill at the advancing Italians.

Rotunno led his men from the front, ordering them to find cover and return the Lothians' fire. The two sides fought for five minutes, and then an accurate artillery barrage fell around the Lothians' ridge.

"Heads down, lads!" Tulloch ordered as the shells exploded, sending shrapnel and shards of rock around them. The bombardment lasted only a few moments, and when it ended, Tulloch expected the Blackshirts to attack the disorganised British lines.

"Where are they?" Kinnear asked.

When the shelling had kept the Lothians busy, Rotunno had withdrawn his Blackshirts back up the hill.

"That man's a good commander," Tulloch remarked. "He's used his advantages of numbers and position well. He knows that he'd lose men if he attacked us here."

"I'm not surprised he's repulsed every assault," Erskine said, calmly puffing smoke from his cigarette holder. "The Italians are in a natural defensive position."

"He won't hold us off for long," Hume said. "We'll regroup and try again. Next time, we'll know what to expect."

"When, sir?" Kinnear asked.

Tulloch had not seen Kinnear during the attack but was glad he had survived.

"Tonight," Hume said. "They won't expect us to attack so soon after they repulsed us."

"Tonight?" Kinnear repeated.

"Pass the word to everybody," Hume said. "I'm damned if I'll allow a bunch of fascist Blackshirts to beat us."

Tulloch looked upwards, where the bodies of fifteen Lothians joined the Rajputs and King's African Rifles, who had previously tried to capture the Spike. A slight mist drifted across the peak, hiding some of the carnage.

Hume has a different attitude from that of old Colonel Pringle. He'll alter the dynamics of the battalion.

Tulloch returned to Four Platoon, where the men lay behind rocks, cleaning their rifles or peering uphill at the Italian positions.

"We're going in again, lads," Tulloch told them.

"When, sir?" Sergeant Drysdale asked.

"Tonight," Tulloch said.

Four Platoon nodded, accepting the order.

"Grab some sleep while you can," Tulloch ordered. "It might be a long night."

"Aye," Hogg mumbled. "Bugger this for a game of soldiers."

There was a kind of beauty in the savage backdrop to Keren, with the mountains and the rugged background. Tulloch remembered exploring the Scottish hills as a youth, gradually expanding his area from the Pentland Hills beside Edinburgh to the long Border hills and the rougher Highlands. He knew he could feel at home in this terrain, which reminded him of India's Northwest Frontier.

I understand hill country better than the desert. I can cope with this battle. He looked up as Hume scrambled over the rocks towards him.

"Tulloch!" Hume called tersely. "We're going in at ten

tonight. I'm leading with A Company; Captain Kilner is taking the left flank with B Company, and Muirhead's on the right with C Company. D Company is in reserve to reinforce whoever makes a breakthrough."

Tulloch nodded. "Yes, sir."

"You know the rules; move as quietly as you can. The Italians don't seem to have fixed positions here, so they could be anywhere."

"We'll watch for them, sir," Tulloch said.

"There won't be any preliminary artillery bombardment," Hume said. "We'll rely on surprise."

"Yes, sir."

Surprise is good at night. We'll use the cover of darkness to roll the Italians up before they know what's hit them.

Four Platoon readied themselves, checking their bayonets were loose in their scabbards, their magazines fully charged, and ammunition clips ready to hand. Tulloch inspected each man, muttering words of encouragement where needed until he was satisfied his men were as prepared as possible.

They are all veterans now. They know what to expect.

The sun set in a glorious orange flush, highlighting the serrated peaks to the west, then plunged them into stygian darkness. A hush fell on Keren, with the Lothians aware of the ordeal ahead, waiting silently for the word of command. The wind rose slightly, cooler than Tulloch had expected, brushing through the ragged rocks and scrubby vegetation, and some night-prowling animal howled in the distance.

Tulloch checked his watch. The minute hand crept forward with little jerks, each movement possibly ticking away his last moments of life.

"Ready, men," Hume whispered, and a tremor of anticipation ran through the battalion. They peered into the darkness above, aware of the highly trained Savoy Grenadiers and dedicated Blackshirts holding their positions, waiting for them.

At ten minutes to ten, Captain Kilner led B Company to the

left flank, with the men of Four Platoon lifting their feet high to avoid kicking over loose stones. A bird called somewhere in the night, the sound eerie, and Tulloch knew other hunters were out in the dark.

"Blackshirts!"

Tulloch heard Hardie's voice raised in a warning shout and then the sharp report of a pistol.

"Blackshirts!" The cry came from the centre, and a volley of musketry followed, rifles and light machine guns firing simultaneously.

"Watch your front!" Tulloch shouted. "Four Platoon!"

Gunfire stabbed from above, mingled with the shouts of startled men. Tulloch lifted his revolver and fired, aiming at the spurts of flame.

"Fire, Four Platoon! Fire at the muzzle flares!"

The men responded with gunfire, shouts, and curses all along the Lothians' front.

"Brens! Spray the front! Riflemen, aim at the muzzle flashes!" Tulloch gave rapid orders, firing into the dark and feverishly reloading. "Where's the mortarmen? Borthwick! Fire a hundred yards in front of us." He heard the crackle and whine of passing bullets and wondered how many Italians were ahead of them.

After a few moments of mayhem, the firing died down.

"Keep alert!" Major Muir gave crisp orders. "Stretcher-bearers, attend to the wounded!"

"Casualty report!" Tulloch demanded. "Sergeant Drysdale, report!"

After a few minutes, Drysdale replied, "Nobody hit, sir. All present and accounted for."

"Wait here," Tulloch ordered. "Hogg, you're with me."

"Sir," Hogg hurried up with his rifle at the trail.

"We're going to have a look forward," Tulloch told him. "Guard my back." "Yes, sir!" Hogg replied.

Despite Hogg's long crime sheet and predilection for brawling, Tulloch preferred him to anybody else when on patrol. Hogg would fight until no breath was left in his body, then rise and fight again. Tulloch cautiously led them forward, wary of any Blackshirts waiting in ambush.

Tulloch reached the first body after a five-minute crawl. He searched the Blackshirt for any documents, found none, and continued, finding still-wet blood on a rock and a few dozen empty brass cartridge cases.

He heard movement above, the furtive sound of rustling cloth and a metallic click, as if somebody had knocked the barrel of their rifle against a rock.

"That's enough, Hogg," Tulloch said. "Let's get back to the battalion."

"Yes, sir." Hogg's eyes gleamed bright in his mud-darkened face. Tulloch thought he looked disappointed.

"What the hell happened there?" Kinnear asked when Tulloch returned to the Lothians.

"We bumped the Blackshirts," Tulloch said. "Rotunno must have had the same idea as us and sent his men down to attack us at night."

Kinnear whistled. "I didn't think the Italians did that sort of thing."

"Rotunno does," Tulloch said. "I found one body out there in a Blackshirt uniform."

"What now?" Kinnear looked up as Captain Kilner arrived. "Do we push on with the attack, sir?"

"No," Kilner shook his head emphatically. "Not now, the Italians are alerted." He ducked as an artillery shell crashed down to explode a hundred yards up the hill. Others followed, closer to the Lothians.

"Back to the starting line!" Hume ordered. "We're compromised now."

The Lothians withdrew, unhappy at having their offensive cancelled but relieved they were not advancing through intensive shell fire.

"Bugger this for a game of soldiers," Hogg said. "I feel like the Grand Old Duke of York, marching to the top of the hill and marching back down."

"If your boots marched as much as your mouth, Hogg, you'd be all right," Sergeant Drysdale snarled. "Now shut your moaning mouth and get on with it."

The heavy shelling continued for the next half hour, blasting the area between the Lothians and the Blackshirts. At ten-forty-five, it died away but continued in a desultory fashion for the remainder of the night.

"The guns are ensuring we don't try again," Kinnear said.

Hardie glared up the slope. "Rotunno is a double-dyed bastard."

"Maybe so," Tulloch agreed. "He is also a good soldier."

When Hardie looked at him, Tulloch saw the hatred in the man's eyes.

Major Hume stepped across, ignoring a nearby explosion. "Your men better get some sleep," he said. "We've got a busy time ahead. Where's Atkins?"

"Here, sir," Atkins hurried up, looking worried.

"When you first joined the battalion, Atkins," Hume said, "you told me you were a rock climber."

"Yes, sir," Atkins agreed.

Hume's smile was as pure evil as anything Tulloch had ever seen. "Good. Now's your chance to show how good you are. Tulloch, Kinnear, Hardie, Erskine, join me." Hume strode away, ignoring the desultory shelling.

Hume gathered the officers inside a slight depression, with a handful of sentries watching for possible Italian raids and the fitful moon providing illumination. Tulloch looked around the faces, with Hume looking surprisingly elated, Kinnear worried, and Atkins nervous. Tulloch could not read Hardie's expression. Erskine was as composed as a man in his own house.

"Tenente Colonnello Rotunno is the best Italian soldier we've encountered so far," Hume began. "He's stubborn, bold, aggressive, and sits in a formidable defensive site. Nobody's been able to shift him, and we've tried twice without success."

The officers agreed.

"We need something out of the ordinary," Hume said. "Something Sandhurst never taught us." He looked around them all, with starlight catching the hard gleam of his eye. "What I am about to suggest may not strike you as the actions of an officer and a British gentleman. Well, if so, you may leave."

The officers glanced at each other without comment. Kinnear shifted uncomfortably.

"Atkins, you are our rock climber. I want you to climb up the cliff behind the Italian positions and drop a rope for a handful of desperate men to follow. Only volunteers."

Atkins visibly paled as he nodded. "I'll have to pick a route, sir."

"You have all tomorrow to do that," Hume promised. "Take a pair of binoculars and plan out a route. Has anybody else any experience of climbing?"

"I have, sir," Hardie said immediately.

"I have a little," Tulloch volunteered.

"You, Tulloch, can lead the men up the cliff when Atkins has secured the rope. Not you, Hardie. I have another use for you."

"What's that, sir?"

"I'll tell you in a minute. Atkins, when Tulloch and his men join you on top of the cliff, I want you to cause as much mayhem as possible. Shout, yell, fire your weapons, anything that makes a noise and distracts the enemy. Got it?"

"Yes, sir," Atkins said.

"That goes for you too, Tulloch."

"Yes, sir," Tulloch contemplated climbing that sheer rock face.

Hume pointed to Erskine. "You wanted to teach the men some unpleasant combat skills if I recall?"

"That's correct," Erskine agreed languidly.

"Good. How are you with a knife?"

"I can use a knife, sir," Erskine said with a hint of a smile. "What do you have in mind?"

"I want you to dispose of the sentries," Hume said. "As I said, hardly the actions of a British officer and gentleman."

Erskine smiled. "I can do that. Do you want me to climb the rope, sir?"

"No." Hume shook his head. "I want you to climb the hill unseen and kill as many sentries as possible without making a noise."

Erskine nodded, lit a cigarette, attached it to his holder, and drew deeply. Tulloch thought he looked pleased with the idea.

"Now, Kinnear, Kilner, and Hardie, you and I will lead the main force. We'll advance up the hill half an hour after Erskine begins his assassinations. I'll arrange for the artillery to bombard Keren to distract the defenders; Rotunno won't expect us if the guns are hammering a different target."

"When do we start, sir?" Tulloch asked.

"That depends on Atkins," Hume said. "He'll work out how long he'll take to climb the cliff and how long your men will take to join him. We'll all work to Atkins' timetable."

Tulloch glanced at Atkins, who looked appalled at the responsibility. "We're in your hands, Atkins. If you need help, give me a shout."

"Yes," Atkins sounded strained.

"All right," Hume said. "You all know your duties. Get on with it."

Atkins spent the next day circling the spur, examining the cliff face from every angle, and writing notes in a small book. The battalion quartermaster was equally busy trying to find lengths of rope and climbing equipment at short notice. In the meantime, Hume sent small parties of men up the hill to harass the Italians and return without risking casualties.

"Keep them occupied so they don't see Atkins and guess what we have planned," Hume said.

The Italian artillery was busy all day, hammering at the road below and making life precarious for any British soldier on Cameron Ridge. Tulloch saw three destroyed British trucks on the road and a thin trickle of casualties from Cameron Ridge.

"That's Rotunno making his presence felt," Kinnear said.

"A reminder why we must capture the Spike," Tulloch replied.

Tulloch patrolled B Company's perimeter, checked the sentries, and stared upward at the now misty hill. Somewhere up there, Tenente Colonnello Rotunno was planning the demise of the Lothian Rifles. Somewhere up there, the Grenadiers and Blackshirts were preparing something unpleasant for his platoon.

"I want volunteers for a hazardous enterprise," Tulloch told the whole of B Company. "You must have a good head for heights and a sense of balance."

"What are we doing, sir?" Hogg asked.

"Going up there," Tulloch jerked a thumb towards the Spike. "By the back door."

"Up the cliff?" Innes asked incredulously. "Not me, sir; I get dizzy standing on a chair!"

"I'll come, sir," Hogg volunteered.

"Have you done any rock climbing, Hogg?"

"No sir, but I was a roofer in Edinburgh," Hogg said.

Tulloch thought of Hogg working on tenement roofs in a windy Edinburgh autumn. "Well done, Hogg. That's one." *And a damned good one.*

Others came forward: an ex-scaffolder, a crane operator, and a couple of men who had climbed hills when they were in the Scouts. When he had a dozen volunteers, Tulloch called a halt.

"That's enough, lads. Thank you."

A dozen men. I hope I still have twelve this time tomorrow.

The raiding parties returned with one minor casualty and no success against the defenders.

"You did fine," Hume said. "If we sat quietly, Rotunno would guess we're planning something." He raised his voice. "Atkins! Have you worked out the times yet?"

"I'll start climbing at six in the evening, sir," Atkins spoke more confidently than Tulloch expected. "If you could arrange a small diversion to keep the garrison away from the cliff top."

Hume nodded. "I'll do that."

"I estimate it will take three hours to reach the top, so at nine, maybe another small diversion."

"You'll need to attach the ropes to the cliff," Hume said. "The noise might alert the Italians." He thought for a second. "I'll ask the Royal Artillery to drop a few shells now and then to distract them."

"Thank you, sir," Atkins said. "I'll climb up with pegs and drop the ropes to Tulloch's men. With ropes, they won't take much more than half an hour, forty-five minutes at most, to reach the summit."

"Quarter to ten," Hume said. "Erskine will begin his work at quarter past nine and dispose of some of the sentries, and I'll lead the bulk of the battalion up the Spike. Once Tulloch's boys begin their mayhem in the rear, we'll attack in the front."

"Yes, sir," Atkins said.

Hume grinned. "We'll show Colonel blasted Rotunno that he can't take the Lothians lightly!"

"Right, lads," Tulloch addressed his volunteers. "Cap comforters, rifles, bayonets, fifty rounds of ammunition, a biscuit, and water. That's all. It will be cold on the rock face, but we'll have to cope."

"Will fifty rounds be enough, sir?" Hogg asked.

"We'll have a man carry up extra ammunition, Hogg," Tulloch reassured him. He looked up at the Spike and shivered.

Chapter Twenty-Nine

The volunteers shouldered their rifles and followed Tulloch to the base of Cameron Ridge and the foot of the Spike.

"Remember the spare ammunition, Dalgleish," Tulloch reminded.

"I've got it, sir!" Dalgleish was a smiling, freckle-faced youngster from C Company with a broad back and impressive muscles. While McAllister carried his rifle, Dalgleish hefted the box of spare ammunition for the rifles, and fifteen extra Bren gun magazines.

Atkins had already started climbing, with his tiny figure a third of the way up the cliff. Every few moments, Atkins stopped to hammer pegs into the cliff, with the sound terribly loud in the night.

"He's making good time," Tulloch said.

"Yes, sir," Hogg agreed.

Atkins may not be the battalion's best soldier, but he's no slouch climbing a cliff. We'll see how he progresses when the light dies.

Tulloch heard the crump of artillery and silently thanked

Major Hume for arranging another diversion to keep Rotunno's attention from the cliff. That metallic hammering was alarming, though.

"You three," Tulloch pointed to the first three men, "you're on stag. Watch the perimeter and listen for Italians. The rest of you settle down. We can't do anything until Lieutenant Atkins drops the rope."

The volunteers watched Atkins until darkness fell, then tried to sleep or just lay on the ground, contemplating the cliff that soared into the dark.

"Imagine climbing in this," Pearson, the scaffolder, said.

"You'll be climbing in this in a few moments," Hogg reminded him.

"I ken that," Pearson said. He nodded. "Aye, we'll be fine. There's no' a breath of wind."

Tulloch checked his watch, realised only an hour had passed, and forced himself to relax.

Something fell from above, landing with a crash that woke two men. Tulloch started, thinking that Atkins had fallen. He rose, saw it was only a fist-sized rock, and settled back.

If the rock is as fragile as that, we'll have difficulty climbing. I hope Atkins is all right up there because the entire plan revolves around him.

The minute hand on Tulloch's watch seemed to crawl, hesitating to move. He closed his eyes, found he could not sleep, and toured the sentries. Something, a bird or an animal, called in the night, followed by a curious swish he could not identify.

The sound was terrific, crashing down a few feet from Tulloch, so the sentries started, and one called out.

"What the hell was that?"

"The rope!" Tulloch replied. "Silence!" He waited for two minutes in case the sound of the rope hitting the ground had alerted the Italians. Atkins must have reached the top of the cliff, but Tulloch had not expected the falling rope to make so much noise. He tested it to ensure it was secure and signalled to his volunteers.

"Right, lads. Up we go."

Tulloch led from the front, with McAllister, the only man with any real climbing experience, at the rear.

I've not climbed up a cliff since I joined the army. Let's hope I remember what to do.

Atkins had hammered in pegs in various places, but Tulloch still found the climb hard. He relied on the rope as his feet sought cracks and protuberances in the rock face, slowly and carefully pushing himself upward. Although the cliff had seemed steep from the ground, Tulloch found the reality worse, with sections nearly sheer, and he marvelled that Atkins had managed to find his route and hammer in pegs.

You're a better man than I am, Peter Atkins.

Tulloch reached for the rope, pulled himself up another few feet, and heard the gasps and scrapes from below as his volunteers struggled up the cliff.

"Keep on, lads!" That was McAllister's Penicuik accent. "We're getting there."

For a moment, Tulloch wondered what would happen if the defenders discovered them climbing the cliff. The prospect was appalling, and he moved faster, desperate to reach the top in the allotted forty-five minutes. Atkins had been ten minutes ahead of his time, allowing the volunteers a slight window in which to work, but ascending a cliff in the dark with minimal training was an incredibly hazardous business.

Old Colonel Pringle would not have approved.

Colonel Pringle's day is gone. The old days of gentlemen soldiers, where war was a sport, have passed, and we're in a new era of brutal professionalism, Tulloch realised. *We can't win this war by playing to the rules.*

The cliff seemed to continue forever, soaring into the darkness above with the rope as a slender lifeline. Tulloch slogged on, panting with effort, listening to the pants and occasional curses from his men below.

"Keep going, lads," Tulloch breathed, "nothing lasts forever. Not even this damned cliff."

He stopped, clinging to the rope, when something heavy hurtled from above to land with an audible thump on the ground.

Was that a man?! Dear God, was that one of my volunteers, or has Atkins fallen? Or has an Italian pushed him over the edge? It can't be a volunteer, as they're all below me. Please, God, it wasn't Atkins.

Tulloch pushed harder, trying to race to the top before an Italian soldier cut the rope or began firing downwards. The lip seemed impossibly far off, yet every step, every drag up the rope, brought Tulloch closer, and eventually, he rolled over the top and lay for a second. The others joined him, one by one, with McAllister last.

"That's us, sir," McAllister said. "And not a man lost." He looked around as Dalgleish peered over the edge of the cliff. "What's your game, Dalgleish?"

"I felt all dizzy there," Dalgleish said, his smile fading. "You'd better take this, sir." He tried to hand the ammunition box across, stumbled, and slid over the edge, with the box of ammunition tumbling end over end to the distant ground.

"Dalgleish!" Tulloch was too late. Dalgleish was gone.

That's one man gone already, along with all our spare ammunition.

"Poor bugger," McAllister said. "It's a long way down."

"He was a good man," Tulloch said. "Where's Lieutenant Atkins? Has anybody seen Atkins?" *We'll have to manage with the ammunition we have. That's a blow.*

"Here I am!" Atkins emerged from the gloom.

"I thought you fell over the cliff," Tulloch said.

"That was an Italian sentry," Atkins said. "The poor fellow was too inquisitive."

Tulloch nodded. "Well done, Atkins." *You're a soldier now, Atkins, not the raw laddie who joined the Lothians.*

They checked their watches. "Ten minutes to go," Tulloch

said. "Hogg, patrol to the west. McAllister, patrol to the right, and the rest form a semi-circular bridgehead."

The men obeyed, moving as silently as possible across the ground with the great sucking drop behind them and low clouds blocking out the stars.

Tulloch rechecked his watch. "Five minutes," he said and swore when a man shouted in Italian.

"*Chi è quello?* Who is that?"

"*Amico!* Friend!" Tulloch responded with one of the few Italian words he knew.

"Enzo? *Sei tu?* Is that you, Enzo?"

"*Sì!*" Tulloch replied, guessing what the questioner asked.

"*Mostrati!* Show yourself!"

Tulloch replied "*Sì!*" again, without knowing what was said.

"Sir!" McAllister shouted. "Italians! Grenadiers!" A shot followed his call and then another.

"Open fire!" Tulloch ordered. His men knew to make as much noise as possible, so every weapon fired at once, with two Bren guns and ten rifles. The storm of shots must have taken the Italians by surprise.

"Shout, lads!" Tulloch yelled.

The volunteers responded with a medley of oaths, curses, and Hogg's expected, "The Gorgie Boys are here!"

"Move out by the centre!" Tulloch ordered. He did not want to be pinned with his back to the cliff edge, although he knew the drop would guard his rear. The volunteers inched forward, firing to clear a path in front.

Watch the ammo, boys! We've no spare!

The Grenadiers, confused by the unexpected assault, withdrew, with officers shouting orders through the dark.

Tulloch's men made good progress, pushing the weak Italian defence aside as they made space for themselves.

"They're coming around the flanks," Hogg warned, firing and working the bolt of his Lee-Enfield.

"Close up!" Tulloch ordered. His job was to create a diversion

321

to draw the Italians from the main frontal assault. He hoped he had sufficient firepower to defend the position against the Grenadiers and Rotunno's Blackshirts.

"Form a circle facing outward," Tulloch ordered. He saw Atkins take his place with the volunteers and heard firing from further down the Spike but was unsure how far away.

Has the main attack begun? I hope so.

"Fire, lads!" Tulloch roared. "Make as much noise as you can. Come on, Rotunno! The Lothians are here! Gin ye daur!"

The volunteers kept low, sheltering behind rocks on the hard surface. To their left, mist shrouded the invisible final peak, while muzzle flashes showed where the Blackshirts and Grenadiers were creeping up to the volunteers' position. Bullets hissed and whined around them as the volunteers returned fire.

We're getting through a hell of a lot of ammo.

"Where's the relief force?" Pearson asked.

"Not here yet," McAllister replied.

The man beside Tulloch yelled, staring at the spreading stain on his shoulder. Lifting his rifle, he tried to fire left-handed and shouted again as a bullet burrowed into his thigh.

"They've got me," he said in surprise.

"Keep under cover!" Tulloch ordered, pushing the wounded man behind a rock.

Where the hell is the main assault? We can't hold out much longer. We must have used two-thirds of our ammunition.

Tulloch fired his revolver, saw dark shapes ahead in the gloom, and heard the long chatter of a machine gun. Stone chips flew from the ground before him, and another volunteer yelled, holding his leg.

Atkins was firing steadily, using a rifle from an injured volunteer.

"Get the bastards!" McAllister shouted, fired his rifle, worked the bolt, and fired again. "Has anybody got any spare ammo?"

"Use the bullets from the casualties," Tulloch shouted.

On the extreme left, Hogg was firing and swearing with equal skill. "Come tae me, you Blackshirt bastards! Come on, you Savoy Grenadiers! The Gorgie boys are here!"

Somebody cheered ahead, and a dozen Blackshirts burst from cover, firing as they charged. Tulloch fired into the mass, saw one man fall, and the closest Bren gun opened up, scything into the attackers.

Our distraction is working, at least. We're attracting the Blackshirts.

"Gin ye daur!" Tulloch shouted. "Lothian Rifles!"

The Italian attack faltered and ended, with men retreating as quickly as they had advanced. Two Blackshirts lay on the ground, one dead, one moaning.

"Cease fire!" Tulloch shouted as the Blackshirts vanished into the scrub-covered rocks. He did not want Rotunno to count his men. The Lothians lay quiet as the Blackshirts and Grenadiers probed their defences with rifles and a machine gun.

"On my word," Tulloch said. "Everybody fire to the left flank. Make them think we're going to advance that way."

The volunteers shifted position, keeping down as Italian bullets whined around them.

"Five rounds rapid!" Tulloch ordered. "Fire!"

The volunteers fired into the dark, with their muzzle flashes illuminating the stark surroundings.

"Now lie still and yell your heads off!" Tulloch ordered.

Keeping low, the volunteers shouted anything that came into their heads, with Tulloch leading the way with "Gin ye daur!"

The Italians responded with a flurry of shots aimed in front of the Lothians' position. Bullets ripped through the harsh scrub and ricocheted from the rocks. As half a dozen artillery shells also crashed down where an advance would have taken the Lothians, Tulloch knew he was correct to remain in position.

The Italians began to sing, roaring out an already familiar song.

"La legge nostra è schiavitù d'amore
il nostro motto è libertà e dovere
vendicheremo noi Camicie Nere
Gli eroi caduti liberando te!"

"Sir!" When Hogg lifted his head from the ground, rock fragments and dust trickled from his steel helmet. "I can hear the pipes."

"What?" Dazed by the noise and the music, Tulloch tried to concentrate. "You're right, Hogg!"

High above the crash of bursting shells and the staccato rattle of machine guns, the distinctive wail of the Lowland Pipes gave hope to Tulloch's volunteers. Tulloch listened for a minute, hardly daring to believe that the Lothian's main attack could be successful.

The singing ended abruptly, and the artillery fire died away as the Italians switched their target to the Lothians' main attack.

Tulloch took a deep breath. "Fire again, boys. Help Major Hume's offensive."

Only eight unwounded men remained from Tulloch's original dozen. They dug themselves in and fired towards the Italians' machine guns, shouting furiously. The reply came in seconds, with a Fiat 14 machine gun searching for the volunteers, hacking chips from the rocks and sending men into deeper cover.

The second the Fiat 14 traversed past the volunteers' position, Tulloch ordered them to return fire.

"Keep them occupied," he ordered. He lifted a wounded man's rifle, checked it was loaded, and fired three rounds towards the machine gun. The pipes were still calling, seemingly no closer as the breeze lifted the music and wafted it away.

A shell burst ten yards outside the Lothians' position, scattering shrapnel and small stones. McAllister grunted, lifted a hand to his head, and swore.

"The buggering thing went right through my helmet," he said. "I'm going to return it to the shop for a refund."

Tulloch saw blood on McAllister's face. "Are you all right, McAllister?"

"I'm all right, sir," McAllister said and collapsed with his eyes and mouth wide open.

"Here they come again!" Hogg roared.

The Italians raced against Tulloch's depleted men, firing and shouting.

"Send them back!" Tulloch said. He aimed at a tall officer, fired, saw the man stagger, worked the rifle bolt, and saw a score more Blackshirts following. His men were tiring now, with depleted numbers and little ammunition.

"Let's hope the battalion comes soon," Hogg shouted with a wild grin. "I've never wanted to be part of a last stand. I wish Dalgleish hadn't lost the ammo!"

Tulloch heard the pipes again and saw a stocky Blackshirt officer standing on a rock.

"There's their commander!" Atkins pointed with a steady finger.

"That's Rotunno," Tulloch said. He took quick aim with his borrowed rifle, fired, missed, and swore.

Rotunno looked directly at Tulloch and shouted an order. The Blackshirts surged forward, singing in a seemingly unstoppable wave. Half-seen in the gloom, they seemed to number in the hundreds.

"Last bullet, sir!" Hogg fired, wounded a man, and stood to face the charge with his bayonet held at an angle and a strange smile on his face. "Come on then, lads! The Gorgie boys are here!"

Only six of Tulloch's volunteers remained unwounded. With his rifle empty, Tulloch unholstered his pistol.

Rotunno smiled as he strode forward, guessing the volunteers' lack of ammunition.

Tulloch saw the khaki uniforms before he heard the shouts, and Hardie led the surge from the flank.

"Colonello Rotunno! Remember me?"

Chapter Thirty

Rotunno turned towards this new threat, shouting in Italian. When Hardie replied in the same language, the two men snarled at each other in mutual dislike. The rest of the battle seemed to fade away as the old protagonists faced each other.

An artillery shell exploded thirty yards away, unheeded by everybody, as Hardie pointed his revolver at the Italian colonel.

They were shouting in Italian, oblivious to the larger battle raging around them.

Rotunno fired a quick shot, Hardie responded, and both men ran together.

"Lieutenant Hardie looks a bit angry," Hogg said.

"He does," Tulloch agreed.

As if by mutual consent, the Blackshirts stopped to watch the officers fight.

Is this a twentieth-century war? Or is it some medieval duel? Leave them to it and take the Spike.

"Fire!" Tulloch shouted. "Send the Blackshirts back to Mussolini!"

Hardie's Six Platoon joined what remained of Tulloch's volunteers in firing at the Blackshirts. When the rest of the Lothians came roaring up the slope, the Italians realised they were outnumbered and withdrew, with two throwing up their hands in surrender.

"There's the lieutenant!" Innes shouted, and Tulloch saw Four Platoon advancing, using any cover they could as they fired and moved and fired again, pushing back Grenadiers and Blackshirts with equal skill.

"To me, Four Company!" Tulloch roared. He saw Sergeant Drysdale, the indestructible veteran, leading from the front with Corporal Borthwick further back. Smith was there, his flat face screwed into a scowl, and Elliot shouting, "Rummel them up!"

Home again.

"After me, Lothians!" Major Hume shouted, and Tulloch led Four Platoon forward, happy to be back where he belonged. Four Platoon was his family now; he knew them like brothers, with their faults and foibles, their strengths, and occasional weaknesses. They were his men, and he was their officer; they belonged together, bound by blood and shared experiences.

The Lothians' advance continued, overrunning the Italians' artillery positions, bayonetting, or capturing anybody who resisted, and herding the remainder, Grenadiers and Blackshirts, up to the peak.

"Halt," Major Hume gathered his battalion around him, organising them back into their companies. "Where's Lieutenant Hardie?"

"Here, sir," Hardie was his old, calm self again. "Rotunno's dead, sir."

"Good," Hume said. "One last push, and the Spike is ours."

The last of the Italians, Grenadiers, and Blackshirts gathered on the summit of the Spike. They began to sing, the words familiar.

"La legge nostra è schiavitù d'amore
il nostro motto è libertà e dovere
vendicheremo noi Camicie Nere
Gli eroi caduti liberando te!"

"I know that song," Hardie said grimly. "These men don't intend to surrender."

Tulloch counted his men, frowning at the gaps in the ranks. "What do the words mean?"

Hardie closed his eyes. Tulloch noted the blood on his tunic and wondered if he was injured.

"It's a Blackshirt song," Hardie said. "It says:

Our law is slavery of love,
Our motto is freedom and duty,
We, the Blackshirts, will avenge
the heroes that died to free you!"

Hardie shrugged. "It's a fascist song about the Ethiopian war."

"You killed Rotunno," Tulloch said flatly.

"I did. It's over now," Hardie looked away, and Tulloch knew it was not the time to ask questions.

Machine gun and rifle fire hammered around the Lothians as the Italians on the summit sang their defiance.

"How the hell do we get up there?" Tulloch stared at the summit of the Spike. The Italians had bolstered the natural defences with walls built from loose boulders. They stood, sat, or crouched behind them, already taking a toll on the Lothians.

"They've got a killing zone in front of them," Major Hume was bleeding from a cut on his cheekbone. "Any ideas?"

"Yes, sir," Tulloch ducked as machine gun fire crossed the clearing, making any advance fatal. "We can call down artillery."

"We're too close," Muir said. "We'd lose half our men."

"Smith!" Tulloch shouted. "Bring the elephant gun!"

Smith staggered up, bent nearly double with the cumbersome Boys on his back.

"I knew old Betsy would come in handy, sir!"

Smith lay beside Tulloch, set up the tripod, called for ammunition, and aimed at the closest Italian machine gun nest.

"Fire when you're ready," Tulloch said.

A moment later, Smith fired, missing by a yard. The machine gunner altered his aim, with the bullets crackling over Smith's head.

"The bugger's seen me," Smith said calmly, loading the Boys.

"Fire at the machine gun!" Tulloch ordered. "Try to distract him from Smith."

"Distract him?" Innes said. "He's distracting me!" He aimed his Bren, with Elliot placing three spare magazines at his side.

Half a dozen Lothian Riflemen opened fire, with some aiming and others hoping the sheer volume of bullets would make the Italian machine gunner lose interest.

With the Boys reloaded, Smith aimed, flinched as a stray bullet whined past, and fired again.

"I scared him that time," Smith said, wincing, for the Boys' terrific recoil easily bruised a man's shoulder.

"That machine gun nest is holding us back," Hume said.

Innes lay beside them, firing short, controlled bursts from his Bren as the riflemen continued to aim at the nearest nest.

"This is getting us nowhere," Hume said. "I want three volunteers."

"For what, sir?" Tulloch asked.

"To quieten that blasted machine gun. Not you, Tulloch. You remain here with your platoon and put down suppressing fire. Kelly, Cattanach, and Gordon, you're my volunteers. We'll go wide and take the bastard on the flank."

"You heard the major, Four Platoon!" Tulloch said. "Suppressing fire from everybody. Fire a complete mag, Innes. Smith, another round from the Boys." He picked up a rifle from a dead man. "Fire!"

While Four Platoon fired everything they had, Hume and his three men broke cover and ran to the side, moving quickly as the machine gun traversed towards them. Tulloch aimed and fired, watching the spurts of dust and chips of rock fly upward as Innes emptied a magazine. Smith fired, grunting as the clumsy weapon slammed back against his shoulder.

The machine gun fell silent momentarily, and Tulloch heard a prolonged yell as Hume and his men charged.

"Cease fire! We might hit the major!" Tulloch saw the orange flash of a grenade and then another, and Hume was in the nest. "Come on, boys! Follow me!"

Four Platoon rose, some crouching, others moving quickly as Tulloch ran, zig-zagging, towards the Italian position. The hill steepened further as he advanced, so he leaned forward for purchase on the steep slope. To his right, Hardie was leading a dozen men, with Atkins fifty yards to his left. Tulloch heard the insane chatter of another Italian machine gun, saw a man stagger and felt something smash against his shoe.

They've hit me.

Tulloch looked down and felt another thump as if somebody had punched him in the ribs. He glanced down, grunted in surprise, and collapsed.

Chapter Thirty One

KEREN, ERITREA, MARCH 1941

The ground was hard beneath Tulloch as he fell, lying still for a second as he tried to work out what had happened. Somebody had shot him, but he was still alive. *Was there any pain?*

Tulloch wriggled his feet and hands. There was no pain.

Have I lost anything?

He looked down at himself. Both his feet and hands were still attached to his body.

No, everything is in place. Can I move?

Tulloch rolled onto his face and pushed himself upright. His right foot ached damnably, but he could place it on the ground. His body seemed numb, devoid of any feeling.

Can my legs take my weight?

Tulloch pressed gingerly down. The pain in his foot and side made him gasp, but it was bearable. He suddenly realised the firing had stopped. The Italians should have shot him the moment he stood upright.

What's happened? I only lay still for a moment. Where is everybody?

Only the injured and dead lay on the ground, some

ominously silent, others writhing and moaning. The stink of cordite and raw blood polluted the air while a thousand flies quested for sustenance.

The battle's over. Either the Italians have won and pushed us off the Spike, or we've captured the damned place.

The sky was darkening as evening closed in. Tulloch heard voices nearby and reached for his revolver. British, Indian, African, or Italian? He found three chambers empty and hastily reloaded. *Come on then, boys. Here I am.*

Flies buzzed around him. He brushed them away irritably, lifted his revolver, and shouted, "Who's there?" His voice sounded strange, weak. He tried again. "Who's there?"

"Stretcher bearers!" the reply came at once. "Who's that?"

"Lieutenant Douglas Tulloch, Lothian Rifles," Tulloch croaked.

A group of men emerged from the gloom, carrying three stretchers between them.

"What was your name, sir?" one asked curiously.

"Lieutenant Tulloch," Tulloch repeated.

The men stared at him. "I heard you were dead, sir," a fair-haired medical orderly said. "We got told you were shot in the head and the body."

"My head?" Tulloch put a hand to his forehead and felt the mass of congealed blood. "I didn't know."

"You're covered in blood, sir," the fair-haired man said. "Your head and your tunic."

Tulloch remembered the punch on his ribs and looked down. His tunic was ripped, and dried blood caked his shirt.

"I didn't notice," he said.

Tulloch had felt no pain in his head or side, but now they started to ache. "Where are the Lothians?"

"Down the bottom of the hill, sir," the fair-haired man said.

"Did we take the Spike?" Tulloch felt himself suddenly dizzy.

"We did, sir," the fair-haired man told him.

"That's good," Tulloch said, feeling himself swaying. "Could you give me a hand here?" He tried to smile, but the ground was rising towards him. He felt himself land but no longer cared because everything was dark and soft.

HE WAS COMFORTABLE IN THIS COCOON OF DARKNESS, WITH NO need to worry about the war. Tulloch lay still, enjoying the sensation of floating. He heard voices without knowing who they were and hoped somebody else was caring for Four Platoon. *Keep Innes and Hogg apart,* he tried to say. *They don't get on.* And then he drifted further away, and it did not matter anymore.

Nothing mattered for a while. Tulloch allowed the pain to take over. He felt very little when the bullets hit him, but now the results dominated his life. Tulloch felt people probing at him, and somebody examined him with concerned eyes. A man's voice murmured in the background, and he smelled anaesthetic. Tulloch felt the keen cut of a scalpel and tried to protest, but the words would not come.

Where am I?

Nobody replied to his wordless question. Tulloch felt hands on him, felt the sharp prick of injections, and heard murmuring voices. Somebody leaned over him, and somebody else screamed nearby.

There was an aircraft's drone and the clamour of a city. Tulloch tried to sit up, but straps held him securely in a bed or perhaps a stretcher. He closed his eyes and allowed the pain to creep over him. He understood pain more than he understood the confusion within his mind.

Vivat Schola Edinensis
Schola Regia venerabilis.
No, hang it, that's not right.
Gin ye daur. That's the phrase. Gin ye daur.
Lothian Rifles!
Take the Spike, Lothians!

Tulloch woke in a hospital bed with a crisply dressed nurse speaking beside him.

"He's lost a lot of blood, and he'll probably carry the scar all his life," the nurse was saying, "but he'll be up and about in a few weeks."

Tulloch stirred slightly and saw he was one of a long row of wounded men, with a fan stirring the air high above and the smell of disinfectant fighting the raw blood and fear in the air.

"Hello," he said, hearing his voice as if it came from a long distance off. "Where am I?"

The nurse was young, pretty, and efficient. "Base hospital in Alex," she informed him with a smile.

Tulloch struggled to sit up. "How did I get here?"

"By ambulance," the nurse told him. "Lie still; you've lost a lot of blood."

Tulloch realised bandages swathed his middle, his head, and his right foot. "It was only a scratch," he said.

"Of course it was," the nurse said. "You had a bullet in your side and a wound on your foot that caused extensive bruising. When you fell, you must have banged your head because you have a dashing scar above your eye. Either that or somebody shot you."

"How long have I been here?" Tulloch asked.

"A few months," the nurse replied, smiling.

"Months!" Tulloch repeated. "When can I get out?" He heard sharp footsteps in the ward. "Who's that?"

"Me, Tulloch," Captain Muirhead stepped into the light. "I was just passing by and thought I'd come in."

"Glad to see you, sir," Tulloch said. "We took the Spike, I hear?"

"We won the entire battle, Tulloch," Muirhead said. "Keren was our hardest-fought victory of the war so far."

"How is Four Platoon? How are my men? How is the battalion?"

A slow smile eased over Muirhead's face. "It's different, Tulloch. Major Hume has been promoted to Lieutenant-Colonel with immediate effect, and he's altering things."

"For the better or worse?"

Muirhead was silent for a moment. He sat beside my bed and lowered his voice. "Colonel Pringle was a gentleman, Tulloch, and he fought a gentleman's war. Colonel Hume is..."

"Colonel Hume is making the Lothian Rifles fit to fight Hitler," Hume strode the length of the ward. "Why are you lying in bed when you should be on duty, Tulloch?"

"Just waiting for orders, sir,"

Hume eyed Tulloch up and down. "I'll give you orders. I'll order you to get fit and rejoin the Rifles. We've proved ourselves against the Italians, smashed them in Egypt, Libya, and Eritrea, and now we have to defeat the Germans."

"I'll get fit, sir," Tulloch said.

"Good," Hume said. "The battalion needs experienced officers." Hume nodded, turned on his heel, and strode away.

"That was well said," Muirhead murmured. "Hume has allowed Erskine to train the men with all his nasty tricks and ordered Hardie to create a unit of snipers. He's sent Kinnear away as not being sufficiently aggressive. You'll come back to a different battalion, Tulloch." He smiled. "The battalion has iron in it now; it has found its soul."

"Yes, sir," Tulloch said. "How is the war going, sir?"

"It's not gone well since you decided to leave, Tulloch," Muirhead said. "As we feared, Churchill split O'Connor's Desert Army and sent half to Greece."

"That's not good, sir," Tulloch said.

"It gets worse," Muirhead told him. "A German general named Rommel arrived in Libya with twenty-five thousand troops and tanks and shoved us right back towards Egypt. The Germans captured O'Connor and defeated us in Greece and Crete as well. Even as we speak, Admiral Cunningham is evacuating Crete and bringing home whatever he can of our forces."

"Another Dunkirk," Tulloch said.

"Aye, another Dunkirk." Muirhead looked up. "The ships might be arriving in the harbour now. Can you walk to the window?"

"If you help me," Tulloch said.

Dusk fell over Alexandria, with the harbour crowded with shipping. Vessel after vessel limped in from the evacuation of Crete, some undamaged and others showing the results of Luftwaffe bombs.

A badly damaged cruiser steamed into harbour, smoking from bomb damage.

"That's HMS *Dido*," Muirhead murmured to Tulloch. "She was carrying over a thousand soldiers from Crete, including many from the Black Watch."

"What's that?" Tulloch heard the Highland bagpipes. He saw a piper wearing the dark green tartan of the Black Watch standing beside the bridge of HMS *Jackal*. The piper faced the damaged cruisers *Dido* and *Orion*, both of whom carried troops rescued from Crete.

As the piper played the survivors of the Black Watch into Alexandria, the Royal Navy highlighted him with a searchlight.

"I wonder if anybody will ever pay such a tribute to the Lothians," Tulloch said.

"I wonder if we'll ever deserve it," Muirhead said. "Hitler might think he's winning the war, but with men like that," he nodded towards the crippled ship and her battered passengers, "he hasn't got a chance."

They both turned around when heavy footsteps crashed into the ward.

"Did you hear the news?" the young subaltern sounded excited.

"Not a word," Tulloch said.

The subaltern was around eighteen, with sunburned skin peeling from his nose. "The Germans have invaded Russia. They've sent hundreds of thousands of men from Poland and are slaughtering the Russians in droves."

Tulloch drew in his breath. "Dear God, that's put the cat among the pigeons. At least we know Hitler can't invade Britain if he's committed so many men to his eastern flank."

Muirhead shook his head. "I wonder why he didn't invade sooner? He's only got a few months before winter, and you remember what a Russian winter did to Napoleon Bonaparte."

"I remember," Tulloch said. He thought for a moment. "Do you know why Hitler didn't invade sooner, sir?"

"No," Muirhead said.

"Hitler had to commit troops to fight us in Greece. That's why Churchill split our desert army; he wanted to delay Hitler by tying him down in the Balkans and Greece. Now Hitler has a tight timetable to defeat Stalin before winter sets in."

Muirhead nodded slowly. "Churchill sacrificed thousands of our men to delay Hitler. His strategy cost us dearly, but he might have won us the war. Russia will swallow Hitler's armies up."

"Perhaps so," Tulloch said. He glanced at the clock on the wall. Amanda was due to visit in half an hour, and when she was present, the war could wait.

Historical Note

General Sir Richard Nugent O'Connor KT, GCB, DSO and Bar, MC. (1889-1981)

General O'Connor, the Little White-Haired Terrier, was one of the most successful and most unlucky British generals of the Second World War. Born in India into an Irish military family, O'Connor was educated in England and attended Sandhurst, two years below Bernard Montgomery. After Sandhurst, O'Connor joined the Cameronians (Scottish Rifles), a regiment with which he had a life-long association.

During the First World War, O'Connor served as Signals Officer with the 22nd Brigade in the 7th Division and later as Brigade Major of the 91st Brigade, 7th Division. 1915 was a busy year, for he won the Military Cross in February, and in March, he fought at Arras and Bullecourt. In 1917, O'Connor won the DSO and then moved to support the Italians – then our allies – against the Austro-Hungarians.

Between the wars, O'Connor held various posts, including a brigade major experimenting with using tanks and aircraft in conjunction with infantry. He also served in Peshawar in British India and in Palestine, always a trouble spot between the wars.

Shortly before the Second World War broke out in September 1939, O'Connor was posted to Egypt, where he organised defences against a potential Italian attack from Libya. When the attack came in September 1940, the Italians penetrated sixty miles and dug themselves in while O'Connor prepared for a counterattack. In December 1940, he launched Operation Compass.

Vastly outnumbered, the 31,000 British, Indian, and Australian forces smashed through the Italian defences, captured tens of thousands of prisoners, and chased the Italians back into Libya. Eventually, O'Connor captured Benghazi, but orders from Churchill denuded his army of many experienced men and much of his armour. Churchill ordered O'Connor to halt his offensive.

The situation became worse when Hitler sent Erwin Rommel and 25,000 German troops to reinforce the Italians in Africa. While driving to his headquarters, O'Connor was captured by a German patrol and spent over two years as a prisoner of war. He escaped in 1943 and returned to the British Army, commanding a core in Normandy in 1944. He met with mixed success in his new role and retired from the army in 1948.

We shall never know what would have happened if O'Connor had remained in command of his 30,000 and met Rommel in Libya.

The Battle of Keren

Often neglected by Second World War historians, Keren was arguably the most fiercely fought battle between the British Empire and Italian forces.

The battle was one incident in the East African Campaign. The fighting began on the 5th February and finally ended on the 1st April 1941, with the British, Commonwealth, Indian, and Free French forces defeating a larger army of Italian and colonial troops.

The British and Commonwealth forces lost 536 killed and

nearly 3,300 wounded, while the Italian and Colonial forces lost about 12,000 killed and 4,500 wounded. These figures are disputed and seem to have a large ratio of killed to wounded.

The prize was the town of Keren, which was strategically important to both sides. It had railway and road connections to Asmara, which was then the capital of Eritrea, and Massawa, a port on the Red Sea. After the battle, the British captured both towns, marking a successful conclusion to the East African campaign ended.

About the Author

Born in Edinburgh, Scotland and educated at the University of Dundee, Malcolm Archibald has written in a variety of genres, from academic history to folklore, historical novels to fantasy. He won the Dundee International Book Prize with *Whales for the Wizard* in 2005 and the Society of Army Historical Research prize for Historical Military Fiction with *Blood Oath* in 2021.

Happily married for over 42 years, Malcolm has three grown children and lives outside Dundee in Scotland.

To learn more about Malcolm Archibald and discover more Next Chapter authors, visit our website at www.nextchapter.pub.

Notes

Chapter 1

1. In October 1939, the Luftwaffe attacked Royal Navy ships in the Firth of Forth. 602, City of Glasgow and 603 City of Edinburgh squadrons repelled them, inflicting casualties. Many people believed the Luftwaffe had targeted the Forth Bridge.

Chapter 10

1. EPIP: Eight Person Indian Production tents were used extensively throughout the North African campaign.

Chapter 11

1. Duffy: a fight, battle.

Chapter 12

1. This incident occurred when a single tank approached Tummar East and asked for it to surrender. The Italian garrison asked for a token bombardment and a more senior officer. When the British obliged, the fort surrendered.

Chapter 14

1. A form of crook-handled walking stick carried by colonels of Highland regiments.

Chapter 18

1. Orde Wingate was one of the most eccentric British officers in the Second World War. Of Scottish stock, he occasionally greeted people while stark naked, either to make an impact or because it unsettled them. He later led the Chindits, operating behind the Japanese lines in Burma.

Chapter 20

1. The Rocks is a waterfront area of Sydney that was once notorious for violence. It is now gentrified and upmarket.

Chapter 23

1. When the Australians captured Tobruk, there were women with the Italians. Their status seems to be ambiguous.

Printed in Great Britain
by Amazon